VEILS OF CONSPIRACY

Karen' With Warm Regards Always. Ruth

BY RUTH R. LEGG

PublishAmerica
Baltimore

ISBN: 978-1-4489-7837-3 (softcover)
ISBN: 978-1-4489-6656-1 (hardcover)
PUBLISHED BY PUBLISHAMERICA, LLLP
www.publishamerica.com
Baltimore

Printed in the United States of America

Dedication

For Lynn
For your trust and belief in me
I will always try to make
you proud.

Veil after veil will lift—but there
must be
Veil upon veil behind.
—Sir Edward Arnold

PROLOGUE

The five sat motionless around the long, polished oak table. The leader's chin rested on folded hands. There was absolute silence in the room. The leader's penetrating eyes looked at each one briefly then drifted upward toward the clock on the wall. No one spoke. They all sat and waited.

"It's time. We've planned every possible scenario and now, it's time."

"Are you sure? We can't make a mistake, you know." The nervous man to the left of the leader spoke rapidly, running the words together. His fear was obvious. He could feel perspiration soaking his armpits.

The leader's eyes shifted to the speaker. The look was cold and frightening, "It's time," was all the leader said.

"Of course, of course." Heads nodded up and down in agreement.

"We will begin immediately." The leader rose, said "good night," turned and left the room.

Reality overwhelmed them.

My God...my God, what are we doing? How in the hell did I get caught up in this? It was only supposed to be a game—a what if game, the man at the end of the table thought. His fingers drummed nervously on the table and he felt the thumping of his heart in his chest. He knew better than to say anything and, like the others, rose and left the room in silence.

The meeting was over.

#

The shrill ringing of the phone cut through the night and echoed in the rooms of the dark house. The woman tried to force herself awake and struggled to focus on the sound. She heard her mother's bedroom door open and the familiar shuffle of feet in the hall. The voice was muffled and the sounds made no sense.

She fumbled for her robe as the door opened.

"There's been an accident." Her mother's voice was emotionless.

"David?"

"Yes."

"Where is he?"

"At the hospital. I'll go with you."

Shock obliterated the senses. He was dead. Everything was suddenly a kaleidoscope of muted words and drawn faces. She did not recognize friends, bending close, whispering their sympathy. The sweet smell of the flowers over whelmed her as she looked at her love…her precious love…unmoving, lying at the end of the room…so still with his face wax like and frozen.

People kissed her cheek and held her hand, but they could not touch the pain in her heart. She tried to sort out the events, seeking an explanation, anything plausible for a reason why he was on that road in the middle of the night. He should have been at work. One train a night and his car stalled on the tracks in front of it. It didn't make sense. Why didn't he jump? Why the hell hadn't he jumped out of the goddamned car?

The act was finished, the sod back in place, the flowers wilted. People went back to their lives and she began to search for the strength to face each day.

tum tum tum ta tum…

tum tum tum ta tum…

The glistening stainless steel table with its holes and faucets and hoses stood waiting under stark, clear lights. Instruments, aligned side by side, sat on another table…rubber gloves waited for hands. What would happen to him here would be one more atrocity for a good and decent human being. But he was not that anymore—now he was a body to be cut and examined and studied and cataloged. For years to come, strangers who never knew him would pour over the information and spew forth theory after theory about what had happened on that fateful day. It was a hell of a way to pass into history.

tum tum tum ta tum…

CHAPTER I

The story begins in a land of rolling hills and tumbling waters, sky blue lakes, green vineyards and white farmhouses. Geologists are quick to explain, in cold, scientific terms, how Ice Age glaciers formed the picturesque lakes, blocking southward flowing streams with debris. Lovers prefer the Indian legends, passed from generation to generation, of the day when the Great Spirit placed His hand on the earth and created a lake for each tribe.

You can drive for days around the lakes, enjoying the quiet tree-shaded villages, winding country roads and fields of rich crops and stately barns. If you stay for the fall you can watch the frost turn the countryside into a shimmering van Gogh of colors. Red apples dot the trees and large, plump, orange pumpkins lie in the fields, waiting for the trip to the canning factory. Deep purple grapes hang in clumps from vines also awaiting a trip that will begin the process of turning them into wine...perhaps to be sipped by lovers as they rendezvous for an evening of passion.

When the days grow short, winter, far north in Canada, gathers strength for the southward rush. Soon this land will be snuggled under a cold blanket of snow, resting for the rebirth that will come with the warm breezes of spring.

The natives dislike the winter and curse the snow and vow that never again will they endure the icy winds and endless white drifts. Then, one morning they wake to be greeted by warm winds and the snow is gone and tiny green shoots appear. Spring brings new life and the memory of winter fades.

Then come the first warm days of June—days that promise a coming summer of sun and heat and clear blue skies and sometimes frightening thunderstorms. June—a time to begin a story that will end in the cold of a January snow, in a city many miles away, with the world watching and asking why.

Cameron Marshall is forty-six. He inherited his mother's classic Latin looks—jet black hair, that is now sprinkled with gray and defies the touch of a comb; flashing dark eyes that burn deep and sometimes offer a glimpse of the pain he hides; and a healthy, ruddy complexion. His dark rimmed glasses add a touch of mystery to his somber persona. He is just under six feet tall and by any woman's standards, a handsome man.

Once a glistening smile marked him as an amicable man you would enjoy having for your friend. But, the frustrations of his life have taught him to hide his emotions and now he guards every moment...almost as if he were afraid to be happy.

He has wealth, inherited from his father; two-children, the legacy of a short, passionate but quickly unhappy marriage; and a recurring dream, a nightmare, that wakes him in the night and leaves him in a cold sweat, confused and frightened.

Cameron's life has been full of mistakes and disappointments. When he finally resigned himself to a career in the Marine Corps, he found himself in combat, wounded, and discharged from the service. He retreated to a small farm in Virginia and took up with a companion named Jack Daniels. The two became inseparable. Like an infant's pacifier, the glass of tepid liquid was ever present, offering solace, companionship and a way to postpone facing reality.

How many days were lost? He couldn't remember and didn't give a damn until one morning when he dared to look into the bathroom mirror and saw a red-eyed, bearded demon staring back. He ran his tongue over his teeth—they were fuzzy and his mouth tasted like shit. The face was no longer recognizable as his own. The cheeks were hollow and the complexion pasty white. It was the face of a dead man—a living dead man with a soul preserved in alcohol— a grotesque figure with no self-respect, no dignity. Tears streamed from his aching eyes. He leaned against the sink and threw up a vile smelling acrid liquid. "Oh, God, what have I done? Help me...please, somebody, help me..." he cried as his trembling body slid to the floor. When he came to, he had fouled his pajamas and he lay in his own filth.

He pulled himself to his feet and found the energy to charge through the house, grabbing all the bottles he could find. He carried the armful into the kitchen and, before his terrified housekeeper, poured the contents down the drain. She dared not say a word to him.

He had lost three years of his life—gone—three years he couldn't remember—time he could never bring back—days—weeks—months— vanished in a haze of alcohol. He didn't like himself very much sober—but there he was and somehow, some way he would have to find a way to live with himself.

What could he do with his life? His body was patched together and hurting. Returning to the Marines was not an option. He sure as hell wasn't going to go near his father's business. When his besotted brain finally cleared, he vaguely remembered a call from his father's attorney.

His father had been in a small town in Venezuela on a business trip and did not return to his hotel room one night. The American Embassy offered some assistance, but he was never seen again. The Ambassador explained that he had probably been kidnapped and murdered for his money. Cameron wondered what kind of business had taken his father to South America, but doubted he would get the truth if he asked.

A friend from his days in Vietnam was sympathetic and now that he was sober, was willing to help him get a job at the Pentagon. Cameron was excited about his future for the first time in his life, because he knew his knowledge and training would be utilized and he would be participating in important, strategic planning sessions and making decisions that would impact on the security of the nation.

Once again, Cameron had deluded himself into thinking that he could be more than he was. He was little more than a file clerk. He put in his days, in a mechanical sort of way because he had nothing else to do and no place else to go. He decided to write a book on military history and spent his free hours digging through the Pentagon's archives. He found the research interesting and he worked with enthusiasm making notes on long, yellow tablets. His notes were first written in the shaky hand of a man whose nerves screamed in anguish as they tried to recover from the devastating effects of alcohol. As time passed, the writing because more definite and the hand moved once again in firm, broad strokes.

The book never materialized and eight years slipped by before he realized it. He had let himself exist in a vacuum because it did not require a decision or much thought. Looking at his face one morning as he was shaving, he started laughing. "You aimless, worthless bastard," he said aloud and wondered if it was possible to slit his throat with a twin bladed razor.

Cameron resigned his job, got into his car and headed for Milwaukee to run the family business. When he got there he discovered it was no longer a family business, but a giant public-held international industrial corporation. His father had been dead for nine years and was all but forgotten. In fact, the Marshall family wasn't even the majority stockholder. He had fifteen percent of the stock, which was worth millions but provided no power. His father's picture hung in the boardroom as a token of the company's history, but the Marshalls had no role left to play.

Out of some misguided sense of courtesy, they offered Cameron a mid-management position, which he accepted rather than beat a retreat back to his dead end job at the Pentagon. He discovered he had good skills and a keen mind—like my father—he thought—and within three years was a vice president.

Deep inside he knew that working for the company wasn't his future, that he was still playing games with himself and avoiding his true responsibilities and future.

Without warning, the company became the target of a hostile takeover and in six months, JM Industries no longer existed. Cameron found himself much wealthier, but once again in limbo. He took his father's picture off the boardroom wall, packed the few personal things he had in his office and headed home to Virginia.

"Time for a new plan," he said as he pulled on to the interstate highway and joined the flow of traffic traveling south.

Then the dreams began. At first he paid little attention because it only happened occasionally. Then the frequency increased and it was always the same—he would wake in a cold sweat remembering the phone ringing and a low, whispery voice when he answered. He could never remember what the voice said.

He decided that maybe politics was the road for him to follow. He enrolled in the University of Virginia and started working on a master's degree in political science. He was surprised at how comfortable he felt in the educational setting and he spent hours in the library reading and doing research. He loved debating with his fellow grad students and he worked hard on reports and his thesis. The dreams had stopped and he felt at peace with himself for the first time in many years. He graduated with honors.

On graduation day, he felt an overwhelming loneliness as he realized there was no one there to share his accomplishments. He thought of his children. He had not seen them since they were babies.

He went back to his farm in Virginia and after dozens of phone calls, managed to talk his children into spending part of the summer with him. It was Gillian who had given in first and said that she would talk to Ryan. He knew it would be an awkward time, because they did not know him, but he was determined make it work.

The twins were twenty. Ryan was his image, but he lacked the exuberance of a young college man. He had been educated in military schools and had taken, all to easily, to the restraint and discipline. His grandfather had used his influence to get him into the Naval Academy. He would start his junior year in September.

He's like a little old man, Cameron thought, as he leaned against the doorway, watching his son unpack. He looked at the closet and saw all the jackets, shirts and trousers separated and hanging straight and even.

"You're precise with everything, aren't you, Ryan?" Cameron commented.

"Yes, sir." Ryan responded.

Just once call me Dad, not sir. He decided not to comment. He turned and crossed the hall to his daughter's room.

Beautiful Gillian—the image of her mother with fair skin, shiny blond hair and clear, blue dancing eyes. Even the toss of her head was Dorothy's. For an instant Cameron saw Dorothy on their wedding day—laughing and happy—close in his arms as they danced together for the first time as man and wife—Dorothy—the mother Gillian had never known. Gillian and Ryan had been given life in a painful, difficult birth that had caused their mother's death. After much prodding, Gillian had gotten her grandparents to tell her the truth. She had never asked about her mother again. There was a deep hurt buried inside of her and she needed someone to help her understand her feelings.

"Do you need a hand?" Cameron asked.

Gillian smiled at him. "No, thanks, I'm almost finished."

It was her mother's smile and Cameron ached for Dorothy. *I haven't put it all behind me and as long as I have Gillian, I never will.*

Lately, when he sat alone at night and watched the fire die out in the fireplace, Cameron had been thinking of his own childhood, with a father who could not bring himself to love his son and he knew he had done the same to his children. They were young adults and embarking on lives of their own and he didn't know them. He had never shared their hopes and dreams. They were related genetically but not emotionally. There was no bond. He was just someone who, long ago in an act of fevered passion, had provided the sperm that gave them life.

"Thanks for coming home, Gillian." He walked over and sat on the edge of her bed. "I haven't been much of a father—I guess I haven't been a father at all. I'm trying to get my life together now. I'm asking a lot of you and your brother by hoping you'll forgive me—and I haven't got a good reason for what I've done. It was stupid to shut you out of my life."

"It's behind us. Grandma and Grandpa did a good job of giving us a home and love. We grew up pretty normal." Gillian took clothes out of her suitcase and turned away to the bureau.

"I missed watching you grow up. I missed all the things you shared with your grandparents. I don't even know what you're studying in college."

"I'm premed at Georgetown. Grandpa wanted mother to be a doctor. I'm trying to make his dream come true."

"What about your dreams, Gillian? Shouldn't you be trying to make your dreams come true?" He knew immediately that he had said the wrong thing.

"It brings me closer to the mother I never knew," Gillian said in a cold, emotionless tone.

"I'm sorry, Gillian. It was thoughtless of me to say that." He was afraid he had slammed the door between them. "I had dreams, too." It sounded lame.

"I don't know anything about you or your dreams. I just knew you were out there, somewhere and that you didn't give a damn about Ryan or me.

"Can we ever put all this behind us, Gillian?"

"I don't know. Actually, I don't know if I want to. It wasn't easy growing up, knowing you didn't care enough to want us to live with you or even see us. I used to pretend I was an orphan."

"I can never undo what's happened, Gillian. It's trite to say if I had it all to do over again it would be different. The truth is I'd probably make the same stupid mistake."

"I don't think we can dismiss this as a mistake. You're an intelligent man. I know about your record at Annapolis and I know what happened to you when you were in Vietnam."

"You're right, Gillian. Coward is a more appropriate description. Maybe someday, we'll be able to sort this out and understand. I'm not sure I can even tell you what's happened to me or make any sense out of it myself."

Gillian looked straight at her father. "Did you love my mother?"

"Yes." Cameron did not hesitate for a moment. "We loved each other with great passion, but we were not good for each other. Your mother had plans for me I just couldn't fulfill. I ran away to 'Nam. Maybe I was carrying a secret wish to die, I don't know. I could have stayed in Washington—stayed with your mother—been here when you were born."

"Why didn't you come back when she died? I know you could have."

"I think I was too busy feeling sorry for myself. And I didn't know what to do about having two babies. It was the easy way out to let your grandparents have you."

"They were good to us," Gillian said.

"They did a good job of raising you. You're a beautiful, intelligent young lady."

They were silent for a moment.

"Do you think you will ever be able to forgive me?" Cameron asked.

Gillian stopped unpacking and looked at him. "I don't know. I have to get to know you first. I'm not sure right now what we have to share. This is a big change in my life." Almost as an after thought, she added, "and Ryan's."

"Ryan worries me a little."

"I think Ryan takes after his father."

Cameron was not certain how to respond.

"He's very much the military man," Cameron said, after a silence.

"He hides his pain that way." Gillian went back to her unpacking. "We're both hurt. You never came to see us, you didn't write or call. It's like we never existed to you. Now you want us to be together and act like a family. We didn't send us away, you did. You took the easy way out instead of facing your responsibilities. Our grandparents gave us a lot of love. We've never had anything from you. I'm not sure why you have asked us here now or what you want from us. I do know we can't pretend the past hasn't happened."

"I think it took a lot of courage for you and your brother to come here. And, maybe, it's a mistake. I probably have no right to want to be in your lives now. I regret what I did. I will always regret it and I know there isn't anything I can do to make up for what's been done. I have no right to consider myself your father."

Gillian's tone softened. "I think we should spend some time together and see if there is any hope for us as a family. I'll talk to Ryan. We'll give it a try." She did not tell her father that Ryan was there only as a favor to her.

Gillian walked over and kissed Cameron on the cheek. His eyes filled with tears. He wanted to reach out and pull his daughter into his arms, but he was afraid. He got up and left the room.

Gillian was true to her word and the three of them began to make an effort to get to know and understand one another. After a few days, the tension eased and they became more comfortable. Gillian opened up the most, sharing her hopes and experiences in high school and college. Ryan was still reticent, but he began to seem a little more relaxed.

Cameron looked at the letter in his hands. It was a simply written invitation from the wife of the man who had served as his first sergeant in Vietnam. They had been close in the days when they faced death together, but their friendship had not bridged the years. There was always a Christmas card and what seemed to him a half-hearted invitation to visit. This was different. Ann had written and he felt a strange compulsion to accept.

This is the thing I should do now. A change of scenery and others around would be good for all three of them. A family vacation, he thought. God, they'll never buy into anything as hokey as this—they're barely tolerating me.

He was pleasantly surprised when they agreed. What he didn't know was that his children realized that by visiting someone, they would not have to be alone with him.

#

The Sheridan home was an attractive two-story white house, with a professionally landscaped and maintained lawn. It stood on a hill, above the often-turbulent waters of Bristol Lake. The picture said Better Homes and Gardens—carefully tended lawn, pruned shrubbery, oval flower garden showing the colors of early summer flowers, and two large, spreading maple trees. The garage door was open, displaying a collection of garden tools, motorcycle and other odds and ends that the Sheridans had collected. Two cars were in the driveway.

Cameron and Guy had met a few months before they were shipped to 'Nam. He had made friends easily then and he and Guy became close. Guy learned to anticipate his Lieutenant's needs and they were, by the time they faced combat, a good war team. Cameron spent many nights listening to Guy talk about his future. He was going to complete law school, find a nice, quiet town, open a practice, meet a woman, fall in love, get married, have a family and play golf on Saturday afternoons.

Cameron had long before given up his dream. His wife wanted to be part of Washington's society and he had promised her that when he returned from Vietnam duty, he would seek a permanent assignment in the Capitol.

Everything changed in one hellish night on the battlefield. Cameron finished his tour of duty in hospitals—first in Saigon and then one in Japan and finally one back in the states. Guy stayed to serve another Lieutenant and return, unscathed, to his hometown.

Cameron smiled when he saw Guy's wife. She still looked like the photograph Guy carried in his wallet and had taken out and kissed before he curled up to sleep each night. Her black hair was short and tossed back from her face, which was wearing the years well. She had kept her slim figure and the smile on her face said she was happy with her life.

Guy met Ann in Saigon, where she was serving as an Army nurse, and fell immediately in love. Cameron remembered Guy returning from leave babbling about the woman of his dreams. Guy's plans for his future had suddenly gotten out of order.

"I've met the woman I'm going to marry." Guy was on cloud nine. He showed Cameron a photo and she was indeed, as attractive as Guy had said. Guy spent all the free time he could manage in Saigon with his Annie. Guy junior was on the way before his parents had a chance to marry and return to the states.

Cameron felt uneasy about the relationship right from the start. Guy had fallen fast and hard for a woman who was aggressive and possessive. Despite his fears, the union had survived and they looked happy and comfortable with each other.

Life has been kind to you, Cameron thought, as he looked at the Sheridans, standing in the yard, waiting for them, as they pulled into the driveway.

Guy towered over his petite wife. Why is it lanky six-footers always marry women who are only five feet tall? Cameron wondered.

It pleased Cameron to know that they were so eager to see him. He stopped the car, drew a deep breath, got out and said "Hi."

All the greetings he had rehearsed during the trip were gone and all he could think of was, hi.

Ann ran down the walk, flung herself into his arms and kissed him on the mouth. Guy grabbed his free hand.

"Wow! This is some welcome."

"I guess it's a little late to introduce you to Annie," Guy said. "You two act like old friends."

For a moment, Cameron had the feeling he had met Ann before, then he realized that Guy had shown him her picture so many times, the image was etched in his memory.

"You look a lot thinner." Guy's voice pulled him back to the moment.

"I haven't put much effort into keeping myself in shape."

"I went to Saigon to see you and they said no visitors. I thought you had bought the farm," Guy said.

"Where's your wife?" Ann asked in an attempt to save what she sensed was an awkward situation.

He had spent hours going over in his mind what he would say when asked that question. But he couldn't answer the way he planned. "She died...while I was in 'Nam."

There, he had said the words. She died. She is dead. She is in a Maryland cemetery and I have never seen her grave. I don't know how she looked in her casket. I made none of the arrangements. I decided to cope by pretending she never existed—she simply disappeared from the earth—forever.

"I'm sorry, Cam. Why the hell didn't you write us? We would have helped you through this. We didn't know." Guy said.

He felt the weight of Guy's hand on his shoulder and he stiffened slightly. *I was too busy playing lost weekend and feeling sorry for myself. Hell, I couldn't even hold a pencil, let alone put words on a piece of paper.*

"I wanted to, but I couldn't figure out what to say. It was a long time ago." *Change the subject.*

"God, this is beautiful country." He let his arm slip around Ann's waist. "Hey, Guy, what happened to your hair?"

Guy rubbed his hand over his barren scalp. "Gone with the wind. It's the result of a certain young Lieutenant, who thought he was superman."

Guy had a slightly tanned face and large, dark brown eyes. His features were sharp and his nose looked too big for his face.

"My children. You haven't met the kids—well, they're not kids, any more—they're adults." He turned and looked at Ryan and Gillian, waiting patiently for him to finish greeting his friends.

"This is my daughter, Gillian and my son, Ryan." Ann hugged Gillian and Guy shook hands with Ryan and put his arm around his shoulder.

"I hope you can stay all summer, Ryan. Come on, let's get the suitcases into the house so you can change and join my boys down at the beach. I hope you water ski."

"You're going to live on the new boat while you're here, Cam. Guy had it delivered yesterday and he's been like a kid with a new toy waiting for you to arrive," Ann chided.

"We'll have to fight the boys for the boat, Cam. I lost it to them the minute it touched the water," Guy's tone was that of a happy, proud father. "Guy, junior talked me into this whole thing. I think he wants to impress your daughter and I can't say that I blame him."

Gillian blushed.

Cameron opened the trunk of the car and Guy grabbed two suitcases. He and Ryan took the others and hurried after Guy, who was halfway to the front door. Gillian followed, while Cameron lingered for a moment with Ann.

They smiled at each other and Cam struggled again with a fleeting memory. She took his hand and they headed into the house. "I thought I'd never get to meet you, Cam."

"Actually, I feel like we've met sometime…somewhere."

She laughed. "I must remind you of someone else."

"I guess."

They stepped through the front door into the carpeted hallway, hung with pictures of the family. Cameron stopped to look at them—photos of the boys in little league uniforms and in high school football and basketball uniforms. There were a number of action shots of young Guy, in the blue and white of Penn State's basketball team.

"That kid's the jock, Brian has the brains, which means he will struggle for a living like his father," Ann said.

"From what I see, you aren't having much of a struggle."

"Go into the living room and grab a look at the view," Guy shouted from another room. "I'll get the kids squared away so they can start enjoying themselves. They sure don't want to hang around and hear us ramble on about the good old days."

"This way," Cam." He followed Ann through a doorway and into the living room. He stopped for a moment and looked at the neat, modern furniture, the ceiling high bookcases and the huge stone fireplace. It was a warm attractive room and the wear on the furniture told him the Sheridans enjoyed their home. He followed Ann out onto the patio. Below, on the beach, he could see the boys—young men really, not boys anymore, but young adults like his children.

"Quite a sight, isn't it?" Guy called as he passed by the door.

"What do you think of our home?" Ann asked. She moved close to Cameron and slipped her hand into his.

"You can't look at this countryside and not believe in God. You're lucky—and I can't help but envy you."

"You seem so unhappy, Cam. You still miss your wife, don't you?"

At this moment, more than I ever imagined.

"I'm not much of an extrovert, Ann." He followed her back inside.

"We're going to change that while you're here. This house has enough energy for an army when the boys are home."

Cameron saw a photograph on the end table and picked it up. It was Ann when she was pregnant with one of the boys.

Why haven't you remarried?"

"I'll never remarry." There was coldness in his voice that kept Ann silent for a few minutes.

"You've missed a lot in your life, haven't you?" Ann continued.

"Yea. I never even saw my wife pregnant. You know what I mean—bulging. We were married when I graduated from Annapolis and we had all of a year together before I went off for combat training. She didn't want me to leave Washington. I think we were growing apart right from the start."

"She begged me not to get involved in the war," Cameron continued. "Her father could have gotten me out of it, but I needed to be a hero, I guess. I was home for a short leave before I went to 'Nam. I guess that's when she got pregnant. Jesus, what a mess we make of our lives."

Ann was startled by his sudden confession and thought it best not to comment.

tum tum tum ta tum…
tum tum tum ta tum…

The catafalque was old and tired and content to rest in the dark silence of the storage room. It's life had begun long ago with an unbelievable tragedy and now, without warning, it was time again to hold a people's shattered dreams. There was still strength in the solid oak wood, an enduring resiliency, but each burden took its toll. It knew what to expect. There would be miles of black bunting and whispering voices and tears—always tears. Soon the door would open and men would come and transport it to the majestic rotunda with frieze and statues and great paintings and the echoes of a Nation's history. Soon. For now, the stately catafalque waited.

tum tum tum ta tum...

CHAPTER II

The days flew past…sunrise fading too quickly into sunset…a page torn from the calendar and then another…and another…morning slipped into night and night into dawn. Cameron and Guy spent their time on the lake, fishing and talking, trying to relive all the years in the short time they had together. Two weeks came and went. Guy and Ann insisted that they stay longer. It was July.

The days grew warmer and summer was in full swing. They all tanned brown from the days on the beach. Young Guy and Gillian were in love. Cameron watched his daughter and hoped that when the summer love ended, she would not be too deeply hurt. She was beautiful and full of life and it was easy to understand young Guy's infatuation. Cameron enjoyed seeing her so happy and forced himself not to show the usual fears of a father.

She's a woman, he told himself, *and old enough to face responsibilities.*

"She's premed, for Christ's sake," he muttered to himself and laughed.

He remembered her mother and the love they had once felt for each other. He was embarrassed as he recalled his youthful passion and felt a pain surge through his loins.

Despite the fatigue from the activity filled days, he had trouble sleeping. By night he was exhausted and ready to welcome the pleasant, refreshing rest that renews a man's body, but it wasn't there. He would wake with a jerk, in a sweat, thinking he had heard someone whispering to him.

There was a dream swirling through his mind and he couldn't imagine where it had come from. *Who the hell am I to think I have the intelligence and ability to be a leader? What I need is a wife, a job and a home. Damn it, I'm losing my mind.*

He turned over and pulled the extra pillow into his arms. *I can never have what the Sheridans have. Damn you for dying, Dorothy. Damn my life. Damn this throbbing in my head. Why do I always want something I can't have?* Suddenly he felt like he had lost his own thoughts and he shivered with fear.

#

He was sitting on the patio with Ann, waiting for Guy to return from a meeting with a client. The kids had left early for a cookout at a neighbor's cottage. The gentle westerly breeze was chasing the day's heat across the hills. He did not want to talk. He wanted to sit in silence and try to understand his troubled thoughts.

"Are you always so reticent?" Ann asked. "I've been watching you these past weeks, Cam. Don't you ever let yourself have any fun? You seem afraid to be happy."

"I am what I am, Ann. Guy remembers someone else. And I'm not looking for a shoulder to cry on."

"I'm not offering one. Can't you let a friend care about you? You can't continue the way you're going, with so much bottled up inside. Your kids don't even know you, Cam."

"I love my children."

"I know you do, but you ignore them. They want your love but you insist on being a stranger to them. Have you even held Gillian in your arms? She doesn't have a mother. You're the only one in the world she can turn to and she needs you now. You must be able to see that she's fallen in love with young Guy?"

Cameron nodded his head as Ann continued.

"She had a long talk with me last night. She has a lot of things on her mind. She and Guy are a man and a woman and their emotions are putting a strain on their relationship. They're good kids and they don't want to be foolish. Gillian needs you, Cam. She needs your love and understanding. You're afraid to love her, aren't you?"

"No."

"Yes you are. You're afraid you'll lose her like you lost her mother."

"That's not true, Ann"

"It is, Cam. I hit the nail on the head. Oh, Cam, I feel so sorry for you. If you don't change, you're going to destroy yourself and your family."

"I didn't come here for you to start rearranging my life."

"Well, I intend to rearrange your life. I can't stand to see you so damn unhappy." Ann picked up the pitcher from the table between them and refilled her glass of iced tea. Cameron had not touched his.

"I am not unhappy," Cameron mumbled, half aloud.

"Yes, you are. I haven't heard you laugh once. When Guy talks about his plans for the future, you get this pitiful look on your face. Guy has noticed it too. He's worried about you. If you aren't careful you'll pick up a bottle and drink yourself to death."

"I tried that...once," Cameron whispered.

Ann looked at him for a moment before continuing.

"And you have the nerve to sit here and tell me you're not an unhappy man. I think it's about time you started making some changes. Your kids are growing up and you're going to wake up damn soon, alone. It's about time you found someone who wants to love you. Try it, Cam, you might like it."

"No...never again will I let myself love someone." The words slipped out in a plaintive cry and his thoughts sped backward—to a day a long time ago...

#

How long had he been in the damned hospital? How many days of staring at the ceiling—counting the acoustical blocks—listening to those infernal, muted bells? How many nights without sleep? He was institutionalized and so used to the routine that days no longer had individuality. He wanted to die. He knew he was back in the States now but what difference did that make? There had been another operation and still the pain continued. He wanted to be free of the world.

His pelvis has been shattered. The damned shell had blown a hole right through him. That had capped his future nicely. Sure, they had put in some nice metal plates and now some fuckin' do-gooders kept trying to force him through physical therapy to get him on his feet and walking again. They kept telling him that with time the pain would ease and he would walk without a limp. They kept saying how damn fortunate he was to be alive—telling him how close he had come to being killed. What the hell did they know? His life was so screwed up that all the therapy in the world would never put it back together again.

He lay there wandering through the past, weeping inwardly at all the things that should have been...all the things that might have been. He remembered his childhood dream of becoming a major league baseball player. He had been good in high school; so good that two pro teams had offered him tryouts, but his father had decided on the day his first and only son was born that he would attend the Naval Academy. No one ever dared to defy his father. Cameron had learned that the hard way, so he took the examination, praying all the time he would score too low to be accepted. It would have been so simple to mess up the answers. But he had an innate sense of competition, so he did his best. The appointment came and his goddamned father didn't even bother to accompany him to Maryland. He never set foot on the Academy grounds the four years Cameron was there.

The drive to succeed did not wane and he excelled at the Academy, graduating fourth in his class. He accepted a commission in the Marine Corps, his private defiance of his father, and married Dorothy Cammet, youngest daughter of Wesley Cammet, Democratic Senator from Maryland, on graduation day.

He was so deep in the memories of his past, wishing he could go back and undo the mistakes he had made, that he was unaware of someone entering his room, until a soft, feminine voice crooned, "Hello, Lieutenant."

Cameron's eyes shot open and his vision was filled with the image of a woman with dark red hair framing a china doll complexion. He sucked a gulp of air into his lungs.

She smiled and he smiled. Oh, the red, full lips—glistening—wanting to be kissed—begging for the touch of his lips on hers—and the heavenly scent—filling his nostrils—burning into his soul…

"I'm dead and you are an angel," he whispered, hoping the sound of his voice would not break the spell.

"No, but I'm very flattered. I'm Gloria Kenwood…" Her deep, throaty voice sent chills down his spine.

"Hello, Gloria Kenwood, whoever you are." He couldn't believe the beauty of the woman beside his bed. His eyes moved downward from her face and he stared at her blouse, taunt over full breasts. Tiny beads of sweat formed on his upper lip and he licked them off with his tongue.

She leaned close and spoke softly to him. "I really don't believe that you don't know who I am, with all the movies I have made."

He cut her off quickly. "I don't go to movies."

She moved away from him and her tone changed. "You just lie here on this bed?"

"Twenty-four hours a day. I'm making a survey of the blocks on the ceiling. Do you know there are 22 blocks in each row?" He remembered how long it had been since he had had a woman. He wanted this one, wanted to feel her nakedness close to him, wanted to feel her moving under him. He cleared his throat.

"I sure as hell must have the wrong room. They told me you were the guy who had risked his life saving someone in Vietnam. I didn't expect someone drowning in self-pity."

The dream shattered. He turned his face from her.

"You certainly are the miserable bastard they say you are, aren't you?"

"Get out of here. I'm sick and tired of being a perpetual good deed for every goddamned Girl Scout in the country!"

Gloria made one quick move, picked up the carafe on the table and poured the ice water over Cameron's head. She turned and was out the door while he sputtered in rage.

Cameron was furious. He was trembling and incoherent when the nurses appeared to change his clothes and bed linens. He watched them hiding their silly smirks. He hated them—the whole goddamned world. To culminate his rage, he shattered the carafe against the wall.

"Get out of my room! Get out! Go back to your horny interns who screw you every night. Whores!! Whores!!" He screamed in his rage.

The nurses won the war. His supper was cold when they got around to delivering his tray. They checked his temperature rectally with a thermometer they kept in ice water, every half hour throughout the night.

Early the next morning his voice rang loud and clear as he cursed the nurses and called for his doctor.

Vincent Korbell was a patient man. He had dealt with people more obstinate than Cameron Marshall. He went about his morning rounds, taking a little more time than usual with each patient. He enjoyed hearing Cameron's curses and he had a hard time keeping a smile from his lips when he entered the room. He had no idea what had happened and he didn't care. He knew that he was finally going to get this man back on his feet.

"All right. All right. You win. I'll cooperate with the therapy. Just get me back on my feet and fast. No two-bit Hollywood bitch is going to pour water on me again."

Cameron had never dreamed it would be so difficult to walk again. First, they made him work on parallel bars, until he regained his strength. Cameron was impatient with the time it was taking, but he had lain in bed so long, he had lost muscle strength. He was weak and tired easily. When he got tired, the pain was worse. When he took hot baths, he could feel the metal plates rubbing on the bottom of the tub. He would collapse in bed at night exhausted and convinced that it was all a hopeless task.

As the days passed, the pain grew less and muscles began to respond to the exercises.

Gloria came back.

She went straight to his room and was surprised to find it empty. She had come to apologize. She stopped at the desk and asked if he had been discharged. She was directed to the solarium at the end of the hall. There she found him, feet propped up, reading a book. He looked up as she approached.

"No more water," he said, placing his hands over his head in mock defense.

"It's good to see you out of bed, Lieutenant."

She was even more beautiful than he remembered.

"When I found your room empty, I thought maybe you caught pneumonia from the water and died."

"Not me. I'm too mean for anything that easy."

She smiled. "I guess you'll be leaving the hospital soon?"

"Pretty soon, they tell me. There are a couple of temporary pins they have to remove. What brought you back?"

"I came to apologize for what I did to you."

"I've been reading a lot about you. I'll bet the papers made a big thing out of the water incident."

Gloria's face flushed. "I didn't tell them."

"I guess I'm still a miserable bastard. I didn't mean to say that. To tell the truth, I hadn't thought about it until now. Why don't we start over, just as if we're meeting for the first time? Right now...OK? Hi! I'm Cameron Marshall."

"I'm Gloria Kenwood."

"Hi, Gloria. You are the most beautiful woman I've ever seen."

"Flattery will get you everywhere, soldier." She perched on the arm of his chair, letting her skirt slip above the knee.

"Marine, if you please. Don't confuse me with a dog faced army man." He couldn't keep his eyes off her thigh. His fingers wanted to reach out and caress the inviting smooth flesh.

"That's right. You're sensitive about those things, aren't you?"

27

"You bet. How long can you stay?"

"I have only this afternoon. I've got two wonderful weeks free and I plan to have one hell of a shopping spree in New York."

"I can't go to New York, yet. Shop in Washington."

They spent everyday of the two weeks together. The weather turned warmer so they drove into the country for picnic lunches and he would lie with his head in her lap and her perfume filled his nostrils. He wanted her so much that he was trembling inside. He ached for her touch. Her image filled his mind when he slept and he would wake in the night and reach for her. It had been too damn long since he had made love to a woman.

His heart beat faster when she was near. He wanted to consume her—carry her off somewhere where they could be alone—where they could shut out the world and make love—somewhere...anywhere.

His body screamed for the feel of her flesh against his. Sometimes, when they were lying side by side, he would caress her breasts and probe his tongue deep into her mouth. But she was distant.

"Not yet," she said. "Not yet."

He didn't argue with her for, despite his raging desire, nothing was stirring. His goddamned medicine was making him impotent.

They both knew the time was gone. Neither could bring themselves to mention it, to say the words, to admit that with the new day, she would have to leave.

He graduated to a cane and the limp was hardly noticeable. Even the pain was almost completely gone. But, the doctors had one more pin to remove, so it would be a couple of more weeks before he would be discharged.

They walked across the hospital grounds to their friend, the big oak, standing majestically in east corner of the hospital grounds. Here they had shared private moments and long, deep kisses. He leaned against the rough, aged bark of the trunk and she moved into the warm circle of his arms.

"I have to leave, Cam. Please understand. The studio is sending me on a tour. They have everything arranged. The schedule can't be changed." The words rushed out as she pressed against him.

"When will I see you again?"

"Three weeks isn't the end of the world."

"It is when you're away from the person you love."

"Please don't make this any harder than it is, Cam. We're adults. We knew

I couldn't stay here forever." She brushed her lips against his cheek.

"What should I say? Thanks for the long walks in the sun. Thanks for getting me out of bed. You did a good job. The charity assignment is over. Drop me a postcard now and then—if you have the time. Do we shake hands now, like a couple of good sports?"

She was crying. "No—you kiss me and I cry." She pressed her body tight against him. Their lips met—again—and again. A searing flame rushed through his loins and suddenly he felt life in the old boy. He ran his tongue over her teeth. She pulled back and gasped for breath.

"I'll call."

"Every night?"

"Every night."

"I'll miss you every moment you're gone."

"Oh, Cam, why is this happening to us?" He kissed her again. She tasted of salt from the tears that streamed down her face.

"Let me make love to you—here, right now," he whispered, his hand slipping under her blouse to cradle her breast. "Let me keep that memory with me."

"No, Cam. I can't. Not here—not now."

"Why not? Please, Gloria. I love you so much. Goddamn it, I'm functioning again. Do you understand what that means to me? Why can't I make love to you?"

All her life, Gloria had been consumed by the dream of stardom—visiting different cities—greeted by crowds—the excitement—the fun—parties—handsome men to escort her—everything glamorous and breathtaking. She just hadn't counted on falling in love. That had never been part of her plan. Now that the world was hers, it was taking her away from the first man she had truly loved. She wanted him to go with her. She knew he needed her.

Why am I offering him only a phone call every night? The publicity department of my studio would love the story and could arrange for them to be together. But that would spoil everything. He's too proud. And I'm not about to give up my career—not when I'm at the top—not when I'm finally starting to live my dream.

She wanted desperately to win the Academy Award. That was the reason for the tour. Boost her popularity—show her as the people's choice. Hell, the acting job was good, but support of the public was what garnered the votes, the studio said. She had to win that award. Cameron would understand. Or would he? Did that shiny gold-plated object mean more to her than a man who loved her? He didn't love her because she was a movie star. He loved her because she was a woman—a sensuous woman who needed a man. It had been a long time for her too—too damn long for Daisy McCroy.

tum tum tum ta tum…
tum tum tum ta tum…

The strain of concentration showed on the faces of the eight young men as they lifted the casket—sandbags had been added for his weight—slowly upward. They turned, obeying hand signals noticeable only to the trained eye, and started moving forward, the casket they carried suspended in the space between them. Their arms ached and perspiration was staining their uniforms. Then a halt, another turn and forward into position on each side of the sawhorses, representing the catafalque. They eased the box down slowly, back away a few steps, turned and marched away, backs ramrod straight, heads high, eyes staring straight ahead, feet barely rising from the floor. The Commander's voice broke the silence. "Again," he said, "again."
tum tum tum ta tum…

CHAPTER III

Daisy McCroy had come screaming into life in the world of a West Virginia coal mining family. Her earliest memories were of a cold and dirty four-room house that never looked clean, no matter how hard or how often it was scrubbed. A fine, black coal dust settled onto everything. She hated her home—hated the kitchen, with its smelly coal stove, where they ate their meals on dishes, cracked so long that they were filled with crooked, black lines—and the table, painted and repainted so many times that the enamel was cracking and chipping and you could see the many layers of paint, tell every color that had been on sale at the Company store, tell the number of times her mother had tried to make the room look cheerful.

There were eight—her parents, two sisters, three brothers and herself. Carl McCroy and his sons worked deep in the mines, going down into the bowels of the earth in the dim light of early morning on a creaky, slow moving elevator. The women who waited in the sunlight lived with the constant fear of the day when the whistle would blow and tragedy would stalk the town. It had happened before and in their hearts they knew it was only a matter of time before it would happen again.

Daisy didn't worry about a mine accident. The dream of leaving Hinton consumed her. Escaping from the life that was strangling her mother and sisters was her goal—and she would make it someday—some way—any way.

She developed early into a beautiful young woman, with long red hair and dark green eyes, accented by long, fluttering eyelashes, and round, firm breasts. Her full lips took on a pouting look and she soon learned to enjoy the glances of the boys as she walked down the street. She relished their attention and two days after her twelfth birthday, she was no longer a virgin.

Homer Bleck was sixteen and already working in the mines. Like most young men in Hinton, there was no point in going to school beyond the eight grade, so he had quit and joined his father and brothers in the dark regions of the earth. He had always had a fancy for Daisy, but Daisy couldn't stand him. She saw him like she saw all the boys in Hilton—dirty, ignorant and content to live the same lives as their fathers.

Daisy did, however, enjoy teasing Homer. It amused her to watch him sweat and become so nervous that he stuttered when he talked. She would mock him and laugh, unbutton her blouse and run her tongue around lips. She took delight in watching him grow excited and she would swat at the bulge in his jeans with her purse. The she would elude his attempts to grab her and skip away, leaving him bent over and moaning to himself.

One day the game went further than she intended.

It was an early spring Sunday afternoon and most of the boys were playing baseball on the dirt field behind the one-room schoolhouse. Homer wandered over to Daisy and asked if she wanted to go for a walk. She shook her head no. Homer responded by grabbing the ribbon from her hair and dashing into the woods. She ran after him and found him waiting. Without a word, he took her hand and they started walking down an old logging road. They laughed and whispered together. Birds were chirping loudly in the budding trees and the woods seemed to be coming alive with tiny shoots of spring growth poking through the damp leaves beneath the bushes.

She broke away from him and ran ahead. He hurried to catch her. They came to a mountain brook, still hurtling small pieces of ice downstream—more evidence of the fading winter. Daisy climbed onto a large rock, sat down and threw her head back, letting the warm rays of the sun caress her face.

"Oh, how I love the feel of the sun," she sighed.

Homer sat beside her. He covered her hand with his. "Let me kiss you," he begged. "Just once."

Daisy turned her head and met his lips. It was a childish kiss that aroused no emotions. Homer took her hand, helped her to her feet and led her toward the shade of some towering pine trees. He took off his faded denim jacket and spread it on the ground. When she sat down, he fell to his knees in front of her and started kissing her again and rubbing his hands over her body. Daisy leaned back contentedly and let Homer undo her blouse. She felt a warm, tingling sensation as his large, rough hands passed over her breasts and rubbed the hard nipples.

She lifted her arms above her head and sighed. She felt good—alive—

happy that it was spring and that she was a year older and a year closer to fulfilling her dream. She didn't seem to mind Homer's fumbling and that surprised her. She shifted her weight so he could remove her blouse and skirt. She was wearing an old pink bra that had once belonged to her sister Martha. Most of her clothes were hand-me-downs. All that would change when she was rich and famous. She closed her eyes and her mind drifted away. She pictured herself as a beautiful, famous movie star—dressed in a shimmering golden gown—and a long mink coat. She would wear her clothes one time and then donate them to the poor. Maybe she would have them shipped back to Hinton. The thought pleased her. She made a mental note to specify that when she made her donations.

Her mind was a hundred thousand miles away from Hinton and Homer Black. She was no longer conscious of his touch or words. When he lifted her up to unfasten her bra, she offered neither help nor resistance. So entrapped in her dream was she that she was hardly aware of Homer's lips and the cool mountain breeze on her bare flesh. The pain as he nibbled her left breast brought her back to partial reality for a moment She moved a little, then surrendered to what was not an unpleasant sensation and once again let her thoughts take her far from the West Virginia hills.

She sighed as she drifted away and Homer took that as a signal that all was going well. He worked harder to arouse her. Daisy felt a tingling sensation between her legs and then Homer struggling to remove her panties. She closed her eyes. In an instant she was transported to her imaginary world and the childish dream—a thick, feather-filled mattress—there were no servants in the house—she had sent them off on a holiday so she could be alone with her lover—the handsome prince come from far across the sea to beg the favors of her beautiful body.

The dream shattered in a scream as Homer plunged himself into her body. She screamed again, but it was too late. Nothing could stop him now. He was like a train laden with coal running full tilt down the mountainside. He buffeted her body. She had never imagined that there would be pain. She bit her lip as he plunged—again—and again—faster and faster. Then, she found herself arching her body to meet his hammering thrusts. She had no control over her body now.

"My, God!" Don't stop," she cried. "Please, don't stop!"

He rammed himself deeper and deeper into her body.

"Homer—Homer," she whispered and then a scream burst from her—but it wasn't a scream of pain—but a yell of passion as Daisy knew the ecstasy of her first orgasm.

It ended with blood on her legs and a pleasant ache deep inside her body. Homer rolled over on his side and struggled to catch his breath.

"I never dreamed it was like this," he panted. "Can we do it again, please?"

She looked at his body. His limp penis was short and wrinkled and for a moment she was consumed with disgust. But she felt a need—a burning—a hunger—"Yes, yes—Homer, yes," she whispered remembering the pleasure of the spasm that had racked her body.

Three times that afternoon she lay in his fervent embraces. Three times and each time better than the last. When they were finished, she could hardly stand. Homer was on his knees with exhaustion. But she wanted more—had to have more.

"Tonight," she promised. "I'll slip out of the house and meet you here."

Homer was just the beginning. Daisy could not be faithful to one person. My lovers, she called them in her dreams. And they were her lovers, as young as they were. Sometimes it was two different boys on the same day. She seldom went back to school after lunch and there was always a boy absent, too. The teacher was too tired and disinterested to care about the mountain white trash, which is how he described the students to his friends in the city.

Homer had unleashed a surging tide in Daisy that she would never be able to satisfy or control.

A year passed and she was thirteen and soon after, physically a woman. She hated herself when she menstruated because now she would have to be careful. Her mother gave her long lectures. Daisy knew what to do. She made Homer buy her a supply of rubbers, which she was never without. She kept the package wrapped in an old handkerchief, which she carried in her red, plastic purse.

Boys marked their passage into manhood with Daisy, either in the woods or in the back seat of a car. One night, in the back of a battered sedan, it was three in a row. It was always the boys who had enough long before Daisy had her appetite satisfied. She began to make them pay for her favors—with a pretty blouse, a skirt and shiny, patent leather shoes—clothes she kept carefully hidden from her mother and sisters. She would slip out of the house after supper, hurry to the old tool shed out back, change into her fancy clothes, sweep her hair up into a pile on her head, paint her lips red and meet whoever it was waiting for her. And someone was always waiting for her.

Time passed and seasons changed—the leaves fell from the trees and were blown across the barren hills. Then it was winter and with the first snow came tragedy. An explosion left eighteen men to rest forever in the earth. Among them were her father and Homer Bleck. Daisy shed no tears for Homer. It didn't matter to her that he was dead. She was tired of him. Besides, Daisy didn't cry for anyone.

The mine closed. People were out of work and lost and confused. The door was slammed shut on a way of life and the miners and their families had no idea how to pick up the pieces and begin again. Many left Hinton, but the McCroy family remained because her mother was too afraid to leave the only life she had known. Daisy begged and pleaded and screamed at her mother, but it was no use. The family had always been tied to the mines and soon they would reopen and there would be work for her brothers again. After all, the mines had always been there.

The men grew restless as days passed into weeks and weeks into months and months into a year. No word came of the reopening. There was talk on the news about the growing poverty in Appalachia.

Daisy watched her mother grow more tired and haggard every day. Hope was gone and with it her mother's soul.

In the summer of Daisy' sixteenth year, a group of men came to Hinton to film scenes of the West Virginia poverty for a television show. The men were easy to identify in their clean, pressed shirts and chino slacks. Daisy walked the streets and watched them. She was secretly glad now that her family had not left Hinton. Maybe she would get to be on television and the whole world would see her.

She smiled suggestively at the man who seemed to be in charge. He was older than the others and dressed in a light colored summer suit. She winked at him and enjoyed his look as he appraised her figure. She watched the pleasure in his eyes as he stared at her breasts, straining against the faded blue material of her blouse.

She walked toward him, swinging her hips from side to side.

"My mama always told me it ain't polite to stare, mister."

"The man's face flushed. "I'm sorry. I didn't mean…"

"Ya got a car?"

He pointed across the dirt street to a convertible.

Daisy' eyes grew wide. "Will ya take me for a ride in it? I ain't never rode in a new car before. I ken show you around the town."

He took her by the arm and led her across the street. He opened the car door for her. Daisy had never been treated like a lady before. She got in and scooted to the center of the front seat, so that she was close to him when he got behind the wheel. As they drove, she rubbed her hands across the red vinyl. The came to a narrow dirt road leading off into the woods. Daisy directed the man to turn. The drove along the edge of a creek until the road ended. He stopped the car and turned off the engine.

"Do many people come here?" he asked.

"Sometimes. I know a place where nobody goes, 'ceptin' me." In a flash, she was out of the car and running along her familiar path. When she reached the top of the hill, she sat on the gnarled trunk of a fallen tree, hiked her skirt up high on her legs and waited. He was breathing heavily when he caught up with her.

"Ya ain't gonna do anything bad to me, are ya, mister? I ain't never been with a strange man before," Daisy lied, making her voice sound like a little girl's.

"John—Johnny—my name is Johnny." His voice was a hoarse whisper. "Of course, I won't hurt you." He knelt beside her, took a handkerchief from his pocket and began mopping the sweat from his face. "Boy, it sure gets hot down here. Do you mind if I take off my jacket?" He slipped out of his jacket and loosened his tie.

"I'll tell ya a secret, if ya promise not ta tell anyone. Sometimes when it's hot like this, I come up here all alone and take off all my clothes. Then I lie here neked in the cool grass. It feels so good." She watched the man's face. He was flushed and struggling for control.

He's almost as funny as Homer, Daisy thought. *Stupid, dead Homer.*

"I'd like that," Johnny whispered. "I'm awfully hot. Why don't we?"

"We what?"

"You know—take off all our clothes and lie in the cool grass. It's such a hot day. We'd both feel better."

"Ya ain't gonna tell on me, are ya, mister?"

He helped her to her feet and she began to undress, first her skirt and then she started to unbutton her blouse. She watched the man's face out of the corner of her eye. One by one, she undid the buttons and slid the garment over one shoulder and then down her back. She heard a gasp and turned to see him naked with his long shaft hard and throbbing.

"I ain't never seen a man without his clothes on," she teased.

She stopped removing her own clothes and stared at him. Nothing had ever given her as much pleasure as she felt right now, teasing this man she hardly knew. She slipped out of her slip and folded it neatly and placed it on top of her skirt and blouse. He was clenching his fists now, fighting for control. She turned her back and slipped off her bra. She heard a groan and turned to face him as she ran her fingers around the elastic of her panties.

He could control himself no longer. In one quick move he pushed her to the ground, tore off her panties and entered her. She forced herself to cry in mock pain throughout the experience, fighting hard to keep her hungry body in check so she would not thrust herself upward to meet his rhythm and match his emotion. He came fast. She dissolved in uncontrollable sobs when he finished. It was not difficult for her to cry. She was furious that he had finished so fast and left her on the brink of a climax.

He tried to comfort her. "How old are you?" he whispered, cradling her in his arms, brushing her hair and then rubbing one hand over her taunt breast.

"Eighteen," she lied. "It's all right. It only hurt a little." She continued to cry softly and pressed her head against his chest. She let one of her hands drift down and fondled him.

"Will ya take me with ya, when ya go, Johnny? Will ya take me away from this awful place? Please?"

"Oh, God, yes. Anything. I'll do anything you want."

#

New York City. Nothing Daisy had read or seen on television prepared her for the excitement she found when she arrived in the city. She stared at the crowds of people: models, dressed in the latest fashions, hurrying to an appointment—neon signs flashing messages to the world—street vendors hawking hot dogs and cheap watches—the honking horns of the traffic—taxis dodging through traffic with passengers—all the colors and sounds of the world—stiff mannequins in dress shops windows staring into space—the smell of charcoal from roasting chestnuts—people speaking in different languages—this was going to be her world now. She loved the noise, the confusion and the smells. She wanted to stop strangers on the street, grab them and hug them and tell them her name and tell them that she was going to be famous.

She had lost track of the man who had brought her to the city. *What was his name? Johnny. Right. Hell, that bastard never even told me his last name. Shit, that don't matter. I'm here. That's all that matters.*

She stared at the towering skyscrapers, standing transfixed in the center of the crowded sidewalk while people cursed as they moved around her.

It had taken them a week to drive up from West Virginia. All those goddamned cheap motels. But, he had taught her some tricks. He rented her a dismal little apartment. All he could afford, he had said, because he had a wife and three kids. Things were good for a few weeks, and then, without warning, he pressed a fifty-dollar bill into her hand, kissed her on the cheek and said good-bye. Daisy closed the door behind him, listened as his footsteps faded from the hall and then let out a big, "Yowie!"

She didn't want to be tied down with him or with anything right now—not now—not when she was getting a taste of life—not when she was beginning to live.

She used Johnny's fifty dollars to buy a cheap suit in a Salvation Army Thrift Store and a copy of Variety. She began making the rounds of auditions, even though she didn't have the slightest idea what auditioning was about. Daisy knew only one way to get what she wanted and it always worked.

In a week, she had landed a bit part. It was a three-line walk on role, for which she granted the producer certain liberties on the sofa in his office. It was a start.

He liked Daisy and wanted more. He bought her new clothes and moved her into a better apartment, with wall-to-wall carpeting, all-be-it a little worn, almost new furniture, a kitchen she would never use and a big, soft double bed that rattled and creaked with their lovemaking. He, too, was married, but he seldom went home to his wife. The day the play left for road tryouts, Daisy turned the key in the lock for the last time and dropped it into the trash barrel in the alley.

On the road, Daisy discovered the advantages of hotel living with convenient room service, provided, free of charge, by handsome, horny bellhops.

The show closed in Philadelphia. That was where she met Adrian. Adrian, hell, his name was Isaac Steinberg. He put on a phony French accent, but he didn't fool Daisy for long. She had noticed him backstage, looking at the girls. He was a tall, thin man with more hair in his goatee that on his head. He called himself a drama coach, whatever that meant. The day the closing notices were posted, he took Daisy aside.

"Cherie…with work, with the proper coaching, you could become a great actress." He punctuated his words with jabbing gestures.

She had no idea what he was talking about, but she needed a place to live, so it was back to New York with Adrian to live in his cramped, studio apartment. Maybe he could help her reach the stardom she kept dreaming about day and night. Maybe he was the one.

Daisy was grateful for the acting lessons, but after three months, she couldn't stand Adrian. He was like a character straight out of one of those cheap, trashy novels she liked to read.

He hounded her, hour after hour, day after day. This was necessary, he said, because she had so much to learn. The West Virginia accent had to go— she had to learn how to walk properly—nothing she did was right and he would scream and yell at her. Once, he sent a chair flying in her direction. She managed to duck and for a moment, frightening terror gripped her.

She had no choice but to endure his abuse…she didn't have any money so she couldn't move out. Night after night, he would tie her to the bed and beat her with his belt while she screamed and cried for him to stop. Then and only then, was he able to take her. Afterward, he would hold her and beg for her forgiveness. The beatings got worse and she knew, deep inside, that if she didn't get away, he would kill her.

She managed to get a part in an off-Broadway play and moved out. She didn't even bother to leave him a note. She saw him once after that, with another girl on his arm.

Two years passed and for Daisy the progress was painfully slow. She was depressed because the lightening bolt of stardom had not struck. So she wasn't the world's greatest actress. Hell, half of the stars in Hollywood weren't either, they just screwed the right men. Sitting along in a bar one evening, trying to wash away her black mood and perhaps find someone who would buy her dinner, she noticed a man watching her. She smiled and he moved to the stool next to her. He introduced himself as Kurt Randall and asked permission to join her. As he sat down, he handed her an engraved card: "Kurt Randall—Artist Representative."

"So what." Daisy flipped the card back to him.

"That means that I am an agent. How would you like to leave Broadway and start making movies?"

"By tomorrow?" she snapped. "That's when I'm bein' thrown out of my apartment."

"I'm serious. I've seen you work. You're not great, but you are also not terrible. You've got looks and a great body and that counts for a hell of a lot, baby."

"So, tell me more." She motioned for the waiter to bring her another drink. She looked him over, from his Ivy League haircut, to the small, almost unnoticeable scar on his left cheek. He was more handsome than the other men she had been involved with in New York. No wedding band on his left hand, not that that meant anything, she told herself.

"I've got a plan." He took a cigarette from a gold case and tapped the tip on the back of his hand. "You, my pet, will be my personal Eliza Doolittle."

She didn't have the slightest idea what in the hell he was talking about, but it didn't matter as long as he was good for a few drinks and dinner.

She watched him fit the cigarette into a holder and light it with a gold lighter. She almost laughed out loud at the funny way he tossed his head back and gripped the holder between his teeth. It reminded her of a picture she had seen somewhere.

"If you want to be a star, you will have to play the game by my rules. This is an idea I've had since college. In fact, I have a hell of a bet with my former roommate. He thinks I'm crazy. But, you are my chance to make this work. Let's go to your apartment. I want to see what kind of a place you're being evicted from tomorrow. You can show me your portfolio."

Daisy smiled at him. The same old story. At least he was good looking and she had not had sex for two weeks. It would be good to feel him in bed with her.

Daisy opened the door to her apartment and was immediately ashamed. She cursed herself silently for not having cleaned the place up. This man was used to finer things. She could tell from his clothes and he had been to college.

"Make yourself comfortable while I change." She grabbed some clothes that had been tossed onto the sofa and hurried into the bedroom. She wanted to make sure the bed was made and the dirty clothes picked up. She pushed some dirty dishes under the bed. She opened a dresser drawer and selected a brand new, white negligee, a gift from the last man who had enjoyed her favors. She was proud of her body and she paused for a moment in front of the mirror to admire herself.

She thrust her breasts forward and moved her hands downward. "This is your ticket to Hollywood, baby, no matter what anyone says, this is your ticket," she whispered to herself.

He was visibly startled by her appearance. "Wait a minute, my dear, somehow you see to have gotten the wrong idea. I was talking about a business proposition. I never tumble with a client. This, my dear, is an image we are going to eliminate." He pulled open her robe and let his eyes sweep down her body.

Daisy took a deep breath, let it out slowly and wet her lips with the tip of her tongue.

"Nice. You've got great tits, baby, and a good shape. Too bad women don't turn me on," he sighed, closing the robe. "It might be fun for a change." He shot a longing glance toward the bedroom and the waiting double bed. Then he turned and walked across the room.

"Go put some clothes on." His voice was cold and harsh.

He moved her into his apartment and enrolled her in City College. She was taking English, voice and diction, acting, singing lessons and a class about the history of the theatre. Daisy had always hated school. She had quit after the eighth grade in Hinton and here she was, letting this man force her into going to classes. At night he would drill her on the lessons.

He bought her new clothes—dresses and tailored suits—all expensive, but nothing that Daisy would have selected for herself. They had high necklines and long sleeves. Not a single one showed off her best assets. And gloves— pairs and pairs of white gloves.

He kept a record of the money spent. It was an investment, he explained, and he expected her to pay it all back, with high interest.

One day, her afternoon classes were cancelled and she came home early. She heard noises in the bedroom when she entered the apartment. She tiptoed across the living room and pushed the bedroom door open a crack. She saw Kurt in bed, with a man on top of him. Kurt was wiggling and moaning like a woman.

She had never known a homosexual. She had heard people back home laughing and calling them queers, but she never knew what made them different. She had a hard time understanding why a man would not be turned on by a beautiful woman and the thought of two men in bed together made her sick at her stomach. She stepped back from the bedroom door and left the apartment. She decided not to say anything to Kurt about what she had seen.

Kurt hired a woman to teach her how to dress, do her makeup and walk properly.

"You will never appear in public without white gloves," Kurt ordered.

Daisy could not comprehend what he had in mind. She was going to the damn classes and, much to her surprise, enjoying them, although she would not admit that to Kurt. And she did talk better. The West Virginia twang had disappeared and she now knew something about plays and playwrights, except that damn Shakespeare and his crazy language.

But it was Kurt who was driving her crazy. How the hell did he expect her to keep living without sex?

She was grateful for what he had done for her, but she was going to have to get ahead on her own. He was nothing but a damn nut with a white glove fetish.

Damn...damn...damn...all I ever get involved with is nuts. At least most of them gave me a good screwing. But, not this queer.

She made up her mind that when the semester ended, she would leave him. After all, she had been good for a year. That was long enough.

When she walked into the apartment after her last class, she found him waiting with a bottle of champagne. He held the bottle aloft. "Welcome, Gloria Kenwood."

Just like that, he changed her name. Gloria—and from the Manhattan telephone directory—Kenwood. They drank a toast to Gloria Kenwood and a farewell to Daisy McCroy—long live Gloria Kenwood. She forgot that she had planned to leave him.

He launched a new phase of her preparation and she loved it. She was being introduced to the public and she began to grow fond of Kurt. But, he was still more like her brother. He'll change, she thought. If I keep trying, he'll change.

He took her to movies, plays and parties. He danced with her and was attentive and loving in front of other people. But it was still a sham. When they were alone he was all business. He never kissed her or took the liberty of a little feel when there was one around. He told her nothing of himself. It was by accident that she learned his name was Marvin Smith.

"Not colorful enough," he told her with a laugh. "I think Kurt Randall has more virility."

"What the hell do you know about virility?"

"Getting horny, my pet?"

"Getting isn't the word for it. I'm going right up the goddamned wall and you haven't got the balls to do anything about it."

"Oh, I've got the balls. You're just not my type."

"Yea. Maybe I better find someone who appreciates me."

He grabbed her arm and pulled her close to him. "I told you never to say yea."

"What the hell kind of man are you? Can't you get it up?" She grabbed his crotch and saw him wince in pain.

"Not for you, my pet. Not for you," he gasped and she released her grip.

She saw him the next day with a handsome, blonde young man. She never mentioned sex to him again.

Their names were linked in gossip columns. They were seen in the right places, with the right people. She was always aloof and dignified. After a few months, they flew to Hollywood. Kurt had done his work well. Two days after their arrival, she signed a contract for a movie. Kurt had managed to create a legend by making her untouchable and a mystery woman. She was an ice Madonna and the big shots in Hollywood were so damn curious that they never even bothered with a screen test.

Producers fell in love with her, but she forced herself to remain the lady. What a change for little Daisy, the easiest lay in Hinton.

God, men go crazy when they find something they can't have, she thought, as she lay in bed thinking back over the day.

"Jesus Christ," she muttered. "I feel like a nun." She rubbed her hands down her body and contented herself with the only way she knew to find relief from the burning inside her. She moaned once and the drifted off to sleep, hating and loving Kurt Randall at the same time.

tum tum tum ta tum…
tum tum tum ta tum…

Muffled drums began the beat…at first tentative and soft…the hands of the drummers seemingly uncertain of the beat and the fingers unexpectedly reluctant to move…emotions were fighting to claim the minds of the young men and they struggled to shut them out and perform, with practiced dedication, the duty for which they were so well prepared. Then slowly…slowly…the mournful sound became louder…and the beat steadied…*tum tum tum ta tum…tum tum tum ta tum*—the men became one with each other as the rehearsal progressed. Perfect—everything had to be perfect for him—each breath, each note, each movement, each sound. He deserved nothing less from them.

tum tum tum ta tum…

CHAPTER IV

A week passed—then two. The last of the temporary pins was removed and the pain was easing. Cameron still carried the cane, but he only needed it when he was tired. He was steady and strong on his feet most of the time.

He had trouble sleeping nights because his mind was filled with visions of Gloria. He saw her face in the ceiling. He relived all the moments they had spent together. Her voice rang in his ears. He felt her kisses on his lips and in his dreams he made love to her.

He had their future together all mapped out. They would be married in the chapel at the hospital. It would be a new start and he would not make the mistakes he had made with Dorothy. Dorothy—Jesus, he had not thought of her for such a long time—Dorothy—oh, what passion he had felt for her—so long ago, it seemed. So damned long ago.

He squeezed his eyes shut and saw Gloria's face again. They would buy a house in the country—and there would be children—a lovely little girl who would have her mother's beauty.

He bolted upright in bed. *My God—my kids—I haven't seen my kids— my little girl—I've never even seen her—who does she look like—her mother? Is her hair blonde? Is she fair? And my son—I have a son. I have to see them. Their grandparents—I'll call them tomorrow. After we're married they'll live with us—Gloria and me.*

Gloria, of course, would give up her career—no more traveling—no more distance between them—she would be a wife and mother and homemaker. She would be his wife and he would be a dutiful, loving husband this time.

Saturday. Gloria was due in Washington on a three o'clock flight. He was as giddy as a lovesick teenager about to have sex for the first time. He calculated how long it would take for her to get her luggage, hail a cab and make the drive to the hospital. Traffic shouldn't be too bad in the middle of the afternoon. Four o'clock. She'd be coming through the door any moment now.

He had intended to meet her plane, but his release process took longer than he expected, so he waited. He was discharged. He was free to go. His clothes were packed. He sat in the lobby and waited.

Five—six—six-thirty—no Gloria and no word. Day faded into night and still no Gloria and no phone call. He sat in the lobby and waited, drifting off to sleep once or twice and waking with a start when his mind tricked him into thinking she was there.

She breezed through the doors early the next morning, babbling about an unexpected change in plans. She urged Cameron to hurry. They had a plane to catch and the taxi was waiting.

"What happened last night?" he demanded.

"A press party I had to attend, darling." She kissed him on the cheek. "You understand, don't you? The studio insisted. I couldn't get away and I never had a chance to get to a phone until it was too late. The only thing that matters is that I am here and you are ready to leave. I've already made your reservation."

"Reservation?"

"To Los Angeles. We have to hurry."

"But, Gloria—I have other plans. I thought…"

She cut him short. "Darling, Monday is Oscar night. They think I have a chance to win. We have to be there. I'll pull some strings and get you a ticket. I have to attend with my agent, of course. I haven't told him about us yet. You don't mind, do you love?"

"Gloria, yes I do mind, damn it. I want to marry you now, right here, today, at that this very moment—in this hospital if I can find the chaplain."

"Now? Don't be silly, Cam. My studio will want to make all the arrangements. They'll even pay for the honeymoon—in Europe."

"I don't want to honeymoon in Europe. I want you. I want a home, in a small quiet town. And I want you at the door when I come home nights. I want to have children. I want a life with you." Cameron saw a look in Gloria's eyes that he didn't understand.

He was silent for a moment and then he relented. "All right, we'll do it your way."

Cameron went to the Academy Awards ceremony alone. There was no ticket for him at the door. He hadn't seen or heard from Gloria since she had dropped him off at the hotel. He had talked an usher into letting him stand in the back of the auditorium and watch. He stood there, with tears in his eyes, when Gloria accepted her Oscar. He ached to be close to her—to share this moment—he would go to Europe with her—he would follow her anywhere—he would do any damn thing she wanted—he would give up his life to be with her.

He made his way backstage and saw her, surrounded by the press. She was clutching the arm of a tall, good-looking man. Her agent, no doubt. Twice she kissed the man as flashbulbs exploded. He tried to signal to her. For a moment he caught her eye, but she looked right through him.

At the airport, he stopped and sent her a telegram:

Congratulations on the greatest night of your life.

I will always love you.

The woman behind the desk gave him a strange look when she saw the name on telegram. He did not include his own name because it didn't matter. She no longer knew who he was.

The big jet taxied slowly down the runway, like a lumbering bird unable to get airborne—its body too big for its wings. *A plane is only graceful in flight, he thought, when the sunlight dances across the silver body.* Cameron looked out the window and watched the drops of rain on the thin, taunt skin. They stopped moving. The air was filled with a tremendous roar as the engines strained to break their bonds and race off to the freedom of the sky. With a lunge they moved forward—faster—faster—faster and then upward, with one swift leap—upward through the heavy, rain filled clouds—upward to the peaceful, tranquil blue of a world where the sun was a fiery orb.

He watched the dancing rays, bouncing and leaping, shimmering and soaring from the wings. He felt alone, removed from reality—he was a rocket on the way to another planet—he was a soul set free from a body—free to dart across the sky—no, he was nothing. He was a reject, a void, an object to be used and discarded. He was transfixed, he could not move, his eyes were glazed.

Tears streamed down his face and he pressed his head against the window, feeling the cold on his face. His lips moved silently.

Forgive me, Father, for I have sinned. And my sins are the sins of my father, who sacrificed his happiness for my mother. Forgive me, Father—for I cannot believe in you—or anything. There is a woman—a beautiful woman—and I love her—I do love her—but I cannot separate my love from my lust. I lust for her as my father must have lusted for my mother.

He sacrificed his heritage and beliefs—a Jew who married my mother, a Catholic, and together they begat an unbelieving heretic.

I cannot be husband to this woman. She could warm my bed and drain the pain from my loins, but she will never be my wife. I was a passing fancy to her and I do not fit into her plans. I am not part of her dreams. I can never share her future.

Oh, God, forgive me, for I am immersed in my remorse. I drown like a man who cannot swim—I cannot fight the tide—my mind is tormented in agony—if you are infinitely good in your way why did you not let me die on the battlefield—I was buried in mud, it should have been my grave— I am not a brave man—I am not a hero—I am not destined to do great things—I am nothing but a stupid lonely man with dreams of grandeur.

Why have I always been denied the things I have longed for in my life? Cursed are those born rich—rich in gold, starved for love. I want to love this woman forever—I want to marry her—I want to look across a room and catch her eye and know that she is thinking of me at that moment— me—Cameron Marshall—have you forgotten me, Lord? Why have you left me to toss about this world—with no purpose—with no destiny?

Father—forgive me—help me—save me—save me—show me the way. Let someone hold a torch for me—let someone light the way—so that I will not continue to stumble in the black midnight of my soul. Forgive me, Father—please...

Sleep claimed his tortured mind and he remembered little of the flight from Los Angeles to New York. He felt weak and exhausted and for a moment, uncertain of what he wanted to do next. He deplaned slowly and was bumped and shoved by others in a hurry. He followed the other passengers down the concourse and claimed his luggage. This was not his destination. He had another stop to make. He walked outside the terminal. A skycap offered to take his bag, but he waved him off. He hailed a cab and spoke three words to the driver, "Grand Central Station."

Cameron Marshall was going home—but there would be no hero's welcome—no crowds to greet him—no bands to play—no one to shake his hand—no one to say, 'welcome home.' No one knew he was coming and if they did know, it would make little difference. He was Justin's Marshall's son and the Marshalls were not part of the community. They lived behind a huge gate, on a hill, overlooking the town and Justin Marshall never, ever came down to mix with the local population.

Cameron rested his chin on his hand and watched the houses fly past as the train traveled north. Soon the train would begin to slow for Dryden Plains. He tried hard to remember what the town looked like. There was Harter's Drug Store—the place where the high school crowd hung out, reading the magazines, munching potato chips, sipping cokes and talking about the big game. Leonard Harter was a portly man who often bragged of devouring a dozen ears of sweet corn at one sitting. He dispensed prescriptions with a comforting smile, practiced a little medicine on the side and never missed a high school basketball game.

Cooper's Meat Market would still be there. Cooper's, with few groceries on the shelves but the best cuts of meat in the area, had made regular, weekly deliveries to the Marshall home. Cameron could still see the white panel truck, with the big, black lettering, pulling up to the kitchen door. Cooper's was a place where you could get venison in the fall, if you were a regular, trusted customer. The chain market next door ran the specials that attracted the new residents, but the older folks remained faithful to Cooper's, out of habit.

The train was slowing and Cameron saw the First National Bank of Dryden Plains. Every town has a First National Bank, he thought. This was a small, one story brick building—the closest thing to modern construction in the town. Across the street stood the cigar store, with its windows full of faded, out-dated posters. Here you bought the Sunday papers, some penny candy for your kids and slipped a bet across the counter.

Next, the train passed the local mortuary. Cameron recalled the village undertaker, with his shuffling gait and fondness for rum. No doubt he himself was dead now and his sons were carrying on the family business and probably, the family drinking.

Cameron turned his head and caught a glimpse of Webber's Feed Store, where the farmers gathered on rainy days to discuss their problems. As a boy, when he came into town with the gardener, he had been fascinated by the cars and old trucks parked outside the store. One time, when they had needed some fertilizer, he had gone inside and was enchanted by the smell of fresh ground feed and molasses. For an instant, Cameron wanted to smell that aroma again.

Through this time forgotten village, nestled close to the Connecticut border, ran two railroad tracks—one taking people north to Albany and one taking people south to the big city. Seldom did a visitor arrive on the train.

The train inched to a stop at the unpainted, antique depot. A young girl got off ahead of Cameron. He did not recognize her face. The conductor reached up to help him step down, but he pulled back. He was capable of leaving the train without aid.

He stood and watched the girl hurry toward her family. He saw the hugs and the man, obviously her father, take her suitcase. They were glad to have her home. He dropped his head. He was home and no one cared. It had been a mistake to come back. He didn't know these people—they were alien to him—or he was alien to them—take your choice.

He sat on the paint-chipped wooden bench and looked across the street to what Dryden Plains claimed as a department store. He shook his head and thought of the summer when he had been seventeen.

His grades had been good and his mother nagged his father into giving him a bright, red Ford convertible. How he had loved that car. He would drive through the town, with the radio blaring, whistling at the girls. He gathered a crowd around him. It was a rowdy bunch of guys from the baseball team and their girl friends. They hung out with him because he was the first to have his own car. He was the king with his court of fools. They bragged of their conquests, mostly imaginary, and planned wild crazy things to do after school and on weekends.

He loved the sense of power the car gave him. He was a big man, sitting behind the wheel, driving too fast and drinking beer bought with a phony ID. For the first time he felt like he was accepted by the others in town. And there was his first girl.

Her face flashed into Cameron's mind and he let out an audible sigh... *Linda—Linda—his teenage love... his first love.*

They were complete opposites. She, ladylike, reserved, and he, boisterous and crude. He could not understand what she saw in him, but then, some girls like to collect characters and he was working hard to live up to his reputation. She was the first love of his life and he felt important as hell with her.

A woman, carrying a child, was climbing the broken concrete steps to the department store across the street. Cameron watched, but she entered the store before he could see her face. It was Linda. Or was it?

Cameron started to follow. They would remember him. They would be glad to see him. He wanted to apologize—talk to her and tell her he had changed— grown up—not the same as a man as he had been as a boy. He stopped in the

50

middle of the street. The letters on the sign jumped at him—Redlin Department Store. Without stepping inside, he could see again the dirty floors, oiled and soiled with the steps of time. He felt dizzy. He couldn't face them. Not after the humiliation. He turned and limped back to the depot bench. He dropped heavily, his breath short and his hands shaking. He would sit for a few minutes and think. He placed his cap beside him, took off his glasses and began to polish them with his handkerchief.

He had planned his actions to perfection, going over and over the evening in his mind. He was careful not to tell the gang that he had a date with Linda. He would give them the details afterward. He picked her up at her house and they went to a movie. He was nervous from the start. First he dropped the change when he bought the tickets, then he caught his arm in the sleeve when he tried to remove his jacket. She laughed and helped him out. The movie was long and dull and he couldn't even force himself to be interested. He held her hand, and then slipped his arm around her shoulder. He let his hand ease down, so that his fingers touched her breast. She pulled away. He wanted the damn movie to end.

Nothing was going the way he had imagined. She was full of talk when they left the movie theater. Then she wanted something to eat. He gunned the car through town, paying no attention to her angry silence. He turned from the main road and took the dirt road that ran behind the quarry. He parked the car and grabbed for her. She pushed him back. He was furious and confused. He tried to force her out of the car, but she scratched his face. The he slapped her—hard—across the face—cutting her lip. The moonlight played on her face and he could see a little trickle of blood. He felt sick at his stomach.

"All right," she whispered. "Do what ever you want to do."

There was no pleasure, only disgust. He hated himself. He stood up over her and saw her form on the ground. She was crying. His stomach lurched and he raced to the bushes and vomited.

He took her home. Neither spoke a word. He pulled up in front of her house and let her out. He didn't walk her to the door...he had to get a way. He jammed his foot on the accelerator and left in a storm of flying gravel. He knew a bar where they would not ask his age as long as he had money. He drank himself into a stupor and could not remember how he got home or where his money had gone.

He woke the next morning with a pounding headache and sour stomach.

A putrid smell filled his nostrils. He had vomited on his pillow. He looked out his bedroom window and saw his car parked in the flowerbed. There was going to be hell to pay and he knew it.

His father came crashing into his bedroom with rage in his eyes. He had never seen his father so angry. Again and again, Justin slapped his son's face. The pain from the blows sent bullets through Cameron's muddled brain. "You stupid bastard," his father screamed.

"I've told you time and time again, not to mess with the people in this town. But not you, Mr. Big Shot. Get dressed and pack your things, now! I want you out of this house in five minutes"

He came down stairs in time to see Linda's father fold a piece of paper and slip it into his pocket. Good old Dad and his instant checkbook cure.

Cameron spent the summer working in one of his father's factories. He lived with a foreman and his family, who tried hard to be nice to him. His father kept his paycheck to repay the cost of his great adventure. He grew lean and strong from the physical labor. He was glad to see September. His father sent him to a private school. He was not to go back home again.

#

"Hey, buddy, ya waitin' for somebody?" A coarse voice cut through his memories and snapped him back to reality.

"What?"

"A simple question. Are ya waitin' for somebody or do you wanna a fuckin' lift somewhere?"

"Yes." The voice had startled him so it took a moment for Cameron to get his bearings. "I would like to go up to the Marshall place, please."

"Ain't nobody up there but the old butler and his wife. Nobody goes up there since the old man died."

Cameron did not like the appearance of the man standing before him. His pants were patched and his shirt dirty. He could see that his nose had been broken and one eye was white, unseeing. He had not shaved that day.

"Never mind," Cameron snapped.

"Look buddy, I'm the only damn ride in town. So, ya either ride in my cab or ya walk. I don't think ya can even haul your ass across the street. I'll take ya where ya want to go, if ya got the bucks."

"That's one thing I've got plenty of—money. All right. You can take me up the hill." Cameron picked up his cap and cane.

"This little suitcase all ya got? Must be ya ain't staying long." The man grabbed his suitcase and tossed it into the back seat of the cab.

"No. I won't be staying long."

"Ya know somebody up there?"

"It's my house."

"I'll be a son of a bitch, I'll bet you're old man Marshall's kid, ain't ya? Don't ya look like a hot shit in that fancy uniform. God, ya ain't been around this town fer years. And jest look at them medals. Wowie. The rich man's kid's a fuckin' hero."

"I earned the right to wear this uniform." Cameron wished that he had not worn the uniform, but in his foolish state of mind, he felt that perhaps if they knew he had served his country, they would somehow forget what he had been as a youth. It had been a mistake. The town had not changed. The Marshalls were still hated.

Cameron climbed into the backseat. "I'm tired and don't care for any conversation, thank you."

"It's gonna cost ya twenty bucks for the ride."

Cameron nodded and waited for the man to settle himself behind the wheel and get the vehicle moving.

"My name's Dempsey. Care to take a little trip around town fer ole times' sake? Ya know, jog the memories a little. No extra charge."

"No. Just up to my house, please."

Dempsey started the motor and the car started forward with a jerk.

"Gonna live here now that your old man's dead?"

"I plan to sell the house."

"Man, ya ain't never gonna find a sucker for that place. People in this town don't care for the Marshalls. Ya rich bastards sitting up there on the hill—like some kinda goddamned gods."

"I don't need your advice, Dempsey."

"Jesus—ya got a hell of a burr up yer ass, General. I was jest tryin' to be friendly."

Cameron cringed at the word general. Ignorant bastard, he thought.

"Does the old town still look the same, ta ya?"

How the hell can I tell, Cameron thought, looking at the dirt covered windows. The car hadn't been washed in weeks. He ran his fingers over the vinyl and felt the grit. He pushed some empty beer cans under the front seat.

"It doesn't appear to have changed much."

"Hell, no. Even the people are the same. They hang around here until they die."

"A lot of things die in this town."

"I know what the hell ya mean. Look what this damn town has done to me. I had me some dreams once. But, all I got is a naggin' wife and six pain-in-the-ass kids, always needin' shoes, wantin' something—my life is shit."

Cameron was trying to figure out how old the man was. The broken veins that coursed his face made it difficult to determine his age. Alcohol, Cameron figured, and a bar fight that left him blind in one eye.

"Did you finish high school, Dempsey?"

"Hell, no. Got myself in some trouble with a broad—ya know what I mean, General?" Dempsey turned, his mouth twisted into a sly smile and he winked at Cameron. "I was a little behind—I wasn't always this slow—just a little slow—anyway, I got this babe knocked up. I had to quit school and marry her. I woulda quit anyway. If I had yer money things woulda been different—man, would they have been different."

"Money can be as much a hindrance as a help."

"That ain't how my old lady feels. Linda's after me all the time to stop drinkin' and earn more money."

The blood in Cameron's veins went cold when he heard the name. *No— it was a coincidence—it was someone else—she would never have gotten herself involved with this son-of-a-bitch.*

"I had me a good job once. Then I had a little bang up with my cycle. I drove my head into a tree. I ain't thinkin' like I use ta. Get headaches all the time. Then the old lady nags me. My life sure as hell ain't been easy like yours."

Cameron smiled. *Sure, buddy, my life has been one big joy ride.*

"How old are you, Dempsey?"

"Twenty-six. Why'd ya ask?"

"No reason. I took you to be older."

"Like I said, General, it's been a rough trip. Ages a man. I get ma ass home at night and the kids are screamin' and fightin'—the bitch is yellin' cause I'm late—and maybe I stopped for a beer or two—there ain't no peace. Bein' married sure ruins a woman. My old lady used to be a real looker. A hell of a broad. Not now, not any more. Damn, is she fat. And the goddamned kids keep comin'."

"Try staying away from her for awhile."

"Come on, General, a guy has got to have some pleasure in life. I ain't got money to buy broads, like ya can. Hey, how about a big tip? I'll go get me one of them babes on the street in the city and the old lady will thank ya. Whatta ya say, General? I'll bet you ain't even married."

"My wife died," Cameron made his voice cold, ending the conversation.

He had a strong dislike for people who shared the intimate details of their lives. He hated Dempsey and wanted him to shut up. He could imagine him that night, bragging to his wife about who was back in town. If it were Linda, would she remember him? How the hell could she forget? He had raped her. She had to still hate him. He had driven her to this character. He hadn't meant to do this to her. They were young, too young to think about the consequences. He had loved her or been infatuated with her, in his stupid, boyish way. He had so wanted to belong, to have friends, to have a girl. What a mess he had made. He wanted to make it up to her some way. How? All the money in the world couldn't undo what had been done. He couldn't buy back the years and the youth she had lost. All because of a foolish act that was committed when they were too young to understand the emotions of their bodies. He could give Dempsey a big tip, but he would waste it at the local bar.

Dempsey swung the car off the main highway.

"Stop here," Cameron ordered.

"Don't ya want me ta drive ya up to the door, General?"

He could not bear the thought of Dempsey trespassing on his property. "No. Just stop here. I'll walk up to the house. I want you back here in two hours to pick me up." Cameron took a fifty-dollar bill out of his pocket, tore it in half and offered one piece to Dempsey.

"I'm leaving my suitcase with you. Don't open it and mess up my clothes."

Dempsey looked at the bill. Without a word he took the piece and put it in his pocket.

"Two hours, Dempsey. Don't get so involved spreading the word that I'm home that you forget."

"Ya want it to be our little secret?"

"I don't give a good damn who you tell. Have your ass here in two hours." Cameron climbed out of the car and slammed the door hard.

"Right, General."

"Lieutenant. Damn it, I'm a Lieutenant," Cameron growled.

Dempsey gave a mock salute and drove away.

Cameron turned and faced the house. *God, it is formidable…and, it is absolutely the same…a cold, majestic cobblestone with towering white columns and marble steps, and those big, high windows. It looks like a goddamned Southern mansion transported to downstate New York.*

Cameron paused at the gate and then pushed it open carefully, as if he feared a sudden alarm. The brick wall that separated the Marshalls from the rest of the world was still intact. He started up the gravel driveway. The lawn was manicured and the flowerbeds were clean and ready for spring growth. Gus, Cameron thought, poor old Gus. So used to stern discipline, he can't relax and take life a little easier. How much fun it had been to follow Gus when he worked on the lawn. He'd jabber a hundred questions and Gus would answer each one in his quiet, patient voice.

When he reached the front door he started to knock, changed his mind and tried the knob and the door opened. He stepped into the dark hallway and looked at the stairs and the long, polished banister. His father's voice echoed through his mind: "Stop that running. I will not tell you again that a gentleman always walks…"

Nothing has changed in this house and yet, everything has changed. My father is gone—buried somewhere in South America—yet, he is still in this house. I can still feel his eyes watching me.

"Don't worry, father, I won't run down your precious stairs. I'd have a little trouble doing that now." Cameron whispered.

A door at the end of the hall opened and a woman appeared.

"Who are you? What do you want? Get out of this house!"

He stood for a moment, staring at her. "Helga?"

Her hands flew to her face and she seemed unable to speak at first. "Mr. Cameron…is that you?"

"Yes."

A man appeared behind Helga. "What is going on?" he said, in a slight German accent.

"Look at him, Gus, a grown man. A soldier."

They both embraced him and even Gus gave him a kiss. Cameron could see tears in the old man's eyes. His own eyes began to water. He had not been prepared to see them so much older and looking so tired.

"Let me take your hat and coat, son." Gus almost tore the coat off his back in his excitement. Cameron extended his arm to Helga.

"Welcome home, son," she whispered, kissing him again. She led him into the library. Cameron turned away from her and walked around the room.

"All these years—and my father is still here."

"Didn't they tell you?" Gus asked, glancing at his wife with questions in his eyes.

A faint smile crossed Cameron's lips. "That's he's dead? I know all about that. One of his attorneys called me. But, he's still here, isn't he? He'll always be here. And you will always continue to live his kind of life."

"Please don't be bitter, Mr. Cameron," Helga pleaded.

Cameron tightened his grip on his cane. *No, don't be bitter. Pretend it never happened. Pretend that you loved your father and that he loved you. Pretend he was like other fathers.*

Helga tried to change the subject. "I'll have Gus take your suitcase up to your room. I haven't changed a thing. It's still like the day you left."

"When I was seventeen and disgraced my family? I have nothing with me. I'm not planning to stay. I'm going back to the city this evening. Tomorrow, I'm flying back to Virginia. I have a home there. I bought it some time ago, right after I got married."

He saw the surprised look on their faces. "He never told you about my wife, did he? That doesn't matter. She's dead, too."

Cameron crossed the room and looked at the large Morris chair—his father's chair—the chair where he sat every morning reading the Wall Street Journal. He motioned for Helga and Gus to sit on the sofa.

"I want to know about my parents," he said, settling into his father's chair.

tum tum tum ta tum…
tum tum tum ta tum…

The word raced like a raging storm across the land, shattering a placid afternoon. He had been shot—murdered—assassinated. At first it seemed impossible, but the ever-present television cameras brought the stark reality into homes and schools and bars and stores around the world. Unashamedly, strangers wept in the arms of strangers, children went home to find their mothers in tears, and even strong, stoic men put their hands over their faces and made no attempt to stem the flood of tears. They wept for a man they did not know, but a man they had come to trust and love. A good and decent man who sought to make the world a better place for all mankind had been struck down. Why? Why, God, why? Why him? Why now? Where in your great plan does this tragedy fit?

tum tum tum ta tum...

CHAPTER V

The undertaker's assistant held an umbrella over their heads as they walked toward the tent sheltering the tiny gravesite. The rain had almost stopped. It was a light, cold mist, although the morning clouds looked more like a heavy down pour was imminent. Justin scowled at the rosy-cheeked assistant. He hated the solicitous attitude of the young man. Justin hated anyone hovering over him, trying to make an impression. He stopped at the first chair and then realized that he was expected to move in, beside his wife. The others came behind him. He glanced to his left and saw the assistant scurrying to get in place beside his employer.

Justin studied the man. His inexpensive black suit, crumpled with the rain, bulged over the rolls of fat. Justin did not like to see a man overweight. He glanced at the man's protruding stomach. Instinctively, he sucked in his own stomach and pushed his shoulders back. Elaina mistook his movement for grief and reached for his hand. Justin pulled away from her and shifted his gaze to the white-vested priest. He had the same facial effeminacy as the undertaker's helper. They were not men and never would be men. One denied his body's desires to serve God and the other never knew the desire.

Justin was a proud man and he was especially proud of his build, which belied his fifty-two years. Few people were aware of the twenty-year age difference between him and Elaina. Justin brushed his hand over his upper lip. He had been considering a small mustache. A small, trim mustache would add dignity to his face, he thought. He regretted that he did not need glasses.

Justin glanced at his wife. She had a beautiful face, framed by dark hair, with glistening brown eyes, long, silky lashes and a firm, full lip line. The boy had inherited his mother's face. He would be a handsome man when he grew older. Justin did not like his own face. He looked too Jewish. But, he was proud of his heritage, a heritage that he had to hide because of Elaina. He should never have married an Italian Catholic. Eating fish on Friday, standing alone while his son was christened…christened! He had always dreamed of the day when his son would celebrate his Bar Mitzvah. It would never happen. He had signed that goddamned paper. And now this funeral for his daughter, with a priest. It had been a terrible mistake marrying Elaina. He had a son he could not claim. And now he was burying his only daughter. She's an angel now, he thought. Justin smiled to himself. A little Jewish angel. He wondered how all the good little Catholic angels would like that.

For an instant, Justin felt the urge to hold his wife in his arms and cry with her. But he couldn't in front of his friends. Tears were a sign of weakness and Justin Marshall was not a weak man.

#

His father had been a sniveling merchant in Warsaw, eking out a living in his cluttered, musty junk shop. The man had been afraid of his own shadow. When Justin was sixteen, he ran away from home and worked his way to America, shoveling coal on a rusty freighter. Then, with careful planning, sheer determination and sacrifice, he set about carving a new life for himself.

His needs were simple. He rented a single room, furnished with a small cot, one dresser, a poorly painted table and two chairs. On the table rested a one-burner hot plate. Here he prepared his meager dinners. He packed his lunch everyday—one sandwich. His work was hard, dirty factory labor, but he was determined and faithful. He learned quickly and in six months was promoted to shop foreman and given a small raise. He saved his money like a miser and was surprised the way his wealth grew as the years passed.

He became a citizen and was made manager of the factory. He took night classes in accounting and bookkeeping. He continued to live in his one room apartment and carry his lunch. His employer was an old man and he treated Justin like the son he never had. When the old man's wife died, the life seemed to go out of him. He lost interest in his business and Justin assumed more and more responsibility. The old man signed his business over to Justin when he was thirty-six and he went to live with his sister. Justin honored the old man by dropping his Polish surname and becoming Justin Marshall. Six month later, the old man joined his beloved wife.

Without warning, Elaina came into his life…beautiful, Latin Elaina—seventeen going on thirty—how she teased him—swinging her hips and throwing kisses at him. She tormented him until he felt like he was coming apart at the seams. He had to have her. But, it could only be with a wedding ring, so he agreed. Agreed to all the nonsense with the priest and the papers he signed saying the children of their union would be raised Catholics.

#

Justin blocked out the words of the priest. His eyes looked beyond the tiny white casket, which held their baby girl. He wanted to be free of this spectacle. He fought back the urge to look at his watch. He had to catch a six o'clock flight to Chicago. At least he would be spared all the people at the house. Elaina would invite all of them home. And they would sit around, drinking his scotch and feeling sorry for him.

When they returned from the cemetery, he went upstairs to his own room, at the north end of the hall, to pack. His wife's room was at the other end. They had not shared the same room in more than two years. Little Angela had been conceived after a party when he had let someone force one too many drinks on him. He had taken his wife, without love, in her bedroom. He never touched her again. A man can do without bodily pleasures, Justin told himself. *A man must be strong willed. I can do anything I set my mind to.*

#

Helga stopped her story. Her mind was clouded with her own memories—of the day when she and Gus had arrived in New York from Germany. They had only the clothes on their backs and a few personal things packed in an old cardboard suitcase that Gus guarded with his life. They had the address of an employment agency. They spoke only a few words of English. They stopped people on the street, showed them the card that bore the name and address of the agency and people pointed in the direction they should go. It had taken them all afternoon to find the agency. They were sent to the Marshall home. How frightened she had been. She had cried all during the train ride. She wondered what Mr. Marshall had thought when they arrived—Gus too nervous to speak and she, with eyes blood red from weeping.

The made a home there. Gus had learned to drive a car, tend the grounds and serve as the butler. She cooked, cleaned and cared for the boy. She had raised the boy who now sat across from her as a man. She worried about him. He seemed too much like his father—cold and distant—his eyes showed no love, no compassion.

The silence was too long.

"It was after they buried your sister that things became so bad," Gus added. "There were terrible fights. All of the stores were forbidden to deliver liquor to this house. But, somehow, she always managed to have a supply."

#

"Where is it?" Justin yelled at his wife. He stormed around the room, emptying bureau drawers onto the floor. Like a mad man, he took the room apart. "I'll find it, Elaina, if I have to take this goddamned house apart, board by board." He started toward the closet, but his wife blocked his path.

"Please—Justin—please—" she sobbed. "Please—I need it—please you don't understand." Justin shoved her aside and in her drunken state, she fell, striking her head on the dresser. Justin towered over her limp form.

"Get up, you tramp," he bellowed. In his rage, he grabbed her and yanked her to her feet. Her head rolled backward and a tiny rivulet of blood appeared on her forehead.

"Tramp!" He pushed her toward the bed and let her fall. He turned back to the closet and found the liquor—four quarts, hidden in shoeboxes. He unscrewed the cap from one bottle as he walked back to Elaina.

"Please..."she whimpered.

"O.K. Here's your bottle," he said, pouring the contents in her face.

"Bastard!" she sputtered. "Bastard!"

Justin slammed the empty bottle against the wall, showering the room with pieces of broken glass.

"You knew how important this dinner was to me, but you had to get drunk. Couldn't you stay sober for one night—one lousy night?"

"Everything is so damn important to you, except me. I need you, Justin. Please help me." She clutched at his jacket as tears mixed with the liquor on her face.

He hated her touch. He hated anyone who touched him. He tore her hands loose.

"You're a fuckin' pig, Elaina."

As he stomped out of the room, he failed to notice his son, crying softly in the hall. Helga found the boy and took him to her room. She rocked and crooned to him until the sobs stopped and he fell asleep.

#

"Your father's trips became longer and longer. She was all alone." Helga dropped her head, not wanting to continue the story any further.

"Was she really alone, Helga?" He watched their faces. "Tell me. Was my mother ever really alone?"

"No," Gus answered. "She was seldom alone. Try to understand, son. Your mother needed someone to love her."

"So any available man was suitable?"

#

Elaina snuggled close to the blonde man who was driving the convertible. She rested her head on the back of the seat and let her fingers find his leg. Robert was driving fast and Elaina loved the exhilarating feeling that surged through her body as the wind stung her face.

"Love me?" she whispered, kissing his ear.

"You know I do." His voice was deep and resonate.

"Kiss me."

"Not while I'm driving, honey. When we get to the cabin there will be plenty of time. Your husband won't be back for three days. And I am ready to give you three days of the greatest lovin' you've ever had."

Elaina jerked away from Robert. "You don't love me. You just want to screw me," Elaina pouted.

"Don't be childish, Elaina. You know I love you."

"You won't kiss me, when I ask." She opened the glove compartment, removed a silver flask, and took a long drink. She felt better as the whiskey sent a warm wave through her body.

Robert shoved his foot harder on the gas pedal and the trees few by faster. "I'll hurry." The speedometer registered eighty-five.

"I'm going to leave Justin for you." Elaina took another drink from the flask. "Then I won't have any money. Will you love me then?"

Elaina was always threatening to leave her husband and the thought made Robert furious.

Elaina was Robert Kriss' escape from the daily hell he lived. Five years ago he had picked up a girl in a bar, plied her with liquor, coaxed her back to his apartment and spent the night screwing her. He turned her out the next morning, never expecting to set eyes on her again. Boy, had he been wrong. Her father was a cop and daddy wasn't about to let anyone who diddled with his little girl off the hook. He didn't give a damn if his precious little girl was a tramp. He had nailed her a husband.

Robert remembered his wedding day and the way dear old daddy had threatened him. He was married now, with two screaming, snotty brats and a wife who never cleaned the house, the kids or herself.

He was desperate for an escape from his four-room prison, reeking with the smell of sour milk and shitty diapers. He wanted beautiful things in life—he deserved beautiful things in life—things that a woman like Elaina Marshall could give him. He smiled as he felt the power of the sports car he was driving vibrating through his body. They were heading for a cabin Elaina kept for them. They would spend the rest of the day making love. Soon, he would have the big house and the servants and all the money. Marshall couldn't live forever. He was a lot older than Elaina. Everything good in life takes money and one of these days, he would have all the money he needed.

Elaina was talking that shit about a divorce again. He knew that old man Marshall would never agree and if he did, there would surely be no money. Old Marshall was a shrewd businessman and he had to have the goods on Elaina. Hell, his wife's old man would kill him anyway. Shit, he was going to have to spend the afternoon talking the divorce nonsense out of Elaina's head.

Robert rammed the accelerator all the way to the floor. The car leapt forward. Power, he thought, God—that tingling, sensual feeling of power. He felt himself growing hard as the wind slapped at his face and drowned out Elaina's infernal whining. The speedometer passed ninety-five.

"Kiss me," she cried and threw herself in front of him. He fought the wheel and tried to keep control. He saw the truck and rammed the brake pedal down—down—down to the floorboard—to the pavement.

The shattered forms bore little resemblance to a man and a woman. A young deputy sheriff walked away from the wreck, fighting to keep his stomach under control. He saw a blood covered purse in the center of the road, and picked it up. He opened it, took out the wallet and read the identification.

"Hey, Jer," he called to another officer. "Wait until you see who we've got in this mess. Justin Marshall and his wife."

"God," Jerry muttered. In all of his twenty years on the force, Jerry Carrigan had never seen such destruction. The red BMW was torn in half. The man was still pinned behind the wheel—impaled was a more accurate description. The woman was lying in a field, twenty yards from the wreckage. She was unrecognizable. Her head was mashed to a pulp of blood, bone and brain tissue. She was ripped in half. He threw a tarp over the remains and walked back to the car, fighting the bitter bile in his throat.

"Carl, come here and take a look at this guy."

"I've seen all I care to see."

"I want you to take a good look at the man," Jerry insisted.

Carl Walters walked back to the scene. "He's dead."

"Isn't Marshall an older man? This sure as hell doesn't look like the picture I saw in the paper last week. Remember that story? Marshall had a mustache."

"So what. The guy shaved."

"Damn it, Carl. Help me out here. This isn't Marshall. This guy is too young."

"So Marshall's got a son. Probably the kid."

"Here comes the coroner. As soon as he is pronounced, we can let the fire department cut him out. Maybe we can find some identification on the poor son-of-a-bitch."

"I'm going to call the office, Carl, and let the chief know what we've got here." Jerry picked up the license plate. "I'll see how the car is registered."

#

"They called here, asking for your father. I answered the phone, and told them he was in Chicago. They wanted to call him there. I asked them why. They told me your mother had been killed." Gus explained.

Justin gave his wife a private funeral. He did not take his son. He closed his eyes and ears to Elaina's weeping parents. At the gravesite, the simple cross above little Angela's grave caught his thoughts.

He went home and straight to Elaina' room. There, in solitude, he put his hands over his face and wept.

"Your father went right on with his business," Gus explained.

"Of course," Cameron agreed. What else would he do? He stood up and looked around the room. "His life was like this house—precise and orderly. But, in his way, he did love her. In his will, he asked to be buried beside her."

He saw the looks on Gus and Helga's faces.

"It surprised me, too." Cameron stood up and took a last look around the room. "I have to go now."

"Please stay, Mr. Cameron. This is your home," Helga pleaded.

He took the woman's hand and looked at her sad, wrinkled face. "No—I can't stay here. I won't live with these unpleasant memories. You and Gus can continue to live here. It's your home. I won't change my father's instructions. But I will not live in his house. Nor will I visit it again."

He kissed her gently on the cheek and wanted to throw his arms around her and sob against her shoulder like he had so many times when he was a child. He wanted to feel her comfort again.

He left them as suddenly as he had come. Helga was crying softly and Gus looked bewildered. For an instant, Cameron regretted his decision, but he was afraid to turn back. He was haunted by the fears of a little boy.

He stopped and looked back at the house when he reached the gate. He gritted his teeth and in a burst of anger and frustration, smashed his cane against the iron bars that locked the Marshall world away from intruders. The wood broke and a piece flew upward, arching to a resting place on the lawn. Cameron held the handle. With a laugh, he flung that onto the grass and then turned to the waiting taxi.

Dempsey jumped out and opened the back door for him. "Have some trouble, General?"

"Shut up and drive me to the cemetery."

Cameron realized as they turned onto the dirt road that wound around the graves that he had no idea where the family plot was.

"How long do you want me to drive around this place?" Dempsey growled.

"Until I find what I am looking for. You'll be paid, so stop complaining."

The graves were on a slight rise, protected by two large maple trees, still barren of leaves.

"Stop here," Cameron ordered. "And wait."

Cameron stepped from the cab and walked to the foot of his mother's grave. Her stone was plain, with only her name inscribed. His sister's grave had a cross with angels on the sides. He saw that there was a space for another grave beside his mother.

He stood for a long time, his eyes riveted to the ground. He tried to force himself to remember what his mother looked like. He had been twelve when she died and his father had burned all of her pictures.

"All of my life, I wanted to know you," he whispered. "The other boys had mothers who loved them, but I can't even remember what you looked like. I know you were pretty. I made someone up. She was you—my mother—and I loved her. I missed you. All of my life, I've missed you. There were so many things I would have shared with you. He did love you, after all. I guess he loved us all, in his strange way. He wanted to be buried beside you. Did you know that? So many things should have been different, mother—so many things."

He knelt, crossed himself, and said a prayer. Tears smarted in his eyes and he blinked to hold them back, but they came in a flood. He cried for his mother...and his wife...and Gloria. He cried for all the hell in the world that had descended on his shoulders. The spring sun warmed his face. He sobbed, oblivious to Dempsey's curious eyes.

He did not leave Dryden Plains as he had planned. He had Dempsey drop him at what the town claimed as a motel. His foolish, immature pride would not permit him to spend the night in his own home. So, now he sat alone, in a small weather-beaten cabin.

He stripped, took a shower, put on clean shorts, stretched out on the bed and tried to sort out his troubled mind—the events of the day—the people he had seen—the things he had learned.

He paced the tiny room, mad at himself for being stupid, stubborn and still in a town he couldn't stand. He should have been on the train, headed back to the city, but there was one more stop he had to make, one more piece of his past to confirm.

He put on slacks and a sport shirt and went to the motel office. A bell rang in the owner's house as he opened the door. The man appeared through the curtain that separated the living quarters from the entry.

"Do you have a phone book?" Cameron asked.

"Right here. You gonna make a long distance call? That'll cost you extra." The man tossed the book to him.

"I want to check out an address."

"Who are you looking for? I can tell you how to find everybody in this town."

"Never mind. I have it here." Cameron ran his finger down the page and checked the address. "Is there more than one taxi in this town?"

"Nope. And you ain't gonna get Dempsey this time of day. He's made himself real comfortable in the tavern about now."

"Any place where I can rent a car?"

"If you're gonna go anywhere buddy, you'd better be planning ta walk."

"How far is Quarry Road?"

"Clear the hell on the other side of town. Out in Little Italy. Ya got one hell of a walk ahead of yourself."

Cameron thought for a moment. He could call Gus, but he didn't want them to know he was still in town.

"Would you consider renting your car?"

The man thought for a moment. "How much are ya willing ta pay?"

Cameron took out his wallet. "Twenty for an hour. I'm going to Quarry Road."

"Well, I don't know you, buster."

"Bull shit, you know who the hell I am."

"Sure. That big shot Marshall kid. Make it fifty and ya can take the kid's car. Ain't much, but it'll take you to Quarry Road and back if ya fill it with gas."

He had no trouble finding the house. A couple of dogs ran up to him and barked as he stepped out of the car. He glanced at the front porch, with sagging steps and a broken rail and decided the back door would be better. Once, it had been a pretty house, but now weeds grew in the yard, pieces of shingles lay about and rotting shutters hung in forlorn despair. A half-pirated rusted car with flat tires and a broken windshield rested in the front yard. An old inner tube dangled from a tree branch on a frayed rope.

Cameron knocked lightly at the back door and waited.

Nothing in his wildest imagination could have prepared him for what he saw. A grossly fat woman, wearing a food-soiled apron over a faded print dress, opened the door. Her hair looked coarse and strands poked in various directions, defying her futile efforts to draw the strands back into a bun.

"Hello," was all he could manage before emotions choked his voice.

Her hands flew to her hair and she tried to smooth it back from her face. "It's you," she said.

"I had to come before I left. I wanted to see you."

Her hands passed over her body. "Not like this," she whispered. "Not like this."

He took a step into the kitchen. She made a quick move to clear dirty dishes from a place at the table.

"Here—sit down." She untied her apron and smoothed her dress.

"I'm sorry, Linda. For everything. I had to come and say it. God, I'm sorry."

Tears filled her eyes. "Would you like a beer?" she asked, her voice quivering. "It's all I have." She regained her composure. "You'd probably prefer scotch, but we can't afford it."

"Beer is fine."

She took a can from the refrigerator and placed it in front of him.

"Linda, please sit down so I can talk to you for a minute. I have to try to explain some things to you. It's so damn pointless to be here now. It's too late, I know. Jesus Christ, look what I did to you."

She sat opposite him and he reached over and took her hands. He felt her trembling as his flesh touched hers.

"Linda, I was a cocky, rich son-of-a-bitch and I thought I could have anything I wanted. I guess, in a lot of ways, I'm still that bastard. When you opened the door and I first saw you, I wanted to reach for my checkbook and give you money. But, we did that once before, didn't we?"

He looked into her eyes and saw emptiness.

"There isn't a thing in the world I can do or offer you that can undo what I did. Can you believe me, Linda—honestly believe me, when I tell you that I did love you then. In my own way, I loved you. And I didn't want to hurt you. I was a stupid kid."

"I know, Cam. I loved you, too." She paused. "Then."

"I drove you to him, didn't I?"

"No. I knew what I was doing. I let it happen. I wanted to punish you and my family."

"Oh, Linda, what goddamned fools we are."

She took a handkerchief from her pocket, wiped her eyes and blew her nose.

"Are you married, Cam?" She asked, letting a small smile appear.

"I was. She died while I was in 'Nam."

"Was she pretty?"

He took her hands again, as if by touching her he could make her understand better. "Yes. She was beautiful, but I didn't love her. We had fun together and we had great plans for our future, but I never loved her. I don't think our marriage would have survived."

She pulled her hands free, got up and started clearing the table. "I think you'd better go."

He stood up. "Linda, I can't ask you to forgive me and I can't blame you if you hate me. Try to understand that I am sorry for what I did to you."

"Good-bye, Cameron." The sound of her voice told him that she meant good-bye forever. He would not see her again because that was the way she wanted it. She was trapped in her life and she had accepted that. He would go on his way and face whatever future waited for him, but it would never be shared with her. She had met her destiny and was living it.

He moved close to her and kissed her on the cheek. "Good-bye."

His hand touched the door, but he couldn't leave. He turned to face her again.

Her voice was flat, emotionless. "I had the abortion."

tum tum tum ta tum…
tum tum tum ta tum…

The world found itself awash in bitter tears that could not assuage the magnitude of the awful deed. Flowers and lighted candles were the outward symbols of the deep, retching pain that free people around the globe felt in their hearts and souls. The act was sudden and beyond understanding—beyond mortal comprehension, beyond belief. People reached out for one another as if the warmth of another human being could somehow help them mourn the wasted life. Many longed to comfort the widow and the children, just as they sought comfort themselves. A gunshot had changed the course of history. And now, the world was deprived of his wise leadership, devoid of his love of life, desolate in its despair and older—much, much older.

tum tum tum ta tum…

CHAPTER VI

He was scourged through purgatory—his companion on the journey, a thin, golden liquid that ran free from a bottle—and in his mind were conjured up images. A face floated free—the face of his father—peering at him—examining him—X-raying him—warning him—scorning him—berating him—hating him—loving him—tormenting him.

And he chased the face—and the form was no longer attached—and it was a rocketing chase—through time and space—across the ceiling—down the walls—over the floor—bumping cold against the door—shut up—shut out—locked—sealed forever in his own doom.

Many days he never left his bedroom. His clothes were soiled, his room smelled, his home was defiled, his honor was desecrated, his tongue was foul. His mind was tormented and he was deserted by God and every human being. There was a steady procession of housekeepers. They worked until they could tolerate his animalism no longer, then they left, some not even bothering to collect their pay. He would get sober enough to call the employment agency and have them send him another one. Then the ride to oblivion would begin all over again. By ten in the morning he was dead-ass drunk.

He wished for death, but he was a coward. He could not raise his hand to take his own life, so he screamed in anguish. His mind was no longer a part of him, his hands no longer moved to his directions, his mind obeyed commands from Satan himself, who promised golden, glorious things—things from another world—a perverted world. He wandered aimlessly in the black of midnight and there was no sunrise, only sunset—a dark, eternal sunset.

Night after night, he mounted a form—it was Gloria, no Dorothy—no, his mother. And there was his father laughing at him, pulling him away from Linda—shoving him downward, into a cesspool, his head sinking in the sewage, rising once—rising twice—but no third time, no trinity. Repentance be damned! Laughing, laughing, laughing, always laughing at him. He hated his father. He hated the man who had given him life in a moment of lust for a woman. He lusted for her—for Gloria. *Damn, why did I fall in love with you? Linda—Linda—I loved you—loved you—loved you. Please believe me— please...*

#

A cold sweat soaked Cameron's face. He stopped talking and looked at Ann. Her face was pale. She had been sitting, transfixed, through his confession. He had poured out his soul and he was exhausted. He reached for Ann and found her warm against him. He was aware of her arms encircling him. She was crooning to him as she would a child.

"I'm none of the things you think I am."

"Oh, Cam, my God, I had no idea," Ann whispered.

"Please don't pity me. I don't want anyone to pity me." He pulled away from her.

"Tell me how I can help you, Cam. I'll do anything you ask." Her voice was quiet and seemed very, very small.

"I think I'd better leave in the morning."

"What will you tell Guy?"

"I've been here long enough," he replied, avoiding her question.

"Will you go back to Virginia?"

"Yes."

"To what you had before?"

He got up, walked across the patio and looked at the lights of the cottages on the far shore of the lake. "No. I'll never do that again. There's nothing to be gained by punishing myself."

"Why did you come here?"

Cameron tensed and his mind raced: *What do I tell her? If I tell her about the dreams she'll think I've destroyed my mind with alcohol.* He closed his eyes and heard again the ringing of the phone and the soft whispers.

"I felt a very compelling urge to do something. But what I have in mind is not possible. I know that now. I was reaching for the moon when I couldn't even find the earth."

"I don't understand."

He turned quickly, angered by her. "I want to be something I am incapable of being. Somewhere I got this crazy idea of getting involved in politics. And you want to know how absurd it is, I want to run for some office. You know, do the public service crap."

"Why does this make you so angry?"

"A man with my fuckin' background couldn't be elected dog catcher."

He heard Ann's soft laugh and a smile slipped across his lips.

"There's nothing wrong with your background, Cam. You aren't the only man who tried to drive away unhappiness by drinking too much."

"You know, Ann, I can't explain this feeling. It's like some compelling force has taken hold of me, telling me that this is what I must do with my life."

He moved back to Ann and sat in a chair beside her again. "I am struggling with this nagging sense that I owe something to a lot of people, starting with my father. When I got my mind clear and my feet back on the ground, I knew I had to do something to make my life worthwhile. I want my kids to be proud of me."

"I think your children are proud of you, Cam."

"You know, Ann, when I went to Annapolis and then into the Marines I bought into the whole noble service shit. I was the most patriotic guy you've ever met. And I don't think I've changed that much. I've had a couple of rocky detours but they're behind me now. When I think about the reaction of the people in the town where I grew up, I realized they never knew the Marshalls. My father wasn't the bastard they thought he was or that I thought he was. He did a lot of good things no one knew about. I was in New York City a few months ago, meeting with his attorneys and I came to realize who my father was. He sent children to college, gave millions of dollars for cancer research, helped people start businesses and I could go on and on. No one knew he did these things. I was shocked. He had a hell of a hard shell exterior, but he was a big man inside. Maybe it was because of what happened to my mother, I don't know and never will, because in all my life I never talked to my father. You know what I mean? So, maybe I should do something for other people and this Country, like he did. It's a crock of shit, isn't it?"

"What you say makes perfectly good sense to me. You must be very much like your father—a hard-shelled exterior and so much love inside. Have you talked to Guy about your plans?"

"No."

"Talk to him. He'll understand. He'll help you. You mean a great deal to him, Cam. Can you tell him what you've told me tonight?"

"I don't think so, Ann. Sometimes it's easier to talk to a woman, if you understand what I mean."

"Yes." Her voice suddenly brightened. "You can't leave tomorrow. We're giving a party Saturday night."

"What?"

"It's an end of summer party. We have a cookout and make it a send off for young Guy and his friends before they head back to college. And I did invite someone special."

"For me?"

"How did you guess? You'll like her, Cam. She's a widow." Ann added the last part in a matter-of-fact tone.

"Wealthy, I hope," Cameron snapped.

"There's still time to cancel the party. You can sit here alone and drink all the liquor."

Ann was angry with him and he regretted his flip comment.

"I'm sorry, Ann. I promise I won't embarrass you. I'll meet your friend and I'll be nice to her. I owe you and Guy that much, but I'm not interested in a woman. I promise I will be a gentleman."

Ann got up and kissed him on the cheek.

"We'd better go inside. It's getting chilly."

The next day, as they were getting furniture rearranged and the patio prepared, Ann told him how she had met Sharon a couple of years after her husband had died and about the personal problems she struggled with, and how, despite it all, she seemed to be facing life with a smile. Ann said she had been trying to convince Sharon to start dating again, but her domineering mother made her afraid to see any man. His visit seemed like a good opportunity for Ann to try her matchmaking skills.

Cameron did not tell Guy about his talk with Ann and he didn't know if Ann had told him or not. He occupied his time helping Ann prepare for the party and telling himself that he would have a good time. He owed that much to the Sheridans. He made a trip to town to buy the things Ann forgot. He picked up extra chairs. He dried dishes. He helped Guy get the grill ready for the steaks. He helped unload the keg of beer and was pleased that he had no desire for a glass.

Friends of the boys started arriving mid-afternoon, eager to get in one more day on the lake. Cameron was please to see Gillian and young Guy so happy together. There was laughter in his daughter's eyes. First love, he thought. God, was I ever like that? And if it ended, it would hurt her, but there would be another and in time, the special one. Or was young Guy, the special one? Time would tell.

Ryan, too, had found a girl. It was obvious that for him, it was a summer fling. The Naval Academy would have their bright young, future officer back soon. He was wiser that his sister. So, it would be someone else's daughter whose heart would break at the end of their vacation. But the kids would bounce back. They wouldn't go off the deep end like their old man.

Cameron chatted with the guests as the arrived, keeping his eyes open for the woman who had been invited to meet him. He found himself curious and not at all disturbed by the prospect. He was convinced that she would be fifty pounds over weight, gray haired and full of silly giggles. She would be on the make and he was her target. But, he would be charming and polite. He would play the game for his friends.

A car pulled up and Cameron's eyes were riveted on a tall, willowy blond as she stepped out of her car and waved at Ann. Her straw-colored hair was cut short for summer and blowing free in the light breeze. As she got closer to him he could see the freckles—thousands of tiny freckles across her nose. He smiled to himself. This could not be the widow. He looked behind her for her husband.

Ann grabbed Cameron's hand. "Come on. I want you to meet Sharon."

It was Sharon. The dancing blue eyes were full of mockery and here and there a strand of gray hair mixed with the blond. Her face was fresh and radiant; she was beautiful. Not the way Gloria had been, but beautiful in a warm way, a wonderful way, a delightful way.

"Sharon," Ann said, "I want you to meet a dear friend, Cameron Marshall. Cam, this is Sharon Haynes."

"Hello, Sharon." How easy it was to smile at her. He touched her hand gently. Their eyes were glued together. Her lips parted in a smile.

"Hello, Cameron. I've heard a lot about you from Ann."

Ann drifted away from them. He realized he was still holding her hand. He blushed.

"Do you live on the lake?" What a dumb question, Cameron thought after he had uttered it.

"We did. I had to sell our house. I suppose Ann told you all about that."

"No. I haven't given her much chance to tell me anything about you."

"She told me a lot about you, including how you saved a man's life in Viet Nam.

"That's an exaggerated story. We don't talk about it. Viet Nam was a long time ago." He took her arm. "Let's join the others."

"I have to call home first. I forgot to tell my kids something. If I don't give them very explicit instructions, they give my mother a hard time."

"You have children?" *Brilliant, absolute brilliant question,* Cameron told himself.

"I was married twelve years. Those things happen," she said with a laugh.

"I have two—twins." It was said before Cameron realized it.

"Three. Two boys and a girl. My daughter is a perfect lady."

"So is my daughter—a beautiful young woman." He was babbling like an idiot, talking about children. But, he wanted to tell this woman something about himself and he wanted to keep hearing her voice.

"The youngest, David, is impossible. You wait," Sharon quipped, "the state will educate him."

"The state?"

"Reform school. He can't miss."

"He needs a father." *My God, my mind has deserted me—I just walked into the oldest trap in the world.*

"Gotcha." And she was gone into the house.

He started to follow her and changed his mind. He jammed his hands into his pockets and started toward the others. He was puzzled by his sudden feelings for Sharon. Maybe Ann was right. Maybe he was lonelier than he realized. Maybe he did need a woman to share his life. No, the memory of Gloria was still too painful. For Christ's sake, he told himself, I'm a grown man and my heart is pounding like a schoolboy's.

Cameron busied himself with the other guests. They were fun people and it was a pleasant evening. The steaks were tender and juicy and he was ravenous. He laughed and talked and realized that for the first time in years, the tension was gone.

As the sun dipped behind the hills across the lake, twilight crept into the sky. Guy slipped away and soon soft music drifted into the evening air. Guy reappeared and began to dance with Ann. Other couples began to dance.

Cameron and Sharon were left sitting alone at a table.

"I don't dance very well," Cameron explained, and then wondered why he was making excuses. They sat in silence, both feeling very out-of-place.

Finally, he relented." Would you like to try, anyway?"

"Sure—if you want to."

He slipped his arm around her waist and they moved away from the table to join the others. He tried to remember how long it had been since he had held a woman this way. She moved easily to the rhythm of the music and he pulled her closer.

She put her lips to his ear and whispered, "You lied. You're a very good dancer."

"So are you."

He pulled her tight and felt the warmth of her body pressing against him. Her head rested on his shoulder. He closed his eyes and moved slowly, feeling her against him. It was Dorothy in his arms…Dorothy moving with his body, Dorothy on their wedding night, dancing in his arms. No, this was Sharon, he had to remember, this was Sharon, Dorothy was dead. He did not love this woman he held. He hardly knew her. There would never be another woman in his life to be loved. He would not let that happen again.

"Sharon," he whispered. She moved her head. He let go of her hand, tipped her chin and kissed her very lightly. Instead of pulling away, she kissed him back. They stopped moving and stood, locked in a kiss and each other's arms.

Cameron realized that the others were watching them. He was furious. There was a crack in his armor and he had to stop it before it split wide open. He pulled away from Sharon and whirled to face Ann and Guy. He stared at them for a moment as the anger in him surged.

"Don't look so goddamned surprised. You plotted this whole thing," he spat at Sharon.

Sharon was visibly shaken by his sudden outburst.

"I don't know what you mean," she stammered. "No one planned anything. What did you expect me to do, slap your face?" Tears filled her eyes.

"Look, Sharon," Cameron tried to explain, as he fought to curb his anger. "I don't like people interfering with my life. I've been doing fine since my wife died and I plan to continue the way I am for a long time."

Cameron was angry with everyone, but mostly himself. He wanted to lash out and hurt someone. He felt cold and alone. He fought the urge to bury his head in Sharon's arms and cry for every lonely moment he had known. She had felt so good close to him and for a moment, he had cared. Actually cared. He trembled more from fear than anger.

Tears were flowing down Sharon's face. "I'm going to make a fool of myself," she blurted out as she turned and ran for the safety of the darkness.

Cameron stood, staring at Ann and Guy, ashamed and embarrassed.

"Go after her, Guy." Ann glared at Cameron.

"No," Cameron shouted. "This is my fault. I'll go. Please let this be a lesson to you, Ann. Don't try to run my life."

Cameron turned and started after Sharon. He walked out of the lights of the patio and across the lawn and down toward the beach. In the background, he could hear the party breaking up. He had ruined the evening. Everything he touched, he destroyed. He walked with reluctant steps. He was drawn toward Sharon, yet he wanted to turn and run the other way. He stopped.

"No," he told himself, half aloud. "I've run all my life. No more."

As he neared the dock, he could hear her sobs. He saw her form in the moonlight, huddled like a child, at the end of the platform, near the water. He could not force himself to go to her. He sat on the steps, a few feet away. He whispered her name. She stopped crying.

"I'm sorry. I was out of line. I never wanted to come here in the first place." The words began to come rapidly. "I don't know why I did what I did tonight. I somehow seem to have this knack of hurting people. I don't mean to, I just do. Sharon—there's no love in my heart and no place in my heart for anyone."

Sharon was silent.

"My wife would have done what you did tonight, run off to cry alone. And I would have followed, trying to make up with her. Dorothy—that was her name—she was a beautiful woman." He found himself on the verge of tears.

"Maybe if there hadn't been a war. She was never meant to be alone. She was so afraid of having the babies. When she wrote me that she was pregnant, I could tell she was terrified. That's what killed her—childbirth. Maybe she knew all the time it was going to end that way. It wasn't fair for her to die."

He patted his pockets for his pipe and tobacco pouch. He filled his pipe with tobacco, tamping the coarse bits with his finger and bit hard on the stem. The moon was climbing in the sky and its light danced across the water.

"Do you get lonely on a night like this?" he asked.

"The nights are the hardest." Sharon's voice seemed weak as it floated to him.

"You get used to it after awhile."

"I still cry."

"I'm all out of tears—or maybe I never shed any. There's nothing to weep for, anyway. Bitter memories can't be washed away by tears." Cameron struck a match and held it over the bowl of the pipe. The light spilled over his trembling hands. He lighted the pipe and drew the warm smoke into his mouth. He let it linger there for a few moments before he continued.

"I look at Ann and Guy and I wonder why I can't have a life like theirs. He went to 'Nam and came home with a wife. I came home alone—to nothing.

"David was my whole life." Sharon could feel the sobs building again. She fought to control them. She could hear Cameron moving toward her.

"I loved him, Cameron. I loved him so much."

Cameron brushed her shoulder. "This is too nice an evening for us to be so unhappy. I'd like to walk you back to the house. I'm sorry for the scene I caused. I was very rude."

He took her hand and helped her to her feet. Touching her made his heart pound again. He pulled her nearer.

"I won't make any promises—I may try to kiss you again—when no one is looking," he whispered.

"There's no one here."

He pulled her closer and found her lips as willing as his. He was thrilled by the emotions of the kiss. He kissed her again and felt her arms tighten around his neck. His tongue found hers. He heard a sigh. He eased away.

"Let's walk."

Their minds raced backward through time, each reliving what had brought them to this moment. Sharon had argued with David before he had left for work. She hadn't even kissed him good-bye. Then he was gone and she had a grave to remember. Now, she was walking beside the lake David had loved with a man she had met a few hours ago.

Dorothy had wanted so much to be a part of Washington society and not a Marine's wife. She had plans for them. She had her father arrange for his assignment to be the White House. She wanted a life of embassy parties and invitations to dine with the President. But her father had not foreseen Vietnam and Cameron, like thousands of others, became part of a war that was destined to be a black page in America's history forever.

Cameron roused from his memories and came back to the reality of the night.

"We're not very good company," he said.

"We shouldn't be here. We should be far way from each other living very different lives."

"The night brings back a lot of memories," Cameron agreed.

"I haven't walked along this lake for such a long time," Sharon said. It was almost a sigh.

"Since your husband died?" Cameron prompted. "You know, I used to pretend my wife never existed. That's not easy to do when you have two children. You can't convince yourself that they never had a mother."

"That love doesn't have to die because you make room in your heart for someone new. Some day you'll meet a woman who needs your love and you have to be ready to give it. I think it's easier for a man. A woman depends on her husband for so much and when he's gone, there's a void nothing can fill."

They came to a fallen tree and sat down to watch the moon climb higher in the sky.

"I never had a chance to love my wife. I've never even visited her grave. For some reason, I can't." Cameron picked up a stone and sent it skipping across the water.

Far south, a bank of clouds was building. Lightening cut across the sky. A storm was beginning.

Cameron pulled Sharon close and kissed her again.

"There's something beautiful about lightening. You may not believe this, but I love to sit in the dark and watch a storm move closer and closer," Sharon said.

Cameron laughed. "A lot of women are afraid of storms."

"I'll be afraid when it strikes."

"This one is twenty miles away."

"It'll move up the lake," Sharon explained. "They always do."

Cam put both his arms around her and she pressed close. He was aware of her rapid breathing.

"Do you want me to move?"

"No—please don't. Oh, God, I've forgotten what it feels like to be in someone's arms. Love me, Cam, please," Sharon whispered. "I need you so much, please…" Her voice trailed off as Cameron kissed her again and again. He lifted her from the tree and lowered her to the ground. He knelt over her.

"Sharon—Sharon." His fingers fumbled with her blouse. He tried to be gentle, but the hunger in both of them drove their bodies out of control. Her hands tore at his shirt and she wrapped her legs around him.

The storm moved up the lake and the water grew wild, the waves building until they matched the pitch of the couple on the shore.

"Don't stop—darling—please don't stop—oh—my God—Cam— Cameron!" Her final scream was lost in a rumble of thunder. She fell back limp and exhausted.

They lay, locked in each other's arms, spent, unable to move, not wanting to move. She held him tight inside her.

"We'd better go back. It's going to rain," Cameron whispered in her ear.

"I don't ever want to move. Make it go away."

Cameron moved off Sharon and sat up.

If only I could—if only—but there would be another storm and another and no harbor ever safe, no mooring ever secure. There is always a storm, to change the tide, to thwart a plan, to course the night and then— then—after the fury of the storm, comes the fresh rebirth, the smell of the earth washed clean, the new beginning.

He helped her to her feet and sheltered her in his arms as the rain began to fall. They did not hurry. They did not want the moment to end.

tum tum tum ta tum…
tum tum tum ta tum…

The boundless energy was stilled. No longer would lights burn into the wee hours of the night as he sat, shirt sleeves rolled up, shoes kicked off, listening to the counsel of others, wrestling with one more problem, pursuing one more solution, making one more decision. Never again would his smile and confidence reassure an unsure world. Never again would his strong arms reach for a child who was frightened, comfort a dazed flood victim, mourn with the families who had lost loved ones, or hold the woman he loved. It was all so unfair and yet, it seemed they always knew it was going to end this way. How had Alan Seeger put it…. I have a rendezvous with Death at some disputed barricade…but this was a cowardly act against a brave man. What place in history is reserved for cowards?

tum tum tum ta tum…

CHAPTER VII

It was a long drive home for Sharon. She was soaking wet, but she couldn't bring herself to face Ann and Guy, so she had gotten into her car and driven off. She needed to be alone. She had a hard time seeing the road through her tears. She had been caught in an emotional roller coaster and she was not sure how it had all happened. She had wanted the man to make love to her. A warm glow spread through her body as she remembered and she smiled. He was so different. He had been gentle, but strong. So unlike David. She ran her fingers through her hair and felt gritty sand. They had been wild making love on the beach like a couple of teenagers. It had been good and she needed the feel of a man's arms around her and the thrusting of his maleness, deep inside her.

A stabbing thought brought her to reality—*what if I get pregnant?*

A slight laugh escaped her lips. *Imagine me, at my age, an unwed mother because I was careless one night on a beach with a man I hardly know. I would like to have a baby. It would be good to feel life growing inside me again.* She pressed her hand to her stomach and held her breath, searching for the feel of a tiny imaginary heartbeat.

Sharon was thankful that no lights were burning at her house. That meant her mother was in bed and, hopefully, asleep. She could imagine the scene if her mother were to see her this way. Sharon shut off the engine and sat in the silent car for a long time. She feared entering the house.

Margaret (Maggie) Cerafetti had given birth to her first and only child, a girl, eleven months after her marriage to Nick Cerafetti. She lay in labor almost twenty hours and in her agony, she vowed that her husband would never touch her again. She kept that vow.

Sharon filled Maggie's days. She had no time for her patient, quiet husband. She hardly ever let the child out of her sight. Maggie cried all day when Sharon went off to school for the first time. Sharon had inherited her father's temperament—the patience of Job, the dignity of a queen and the happiness of innocence. Nothing seemed to bother Sharon and she accepted her mother's gripping possessiveness with a smile and a child's unquestioning love.

The bride's mother always cries during the wedding ceremony, but it was supposed to be with happiness for her daughter. Maggie's tears were tears of hate for the man who was taking her baby away. Maggie's feelings toward David never changed and she shed no tears when he died. She was glad because she had Sharon back and was determined never to relinquish control again.

Maggie's family was close, so it was easy for her to encourage her brothers and sisters and their families to visit and include Sharon in their plans. "Help me keep her mind off her loss," Maggie lied. She was using her family to shut Sharon off from the world. She could never understand why Sharon had to have friends outside the family. It was those people who had taken Sharon away from her this night.

Maggie sat in the dark living room waiting. She heard the car pull into the driveway and the engine stop. She knew damn well that something had happened when Sharon did not come right into the house. She pulled her robe tighter, set her jaw, and waited.

#

Sharon Cerafetti met David Haynes her first day at Cornell University. The Cornell campus, high above the waters of Cayuga Lake, stands like a guardian over the city of Ithaca and Sharon was exhilarated by the excitement of the big campus, the people and the brick, ivy covered buildings. She hiked across the campus and finally located the bookstore. When she had purchased all of her supplies and books, she looked in anguish at the load she would have to lug back to her dorm room. David had come to her rescue.

David was also a freshman, a six-two, two hundred and fifteen-pound redheaded, rugged football player, attending college on an athletic scholarship. The load of books looked small in his large arms. Sharon had an immediate attraction to this strong, handsome man. He talked about football as they crossed the quad and Sharon tried desperately to understand.

"Four years here and then right to the pros. It's football all the way for me," he explained.

Before they parted at the door, he invited her to the orientation dance.

Sharon accepted. She had not dated much in high school because no one seemed to pass her mother's critical eye. There had been one special boy and they had gone steady for almost a year. He had given her his class ring, which she kept hidden under the panties in her dresser drawer so her mother would not find it. Then, one September day, he went off to college and forgot to write. Somewhere, she still had his ring.

David and Sharon went steady for three years. They had a special Saturday ritual—he would send her a big football mum, which she wore like a badge as she sat in her special seat in the stadium, cheering her heart out for him and afterward, he took her to dinner and replayed the game for her. She tried hard to understand and share his love for the sport, but she couldn't make herself understand football. It didn't matter. Her eyes saw only one number, one man—David.

He was injured in the last game of his college career. The orthopedic surgeon, who x-rayed and probed his knee, told him it was over. There would be no more football, no career in the NFL. David gave her a diamond two weeks before they graduated and she knew she had to take him home to meet her parents. Her father liked him immediately and the feeling was mutual. David thoroughly enjoyed telling Nick about his football experiences.

As expected, Maggie hated him. It didn't matter because they had decided to be married in July, with or without her blessing.

Sharon had the wedding of her dreams with a flowing, white lacy dress and love blinding her eyes. David crammed his large frame into a rented cut-away and waited at the altar for his bride. Friends and family packed the church. Sharon had never felt happier in her life. Margaret had never felt so miserable in hers.

When they returned from their New England honeymoon to life in Buffalo, where David had a job as an assistant manager of a restaurant, the doctor confirmed what Sharon had suspected. She was pregnant. David was a good husband and eager to be a father. Eight months later their first child, a son, James Gregory, was born. Two years later there was another child, a girl, blond and fair like her mother, and they named her Deborah Margaret. David was promoted to manager and given the opportunity to buy an interest in the restaurant.

These were their happy years—watching the children grow and loving each other. It all went by so fast and before they knew it, Jay and Debbie were in school and Sharon found herself with an empty house and an all too often absent husband. David spent more and more time at the restaurant, not working but drinking. Some nights he didn't even bother to come home.

David had never fully recovered from the fact that his football career had been ruined on a Saturday afternoon by an illegal clip. Eight years into their marriage, he sold his share of the restaurant; borrowed money from a couple of his drinking buddies and opened a sports bar. He gathered a group around him and they spent their time drinking beer and talking football. David's weight shot up to three hundred pounds and he began to gamble in a desperate attempt to pay their bills. The creditors swooped in and the bar was sold along with their home, in a bankruptcy auction.

Maggie talked them into moving back home. David refused, borrowed some more money and bought a house on Bristol Lake. He went through job after job. Finally, he ran out of friends who were willing to loan him money, so they sold the house and moved in with her parents. David kept drinking and brooding.

It was a disaster from the first day. They shared the same bed, but David was afraid to make love to her because Maggie might be listening. He was right. Night after night, Maggie sat in the darkness listening and hating her son-in-law.

Maggie knew when David junior was conceived.

Secretly they planned to move out, but Maggie suffered a mild heart attack and took to her bed for a month. Sharon was heavy with the baby, but she lugged trays upstairs to her mother. She knew that her marriage was dead as long as they lived in the house, but she couldn't see any way out.

David found a way—on a country road in the wee hours of a dark morning, he drove in front of a fast moving freight train.

#

Maggie heard the door open. She switched on the lights as Sharon stepped into the room.

"Look at you! Tramp!" she screamed at Sharon.

Sharon was unprepared for the sudden outburst. It took a moment for her mind to grasp the reality of what was happening.

"Who is he?" Maggie demanded.

"Who?"

"The man you were with tonight. And don't lie to me. I know you've been with a man." Maggie slapped Sharon hard.

#

Cameron was emotionally spent and exhausted, but he didn't want to sleep. He had to see her again. Who was she? A casual acquaintance? A one-night stand who satisfied a burning physical need? A transient passing through his life? Or was she someone special—was her life now to become part of his life? Love had never come to him like this before. With Dorothy, it had taken two years. First casual dates, then a weekend at her place to meet her parents, then his ring. He gave her a small diamond when he started his senior year and on graduation day, with classmates looking on, he slipped a wedding band on her finger. He had not even slept with her until their wedding night.

He was sweating again—like he always did when he woke with a start from a deep, trouble sleep. He sat on the edge of the bed and wiped perspiration from his face.

He dressed and left the house, not knowing where he was going or why. He drove into Seward and through the deserted streets of the town just beginning to waken on a Sunday morning. He saw a church—a Catholic church. He glanced at his watch. There would be an early Mass. He could not remember the last time he has been inside a church. He slipped inside and saw an elderly priest praying at the altar and started to approach the man, but changed his mind. He slipped into a pew, knelt, closes his eyes and prayed to a God he wasn't sure he believed in anymore.

He emerged from the church into the bright sunlight of the day. He felt strangely at peace. He had to find Sharon—had to share the day with her. He spotted a phone booth and dialed Guy's number. Guy would think he was crazy, but it didn't matter. He let the phone ring and ring. He realized the Sheridans were sleeping late after their party last night. Finally, after ten rings, he heard Guy's sleepy voice.

"Guy—this is Cam. I'm in town. How do I find Sharon?"

"Cam? What the hell is going on?"

"I've got to see Sharon. Where does she live?"

"Are you all right? Oh, Christ, don't tell me you're drunk." Guy was waking up.

"I'm fine. Please, Guy, tell me how I can find Sharon. I have to see her."

"Cameron—it's seven thirty in the morning."

"I know. And it's a wonderful day. I don't want to waste a moment. I need to talk to Sharon. I have to put things right."

Guy gave Cameron directions to Sharon's house. Ann was awake and listening to the conversation.

"Is he going to see her?"

"Yes.' Guy replaced the receiver and slipped back under the covers.

"Good."

Guy looked at his wife and laughed. "You women are all alike. You think that everyone has to be paired up to be happy."

Ann did not reply. She simply looked at her husband as a smile passed her lips.

Guy's directions were easy to follow and Cameron found the small, neat white house without any problems. He kept knocking until the door swung open.

There she was, dressed in a soft, pink robe. She radiated beauty in the morning light.

"Cameron! What on earth are you doing here?"

There was no doubt in his mind, this was a special woman.

"Shhh…you'll wake my mother—and there will be hell to pay."

"I'm sorry…I don't want to wake your parents—they might stop me. I need to talk to you—now. We parted last night with things left unsaid."

"Come inside before the neighbors wonder what's going on and call the police. And keep your voice down. Are you drunk?" Sharon was clearly upset with him

"No," he grew serious. "I am cold sober and for the first time in my life, doing something impulsive and wonderful. What a night I spent. You haunted my every moment. This is a beautiful day. Let's go someplace where we can be alone and talk. We have to talk. I have so much to tell you." He was talking so fast that the words were running together.

He looked behind Sharon and saw a gray-haired woman descending the steps.

"What's going on down here?" The voice was cold and harsh.

"Mother, I'd like you to meet Cameron Marshall. He's a friend of the Sheridans. Cam, this is my mother, Margaret Cerafetti. She prefers to be called

Maggie."

"So, this is the man you were with last night. And you have the nerve to knock on my door at this ungodly hour. I would think that the two of you would be too ashamed to show your faces."

Cameron was puzzled. "Ashamed of what?"

"You know very well of what. I suppose you find my daughter a very attractive and available widow."

Cameron looked at Sharon and smiled. "Yes, I do. And I find myself wanting to know her better. "

"I suppose you want to take up where you left off last night."

"Mother, please…" Sharon begged.

Cameron was stunned by the hate in the woman's voice.

"I want to spend some time with your daughter." He made his voice firm and level. He had an immediate dislike for Sharon's mother and knew that the feeling was mutual.

He took Sharon's hand. "Go change your clothes, Sharon. This is our day."

Maggie moved between Cameron and Sharon and shoved Sharon back. "My daughter is in mourning for her husband."

"Her husband has been dead for five years. I'm going to take your daughter out, for the entire day. She's a mature woman and she should be able to make her own decisions."

"She will not leave this house."

Maggie was furious. Her security was threatened and she knew, deep inside, she was going to lose Sharon again. He was handsome, so perhaps it was only a physical attraction. She would get Sharon alone and explain that the man wanted one thing—sex. And he had obviously gotten it last night. Men only dated widows because they were easier to get into bed. She had to get this sexual predator out of her house and make sure that Sharon never saw him again.

"Are you going to leave this house or do I have to call the police?"

Cameron looked up the stairs and saw the slight figure of a man, watching and listening. "I'll leave." He turned his attention back to Sharon. She, too, was looking up at her father.

"Wait for me, Cameron. I'll change." She dashed up the stairs and was out of sight before he could answer.

They stopped at a supermarket and bought food for a picnic, then headed for a nearby state park. It was early and the park was quiet and almost deserted. Two early morning joggers trotted along the lakeside, lost in the music coming through their earphones. Cameron spread a blanket on the ground.

"I haven't had any breakfast. Can we eat what we bought and pretend its cereal?"

Sharon laughed. "Since we have both gone insane, we can do anything we want to do." She made him a sandwich and he ate it hurriedly. She picked at her food. After they ate, they stretched out, side by side on the blanket.

Sharon rolled to her side and propped herself up on one elbow. She looked at Cameron's face.

"You have beautiful eyes." Cameron said.

She bent over and let her lips brush his. It was a gentle kiss.

He reached up and gently let the back of his hand brush her cheek.

She told him about her children and how she had struggled to hold her life together after David's death.

"Do you like teaching?" Cameron asked.

"I've lost myself in my work. I had to do something. The days were so long with David gone and I needed money. Mother takes care of the children. David left me with a lot of bills to pay. It's been hard, but I've almost got them all paid off."

"How do you survive at home?"

"With my mother, you mean? She means well, Cam. She's been like this all my life. I'm the only child she has."

"Your mother has quite a grip on your life. I felt like I was facing a tigress, protecting her cub this morning. Is she always like that when a man comes to call?"

"Well, you were a bit of a surprise. You're also the first man who's come to call, as you put it, since David died."

"You can't be serious?"

"I am." She eased off his glasses and laid them to one side.

"I like you better without glasses. You don't look so serious. You're a lot like my mother, Cam. You've lost the joy in your life."

Cameron was silent for a few moments, thinking about Sharon's words.

"There never has been much joy in my life. I have managed to mess up everything that was ever important to me, including the lives of my children."

"They seem pretty normal to me."

"The damn irony is that despite me, they are two bright young adults headed for very promising careers. They owe it all to their grandparents. I have never been their father."

"I think you're a little hard on yourself. Stop dwelling on the past and move into the present. We all make mistakes…"

"Mine have been beauts."

Sharon laughed and stretched out beside him. "Life challenges us to make a lot of choices. Sometimes we just aren't up to them and, for unknown reasons, we make a lousy choice. People get hurt and lives get destroyed."

Cameron pulled himself up and over her. "You certainly are philosophical this morning. We won't be like them."

"Who?"

"Our parents. You should have known my father, Sharon. What a match he would have been for your mother. It would have been the battle of the Century. Isn't it strange what life can do to people? My father was a very successful businessman and he wound up living a life filled with unhappiness and hate. Does it scare you to think that maybe that's what is going to happen to us?"

Sharon was listening intently.

"My father was almost twenty-five years older than my mother. She was eighteen and Dad was well on his way to being successful, so she felt she made a good choice. At first, he gave her everything money could buy—except love. Or at least, a love he could show. She found that with someone else. But, she never had a chance to marry her lover. They were both killed in a car crash."

"How awful for you."

"I didn't know much about it at the time—just that my mother had died. I was too young. A few years ago I went back home for a visit and our housekeeper told me the story. You know, I think my father did love my mother in his own, old country way. He wanted to be buried beside her."

"Is he?"

"No. He was on a business trip in South America and disappeared. No one ever found a trace of him."

"My, God, Cameron."

"Maybe she understands."

"If you believe in God and heaven, you know that she understands now. I guess we never understand our parents until it's too late to do anything," Sharon hesitated for a moment, reluctant to share the pain. "My parents stopped loving each other the day I was born—physically, at least. They still live in the same house and will until they die. Dad works nights. They hardly ever speak to each other. I've never known them to share the same bed."

"That's why your mother clings to you." He made a move to kiss her.

Sharon pushed him away.

"No, Cameron no more. It's too soon. We can't let what happened last night clouded our minds. We had sex and that's all. It was one night and nothing more."

"I don't think you mean that. Are you afraid of what people might say? You're not being unfaithful to David's memory. He's been dead over five years. You have to live again, Sharon. And so do I. You're a beautiful, vibrant woman, Sharon. You're alive."

"But what if it happens again?"

He saw the fear in her eyes. She was trembling.

"I can't guarantee that it won't happen again, Sharon. No one can. That's a gamble we have to accept when we fall in love with someone. We can't be afraid to love each other because of what might happen tomorrow. It has taken me a long time to believe that, but I think I'm beginning to now. There's a lifetime before us and I'd like to think we might be able to share our lives— no matter how few or many days there may be."

"I need time, Cam."

"We've already had too much time with our unhappiness." He sat up and looked across the green expanse of the park. "We've got to grab hold of today, right now. What happened between us happened because two adults wanted it to happen."

He turned back to her and embraced her with his eyes before he spoke again. "I need someone like you in my life. Maybe I'm being selfish, Sharon, but I want all the things in life I haven't been able to have." His voice trailed off.

"You're living in a dream world. I live in a world filled with responsibility. I don't have the luxury of doing something foolish."

He got up and pulled her to her feet and into his arms. "Give me a chance," he whispered. He looked at her face and saw her eyes sparkling and her heart was beating rapidly as he held her close.

The stood for along time, locked in each other's arms. She felt his hand gently rubbing the back of her neck. She closed her eyes and felt his lips brushing her hair. A slight breeze stirred.

Never lose this moment, his mind echoed.

"Oh, Cam...I don't know you at all. You came crashing into my life last night. I was vulnerable and you took advantage of that."

"It wasn't intentional, Sharon. It just happened."

"Cam, you're confusing a physical act that satisfied our mutual needs with love. They're not the same. We're not teenagers having sex for the first time. We're mature adults. Last night I over reacted. We need to move past it. Go back to your home in Virginia and forget this encounter ever happened."

"And I thought I had a lock on cynicism. If I go back, nothing will change in my life or yours. Maybe what passed between us was meant to wake us up, make us change. Maybe there is some force at work that is greater than we are. Did you ever think of that possibility?"

"You are a damn puzzling man, Cameron. Damn good looking too, but I don't think I would ever understand you."

"Do you think you might be able to love me someday?"

A slight smile appeared on Sharon's face. "You won't give up, will you?"

"No."

"OK. I'll make a deal with you. We'll spend some time together. We'll talk and get to know one another better and see what happens. I won't promise you anything...except I will not sleep with you again. Do you understand?"

"You drive a hard bargain, lady."

"Cameron, I am not ready for someone in my life right now. I have all I can do to cope with my kids and my mother. Can you accept that?"

"Yes, Sharon. I'll respect your feelings. Let's see what time together brings to us."

He squeezed her hand and they looked into each other's eyes. Each had their own private thoughts. Perhaps they had found each other at a time in their lives when they needed someone to fill the terrible void of loneliness. They would take the first steps of the journey into their future and see where the path would lead.

She said a silent prayer that all their tomorrows would be as wonderful as this moment. He kissed her softly.

For Cameron, no more words were needed. Love has snatched him up when he least expected it. It had moved deep into his soul and propelled him into a whirlwind of emotions. It was lightening cutting the midnight sky—it was rain cleansing a parched earth—it was heaven exploding in a cascade of colors. He always wondered if finding love again would bring him a sense of peace and serenity. Would it be a treasure to be guarded forever—a vintage wine to be savored—a peaceful inner glow—a sunrise seen by few. No one ever warned him that it would be a roller coaster ride of emotions.

#

They pledged their love in the quiet of an early fall evening, before their families and closest friends on the patio of the Sheridan house. Father Joseph O'Conner, a Chaplain who had served with Cameron in Vietnam, performed the short, simple ceremony. Cameron had wanted Sharon's parents there, hoping watching them marry would ease Maggie's distress. Nick had wanted to come, but not Maggie. She was confined to her bed, mourning again the loss of her daughter.

Cameron's children had accepted the news without much comment. They were grown and embarking on their own lives, and if their father was happy, it was fine with them. Sharon's children were young and resented someone taking their father's place. Jay was the most difficult. They had asked the children to stand up with them and all but Jay did. He sat sulking in the shadows. It would take a special effort on Cameron's part to heal the young man's pain.

They took a few days for a honeymoon and then moved in with Sharon's parents. Cameron tried his best to persuade Sharon to move to Virginia with him, but she refused to leave while her mother was ill. Cameron sensed that Maggie would never be well again. Nick enjoyed Cameron and spent long hours sharing stories of his life with him. Maggie did not speak to Cameron.

Their marriage was strained right from the beginning. Sharon was afraid to make love because her mother might hear them. One night, they drove into the country and like horny high school kids, made love in the backseat of the car. Cameron knew he had to change their situation or he was going to lose his family again.

A few weeks later, Cameron took Sharon out to the lake. He did not turn into the Sheridan's driveway, but continued to the next driveway and stopped at a large, friendly looking farmhouse.

"There you are, honey, all yours," Cameron said.

Sharon was puzzled. "What do you mean?"

"This is your house. I bought it. We can't continue living with your parents. We're both a nervous wreck. This way, we can be alone and still be close enough for you to keep an eye on your mother."

"I didn't expect this. Why didn't you ask me?"

Cameron was puzzled by her reaction. "I wanted to surprise you, Sharon."

She looked at him for a moment and blinked back tears. "I know you did. I just wish you would share your thinking with me, Cam. I never have the slightest idea what is going on in your head."

"I'm sorry, Sharon. I just wanted us to be somewhere alone."

"It's beautiful, Cam."

"Let's go inside. I have the key."

He took her by the hand, led her across the lawn and through the front door. They walked down the hall to the living room.

"See, it overlooks the lake, like the Sheridan place. Let me show you the master bedroom. We'll put a big king sized bed in there and that's where we'll make our children." He pulled her close and kissed her.

"I love you, Cam."

"I love you, too, Sharon. I promise that we are going to spend the rest of our lives right here. No more surprises."

She kissed him, her lips gentle on his. He caressed her hair and dreamed out loud. "We'll be a real family—with time to spend with the children—the boys and I can fish in the summer—it will be perfect, Sharon."

He let his hand float across her cheek, down the bridge of her nose and then he traced her lips. He leaned close and touched her lips lightly with his own. She sighed and hugged him. For a moment he felt an inner peace he had not known before.

tum tum tum ta tum …
tum tum tum ta tum …

The flag was not extraordinary—just a standard issue, American flag—a red, white and blue piece of cloth—folded in a precise, tight triangle—held in a man's white-gloved hands—waiting. It was a shock the men were steeled against but not prepared for—seeing the casket for the first time—knowing what it held. They kept their concentration as the casket was rolled slowly between the two lines and then they began the ritual of unfolding and draping. It was his flag now—it was the Nation's blanket that would protect and guard him in the days that were ahead—through the ceremonies and farewells. It would be preserved in photographs and in the memories of millions for all time…a simple piece of cloth symbolizing the sorrow of the world.

tum tum tum ta tum…

CHAPTER VIII

Two months later, Cameron flew to Virginia to talk to a realtor and put the house there on the market. As he stood in the backyard looking at the Blue Ridge Mountains in the distance, he was already regretting his decision to sell the house. The ringing of the phone roused him from his thoughts and he hurried inside to answer, knowing it was Sharon.

The next evening, as the fading sun painted the sky with the reds and yellows of a lingering sunset, Cameron opened the front door and admitted Ralph Saunderson, chairman of the Democratic National Committee. Ralph had been quick to accept Cameron's invitation because politics is a rich man's game and even when you do not know the motives, the cardinal rule is never to ignore a wealthy contributor.

"Good evening, Ralph. Nice of you to come on such short notice," Cameron extended his hand. The two men had never met, but Cameron had decided to act as though they had and see what Saunderson's reaction was.

Saunderson was a distinguished looking gentleman in his early sixties with black hair flecked here and there with grey. He had a stern but not unpleasant look about him. He was one of those tall trim men who wore clothes well. He would look dressed up in old jeans and a sweatshirt.

"Cameron, it's good to see you," Saunderson replied, gripping Cameron's hand. "When you called, I had trouble placing you at first—then I remember you had worked at the Pentagon. I think we met there."

Cameron smiled. *You're a big bull shitter. I was so insignificant at the Pentagon that no one remembers me. Your people must have busted their balls to get information on me.*

Cameron led Saunderson into the living room and motioned for him to sit on the sofa.

"What would you like to drink?"

"Scotch and water. Neat." Saunderson settled himself on the sofa, took out a cigar, savored the aroma and then lighted it carefully, moving the match in small circles around the tip.

"What have you got on your mind that concerns me?" he asked, twirling the cigar in his lips.

Here goes, Cameron thought. "The Senate."

"Planning to buy a Senator?" Saunderson said with a loud, false laugh.

Cameron kept his face impassive as he moved close to Saunderson and handed him his drink.

"Aren't you having one?" Saunderson asked.

"You know I don't touch the stuff anymore."

"I admire your self-control," Saunderson commented as a little smirk appeared on his face.

Cameron settled himself in a chair facing Saunderson, took a pipe from the rack on the table beside the chair and packed in with tobacco.

"I plan to run for the Senate."

Saunderson was silent.

"I was born in New York State and I retained the family estate there. I recently married a New Yorker and we're living upstate now."

"What the hell are you, the reincarnation?"

"I'm my own man. With party support, I can win the election."

"The Senate is one hell of a goal. You must have a bigger check book than my sources reported."

Cameron ignored Saunderson's comment and plowed ahead. "I want you to open the door for me—arrange a meeting with the state chairman and other party leaders—tell them I've got your support."

Saunderson drained his glass and set it on the table. Cameron made no move to refill it.

"How long did it take you to think up this goddamned joke? I'm a busy man. Get to the punch line so I can go home."

"No joke—no punch line—a simple statement, that's all. I am going to be elected to the Senate—with or without your help."

Saunderson threw his head back, his mouth opened and a deep, mocking laugh burst forth. "Here I sit, in Virginia, listening to a man I've never met tell me he is going to be the next Senator from New York and I'm suppose to believe this isn't the fuckin' twilight zone. Those years on the booze rotted your brain cells, Marshall. No more of your shit ass games—what the hell do you really want?"

Cameron was surprised that he was able to keep his composure. Saunderson was red-faced with anger.

"What I plan to do will be done—with or without your help."

Saunderson relaxed, sat back on the sofa and shook his head. "You're a real nut case, Marshall. You have no experience, no political organization and an ego beyond comprehension. Spend your goddamned money any way you want. I'll be in my office laughing my ass off every day."

"Don't allow yourself the luxury of ignoring me, Ralph. Let me lay it out for you. You'd do anything for a victory in New York, but the Republicans won't give you a chance. You need a fresh candidate that's attractive to the voters. They're tired of seeing the same old retreads every year. You know damn good and well that winners can be made."

Saunderson sat there, tapping his fingers together and thinking. He got up, took a business card out of his pocket and dropped it on the table. "When you have the chance, see this man."

Without look at the card, Cameron said, "I'll meet with him at ten tomorrow morning. See that I am expected."

Saunderson gave Cameron a cold stare, turned and left the house. Cameron sat down and rested his head on the back of the chair as a pounding headache stuck. His hands shook.

He took a late night flight to New York and checked into a mid-town Manhattan hotel. He was tossing around the bed unable to drift into sleep, when the phone rang. He picked up the receiver and listened to a monotone voice on the other end. He held the receiver to his ear long after the other party had hung up.

He woke tired and irritable the next morning. He showered, dressed and left the hotel without breakfast. He started walking north. After two blocks, he stopped, looked at his watch and started toward a building on the corner. He went in, got on the elevator and punched the button for the fourth floor. He got off and faced a door that read New York State Democratic Committee. He entered the office.

The receptionist was expecting him. She pushed a button on her phone and announced him.

"Go right in," was all she said as she turned her attention back to papers on her desk.

He stepped into a well-furnished office and was greeted by a portly man.

"Well, Cameron Marshall. Saunderson told me about you and I laughed. To tell you the truth, I'm surprised as hell you actually showed up here. Sit down."

Cameron sat down on the edge of the chair. He took an immediate dislike to Virgil Bailey. He represented an era of politics long dead, yet he had control and power. Bailey was a heavy man, with an enormous stomach hanging over his belt in a giant roll. His jowls were loose and flabby. His deep-set eyes were rimmed with dark circles. He had nicotine-stained fingers and food spots on his shirt. He lay back in his chair, breathing heavily. From this mass, came a thin, raspy voice.

"Ralph said you had your sights on the Senate seat. You got big balls, Marshall." Bailey was chain smoking, lighting a new cigarette from the butt of the other.

Cameron scrutinized Bailey. *Our forefathers sure as hell didn't have you in mind when they set forth our form of government. How the hell did you get into the position of party leadership? Apathy, I guess. Goddamned apathy.*

"Yes, Mr. Bailey, I plan to run for the Senate." Cameron was irritated and he fought to hide it.

"I suppose you've come to ask my blessing." Bailey opened his bottom desk drawer and took out a bottle of whiskey. He poured a healthy shot into his coffee. "Want some?"

Cameron shook his head no.

"I have come to inform you of my intentions."

"What makes you so goddamned special, Marshall?"

Cameron looked at the man and thought, *I haven't the slightest damn idea. I have no idea what I am even doing here or how this has all happened.*

"Have you got an organization?"

"Yes, I have," Cameron lied, knowing that he would regret it. As soon as he left the office, Bailey would have his henchmen checking him out.

"Who's your campaign manager?"

"Guy Sheridan." It was the only person he could think of to name.

Bailey looked surprised. "Haven't heard of him before. He know anything about politics or is he another half-assed fool like you?"

"I am quite capable of putting together a sound, efficient organization."

"Using, no doubt, the skills you learned running your father's empire?"

Cameron knew he was treading in shark-infested waters. Bailey was a lot of things, but he wasn't a fool. In less than twenty-four hours they had the book on him.

"Where do you think all this nonsense is going to get you?" Bailey asked.

"Washington."

Bailey sat up and spread his huge hands on the desk. "I like you, boy," he lied. "Yes, I like you. I think we might have us a candidate here."

Cameron let a smile pay across his face while he forced his mind to work. *Too quick, Bailey. I'm missing something in your plan, but your reaction is too quick. You're a damn poor poker player. You should play me along more. What the hell have I walked into here? Saunderson is in this. Why this change? Why are you suddenly so willing to see me as a candidate? I'm a nobody. I don't even know where this cockamamie idea of mine came from. There's a goddamned rat here and I'm not astute enough to see it. I've got to buy some time until I can figure out what the hell is going on.*

"Let's set up a date early next week for my people to meet with you and your staff. I'll have Mr. Sheridan call you." Cameron said, as he got up and extended his hand across the desk. Bailey ignored him for a moment, then rose, came around the desk and shook his hand. Cameron recoiled from the smell of whiskey on Bailey's breath.

Bailey walked Cameron to the door with his greasy hands around his shoulder. It was all Cameron could do to keep from pulling away in revulsion. "Good, son, we can meet right here. I'll have some of my aides here and we can start turning your plans into action." He slapped Cameron hard on the back.

When Cameron emerged from the building into the sunlight, he suddenly felt weak and dizzy. He leaned against the side of the building to get his balance. He pressed his head against the rough texture of the stone and closed his eyes. He felt a hand on his shoulder.

"Are you all right?" a strange voice asked.

Cameron shook his head to clear it. "Yes. Yes—I'm just tired."

"Maybe you should go inside and sit down."

"No—I'm fine." He forced himself to stand upright and smiled at the man. "Thank you for your concern."

"No problem, mister. I thought you were sick." The man disappeared among the walkers on the street.

Cameron made his way back to his hotel room, took off his coat and fell across the bed. When he woke, it was dark. He felt better. He got up, went into the bathroom, showered and then ordered room service. He decided to talk to Sharon while he waited for his dinner to arrive. He did not tell her about his decision to enter politics or that he was in the City. He had to see Guy and talk to him first.

#

"You are one fucked up bastard. You can't keep yourself on track for anything. Now you think you're a goddamned politician. And you want me to go along with your pathetic plan. For Christ's sake, Cameron, grow up. No wonder your children don't have anything to do with you. They figured out you're a spoiled son-of-bitch with too damn much money. And now, you're going to play games with Sharon and her kids. And you want me to fuck up my life so you can feel important. I wish to hell Ann had never invited you here." Guy was almost irrational in his ranting.

"Are you finished?" Cameron asked.

"I'm sure as hell finished with you," Guy added.

"You used to be the one with the political ambition, remember Guy? You even talked about the White House."

"That was a long time ago. I was a kid dreaming a wild dream. Now I have a family to think about and a law practice. And my brain hasn't been rotted by alcohol."

"A man is never too old to have a dream, Guy. I think you told me that this summer."

"Well, I was wrong. Sooner or later, you have to face reality. That's your problem, pal. Look what you've you done with your life…not a goddammed thing worthwhile."

#

"I don't understand you, Cam? How could you go off on your own and do something like this?" Sharon was angry and fighting hard to keep control. She was determined not to yell and even more determined not to cry.

"We're suppose to have a marriage—a marriage is a partnership—you talk to the person you married about things that will change their lives. Don't you have any respect for me?"

"Oh, Sharon, you know I do. What can I say?" He didn't know how to react to her anger. He knew he could not reach out and touch her and try loving her to his side of the issue. She was right—he was wrong. He had jeopardized their relationship, perhaps beyond repair.

"When you called me last night, where were you?"

"I was in New York City."

"And you couldn't tell me that? You let me believe that you were in Virginia. You knew when you left here that you weren't going to sell the house, didn't you? This has always been your goddamned plan!"

It startled him to hear Sharon swear. He started to tell her about the nightmares, but knew that would confuse things more than they were. Besides, it would sound like an invented, half-assed excuse.

"What about the children? This will affect their lives, too. Or don't they matter? I think you're a selfish, self-centered individual, Cameron, and this political nonsense is nothing but an ego trip." Sharon's voice was shaky.

He could see she was losing her resolve and was near tears. "I guess you're right, Sharon. I can't explain why I did what I did, but you should have been part of it from the beginning. If pursuing the nomination means I might lose you and the children, I will stop it all today. You and the children are the most important things in my life."

She was silent for a moment. "Do you think you have a chance?"

He looked at her face and saw that it was softening. "Yes, I do."

"Please don't ever shock me like this again."

He reached over and took her hand. "I promise I will always share my thinking with you."

He pulled her into his arms and he could feel her trembling. "I'm sorry, Sharon. I made a mistake."

She did not answer him.

Cameron sat on the edge of the bed most of the night. Sharon slept restlessly, with her back to him. He watched the hours drag by and finally he heard Sharon's breathing fall into the even pattern of deep sleep.

He got up and went downstairs, moving slowly so he would not wake

Maggie. The last thing he needed was a confrontation with her.

He stood for a long time, looking out the window at the stars. He could hear the west wind blowing. *Maybe this is all a mistake, another ploy to help me avoid reality. But what if it is meant to be, he wondered. What if?*

He rushed into the bathroom and vomited into the toilet.

As dawn broke, he felt better, dressed quietly and slipped out of the house. It took him only ten minutes to get to the Sheridan house, not enough time to figure out what he would say to his friend. He looked in the kitchen window and saw Guy having coffee. He tapped softly on the window and Guy waved him inside.

They sat silently, sipping coffee, each reluctant to break the silence.

"You think I'm crazy to run for the Senate don't you?" Cameron finally asked.

"Yes, damn it I do. Cam, I admire you. I have ever since we were together in 'Nam. You were a damn good leader. But what do you know about politics? I don't know what prompted you to get involved with the politicians while you were away. Do yourself a favor Cam, buy some kind of business. Get off your ass and do an honest day's work for once in your fuckin' life."

"Does my wealth bother you that much, Guy?"

"Look, Cam, forget what I just said—it came out wrong. I do think you're wasting your life. I think you need to grow up. If you want to get involved in politics, start at the local level. Get Sharon and the kids settled, get to know this community and take it from there. Test the water. Run for the damn school board. That'll keep you busy and cure your political ambitions in a hurry. I love you like a brother, but I think you're way off base with this idea."

"There isn't time."

"What the hell does that mean?"

Cameron was silent for a moment. "I don't know, Guy. I don't know."

"You've wasted a hell of a lot of time since 'Nam and now your ass is on fire to be a U.S. Senator." Guy's anger was growing. He shook his head in exasperation.

"I can't buy back those days and years. I know that, Guy. I feel compelled to make my move now. I can't explain it…I just can't. This is something I have to do. Please trust me and help me. I need you to run my campaign."

"What the hell do I know about running a political campaign? If you're so hell bent on this madness, you've got to have someone with experience running your campaign, Cam. Not me."

Cameron smiled at his friend. "I have to have someone I can trust. I don't want any connection with Bailey and his outfit. You're my campaign manager. Besides, I already told Bailey you were it. We can't have a rift in our ranks. Solid front…old boy…and all that crap."

Guy forced a smile. "Damn, I wish I understood you."

"I wish I understood myself, Guy. It would sure make life a hell of a lot easier. We've got a lot of work to do before the convention in August.

The first thing we need is some sort of official headquarters. Can you find an office of some sort? A couple of rooms…"

"Yes, but…"

"Rent it, today. Get someone to paint some type of damn sign and throw up some flags."

"Wait a minute, Cam. I haven't agreed to anything. You can't dump this on my lap—I have a law practice…"

"You've got to help me, Guy. I have to cover every inch of this State if there's going to be any chance of getting the nomination."

"Cam—look—you're in a position where you can go running off any time you feel like it. You don't have to worry about an income to support your family. I'll do everything I can to help, but I can't give up my law practice."

"As of now, you are on my payroll. Consider it the same as a retainer. When we win, you'll be my aide and on the Senate payroll."

"And if you lose?"

"We won't, Guy. We aren't going to lose."

Guy looked at Cameron and shook his head. "You've changed. I've never seen this side of your before. I'd love to know what's come over you all of a sudden."

"We're going to need a staff. Someone has to help us with the press. Any ideas?"

Guy shook his head and crossed to the kitchen bulletin board, took down a card and tossed it to Cameron. "Remember this guy?"

Cameron looked at the card and laughed. "Crazy Carter? What the hell is he up to now?"

"Call the number and talk to him."

"Wait a minute, Guy, this card just didn't happen to be there on your bulletin board by accident, did it?"

"No, I spent most of the night thinking about your idea and I remembered my own dream. We're both probably just crazy enough to make this damn thing work."

Cameron grabbed his friend and hugged him and then he dialed the number on the card.

Cameron recognized the dry, Southern drawl immediately.

"Carter, this is Cameron Marshall, the next Senator from the State of New York."

"Jesus, you're still drinking!" Carter roared back.

Guy could hear Carter's laughter over the phone. He reached for the receiver.

"Carter," Guy said, "Remember when we were in 'Nam and you bragged that you could turn any war hero into a politician the people would love? This is your chance to prove your theory."

"Guy, you're as crazy as that other shit-head," Carter responded.

"I can't talk him out of it, Carter. He's going to run for the Senate. We need a good man planning strategy and handling the press. Are you in?"

The tone of Carter's voice changed. "Let me talk to him again."

Cameron took the phone from Guy. "Yes, Carter."

"You're a goddamn lunatic. Are you sure you're not still drunk?"

"Sober as a church mouse and dead serious. Carter, I'm asking for your help."

"And you're convinced that you can come out of the blue and win a state-wide election? You'll need more than my help—you'll need a miracle. But, I like a challenge and I'm bored on my job. Have you met Virgil Bailey?"

"Yes."

"He's a piece of work, isn't he? Don't buy into the mess in the State, Cameron. Stay home with your family. You're a rich man—enjoy a rich man's things."

"Carter, I can't explain what is compelling me to do this, I just know I have to try. I know I'm not a politician. I don't know how to manipulate people. I don't want to make promises to people I can't keep, but I think I want to go to Washington and be a part of the government of this Country. I need your help to get there."

"I think you're doing a damn good job of manipulating me, right now, Cameron. They'll kill you, buddy. The big boys will chew you up into tiny little pieces, spit you into a corner and then piss all over you. I may be every bit as crazy as you are, but I would love to shove a stick of dynamite up Bailey's ass. Maybe, maybe my theory is right."

"You know, Carter, when I went to see Bailey, he was too friendly. It didn't take long before he was on my side and he didn't even know me. Why?"

"Here comes lesson number one, old friend. Let me spell it out for you. With the President bogged down in scandal and unable to run again, the party is stuck with the colorless, sad vice president as their candidate. He's collecting political IOUs all over the country and no one dares back out of their support. So, the perennial Republican candidate, Mr. Goody-Two-Shoes, ole Nathaniel Mark Richardson, is certain to sweep the country in a Republican landslide. And the Democrats are busy as hell looking for a way to protect their future candidates. Next year's election is not the time to be a Democrat. Bailey had already made a decision to keep the bright Lieutenant Governor out of danger next November. Then you walk in off the street and offer yourself as a human sacrifice. They love you, Cam. Bailey will buy anyone he can sacrifice and emerge unscathed himself. You're an answer to his prayer, you ass hole."

"Jesus, Carter, I had no idea," Cameron responded.

"Of course you didn't. You don't know the first damn thing about politics. I'll sleep on it tonight and tomorrow and decide if I can do anything for you. Where the hell are you camping out?"

"Carter, we'll have to have money." Cameron asked.

"No shittin'. And I'm supposed to have the key to that too, huh?"

"We'll have to raise whatever we'll need to get the job done."

"You crazy bastard. You call up and disrupt my life, now you want blood. I should have stomped on your IV in Japan."

"You missed your chance, Carter, now it's too late."

"I'll do what I can. But I'm not making any promises. I can hear myself telling this story to my friends and then asking them to write checks. I hope to hell they have a good sense of humor left."

"My attorneys will handle the contributions from my own funds. I know there are some laws regulating contributions."

"God, maybe you do know a little bit. I hope Guy is sane."

"He is. Want to talk to him?"

"No. I want a face-to-face talk with him, not another crazy phone conversation. By the way, Cameron, I have to convince my wife of this little adventure."

"When did you get married?"

"Sometime ago—while you were playing lost weekend. You'll like her, Cam. She doesn't understand me, but she loves me."

"Bring her along. We need all the help we can get."

"She hates politics. She'll stay home and wait for me to return to my senses. Cam…"

"Yes, Carter?"

Carter changed his mind. "Nothing. For a moment I had a…nothing. I'll see you sometime tomorrow." The line went dead.

Cameron replaced the receiver and stood up to leave. Ann was standing in the doorway. She had been listening to his end of the conversation.

"Who's Carter?" Ann asked.

Cameron was surprised that Ann hadn't met him in Saigon. "Carter Wilson is an old friend—a newspaperman. He did some freelance work in 'Nam. He got a little too close to a piece of flying metal and lost his left eye. We were roommates in the hospital for a while."

"Losing the eye didn't slow him down, Ann," Guy added. "The last time I talked to him he was in the process of writing a novel. Nothing came of the book and I think he worked for the New York Times for a while. He's a damned good newspaperman."

"And he's going to help you with this campaign for the Senate, Cam?" Ann asked, crossing to Guy.

"Yes. He's a brilliant man. We're going to have a damn strong team." Cameron reached for Guy's hand. "We're going to make a great pair, Guy. It'll be like when we first met. I'm pleased you're going to manage the campaign."

Ann smiled and kissed her husband on the cheek. "Oh, Guy, I'm so happy you're going to work for Cam."

"Hold it a minute, you two. I haven't said yes, yet. I haven't had a chance to say anything."

"Guy, you are the one person I trust with my future."

"Don't make it so difficult, Cam. I don't know a damn thing about politics. I can't play the game with the professionals. I'll ruin everything."

"If I had wanted a professional, I would have hired one. I want people around me who believe in the same things I believe in. It has to be you Guy. You'll tell it like it is. Carter will call and let you know when he's arriving. You two can brainstorm when you pick him up at the airport. I have to go home and talk to Sharon. She was pretty upset with me last night, but I think she'll come around."

Cameron and Ann locked eyes for a moment then Ann smiled and left the room. He felt distracted by the way Ann had looked at him. I've seen that look before, he thought.

"Trust me, Guy. This is right. I know it is. Don't ask me how I know it's right—it just is."

tum tum tum ta tum…
tum tum tum ta tum…

He was coming home quietly in darkness—in the company of those who served, honored and loved him—in the company of his family who grieved beyond comprehension—in the company of silent television cameras—in the company of strangers on the street. The Nation's House had been transformed into mourning—black bunting hung from the doors, windows and chandeliers; flowers and flickering candles waited in the East Room. The shadows of other fallen presidents were there too—silent sentinels to a Nation's moment of madness. They, along with the honor guard, would stand watch until he departed and moved forth to his final resting place. Then they would welcome him and one day, he too, would be a silent sentinel to another act of insanity.
tum tum tum ta tum…

CHAPTER IX

Carter arrived on the scene five days later. He was a short, stocky man with hair that looked like it had never seen a comb. Bushy eyebrows added to his wild appearance. He wore an old tweed jacket with leather patches on the elbows and cigars stuck out of the breast pocket. He was a character from another era.

Cameron was grabbed by Carter's burly arms and pulled into a bear hug that took his breath away.

"Damn, its good to see you," Carter drawled. "Did you get your wife calmed down? Bet she thinks you're a crazy shit-head."

"That's an accurate description of her feelings."

"She'll be fine. Political power is the world's greatest aphrodisiac and there isn't a woman alive strong enough to fight that. And if she does, it won't matter. When we're through, the babes will be hot for you." Carter laughed and pulled a cigar out of his shirt pocket and steered him toward Guy's living room.

"Let's get down to business, my friend."

Guy followed.

"We won't get by with our naive, novice politician act for long. Saunderson's smart. He'll be watching every move you make and when he sees that you putting together a strong organization, he'll suspect we're up to something. We'll try to get as much of a jump on him as possible, but he'll know. He's got informants everywhere. The plus for us is that he's got an ego bigger than his dick, so he'll figure he can always outsmart you." Carter said.

There were three men waiting in the living room.

"I want you to meet the team, Cam." Carter took him by the arm and steered him across the room. "This is Jacob Aarons, our image expert."

Jacob was a small man with close-cropped hair. His round, steel rimmed glasses made him look like an owl. He had a perpetual five-o'clock shadow, which did nothing to enhance his features. The look on his face said he did not want to be there.

"Do you always wear those dark-rimmed glasses?" Jacob asked as he rose to shake Cameron's hand.

"I beg your pardon?"

"Jake has some definite ideas about how a candidate should look and dress," Carter said.

Cameron looked at the man's rumpled suit and muttered, "He needs the advice, not me," under his breath.

"How old are you?" Cameron asked.

"Twenty-four," Jacob replied.

"A little young, isn't he, Carter?"

Jacob walked across the room and looked out the window. He would let Carter handle Cameron this time.

"Did you tell me to raid a nursing home? You want me to assemble a team—well, that's what I'm doing. I'm going to find people who are the best. If you have a problem with that, it's fine with me. I'll head back home."

There was a look on Carter's face and a coldness in his eyes that frightened Cameron for a moment.

"Carter—I had no idea we were going to move this fast." Cameron felt trapped; afraid to tell these men he was ready to change his mind.

"You called me, remember? You were all fired up and raring to take on the world. Well, we're here to help you do that. But, we call the shots. If you can't accept that, we don't have a prayer."

"All right, Carter. Here's what I'll do. I'll listen to what you and your friends have in mind and then I'll make my decision."

Carter glanced at Guy. Cameron did not notice Guy's slight nod of his head.

Jacob turned and faced him. "I've made some notes about how a candidate should look. We have to appeal to women, but not make men see you as competition," Aarons explained. "It is also important that you do not appear too intellectual. That was Stevenson's problem. I've made a detailed study of the personality traits of successful candidates. My recommendations are in this book. They include getting you into good physical shape as soon as possible. Look it over and I'll answer any questions you have."

Jacob walked over to Cameron, handed him a thick, black three-ringed notebook. "I hate being called Jake," he said as he moved to a chair across the room.

"Short and to the point, aren't you? How did you gain so much confidence so young?"

"My senior thesis at Harvard was on the personality quotients of successful and unsuccessful presidential candidates. I studied thousands of exit poll interviews and put together the ideal candidate."

"I'm running for the Senate, remember."

"Time will tell," Jacob shot back.

Cameron started to respond, but Carter jumped in first. "You're not making a very good first impression, Cam."

"I guess that makes my personality quotient zero."

Cameron sighed and walked over to an empty chair. "Sorry. I said I would listen." He sat down and waited.

"This is Lawrence Diamond. He's made a study of your potential opponents," Carter said, introducing a heavyset man waiting across the room.

Lawrence was ruddy faced with a square jaw. He wore his graying hair in a brush cut and his glasses were on a chain around his neck. His gray sweater was stretched tight over his chest.

Lawrence moved over to some charts resting against the fireplace. Guy moved over to help hold the large sheets of cardboard.

"You have five potential opponents for the nominations, two announced and three speculative. Your real opponent, the Lieutenant Governor won't enter the race. He's a smart man and knows what's ahead for the party in November, so he's going to play it safe and sit this race out. He can't afford to endorse anyone who might win with his help and ruin his own political ambitions. He also can't afford to be aligned with loser. He'll be on the sidelines, waiting for his own landslide reelection in two years. That will have him in the driver's seat to make his move in the next National election."

Cameron did not understand the graphs Lawrence was pointing to while he talked. "The other candidates for the nomination will have some regional support. None are known throughout the state. This is where our advertising campaign is going to come in…"

"Advertising campaign?" Cameron interrupted.

Carter broke in. "We are going to start a State-wide media blitz in two weeks. Your media manager isn't with us yet. He has to wind up some things at his agency and then he'll be aboard. He is working out the initial ads in the meantime."

"You've done a hell of a lot of work in a short time, Carter," Cameron said. "It's like you've had this planned for some time."

Carter looked at Lawrence and then back to Cameron. "You've given us an impossible task. I don't have time to sit around and think up strategy. We have to act, these people are my friends and they are willing to help."

"I think this is all getting a little beyond my control," Cameron said.

Carter smiled and crossed over to the bar and poured a shot of whiskey into a glass. "You're the one who said Guy had to be your campaign manager because you trusted him. You called and asked me to help, so I assume you also trust me. We either run a campaign that means victory in November or we pack it in right now. Do you or do you not want to be in Washington this time next year?"

Cameron wasn't quite sure how to answer for a moment. He had about decided not to pursue the nomination for Sharon's sake—but now—it seemed like the forces were moving fast, carrying him along in a swirling, turbulent river.

"Yes...I guess so—I never had an idea about what it takes to run a campaign."

"If you want to run for the Senate and win, Guy and I are the bosses. You will have to do everything the way we want it done. We can't be at odds with one another. Do you understand?"

Cameron felt like a chastised child. "I understand. But, look at it from my point of view, Carter. I'm being hit with a lot in a hurry. My image has to be changed, my potential opponents have been—what's the term?"

"Profiled," Lawrence injected.

"Profiled. I walk into this room and I have three strangers mapping out my life."

"There will be a hell of a lot more on the team before we're finished, my friend," Carter added, sipping his drink.

Resigned to the situation, Cameron asked, "What else do you have?"

Lawrence spoke quickly, as though he was afraid of losing his turn. "I'd like you to review this book as soon as possible." He passed another thick, black notebook to Cameron.

Cameron accepted it and flipped through a few pages. "Have you read it, Guy?"

"This morning."

"Should I read it, Guy?"

"Yes, Cam. Today."

"Well, Carter, press on. This is all very interesting."

Franklin Hargrave was next. He dark hair had been slicked back with some type of pomade and his skin was pox marked and sallow. He had a pencil thin moustache above his thin lips. He wore an expensive pin stripped suit. The chain across his vest held a Phi Beta Kappa key. His left hand drummed nervously on the table.

He looked at Cameron for a moment without speaking. Then he pressed the tips of his fingers together in front of his face and spoke in a surprisingly soft tone.

"Tell us about Vietnam"

"I don't talk about 'Nam."

Carter took out a cigar and began to light it. Franklin tapped his lips with his fingers.

"We're waiting," Franklin said.

#

The rain came down in torrents and turned the land into an infinite sea of mud. Cameron huddled under his slicker, but the dampness crept into his bones. His boots and trousers were caked with slimy black earth and his hands trembled from the cold. He wanted a cigarette but knew that the slightest glow in the dark would attract enemy fire. Like his men, he was hungry and exhausted. He could barely make out the hunched over figure of Guy, shivering in the cold. He started to move closer to his sergeant and then changed his mind.

"Damn," he muttered to himself, "how in the hell did I get us into this mess?"

He crouched forward on his knees and stared into the night. The enemy was out there—somewhere—watching—waiting. *I wonder if they are as miserable as I am? If this goddamned rain would only stop.* The constant rhythm of the drops on his helmet echoed through his brain. *Hell,* he decided as he settled back and tried to find some warmth in his wet clothing, *it'll rain forever.*

Suddenly, the air was electrified with a dull whine.

"You sons-of-bitches, add to our misery!" he screamed as the shells came closer.

Exploding lights that sent eerie shadows across the terrain cut the blackness of the night. Occasionally, there was a glimpse of one of his men as he dodged an explosion and disappeared again, into a hole or trench, seeking safety from the forces of destruction. But, there was no escape. Even the deepest foxhole offered no protection from a direct hit. And there were many that night.

The cries of death began. Cameron shuttered and clutched his knees. He was terrified and he had a right to be so. He was supposed to be strong, but he was frightened. His men were sitting ducks and he couldn't do a damn thing about it. His hearted pounded. Everywhere men were screaming like frightened young girls, their voices high-pitched and desperate. The pleas for corpsmen were first strong and desperate. Then they grew weaker and weaker until they were silenced by the welcome peace of death. It was an endless nightmare as on and on the hammering continued—bringing incessant pain—incessant torment—incessant death.

"Oh, God," Cameron whispered, "please make it stop. Please."

"Help me…help me!" The cry cut through the din and sent a flash of chills down Cameron's spine. He knew the voice.

"Somebody help me—for God's sake—somebody help me—please—don't let me die." The cry was shrill and mingled with the explosions. Cameron leaned forward and listened to the voice.

It's one of my men—he's been hit and he's out there alone. I have to go get him—it's my responsibility—I can let him lie there and die—he's my responsibility—I can't leave him there.

"Don't let me die—please—help me—mama—please—someone—I'm hit—help me—mama—I don't want to die…." The voice trailed off into sobs.

Jesus, what should I do? I can't leave him out there but I can't break my own orders—I can't sit here and let that boy die—what the hell am I going to do?

"Mama—mama…" The voice grew fainter.

"Hell, I'm going. I don't care what the book says—he's one of my mine and I am not going to leave him out there to die alone. I'll be damned if I'm going to sit here and listen to him dying. I'm going after him." Cameron was speaking aloud, but there was no one to hear, to approve or disapprove of his decision.

Cameron inched his way out of the trench and started crawling toward the voice. The slimy mud made his progress slow and before he had gone very far, he discarded his rifle and slicker. He slid forward, his feet fighting for a hold in the yielding mud. He stopped again and tired to rub the mud from his eyes, but it did little good. His beard was caked and matted and his hands felt like they were encased in large, slippery mittens. It seemed like an eternity before he made out the writhing figure.

"Don't let me die—please, God—don't let me die," the man sobbed.

"It's all right, son. I'm here. Everything will OK. Take it easy. You won't die," Cameron whispered. "I won't let you."

He took a chance and yelled for a corpsman. He knew that the yelling was useless, but he had to try. The heavy shelling continued and the few corpsman they had couldn't begin to keep up with the wounded. It was hell on earth.

"Where are you hit,"?"

"My legs—my legs are gone."

Cameron eased his hands down the boy's body and felt the torn flesh. His legs had not been blown off, but he needed a tourniquet. Cameron removed his belt and wound it around the young man's right leg.

"Hang on—I'm going to carry you back."

"Don't let me die—please," he sobbed. "I don't want to die—I don't want to die…."

Cameron slipped his arms around the wounded man and lifted him from the foxhole. The man screamed in pain.

"Hold on, Marine," Cameron urged. "Hold on."

They started moving through the night. The added weight made it almost impossible for Cameron to move. Inch by inch, he worked his way back toward safety. His arms screamed in agony at the strain, but he kept moving. Every few feet he had to stop and rest and shift the weight of his burden a little bit. Then they moved forward again. The shelling grew heavier and in the exploding light, Cameron saw the man's face, twisted and set in agony.

"Can you hear me?" Cameron shouted. There was no answer, but he continued to lug the man on his shoulders.

"Hold on, you son-of-a-bitch—don't quit on me now—keep breathing, goddamn it—keep fuckin' breathing—we'll make it. It isn't much farther. Don't quit on me now—stay with me—hang on."

The night erupted into a thousand fires from hell. Cameron twisted his body to cover the man, but the shock from the explosions sent him spinning backward. Cameron struggled for a moment against the force and then it tossed him through the air like a child's toy. A searing pain ripped his body and he pitched into unconsciousness.

Dawn came onto the scene and the shelling stopped. The men ventured out of their muddy shelters and began the grim task of collecting the dead. The moans of the wounded and dying filled the morning air. Guy Sheridan began looking for the body of his friend.

Cameron heard the sounds and struggled to rise. Blood had streamed down his face and mixed with the mud. He tried to force the mess away from his face, but his hands added more mud to the sticky covering. He tried to rise, but his legs crumbled and he fell face down into the mud. A stabbing pain shot through his body. He couldn't even find the strength to scream. He waited. He knew he was dying.

In the distance, he could hear voices approaching. He tried to raise his head, but couldn't. By pushing with his left foot he was able to inch forward. "Please, God," he prayed, "let them see me."

"Hey!" someone yelled. "That guy over there moved. Get a stretcher quick."

#

He was aware that he was lying on a bed. People were moving about and their voices mingled in confusion. Cameron felt pressure on his head and with his left hand, he felt the bandage.

I'm in a hospital—I don't know how I got here—I don't remember— the mud—yes, the mud—and the man—the cries—the shells, that's it the shells—closer—closer—closer... He screamed.

He heard a scurry of people moving toward him and two strong arms gently pushed him back down on the bed.

"Easy, fellow, everything will be all right," a voice said.

He felt the jab of a needle in his left arm. For a moment, he continued to struggle and then his strength ebbed and he eased into a dreamless sleep.

He had no idea how long he slept. From the quiet, he judged that it was night, but with the bandages over his eyes, he couldn't see. He couldn't be certain of anything. He listened to the labored breathing of a man to his right. Somewhere in the room another man groaned and called for a nurse. Cameron moved his head from side to side and felt no pain. The throbbing that had roused him the first time was gone. He relaxed and slept again.

The hospital came to life and Cameron heard someone beside his bed. He forced himself to concentrate and realized that they were doing something to the man to his right. He knew that the labored breathing had stopped. While he had slept, death had come and claimed the man, but Cameron didn't feel afraid. He had been a partner with death since he had arrived in Vietnam— and he was used to it now—it was just another everyday occurrence. He didn't know who the man was—maybe it was the young man he had tried to save— he could see his face clearly for a moment—so frightened, so afraid of dying.

He heard someone approaching his bed.

"Good morning, Lieutenant. How do you feel?" The voice was deep and unfamiliar.

"Better, I guess," Cameron answered.

"We'll be air lifting you to Japan today," the man continued.

"How long have I been here?"

"A month."

A month—my God, What happened to me? No. The man is wrong. I came in last night—it was last night—the shelling—the boy—last night— not a week—last night.

"I want you to listen, son. There is nothing wrong with your sight, just an infection from the mud. But—your pelvis and right leg were smashed. We've patched you together. They'll need to operate in Japan and put in some plates. You'll be going home soon. There will be a few weeks in Japan and then stateside to Bethesda. You're going to have a long bout with rehabilitation, but you should get back on your feet. You're lucky. I know things seem like hell right now, but you're damn fortunate to be alive, Lieutenant."

What the hell is he trying to say, Cameron's brain shouted. *Plates— where—he couldn't feel his right leg. Oh, my God, they cut off my leg— my leg—the goddamned butchers cut off my leg.*

#

No one in the room spoke for a few moments. Cameron looked at their faces, but no one seemed moved by his story. He felt exhausted, drained. Under his jacket, his shirt was soaked with sweat and these guys looked like they had heard it all before.

"What happened to the man you tried to save?" Franklin asked.

"I don't know. No one seemed to know anything. There were a lot of wounded. Who knows which one I had in my arms."

"Too bad we can't find him. He could be useful to us during the campaign. But, if we don't know, we don't know. Is there anything in your past we should know about now? Anything that might surface and embarrass us?" Franklin continued.

"You know the story of my drinking problem, I'm sure. I don't make a secret of it. I don't drink any more."

"We are prepared to face that head on, when the time comes. Carter filled us in when we discussed taking over your campaign. If we play this right— losing your wife and your parents, the war injury—we can make people sympathetic to your little problem," Franklin explained.

Cameron did not like him. He's too smooth, he thought.

"You do abstain now, don't you? Carter asked.

Cameron looked at him for a moment. "No, I don't. I'm a newly wed. I enjoy my conjugal rights almost every night."

The comment broke the tension in the room and everyone except Franklin laughed. His dark eyes glared a Cameron with a chilling look of disdain.

"There is one thing, Cameron," Franklin said. "You must never be photographed with a glass in your hand, even if its only water. Do you understand?"

"Is it all right if I drink water in private?" Cameron asked.

Carter stepped toward him. "I'm sorry, Cameron, if we've been a little rough on you today. We're all in your corner. The fellows are a little tense because this the first time they've had a chance to get their hands on a candidate. We want to work with you, not against you, believe me."

"I believe you and I trust you, Carter. It'll take me a little time to trust the rest of the team. I think you're a damn smart man, Carter. Don't disappoint me."

"I'll try my damnedest not to, Cam. I promise."

Cameron felt fatigue overwhelming his body. "I'm a little tired. You guys have hit me with a lot. I need to get my bearings."

The men in the room were silent.

"Go home, rest and think everything through. Talk to Sharon—she'll see things your way when she understands how important this is. We'll meet again tomorrow," Carter said.

Guy started to the door. "I'll walk you to your car, Cameron."

As they stepped outside, Cameron stopped and looked at Guy. "What do you make of all this, Guy? I felt like I was in the middle of a damned inquisition. Where the hell did those guys come from?"

"I'm a little overwhelmed, too, Cameron. At first, I thought everything was out of control, then I talked with Carter for a couple of hours this morning. He explained to me what it takes to get a candidate elected today. He said these guys are the best."

"Frankly, Guy, they scare the hell out of me."

"You're over reacting, Cam. My biggest concern is handling your campaign. I think I'm way out of my league. Damn it, I don't even know where to start."

"You're my friend, Guy. I believe that I can always trust you to be honest with me. I'm not sure I like what seems to be going on, but I think Carter is a good man. You'll learn and Carter's medieval trio won't let you screw up, I'm sure."

"If I get in the way, tell me and I'll quit. Is that a deal, Cam?"

"You'll never get in the way as far as I'm concerned, Guy. Keep an eye on those guys. They're interesting, but I guess they're going to do the best job they can for me. I'm going home and do my homework. I'll talk to you later."

Cameron patted Guy on the shoulder as he started toward his car.

When Guy and Cameron left the room, the four men sat in silence for a few moments. Carter was the first to speak.

"How do you assess the meeting?"

"I think that he will be impossible to control," Jacob said. "He's arrogant."

"Control will not be an issue, I assure you," Carter said.

"OK, Carter. We'll go along with whatever you say. You'd better be right."

"I am."

No one else spoke for a minute.

This time Franklin broke the silence. "I think we can get him elected to the Senate without too much trouble. The next step is going to take a lot of preparation and planning. Control must not become a problem."

"I agree with you, Franklin. New York's next Senator just left this room. And if our plans are right we will have him in the White House four years after that," Lawrence spoke with authority.

"Ambitious aren't you, Lawrence?" Jacob asked.

"Someone find where Sheridan keeps his good scotch," Lawrence said. "He has to be worth something."

While the men celebrated their success, Carter slipped into the kitchen, picked up the phone and dialed a number. The answering machine cut in on the first ring.

"Everything is going as planned," Carter said and replaced the receiver.

tum tum tum ta tum…
tum tum tum ta tum…

The great pilgrimage to Washington began almost as soon as the word was flashed. They traveled by train, bus, car, plane, bicycle and foot, from all walks of life, from big cities and small towns, individuals and families. Some made the journey from other countries. Some came out of simple curiosity, some came to be caught up in a moment of history, and some came because they felt a deep need to be near him this final time. As daylight faded from the somber sky, their candles were lighted and the dancing flames became a *danse macabre*, illuminating the drawn, sad faces of the throng that inched its way along Pennsylvania Avenue. The people, along with their country, were in pain and neither would ever be as young or as free again.

tum tum tum ta tum…

CHAPTER X

The painters and decorators finished their work and turned the key back to Cameron an hour before he stood in the sunlight and told the citizens of the State that he was planning to run for the Senate.

Maggie was aghast. "Before you even move into that damn house he bought, that man you married is making plans to move," she screamed at Sharon. "I knew he wanted to get you away from me."

Cameron stepped into the argument, although he knew better. He was tired and tense. "Stop it! Don't shout at my wife. She agrees with my decision."

"You're no better than David was."

Cameron stared at his mother-in-law. "Don't ever compare me to David again. Do you understand."?

"I know what you do to Sharon at night. I hear you." Maggie spat the words into his face.

Cameron felt his face flush with anger. "What my wife and I do in the privacy of our bedroom is our business. You should be sleeping with your husband instead of eavesdropping on us. You might find you enjoy it." He regretted the words the moment he spoke them.

Like a flash, Maggie's hand shot and struck his face, knocking his glasses to the floor. Cameron moved away, shocked by the strength of the blow.

"You men are all alike—pigs!" Maggie was screaming now. "David used to keep on and on, until she'd cry for him to stop. He liked to make her cry from pain."

Cameron felt sick at his stomach. He could hear Sharon's sobs. His head hurt from Maggie's slap. "Stop it—for God's sake, Maggie—stop. You're a sick old woman. Leave us alone."

Maggie smiled at him as she turned and left the room.

Cameron felt Sharon's arms around him. He looked at her. "I love you so much," was all that he could manage.

"Oh, Cam, what a mess I got you into. My poor, poor darling. I'm so sorry."

"It isn't your fault Sharon. I should have kept my mouth shut."

They found freedom in the campaign that they both knew might take them away from their new home forever. By chartered plane and car, they crossed and re-crossed the State, meeting people and building support for the convention in August. Cameron was good at listening to people's problems. They crammed as many stops into a day as was humanly possible.

Sharon learned to stand before a microphone, silently praying that her trembling legs wouldn't be noticed, and ask the crowd to believe in her husband.

"He'll work hard for you," she said shyly. "He'll keep his promises and he'll make the best Senator this State has ever had."

She said it a hundred times, in a hundred different ways, to hundreds of different people, and it was just the beginning. The nomination had to be won first and then the campaign would begin in earnest. These were delegates she was talking to today. She shook hands with them, drank coffee and nibbled on a greasy donut while she answered questions about her family.

She missed the children and they missed her. She called home every night, but it wasn't like being there. Deep inside, she was afraid of what her mother was telling them.

Six men raced against time and each other. Of the group, one was an old party man who's day had come and gone, two ran on absurd platforms, two were trying for the third time, and there was Cameron. He was starting to interest the delegates with his looks, manner and style. They liked his ideas.

People like heroes and the handsome couple was making good press. Carter's connections in the media were serving them well. Charlie Horton's television campaign was arousing curiosity and crowds. Cameron was moving from being an unknown to a favorite and the quest for the nomination had become a two-man race.

The Marshall campaign team was growing concerned that they might be making too much of a showing, too soon. They didn't want Bailey to suspect that Cameron might be a man capable of actually winning the election in November. They knew that Bailey would somehow eliminate anyone who appeared to be a threat to his absolute control.

Cameron made a quiet entrance into Buffalo. He arrived late at night and went straight to his hotel room without being noticed by the press. Jacob,

Lawrence and Franklin were orchestrating every move he made. The unholy trinity, Cameron called them. Carter did not appreciate the humor.

"Everything is ready," Guy explained as he and Carter joined Cameron in his room. "We've got a little demonstration planned after your name is placed in nomination. Nothing too fancy. We want Bailey to keep thinking that you have half-hearted support out there and need his blessing to be successful."

Cameron nodded approval.

"Bailey is a little edgy about Congressman Striker giving your nominating speech. I told him he was the only guy we could find to do it. Probably didn't fool that son-of-a-bitch," Carter said, lighting one of his famous cigars.

"Striker is a renegade as far as the bosses are concerned. It should seem natural that he would team up with me," Cameron noted.

"Natural to you, but not to Bailey. Believe me, Cameron, Bailey has his hooks into Striker, too—big time. If we blow this, Striker is dead politically and he knows it. Bailey will have very quick revenge."

"God, all this makes me nervous. I'm not a politician. How the hell did I get into this?" Cameron got up and started pacing around the room.

Carter looked at Guy and indicated for him to get up and talk to Cameron.

"Hey, buddy," Guy said, putting his hand on Cameron's shoulder. "It's too late to turn back now. A hell of a lot of people will be disappointed in you if you quit. You told the people of this State that you were going to be their Senator. We can't let them down now, can we?"

Cameron was silent for a moment and then he smiled. "You guys seem to have everything under control. Are you sure you need me around?"

Carter and Guy laughed with relief. "We're just using you as a front," Guy quipped.

Despite the confidence of his team, Cameron spent a restless night. He missed Sharon and wanted to hold her. He finally slept, but soon woke with a start, drenched with sweat. The dream again. He did not understand it. Everything was moving so fast.

Sharon and Ann would arrive the next day. He would not get to be with her until after the nominating speeches and the balloting. He wanted to be at the Convention with her, but Carter insisted that he stay at the hotel and meet with people. It would be a long day.

Congressman Stanley Striker was a tall, lanky man, with a shock of uncontrollable sandy colored hair. He was a pleasant man who always wore a smile and was eager to shake hands with people. He was happy with his role of placing Cameron's name in nomination and he kept his head, giving a speech that was perfunctory and placed Cameron into official consideration.

Striker longed to be governor of the State and his chances lay in someone taking control of the party from the old time bosses. Cameron Marshall seemed to be a bright ray of hope. Striker prayed silently that he would be, as he moved back to his seat. It was a gamble and it was too late to turn back now. He had committed himself to the Marshall candidacy. If Marshall was victorious, he would be, too; it they lost, it would be the end of his political career, because Bailey would retain his iron grip on the party and destroy him.

The Marshall demonstration lasted eleven minutes, one minute over the allotted time. The young men and women that had been recruited to parade and wave banners did so with enthusiasm, and got a little carried away, but no damage was done. A few delegates got up and joined in the fun.

Cameron paced his hotel room like a nervous cat. He was finding it impossible to sit still and watch the proceedings on television. Guy and Carter left for the Convention as soon as all the nominating speeches were finished.

Cameron stared at the television screen whenever the cameras panned the crowd, hoping to catch a glimpse of Sharon. His dinner sat, untouched and cold, on the table in the corner of the room.

The balloting began.

It was apparent from the beginning that none of the six candidates would receive a majority on the first ballot. There would be a second ballot. Bailey's men began to move among the delegates trying to change votes. Cameron didn't like what was happening, but he was helpless to do anything.

His team would have to move fast to stop a second ballot.

Bailey was preparing the take control of the next vote and that would not be in Cameron's favor, unless his people were willing to strike a deal and he had been adamant about no deals with Bailey. The game could be ending faster than he had expected.

Tom Kennington, from Long Island, was trying to get the recognition of the chair. The gavel pounded and Kennington was recognized. He changed his vote for Cameron. And then another delegate was calling for recognition and another vote went into Cameron's column.

It was over quickly once the ball got rolling. No one wanted to be left off the bandwagon. Stan Striker worked his way back to the platform and called for a unanimous voice vote. Cameron was the Democratic nominee for the Senate. The Convention moved on to other nominations and business. The drama that most of the people knew nothing about was over.

Cameron was elated when the group got back from the convention hall. He was happy to hold his wife in his arms. He kissed her and whispered, "We're on our way."

Guy overheard. "Yea, you're on your way, all right. Bailey will send your acceptance speech over in the morning. He's mad as hell because you won on the first ballot. You didn't give him a chance to be the kingmaker. What the hell is wrong with you, Cam? Don't you know how to play the game?"

They all laughed.

"By the way, Carter, where is my speech?" Cameron asked.

"You'll get it in the morning. There'll be plenty of time to make any changes you want. Remember, even though you're on TV, this is PBS coverage. You're not going to be high on the viewers' list tomorrow night," Carter explained.

"Most people are going to be more interested in the candidate for Governor. You'll have your twenty minutes in the limelight, but you're not the big show tomorrow night. You're an unknown who somehow is running for the U.S. Senate. They'll be polite, there will be a show of party unity, but you're the odd man out, Cam. Don't you forget that. You're a convenience to them, someone they can sacrifice so that they can protect the real candidates, who can see a Republican landslide on the horizon." Franklin was lecturing them again.

Cameron nodded his head. "I know—it's an uphill battle. I've known that all along. I don't have any delusions of grandeur here. I know we're locking horns with Bailey and company."

"Good boy," Carter said. "You're beginning to act like you know what the score is."

Stanley Striker, his wife Lorraine and their three children accompanied Cameron and Sharon to the convention center. Cameron had acquired his first political debt and he was starting an immediate repayment. Sharon's parents had been persuaded to join them in Buffalo. They brought Debbie and David. Ryan was somewhere on the other side of the world flying jet planes. Gillian and Jay accompanied them to the platform when Cameron was announced.

The delegates welcomed all of the nominees to the Convention with cheers and exuberance. This was a night for fun and celebrating. The candidate for governor looked worn and tired. Cameron shook his hand and the two men waved to the crowd together.

He knows he going to lose, Cameron thought. I wish there was something I could do to change that, but I can't.

Virgil Bailey stood in the shadows watching the action unfolding before him. Cameron smiled at him and held up the manuscript he had received that morning. Bailey nodded his approval.

As Cameron started forward to begin his speech, Guy thrust a black notebook into his hands. The applause died down.

"The lamb is led to slaughter," Cameron whispered under his breath and glanced at Bailey and smiled. They locked eyes for a moment and Cameron saw a strange look on Bailey face.

"My friends—citizens of the great State of New York—fellow Democrats...I am proud to accept your nomination for the office of United States Senator." Cameron continued with praise for the State and his plans when he was elected. Then he closed the notebook, paused, looked over at Bailey and began to speak again.

"My friends, I have to tell you that what has transpired at this Convention in the past few days has been as example of Democracy at its worst. I do not know if I will be a good Senator or not. I have never held an elected office. What I am, you see, is a convenience for the political bosses who control our party. They have conceded the election this fall to the Republicans. And they needed someone like me to be sacrificed. I am an unknown. I couldn't possibly win. So, they arranged for me to run and protect the real candidates from defeat. Virgil Bailey and his crew of manipulators have victimized you. You have been deprived of a free choice at this Convention. Think about it for a moment—if you were not bound by party allegiance, would I be the candidate you would choose? What do you know about me?"

There was silence in the auditorium. Carter turned to Guy. "What the hell is he doing? Where did this stuff come from? Who the hell does this self-righteous bastard think he is?" Carter glared at Guy. "You said you had him under control." Carter left the platform and headed for a pay phone.

The Convention crowd was silent as Cameron continued his speech.

"I have won the nomination, not because I am the best candidate, but because the bosses believe that I can be sacrificed in the Republican victory the party believes will hit this State in November."

There were a few cries of "no! no!" from the audience. In the boxes to the left of the platform, an usher tapped Ann on her shoulder, and whispered something to her. She got up and followed the man out of the hall.

"Let me tell you, my friends, there will be no Republican landslide in this State in November. We are going forward to victory. The political bossism that has controlled your political beliefs and choices for so long, is dead. We are burying bossism tonight—here—in Buffalo.

The delegates began to come to life. Ann returned to her seat and handed Sharon a bouquet of flowers. She smiled as she sat down. "He's electrifying this crowd."

Some of the delegates rose to their feet and began to wave State flags.

"Stan Striker and I are going to Washington. You are going to send us there and we will give this State honest, faithful and true representation.'

Carter returned to the platform and moved behind Bailey. He put his hand on the man's shoulder and whispered, "You're through, Bailey. Get out of here before Cameron throws you to the lions."

Bailey wrenched himself free of Carter's grip. Pain shot down his arm. Sweat started pouring down his face. His shirt was soaked. His stomach hurt. Something had gone wrong. That bastard Marshall was not the man he had pretended to be when he agreed to the plan. He looked through the curtain and saw Carter. "I hate you, you bastard," Bailey mumbled to himself. The room began to spin as he got to his feet and lurched into the back hall.

"Our assignment will not be easy," Cameron told the assembly. "It will be an uphill battle. But nothing worthwhile is ever easily gained. We must fight for victory in November and fight we shall. Stan Striker and I owe our allegiance to you, the delegates to this Convention—to you, watching at home—to every man, woman and child in this State. We owe you faithful, diligent, loyal dedication. The world moves too fast today for our political offices to be treated like pawns. Political offices must be earned by men who believe in this Nation and the principles for which it stands. Men who are not afraid to stand up and say what they believe must be elected if we are to remain strong and free."

Applause interrupted Cameron's speech. He looked back and saw that Bailey had disappeared. He turned back to the audience and continued his speech. Now he spoke with a new force, carrying the audience with him in his enthusiasm. He inspired them and they cheered him.

When he finished, Striker joined him and they posed for more pictures. The candidate for Governor made his way forward from the back of the platform and joined them. He seemed out of place.

As the flashbulbs exploded in his face, Cameron heard Guy behind him. "Bailey's dead. Coronary," Guy shouted into his ear.

Cameron turned his head and looked at Guy. The victory was sour. He had not wanted to kill Bailey, only to break his strangle hold on the party.

"Goddamn it," Cameron muttered. Striker looked at him. Carter was right. Politics was no place for him, but it was too late. What he wanted was within his grasp. Cameron smiled for the photographers and let his hand rest on Striker's shoulder.

#

They lost no time in beginning the campaign. Franklin left the Marshall camp and moved into the State party headquarters as the new chairman. Cameron and his team claimed the leadership role in the State.

The Marshall forces moved quickly around the State. Sometimes Cameron and Sharon were together, but more often they were apart. Cameron would make an appearance in one town, Sharon in another. They wanted to meet as many people as possible, speak to as many people as possible, shake a million hands, find the votes they needed.

Guy and Carter often preceded him into the cities and villages of New York. He seldom saw his friends; they were off to another place by the time he arrived. He had to be satisfied with late night conference calls with them and then a good night call from Sharon.

A tall, young, blond-haired man named Chuck Roswell came aboard as Cameron's personal aide. Chuck drove the car, carried his briefcase and always watched the crowds, searching for anyone who might make an unusual move.

Others joined the staff. There were men who were trained to protect him and for the first time the thought of personal danger entered Cameron's mind, but he dismissed it. Cameron did not know the men, but they were always near and he knew that they rested and slept after they were certain he was asleep.

He could see them talking on the phone, sending telegrams, rushing through different routines every place they stopped. He knew that they were reporting to Guy and Carter. He laughed to himself about Guy and Carter. They had been furious with him about the changes in the convention speech, but it had worked. He had control of the party now. Or rather, they did. Cameron realized that, while he was the candidate, he didn't have control over much of anything.

The candidate's role is small. If the public knew the real truth, they would never believe in the democratic system again. An advertising agency turned out slogans, singing jingles and slick videos. *I'm a goddamned commercial package,* he thought, as he watched one of his ads on television. *They sell me like soap. God Bless America—there isn't another land like it anywhere in the world.*

He flew from New York City to Albany, rehearsing his speech as the engines of the jet roared. Sharon was waiting for him at the airport. He smiled at his wife, gripped her hand and kissed her on the cheek as flash after flash from the reporters' cameras exploded. Sharon looked pale and tired and had little to say. He didn't have time to pursue the problem, as local dignitaries moved in to shake his hand. He was schedule for two speeches in Albany and then they were flying home for a long promised free day. Home to the children and a closed door. A door they could hide behind for a few hours.

The day went as expected and the speeches were well received. A last minute change in plans kept them in the Albany later than they expected. It was past midnight when their chartered plane landed at Lakeland Regional Airport. Ann and Guy were waiting just inside the terminal.

"You look like hell," was Guy's greeting.

"Thanks. It's your schedule that's doing this to me. It's no easy task out there. It's a tough battle. I knew it was going to be uphill, but the hill seems to be getting steeper. What's the latest report?" Cameron asked Guy as they walked through the almost deserted terminal.

"The national poll shows what we figured, a Republican victory. Richardson is a definite bet for the White House. Won't that be a joy?"

"Nathaniel Mark Richardson. It has a nice ring of patriotism. Too bad he'll give away the store to anyone and everyone. I don't think he has the balls to say no to anything."

"This must be what the people want," Guy commented in an off-hand manner.

"Want? Hell! The don't have a choice. The can have the Vice President or Rich. Look what they get with the Vice President—scandal and corruption. I don't know how involved he was, but he never had the guts to stand up and denounce the President. He's incapable of making decisions on his own. Neither man in qualified to lead this Nation. It's a damn sorry commentary on our political system when this is the best we can do for leadership."

"What the hell got you onto the soap box tonight?"

"I'm disgusted by what I see, Guy. I hope to hell you and the boys can continue to keep the Vice President away from me. If he comes into the State, I'll have to appear with him and that will be the end of the ball game."

"So far, we're successful in doing that. And, we've got the opposition worried. Rich is going to increase his appearances here. New York is one state identified as being a possible loss for the great man. They seem to attribute that to you, Cam. The game is going to be very rough in the last few weeks. I don't think they'll write New York off, but we can hope."

They were out of the building and on their way to the car before they realized that Ann and Sharon were not with them.

"Jesus, Guy, we were so damn busy talking, we forgot our wives."

"We'd better go back."

"You go, Guy, I'm beat. Where's the car?"

"Over there, in the fifth row. It's unlocked." Guy gave Cameron a strange look and started back to the terminal. He was puzzled by his friend's lack of concern for Sharon.

Guy found Ann and Sharon standing inside the main door. Sharon looked pale and frightened, sitting on a bench, with Ann hovering over her.

"What's wrong?" Guy asked.

"Sharon was dizzy."

"I'm all right now. Where is Cam?"

"He's waiting in the car."

Guy gave Ann an 'I don't understand' look and helped Sharon to her feet. She supported herself on his arm as she left the airport.

"Sharon's pregnant," Ann whispered to Guy.

"Does Cam know, Sharon?" Guy asked

"Oh, Guy, I haven't talked to Cam in weeks. We've been separated by all the appearances and then there's always someone with him. He's so exhausted, he slept all the way from Albany. He doesn't care about anything but the goddamned election. He's consumed with the idea that he's going to win the damn election." Sharon struggled to fight back tears.

When they got to the car, Cameron was asleep in the backseat. Sharon slipped in and sat close to the right hand door, as far away from Cameron as possible. Guy gave Ann a shrug and walked around to the driver's side. He was furious over what was happening to his friends and he knew he was part of the cause.

They drove in silence for a while, with the only sound Sharon's weeping n the backseat. She was staring out the window, her eyes seeing beyond the scenes that flashed past the car. Guy couldn't stand it any longer.

"Cameron," he shouted. "Damn you, wake up and pay attention to your wife!" Ann was startled by the sudden outburst.

"Guy!"

"Stay out of this, Ann. I've created this problem and I'm going to solve it right now." He stopped the car along the side of the road and turned to face Cameron.

"If getting you elected to the Senate means destroying your marriage, I'm not going to have any part of it, Cam. Do you understand?"

Cameron struggled to grasp what was happening. He had been so tired he had fallen into a sound, dreamless sleep and for a moment, he had no idea where he was.

"When we get home, the first thing I'm going to do is give you my resignation. I refuse to be a party to anything that destroys two people I love as much as I do you and Sharon. I never wanted to be involved in this in the first place. You've lost all sense of reality, Cameron. All you can think about is getting elected. You're as consumed by this as much as you were by alcohol!"

"Guy, that's enough." Ann gripped his arm.

"I don't know what you're talking about." Cameron was confused by the outburst from Guy. He head was starting to ache.

"Look at your wife! The woman you claim to love."

"Guy!" Ann's voice was sharp.

Cameron heard Sharon's sobs and reached for her. "What's wrong? Why are you crying? Sharon—what's wrong? I don't understand any of this."

Ann turned and looked at Cameron and Sharon. "I think we all need to take a deep breath and calm down. Yelling isn't going to solve anything. Let's get going home, Guy."

Cameron looked over at Sharon and reached out his hand. She slid across the seat and into his arms. He pulled her close and whispered, "I'm sorry if I caused you pain." He had no idea what had caused Sharon's sudden unhappiness and Guy's outburst. He would wait until they were home to deal with the problem. Right now the fatigue in his body had him in a vice grip and his head wasn't clear. Tomorrow—it would all be clear tomorrow

tum tum tum ta tum…
tum tum tum ta tum…

The day comes all too soon when the one we love is gone forever Then, and only then, do we stop to consider all the things we should have done, but didn't. The million times we should have whispered 'I love you,' but were too busy…the time we should have offered comfort, but were too tired…the times we should have looked, but were too blind. With death, endless nights bring back memories and memories and memories. It is too late to make amends…too late to go back…too late to recapture the lost love…too late to hear the voice, see the face, feel the touch. Oh, my darling, it is too late forever.
tum tum tum ta tum…

CHAPTER XI

Cameron and Sharon were sound asleep in each other's arms when the phone started ringing. Cameron roused with a start and was surprised to see sunlight streaming into the room. He grabbed the phone. It was Carter.

"We have a problem. I'm on my way over right now." Carter hung up before Cameron could ask any questions.

Cameron's opposition Mackenzie Farrell had launched a bitter, personal attack on Cameron and his family. The Republican Party had tapped Farrell at the last minute to run, when five-term Senator Chester Gamble abruptly announced his retirement after the sudden death of his wife. Farrell was working feverishly to make up ground.

In fifteen minutes, Carter and Cameron were seated at the kitchen table looking at the morning newspapers.

The front pages of newspapers all across the State were carrying the story of Cameron's bout with alcoholism. Farrell called him a carpetbagger and charged that his marriage was a sham. "It is a marriage of convenience," Farrell said in the story, "designed to make Marshall look respectable and give him a strong tie to the State."

Cameron shook his head as he read the article. They had found and interviewed his mother-in-law, who had spewed forth her hate for him.

Sharon joined them in the kitchen and stood reading over Cameron's shoulder when Ann and Guy arrived. They looked at one another in disbelief.

Cameron turned on the TV in time to catch Farrell on an early morning news program. "Marshall is a rich playboy, bored with life and he's found an interest in a new game—politics. He's a millionaire who doesn't give a damn about the common man. He isn't even able to recognize one. He's decided it will be fun to make the Senate his new playground. His interest is self-glory," Farrell charged.

Carter handed Cameron another newspaper and he read another version of the same charges. He felt a sinking sensation in his stomach. What infuriated him most was that Farrell was right. About part of it anyway. It had started out that way, but he had changed—or had he? Did Farrell know him better than he knew himself?

Sharon poured coffee for everyone and she and Ann went into the living room to be alone.

"What the hell do we do now, Carter?"

"I say we ignore Farrell and continue with the campaign as planned. I think people have already made up their minds," Guy suggested.

"We've been expecting something from Farrell for some time, Cam. I think he was counting on Richardson to save his ass," Carter said. "I talked with Franklin and Lawrence this morning. They feel our answer should be the ads we've prepared that play up your hero image. Too damn bad we can't find that dumb son-of-a-bitch you saved."

"I can handle what he said about me, it's the attack on Sharon that has me furious. It's not fair. Damn it to hell!" Cameron shouted.

To add to their problems, Maggie arrived, waving a copy of the morning paper. She stormed through the kitchen and into the living room.

"I told you," Maggie raved, waving the paper in Sharon's face. "You wouldn't listen to your mother. No, you had to marry him. When he's elected, he'll divorce you for some Washington bimbo. That's what they all do."

Sharon smiled and kept her control. "I don't care why he married me. The important thing is, he married me. And, I'm carrying his child."

"That doesn't mean anything to a man like him. With his money, he can buy his way out of everything. He'll erase you with a check. You'll regret this; you'll regret you ever met this man. No, living at home with your father and me wasn't good enough. You had to have a playboy."

"Mother, if you can't make yourself accept Cameron, please stay out of my house." Sharon's voice was calm and firm.

"Now, he's turned you against me." Maggie's voice was changing into a whine. "Oh, baby, look what he's doing to you—dragging you around the State. You're a public spectacle. And I know you had a fight—I saw the look on your face when you got home last night."

"My place is with my husband. I made a mistake with David. I won't make the same one with Cam. He needs me and I love him—very much."

"And you'll go off to Washington and leave me all alone."

Sharon was tired of listening to her mother. "Mother, you don't run my life anymore. Do you understand? Go home. And, for God's sake, never speak to a reporter again."

Guy and Carter were losing their battle in trying to talk Cameron out of answering Farrell.

"You're too angry, Cam. You'll just fan the fire. Let the story die.

Let us do our jobs," Carter said.

"No. The press is camped on our doorstep this morning and I intend to use them. Tell them I'll hold a press conference in fifteen minutes. Where's Sharon?"

"In the living room with Ann and her mother," Carter said.

"I'll bet Maggie is having one of her champion tirades. I did not marry Sharon because she would help further my political ambitions. I admit I've done some reprehensible things in my day, but that is not one of them. I did not come here looking for a wife."

"I know you didn't honey." Sharon's voice was soft and remarkably controlled. Cameron had not been aware of her entry into the kitchen. She came over, bent down and kissed him. "I love you," she whispered.

Cameron took her hand and pulled her down onto his lap. "Say, Carter, did Sharon tell you we're going to have a baby?"

"Yes, we know. Look, Cam, be reasonable. Let us handle the reply to Farrell's charges. We know what we're doing."

"No. I am going to answer Farrell this morning."

"I'll have someone write your statement," Guy said, heading for the telephone.

"Don't bother. No public office is worth this. Tell them that I quit—today. There will be no discussion on the matter. The book is closed."

Guy and Carter stood silent, glaring at Cameron.

Carter found his voice first. "You've got to be kidding. You've come all this way, the campaign begins to get a little rough and you run away. You are a bastard."

Carter stomped out of the room and Guy followed. He was also furious with Cameron over his decision. Cameron could hear them arguing in the living room.

"I'm going to tell the truth, honey," Cameron explained to Sharon. "Farrell is right about a lot of things. But he's dead wrong about you and my intentions.

I'm going to stand in front of this house and be an honest man. And then, honey, it's all over. We can begin our life together again without the world watching. Right here, in this house—with a new baby."

Sharon jumped to her feet. "Are you really going to do that, Cam? Do you believe what you're saying? Is this the kind of man you are? That kind of thinking is how Bailey and his bunch got control of the party in this State. What's the matter, Cam? You look shocked. I know a hell of a lot more about politics than you give me credit for knowing. I also know a lot more about you than you think. I've seen you change. I've watched you listen to people and I've seen the concern on your face. I think I've watched you grow up in this campaign. I think you have a hell of a lot to give. And I also think that you love me. I know I love you and I'll stand beside you all the way, but not if you quit. I can't live with that."

"That's some speech, lady."

"I mean every word of it, Cam. You quit—you let a lot of people down who are learning to trust and believe in you and I walk out the door forever."

"I think you should be the politician in the family."

"I think you're right. It seems I have something you haven't—balls."

Her last comment broke the tension.

"I think yours are bronze. Will you walk out the door with me and meet the press?"

"You aren't going anywhere without me, buster." She bent down and kissed him. "I love you."

"And I love you. If I want to keep you, I guess I'd better get ready for a fight."

"You'd better mister, or you're going to be damn cold nights—alone on the sofa."

Cameron walked over, pushed open the door to the living room and called to Guy and Carter. "I'm going out to face the press."

Guy was beside him in a flash. "You can't. We haven't got your speech yet."

"Screw the speech, Guy. I know what I have to say without any help from anyone."

Cameron felt a surge of confidence as he stepped out the front door to meet the members of the press. In his left hand he carried a folded copy of a morning newspaper. It was a clear, crisp, late October day and he could see the trees in their fading hues of reds, oranges and yellows. The sun was bright and danced in his eyes, sparkling on the tears he was fighting to control. Sharon squeezed his hand.

"Ladies and gentlemen," he began. "You know why we are having this meeting. I'm sure you have been trying to second guess my reaction to Matthew Farrell's charges." He waved the newspaper over his head.

"Let me be honest with you. I was so disgusted when I read the stories that I had every intention of coming out here this morning and announcing that I was withdrawing from the campaign. Then a very beautiful and wise woman gave me an ultimatum." He turned to look at Sharon and winked.

"The truth must be acknowledged. Matthew Farrell's charges are correct." Silence—total silence as the reporters stared at him.

One young reporter turned to the woman on his left and commented. "My, God, it's over. This ass just committed political suicide."

"Or rather, let me say, some of his charges are correct. Yes, I am an alcoholic. I have never hidden that. Yes, I am a rich man, who outside of one compulsive act in Vietnam has never made a serious contribution to society. But, I did not come here looking for a wife. No one can pick the time and place when they will meet someone to love."

"In the past year, my life has changed dramatically and I realized that it is not too late for me to devote myself to a life of service. It is a lofty ambition for me to seek a Senate seat, but I do so because I believe I can make a contribution and serve this State well in Washington."

Cameron turned and looked at Sharon. "Relationships have to grow and mature. My relationship with my wife has grown and it matured in this house a few moments ago when this woman told me she could not live with a man who is a quitter. I was prepared to run away again—as I had done in the past. What I am not prepared to do is lose the love of my life."

"My relationship with the citizens of this State has matured as I have listened to the concerns of people all across this state—people from every economic level. I believe that I can start to make a difference. I say start because it is a tremendous task and no one man can do it alone. But this one man is determined to give his best. I ask the people of this State to give me the opportunity. I am asking for your trust and faith. I know, I am asking a lot, but I promise I will not fail you. This strong, determined lady standing beside me will make certain that I never betray your trust."

He realized that tears were slipping down his face and he wanted to rub them away. "I will continue this campaign and I will continue to speak for the things I believe are important. The personal attacks are painful, but I will not choose to follow that route. I am disappointed in Mr. Farrell's actions, because I always considered him an honorable man, but sometimes in the heat of battle we make decisions that are not always sound. My wife and I forgive Mr. Farrell and we will resume the campaign tonight. The citizens of this State, not an individual, will judge us. Thank you for your time and patience."

Sharon and Cameron waved at the reporters and turned to go back into the house.

"Damn it, man, you got balls," someone shouted.

He put his lips close to Sharon's ear. "He should see the ones my wife has. They're the real things."

Sharon punched him in the ribs with her elbow and they laughed.

Carter and Guy shook their heads and went back into the kitchen, leaving Sharon and Cameron to shake hands with a few members of the press.

Carter was sucking on one of his famous cigars. "He went off on his own at the convention and got by with it. Time will tell if he's right this time. He's a piece of work, Guy."

#

They were back on the road and they felt revitalized. There weren't many days left. Franklin and Lawrence were trying to assess the damage to the campaign. Jacob was working as the advance man, traveling ahead, preparing supporters before his arrival. Everything was moving at a faster and faster pace.

Sharon looked across the car at her husband, his chin pressed into his hand, lost in deep thought. He was worried, she could tell, but she was reluctant to disturb him, so she turned her attention to the countryside.

"Where's the next stop?" she asked Guy. Chuck was driving the car and Guy was sitting in the front passenger seat, holding Cameron's briefcase with the day's briefing papers. Soon he would pass the papers back to Cameron, so he could review important names before they arrived at their destination.

"County Democratic meeting. One of those Sunday barbecue affairs."

"Oh, God, Guy, he'll starve to death before Election Day." She always ate a good meal, but Cameron would fill his plate only to have it set, untouched, while people crowded close to him, eager for a handshake, a word, or the opportunity to touch the candidate. Sharon didn't think that she could stand to watch another scoop of ice cream make an island out of a piece of cake. It doesn't seem to bother him though, Sharon thought. He loves the people. She reached over and rubbed the back of his neck. He turned and smiled at her.

"Better take a look at these, Cam. We're almost there," Guy said, passing Cameron the ever-present note cards.

Sharon took a mirror from her purse and did a little repair job on her makeup. She had a hard time forcing her shoes back on her feet.

"Swollen, again?" Cameron asked.

"Uh, huh."

"Maybe you should buy a pair of larger shoes for evening."

"Do you want a wife with big feet?"

"My dear, I never look at your feet." He leaned over and kissed her on the cheek. "Is my tie straight?"

"You're as handsome as ever."

Guy turned and laughed. "I hope the press never asks me if you two discuss major political issues while you're traveling."

The car swung down a side street and pulled up in front of a white building. People were milling around and began applauding as the car slowed. Two State Policemen took their places beside the candidate as he stepped from the car. Cameron waited for Sharon to join him and then they plunged into the crowd, shaking hands, smiling and happy. This was their life. They were cramming as many stops as possible into a day, trying to overcome any advantage the attack might have given Farrell. The week was a blur to Sharon.

#

Cameron had just stepped out of the shower in their hotel room when he heard loud banging on the door.

"Cam—open the door, quick." It was Guy.

Sharon got to the door first. "What's wrong, Guy? You look like you've seen a ghost."

"You two better sit down, you aren't going to believe this. Farrell has been killed."

"What?" was all Cameron could manage as he struggled to wrap a towel around his waist.

"He was heading toward Albany on the Thruway. Somewhere around Utica a semi went out of control, crossed over into his lane and demolished his car. Farrell, his aide, his driver and the truck driver were all killed. I guess the whole damn thing exploded into flames. A TV news reporter called me a few minutes ago. I don't know what to think, Cam."

"Oh, Cam, this is awful." Sharon could not control her tears.

"Jesus Christ, Guy. What do we do? Who do we talk to? I need to get dressed." Cameron headed back toward the bathroom. "Should we go to his home, Guy? I need to say something to his wife."

The phone rang and Guy answered it. "It's Carter, Cam. He's heard the news and wants to talk to you."

Cameron came back into the main room. He was dressed in slacks and a shirt, but barefooted. "Find me some socks, somebody," he said, taking the receiver. There was another knock on the door and Guy let Roswell into the room. Guy spoke to him for a moment, opened the door and Roswell returned to the hall to stand guard.

"Carter—what the hell do we do now? I need to get in touch with his family as quick as I can. This is hell. How can something like this have happened?"

"Look Cam, I'm as stunned as you are—we all are," Carter said. "We plan for everything—but no one thinks of a candidate being killed. You're right, you need to talk to his wife and children. I doubt if they're going to be heading to the accident site. Let me make some calls and I'll get back to you. Put Guy on for a minute."

Cameron turned and extended the receiver. "Guy, Carter wants to speak to you." He handed the phone to Guy, took a pair of socks from Sharon and sat down on the bed to put them on. His hands were shaking and his heart thumping in his chest. Sharon sat down, put her arms around him and rested her head on his shoulder.

Guy hung up the phone, looked at his two friends and then turned away to give them some privacy.

He waited a few moments and then spoke. "Cam, I know this is difficult, but Carter said you can expect the press to start calling you or turn up at the door. You need to get your thoughts together."

"Yes, of course. I'd like to speak to Farrell's family first." Cameron took a deep breath and stood up. "I think it's appropriate that I express my condolences to Mrs. Farrell and the children before I make a public statement. Someone needs to cancel my schedule for the next few days. I will not campaign again until after the funeral. Two weeks before the election and this happens. It's goddamned unbelievable." Cameron was back in control.

Cameron and Sharon both spoke to Mrs. Farrell and the children and then met with reporters to express their sorrow. They flew to Westchester to pay their respects. They had asked for a private meeting with the family and it was granted. Sharon and Marcia Farrell cried in each other's arms.

They attended the funeral and left after the ceremony at the cemetery. Cameron knew he had to get back to business and salvage his own campaign. The Republican Party was not clear about how to handle the situation and was resigned to the fact that Cameron would win the election.

#

Cameron and Sharon voted early in the morning, so they could have the rest of the day with the children. Ryan and Gillian had flown home the night before and Sharon, with a feigned show of great reluctance, had permitted the three younger kids to skip school. The seven of them ate breakfast as the local McDonald's, Jay's choice, and then headed back home. They walked down to the beach and along the lake, and Cameron tried to explain what the future might bring for them.

I don't know you very well. None of you. Ryan, my son, I'd give anything to share your thoughts right now. You've become a brave man, devoted to protecting your country and I am so proud of you.

And Gillian, you grow more beautiful every day. So, you still love young Guy. I thought that would fade as the year went by, but it hasn't. Maybe, my daughter, he is the one. He's a fine young man and I hope that you understand that it was for his future that I insisted that he stay in college and not work on the campaign. It wasn't to keep him from you.

And David, Debbie and poor troubled Jay, you need a father more than my own two do right now. I even took your mother away from you, didn't I? When you're older, you'll understand, I hope.

He stopped, held his arms out to his wife and his family and they all moved in for an embrace. He hugged the young ones close and Gillian rested her head on his shoulder. He looked up and saw Ryan and their eyes locked for a moment. Ryan gave his father a thumbs up sign and turned away.

The day seemed to drag. Cameron and Sharon tried to nap, but they were too keyed up to sleep. Finally, it was evening and soon it would all be over. Cameron knew it would be a bittersweet victory. He fidgeted and kept looking at his watch.

Sharon walked over to where he was sitting, grabbed his hand and pulled him to his feet. "Let's go for a walk, mister, just you and me."

"You got a deal, lady."

Friends were arriving to watch the returns, so they slipped out the back door. They were so intent on each other that they didn't even feel the cold.

"A few weeks ago, I tried to think about what I would do if I lost tonight. I decided I'd try again. I'd write a book on my views on the political situation in the state and…"

"It seems I've heard that story before. Remember the book you were going to write when we first got married?"

Cameron laughed. "You're right. I'm not much of a writer. Maybe I won't make much of a senator, either."

"I think you'll make the best senator in Washington."

"I don't think you're what they consider an impartial observer. You know, if it wasn't so cold, I'd tear your clothes off and have my way with you—here—now."

"And the two reporters following us would have the pictures of a lifetime."

"What?" Cameron looked over his shoulder. "We can't get by with anything, can we?"

"Let's go back to the house. I know how much you're hurting, Cameron. I know you didn't want it this way—none of us did. Fate played a cruel trick. We have to make the best of it."

Cameron glanced at his watch. "It's almost time for the polls to close. Sharon…" his voice softened. "I love you. I've loved you since the first night we met and I will never stop." He pulled her into his arms and they kissed, long and passionately.

"I've never doubted your love, Cam," she whispered in his ear.

"I promise you that we'll still be hold hands when we're sitting in rocking chairs on the front porch. That's about all we'll be able to do then, but we'll make the most of it."

"You've got yourself a deal, mister."

"This is the right thing to do, Sharon. I've wasted too much of my life as it is. I think I can do a good job for this State and this country. I don't know how we got on this track, but I think I can make you proud of me."

He took her hand and they started back toward the house. In the distance, he could see the lights, spilling across the light dusting of snow.

#

"I don't want to go to Annapolis," the boy shouted. "I want to be a baseball player. I'm good."

"What kind of a life is that? Playing a game every day. You'll do what I tell you to do. No son of mine is going to waste his life on a child's game." The man's voice was firm.

"I can make a good living. It's my life. You can't tell me what to do forever."

The hand streaked out and the blow sent him reeling.

"Who are you to talk to your father like that? You've spent too much time with the people in town and now you're like them—trash. What do you want to do, go find another girl and get her pregnant, too? I paid for one of your mistakes and I won't pay for any more. Get on your feet and stop sniveling like a weakling. You'll take the entrance tests and you damn well better pass them. I know you're a bright kid, so don't play around with me. If you don't pass, I'll ship your ass to my most remote factory and let you rot there. Do you understand me? I'm talking to you. Do you understand me?"

"Yes, sir," he stammered, tasting the blood in his mouth. "Yes sir," and he shut his eyes tight to hide the tears.

Fear and pride drove him to do his best. He scored well, passed the physical and received the official appointment. He knew there was no question about getting appointed. His father made a phone call and everything was arranged. He was at Annapolis. His one bold moment of defiance came when he accepted his commission in the Marine Corps instead of the Navy. Not that his father gave a damn. As long as his son graduated from Annapolis, Justin was satisfied. Cameron guessed that he was at the graduation ceremony, but he never tried to find him.

#

A crowd had gathered at the house to watch the returns. In the northeast, state-by-state was going into the Richardson bag. On the local stations, the commentators were recalling McKenzie Farrell's tragic end and rerunning footage of the accident and funeral.

They sat in silence and watched Richardson greet his supporters. He had won forty-two states, but was playing a little game and said nothing official, claiming he had to wait until all the returns were in.

"I don't like that man," Guy groused. "I don't even know him, and I don't like him."

"He's a crook," Cameron added. "He won't be able to spend four years in the White House without getting involved in some dirty deals. The question is how will the public react when they see him for what he really is. He's also damned smart." Cameron shook his head with resignation.

"It all comes down to advertising and manipulation, doesn't it?" Sharon asked.

"If you're clever you create an image the public will buy. Television is the most powerful force in American politics. It has a controlling influence on millions of people. Richardson uses the medium very well. He had a slick campaign and he ran against a weak sister. Ergo—our new president…the leader of the free world for the next four years. Makes you proud to be an American, doesn't it? You know Cam," Carter commented philosophically, "you may be lucky if you lose this election. Do you want to lock horns with that guy?"

"Yes, I do."

Carter and Guy looked at Cameron. On his face was a look of determination. His eyes had a far away look.

"Yes, I will."

tum tum tum ta tum …
tum tum tum ta tum …

It was taking her forever to dress—her hands were ice cold and they shook as she fumbled with the buttons. She couldn't stop the tears—the time had come—the beginning of the centuries-old ritual—the formal State Funeral—the public, stoic farewell to the fallen warrior. It required her to stand before the eyes of the world and display an inner strength beyond human reason. She could not falter—for his sake. She could not be less than what he would expect. She, too, had a place in history and her actions would be chronicled for generations to study. Her strength had to become the Nation's strength. She had to bear their pain and grief. She looked into the mirror and opened her mouth to scream. No sound emerged.

tum tum tum ta tum...

CHAPTER XII

Dear Diary. Today I am going to take charge of my life. The new Senator from New York is interviewing for a personal secretary. I am so proud because I had the courage to apply. I spent the last cent I have on a new hairstyle and a new suit. I know I'm extravagant and it is probably foolish, but I'm going to try. I've never met him, but I've seen his picture. He looks like a pleasant man. I probably won't get through the interview. I know, diary, I need to have more self-confidence.

Helen Grenadier had been keeping a diary for five years, ever since she had found herself alone. First she had lost her parents—her mother to cancer and six month later, her father to a heart attack—and then Rudy. She had come home from work early one day and found them—her husband and the neighbors' teenage daughter—in bed together. It had taken three months in a hospital to recover from the breakdown.

When they finally considered her well enough to go home, he was gone, along with the furniture and all of their money. She managed to get a job in the secretarial pool at the State Department. She moved into a one room furnished apartment and began the task of surviving each day. With the cost of living in Washington, it was hard. Several times she considered leaving the city, but she realized that she had no other place to go.

At the suggestion of her doctor, she began to keep a diary. She would come home from work, fix a simple dinner, carry it to her desk and write her thoughts while she ate. No one invited her out any more. She wasn't an ugly woman, just plain and quiet. There had been a few dates, but she always left them at the door because she simply could not face the possibility that a man might want to go to bed with her. She was fifty-two now and living the life of a lonely spinster.

She dressed carefully in her new tailored gray suit, with a white, high-necked blouse. She was thin, but the suit fit her well. She selected her best black shoes, a new purse and decided against a hat and gloves.

"Don't over do it," she told herself. She said a silent prayer, crossed herself, locked her apartment door and headed for the bus stop. She watched a mother with two small children. Those could be my grandchildren, she thought, if life had worked out differently. She fought the urge to bolt back to her apartment.

Helen felt very self-conscious sitting in the reception room. There were eight others, all younger and more attractive.

At least I look more like a Senator's secretary, she consoled herself. But what if the Senator wants a pretty face to decorate his office? She had been around long enough to know the stories about politicians and their interests. She was about to get up and leave when she saw the Senator's aide enter the room and look around. "Guy Sheridan," she whispered to herself. *Maybe if I could talk to him first.* She wanted a cigarette but saw that no one else in the room was smoking, so she changed her mind. She was about to look in her purse for a mint when Sheridan turned and disappeared into the inner office. She settled back in her seat, sighed, smiled at the woman next to her and decided to wait ten more minutes.

The phone on the desk started to ring. She waited for the door to open, but no one appeared and the phone kept ringing. She looked at the other women sitting in the room. No one was paying any attention to the persistent ringing. "What the hell, I'm going to answer it," she said aloud. She moved quickly to the desk, sat down and picked up the receiver.

"Good morning, Senator Marshall's office—yes—one moment please, I'll see if the Senator can speak to you now."

She pressed the hold button and then what she hoped was the correct intercom button. She could feel the stares of the other women in the room. She heard his voice say "yes" and for an instant, she froze.

"Excuse me, Senator, Congressman Height is on line two."

"Thank you. Would you step into my office for a minute, please?"

She opened the inner door and stepped inside. Her hands were like ice. She was surprise when she saw him standing by the window. He looked taller in person.

Strange how it's always a shock to see someone for the first time when you know them so well from photographs.

"I don't believe I know your name," he said.

"Grenadier—Helen—Helen Grenadier—Mrs. Grenadier." *My God, I'm making a complete fool of myself.*

"That's a long name. May I call you Helen?"

She nodded yes in his direction.

"Do you always answer the phone in someone else's office, Helen?" Cameron asked.

Helen felt her face grow hot. "I thought it might be important. I guess it was a reflex action. I'm very sorry, sir."

"Where in the hell did you get a name like Height? There's no Height in the House."

Oh, God, why did I answer the phone?

She saw his smile and heard a soft laugh.

"Sit down, Helen." He gestured to a chair close to his desk. "We owe you an apology. Forgive us, we didn't mean to embarrass you. But, if you plan to work in this office, you will have to learn to identify Mr. Sheridan's voice."

She sat cautiously in the chair, clutching her purse in her lap. She was very confused.

"Let me explain this to you, Helen," Guy said. "The Senator and I had a little bet. I told him there wasn't one secretary sitting out there. He looked and said there was one. I now owe him dinner tonight. I'll deduct it from your first paycheck."

"Don't pay any attention to Guy, Helen. He was foolish enough to give up a good law practice to follow me to Washington, so you can't expect much from him. Actually, I cheated, any way. Your boss at the State Department is an old friend and he called me yesterday and recommended you highly. I figured that if you are half as good as he says you are and really take your work seriously, you wouldn't let the phone keep ringing. I was right. If you want to work for me, the job is yours. Guy will work out your salary and other details. Well?" Cameron asked.

"Yes—I would like very much to work for you, sir."

"Good. You can start by sending the other applicants home. I like to start my day early. Will that be a problem for you?"

"No—not at all, sir." It was all happening so fast. She had expected to be asked a lot of questions and she had rehearsed answers most of the night. And here, in a matter of minutes, she had the job. She wanted to cry and hug the man, but she kept control.

"And you don't have to call me sir. Your lordship will be fine." Cameron saw the startled look on her face and laughed. "Don't be so serious, Helen. I'm kidding. Call me Senator or Mr. Marshall." He stood up and reached out his hand.

She took his hand slowly. She wanted to thank him, but couldn't find the words. He hadn't asked her any questions about her background. She had been afraid of those questions, but he hadn't asked.

She closed the door and hid her smile as she sent the other women home. She walked across the room and looked out the window, wiping tears from her eyes. She heard the outer door open and she turned.

"I'm sorry, Miss, but the Senator has already hired a secretary."

"You mean I'm too late?"

"I'm afraid so."

"Are you his secretary?"

"Yes," and Helen felt pride in her voice.

"Good. Tell the Senator I approve." The woman offered her hand. "I'm Sharon Marshall."

Helen was flustered. "I'm sorry—I—of course you are. How foolish of me not to recognize you. I've seen your picture so many times, Mrs. Marshall. I'm sorry."

Sharon smiled. "I think you are a little bit nervous about working for my husband. What's your name?"

"Grenadier—Helen—Helen Grenadier—Mrs…"

"She goes through this every time. Call her Helen, honey, it saves a lot of time," Cameron said as he came into the office.

"I'm making such a mess of this. Really, Senator, I do have my wits about me."

"Relax, Helen." Sharon moved over and put her arm around Cameron's waist. "Don't let him frighten you. He's really a big pussy cat, aren't you darling?" She kissed him.

"Helen is my new secretary, honey," Cameron explained.

"I know. I came to apply, but I guess I'm too late."

"And also too pregnant."

"That will change very soon, love. Helen, we're having dinner in the city tonight. Will you join us? Can you join us? I mean, do you have a family or any thing?"

"No," she hesitated for a moment. "I'm alone. I'd love to join you for dinner."

"Good," Cameron said. "Now that the social amenities are out of the way, maybe we can get some work done."

"Of course, sir?"

"Helen!"

"I mean, Senator." They all laughed and Helen felt the tension drain from her body.

"Helen, welcome to my staff. Let's take a look at the papers on my desk. They don't lose much time dumping work on you around here. Sharon, I'll see you at six." He kissed Sharon and disappeared back into his office.

Sharon smiled, "Well?"

"I think I'm going to like working for him—very much. And thank you for inviting me to dinner. Are you sure I won't be imposing?"

"Not at all. You're probably going to be seeing more of my husband than I am, so I'd like to get to know you."

Sharon was relieved that Cameron was getting some much-needed assistance. Confusion had reigned after the election. They had run a well-organized campaign, but never planned for the aftermath of a victory.

#

A Senator's work begins the day he is elected and never stops. The phones were ringing as soon as the networks declared Cameron the victor.

Representatives of special interest groups moved with skillfully calculated action. Each needed to be among the first to congratulate the winner and make sure his or her name was known to the new Senator. They had to be able to report to their constituents that they were on a first-name basis with the new man and favorite projects would not be in jeopardy.

If Cameron thought he was going to start with a clean slate, he was sadly mistaken. The art of courting legislators is so skillfully honed that no one is beyond the reach of canny professionals. Every election campaign incurs debts and Cameron would soon learn the true cost of his election.

They had two months to get the family packed, moved to Virginia and the children enrolled in new schools. Cameron was absent most of the time, shuttling back and forth to Washington and meeting with State officials. Sharon was exhausted from the chaos and her final months of pregnancy.

Guy had been reluctant to go to Washington with Cameron, but finally relented, sold his law practice and he, Ann and the boys moved into a rented house in Georgetown. Carter and his wife went back to Nyack, where he planned to do free lance writing and help Cameron whenever he could. The others on the team returned to their regular jobs.

Finally, they were moved and Cameron was settling into his office. Despite Helen's warnings, he was determined to be accessible to any and all Constituents.

"The people elected me and they deserve some of my time," Cameron told Helen.

She just shook her head, handed him a stack of phone message slips and went back to the papers on her desk.

In less than an hour, he was hopelessly backlogged with phone calls. Every chair in his reception room was taken and people were standing in the hall.

Helen walked into his office, closed the door, stood with her back against it and smiled.

Cameron looked sheepish and gave her an "I surrender" gesture.

"I've hired a receptionist who will start tomorrow. Mr. Sheridan needs to start finding you staff," Helen said calmly.

Cameron just nodded.

"Now, Mr. Accessible, you need to get out the back door and over to the Senate Chamber for an orientation session. You are already ten minutes late."

He got up without a word and left.

There were so many procedures and rules that had to be followed in the Senate that Cameron didn't think he could possibly grasp it all.

He was bothered most by the intelligence briefings. He learned that things he suspected were true were actually worse than he expected. There were areas of the world that had an unfathomable hate for the United States. The Country he loved and thought of as a haven for people struggling to find home, freedom and security for their families, was viewed as a bully, hell bent on imposing its will on those weaker and more vulnerable.

How the hell did I get into this mess, Cameron wondered, as speaker after speaker droned on with report after report. Cameron fought disillusionment and tried to hold on to his determination to somehow make a difference.

In January of every odd numbered year, one third of the Senate is sworn into office. Prior to the opening session, committee assignments are made within the Republican and Democratic conferences. Cameron was not excited about his committees, but knew that as a new-comer he had to make the best he could out of what he had been dealt. With the Republicans in power—all-be-it by a slim majority—he didn't have any options.

January seventh marked the first day of the new Congress. Cameron was anxious and nervous. He was anxious to finally begin work and nervous about being able to serve the people back home. Sharon seemed to take it all in stride.

She smiled and straightened his tie.

"You look very handsome in your new suit, Senator Marshall," she said as she stepped back and looked as her husband.

"Thank you, Mrs. Marshall. Why do I feel that is not an unbiased opinion?"

She kissed him lightly and turned her attention to the children.

The family, along with the Sheridans and Helen, would be seated in the gallery to watch the Opening Day Procedures. Supporters would watch on television in the Senate reception room across the street. A reception was planned for later in his office.

The Senate adheres to a long established routine. The first order of business was the swearing in of new members.

Cameron waited nervously as senators were called alphabetically, in groups of four, to take the oath administered by the Vice President.

Finally, his name was called and he held Sharon's arm as they moved to the front of the Chamber. Sharon carried her Grandmother's Bible. Cameron had elected to be accompanied by the man he was replacing, Chester Gamble. Some members of his party were upset because Gamble was a Republican, but when Cameron had met the worn out old man for the first time, he made up his mind then, that he would give him one final moment of dignity.

Cameron was trembling as he placed his left hand on the Bible Sharon held and raised his right hand. He hoped his voice would remain strong. He held his head up and spoke with resolution:

"I, Cameron Marshall, do solemnly swear that I will support and defend the Constitution of the United States against all enemies, foreign and domestic; that I will bear true faith and allegiance to the same; that I take this obligation freely, without any mental reservation or purpose of evasion; and that I will well and faithfully discharge the duties of the office on which I am about to enter: So help me God."

He kissed Sharon, shook hands with the other new Senators in his group and the Vice President. Then he moved over to sign his name, thus "subscribing to the oath" in the Official Oath Book.

He looked at the fountain pen he had been given to sign the oath. He smiled, put the cap back in place carefully and slipped the pen into the inside pocket of his suit jacket. In a few years, he would present it to his child, who had attended the ceremony in his mother's womb.

tum tum tum ta tum…
tum tum tum ta tum…

The caisson creaked slowly to a stop in front of the Capitol. Doors of the official limousines opened and the family emerged. The spirited black, rider-less horse, a symbol of a fallen leader since the days of Genghis Kahn, started to rear in protest. For one brief moment, Sharon saw a flash of his indefatigable spirit in the majestic stallion. Sharon drew in a deep breath, held her head up and turned her eyes toward the flag-draped casket being lifted once again by the uniform bearers. The band played *Hail to the Chief* and cannons boomed. It all seemed to be in interminable slow motion.

tum tum tum ta tum…

CHAPTER XIII

He was immediately at home on the hill. Bright and articulate, he made good press. On January thirty-first, they welcomed Nicholas Justin, a healthy boy named for his two grandfathers. Cameron was at Sharon's side during the birth and when the doctor announced their son, he had fainted, striking his head on the leg of the delivery table. The press had a field day with his accident and over night stay in the hospital. It was the beginning of the image the public would come to love.

He quickly earned a reputation as a hard worker and a man who would listen. His colleagues could count on him to have done his homework. He was not afraid of difficult decisions and stood by his convictions.

In two years, he was clearly on Senate Minority Leader Dwight Patterson's radar.

Patterson was a short man—just 5' 2", who had specially designed lifts in his shoes to make him taller. He wore an ill-fitting toupee and always had a cigarette and cup of coffee in his hand.

He had small, intense eyes that seemed to look right into your soul. His effeminate, high-pitched voice led people to misjudge him. He was unquestionably the best politician in Washington. He knew how the system worked and how to make it serve his needs and ambitions.

Patterson had the ability to negotiate, intimidate and cajole people into his way of thinking. He was a formidable minority leader, skilled at keeping the Democratic caucus in line.

He had divorced the devoted woman who had borne and raised his four sons and married a woman half his age and four inches taller. Her sole responsibility in life was to look good on his arm at parties and in photos and keep her mouth shut.

The people of Idaho did not approve of their Senator's personal life, but were apparently too afraid not to reelect him. He was a feisty bantam rooster with power that no one dared to challenge.

The Minority Leader could make or break a new Senator. He had one staff member dedicated to keeping watch over the "FiTerS"—First Term Senators—and providing his boss with private, detailed reports. The Leader wanted to know who would quickly fit in and be of value to him. Those who did not would be unsuccessful, one term Senators no one remembered.

Cameron had caught the Leader's attention early and the confidential file in the locked desk drawer was thick with reports and newspaper clippings. His staff member had made more than a dozen trips to New York State to assess how people back home viewed Senator Marshall.

Patterson had found his FiTer and it was time to make his carefully calculated move. The organizational meetings for the new Congress were about to begin and Senator Marshall needed to be put on high profile committees. Televised committee hearings would provide Cameron with exposure to the Nation and introduce the people to a rising political star.

Patterson sat alone in his office at two in the morning, carefully reading Cameron's thick file. From time to time, he would smile, nod his head and underline certain passages.

He had always envisioned himself as a kingmaker and now, after a couple of failed attempts, he finally believed that Cameron was the one.

Soon the Leader was tapping Cameron to be one of the Senators who stood in the background when he spoke to the press. Then, he assigned Cameron to make a few comments. Business leaders, who owed the Leader favors, received late night phone calls at home and Cameron was suddenly in demand as a speaker at meetings and conferences around the Country.

Cameron was unequivocally a mover and a shaker in the Senate and a man on the way up in the political world. He was appearing on Sunday morning news shows. Some political analysts began to speculate on him as a potential Vice Presidential candidate.

The Leader's lifelong plan to become Secretary of State and control America's foreign policy was finally within his grasp. He had done his job well. He would soon be able to claim his reward.

Cameron continued his yeoman hours, often working late into the evening with Guy and Helen at his side. The dream was beginning to form.

#

"I thought the Senate was going to be enough," Sharon stated, her voice emotionless.

Cameron looked across the table at her. *God, you're beautiful and I do love you.*

"Well?"

"I don't know, Sharon. People are talking. You know how it is. There's always a lot of talk in Washington."

"Are you doing anything to discourage it?"

He sat silent for a moment. "No," he answered softly.

"Why not? I don't understand you, Cam. You're a good Senator. Look at all of the good things you've done, the bills, and the people you've helped. Why can't you be content? We're not a political family. We're plain people. I don't want to live in the White House. I haven't got the slightest damn idea how to be First Lady."

He watched her face as she talked. Her cheeks were flushed.

"You've made up your mind, haven't you?"

He nodded yes.

"Why? Why? Oh, Cam, I don't know what to say to you anymore."

Cameron dropped his head.

"When we first got here, you were open and honest with me and the children. Now you've become so distant. We used to share your dreams and plans. Now you keep everything to yourself. You haven't sat down to dinner with your family for months. Your son doesn't even recognize you. The kids miss you. I miss you. I think I should call Helen and have her put young Guy and Gillian's wedding on your appointment calendar so you won't have some damn political speech that day."

"That's a low blow."

"As low as I could aim it!"

"Honey, please…"

"Don't, Cam. Don't start. I know you too well. Don't start with your damn sweet talk." She was fighting to keep her voice calm and steady.

"You'll come over here, put your arms around me, and we'll be off to bed. That's always your solution. And afterward, I'll lie there and watch you sleep and be filled with love for you. Not tonight. I've got to get all of this out in the open."

"O.K., I'll listen. But when you're finished, please hear my side."

Sharon took a deep breath. "Maybe. I won't promise, because I don't know how I will feel when I'm finished. You know, I think I could deal with this better if you were seeing another woman. Hell, I don't have the slightest idea how to compete with an entire country."

Cameron tried not to smile. "Sharon…"

"No. You promised you'd listen."

He nodded yes.

"I guess I should have realized what was coming when Carter moved to Washington last year. And then all the calls starting coming from other Senators' wives. Just like you, I'm being courted. Foolish me, I thought they enjoyed my company. But they see power. Every move in Washington is orchestrated by someone. It's a big political machine and you love it, don't you? When you decided to run for the Senate I thought you were crazy and I walked into a world that scared the hell out of me. I'm scared, Cam. I'm so damn scared. I see what's coming and I don't know how to stop it. Couldn't you just once ask me what I want?"

"All right. What would you like to do?"

"Have another baby." Tears were flowing freely down her face and she tried to brush them away.

He smiled and moved close to her. "I can grant your wish if you will give me a chance." He knelt beside her.

"You're going to run for President, aren't you?"

"Yes."

"Why you?"

"Why not me? I have to Sharon. Rich can't continue to do the things he's doing. He's a corrupt man and someone has to stop him. That's part of it. There are a lot of reasons, some of them noble and some not so noble. Don't sell yourself short, Sharon. You can handle it. You're a politically intelligent woman."

"What if I can't hold up my end? I'm a small town girl."

"You'll make a lovely First Lady and you'll serve the Country in your own way."

"Oh, Cam, why do you always know the right things to say?"

"Because I love you."

"I know that. I've never felt that you don't love me," her voice was soft.

"But, sometimes you scare me. I'm so afraid of losing you."

"Want to have a baby?"

She nodded yes.

"Good. So do I."

Cameron lay awake after the lovemaking, cradling Sharon in his arms while she slept. He kissed her lightly on the forehead and whispered softly to her, "How can I explain the feeling inside me, darling? It's there. It's there for me. We've been working on it ever since we arrived in Washington. Carter never disassembled the team, honey. They've been planning since the day I announced I was going to run for the Senate. The presidency was always the goal."

He fell asleep trying to figure out how many men in the history of the Nation, had had the opportunity to run for President.

#

The year went quickly. Cameron worked hard in the Senate and was in demand on the speakers' circuit. His star power was rising and some of the press began to speculate about his future.

Cameron and his advisors began to talk about primaries and who might run against him. He told Sharon the decision was made—he was going to run. She took the news in stride.

Carter turned up, unannounced, early one morning in Cameron's office.

"What's up, Carter?" Cam asked.

"You're not going to get Rich."

"What? Why not? He thinks he owns this town. Why the hell wouldn't he run for re-election?"

"You ready for this one? It seems that when we had some foreign visitors a couple of months ago, two of his aides got generous with information. They were convinced that by sharing some military secrets we'd get that nice disarmament treaty. Well, as you know, no treaty and the foreign boys went home knowing a hell of a lot about our work in chemical warfare defense."

"My, God, Carter, you've got to be kidding. The President can't be that stupid."

"I wish I were kidding, Cam. Rich wasn't directly involved according to my source, but they're his people. It's one more of his colossal errors. He doesn't mind the store. So, the word is he's not going to run. The Vice President is going to bow out, too. They know we'll nail their a asses to a wall over this is, so he's going to duck and run."

"Who will the party pick?" Cam asked.

"I think the senior senator from Vermont has a lock on the nomination, if he wants it."

"That guy is a joke. He's too old. He doesn't even know there's a world outside the Washington beltway."

"Maybe, but he's got a hell of a lot of political IOUs and he's going to collect to have his last moment of glory. Screw the party."

"It's going to be a disaster for them anyway, Carter. Rich has made such a mess the people will want a clean sweep."

"I think our job is going to be much easier now that this is happening. But, we've still got to be prepared for the new man. One thing you need to remember in politics—never underestimate the voter. Senator Conklin may come across as everyone's grandfather and find himself in the White House."

Cameron laughed at the thought.

"I've called Franklin and Lawrence. We're going to run a bunch of names through the computer and see whom it thinks they'll run. There isn't any need for you to join us now. I didn't want you to be surprised when you find a reporter under the breakfast table in the morning. Word is leaking fast. The phone lines will be burning all day."

"You're right. This is sort of a good-news, bad news situation, Carter. I was looking forward to tangling with Rich. But, at least we know he's on his way out of Washington. That's good for the Country. Call me when you have some more information. Even at home."

"We'll have some speculations for you later today. We'll also get a statement ready for you to use after the President holds his press conference. Until then, stay low."

"Right." Cameron shook Carter's hand and he left by the back door.

By noon the next day, Washington was on fire with rumors, speculation and people jockeying for positions of leadership in the Republican Party.

Cameron was in a strategy session with his team.

"We figure your primary opposition is going to be Governor Christopher Enfield of Michigan. He's got a lot of his people in key positions on the National Committee. He's a very popular governor with a damn good record in his state.

He's delivered a balanced budget and got one hell of a welfare reform plan working. That landslide re-election catapulted him into the national spotlight. I'll be honest with you, Cam," Franklin said, "If you weren't planning on running I'd work for Enfield."

"I don't like the sound of what I'm hearing. I thought you guys would be on top of the world with the President's surprise. You look glum."

"Enfield's the bright star of the party right now, Cameron. You're the new kid on the block and your day is still a few years away," Carter replied.

"Jesus Christ, yesterday you had me on the way to the White House and now I'm an outsider. What the hell has happened?"

"We've been talking to some people. And you saw who the press went to for an immediate reaction after the President's announcement...Enfield," Carter said.

"And he sure as hell sounded like a candidate," Franklin added.

"We thought he was so committed to his state, he wouldn't run. Obviously, he changed his mind. We didn't count on that, Cameron," Lawrence noted.

"What a sorry team you guys are. What's this we didn't count on that, bullshit? You're the damn political experts. You get paid to count on everything. How the hell do you make a mistake like this?" Cameron was furious.

"Look, Enfield pledged to his people in the last election that he would serve out his term. He has a reputation for being an honest man. What would you think, Cam?" Carter asked.

"Never trust a politician," Cameron quipped.

"Including you?" Franklin asked. It broke the tension.

"Well, guys, what do we do now?"

#

Enfield made his move quickly. He rationalized the fact that he was going back on his promise to the people of his state by claiming he had agonized over the decision and with the problems in Washington, he felt it was his duty. Cameron laughed as he listened to the explanation.

Now, if he challenged Enfield, Cam would be the party heavy, a spoiler. He could find himself responsible for the party losing the election—to a half-senile Senator from Vermont of all the goddamn places. Cameron was furious as he watched Enfield on television, but there wasn't a thing he could do about it.

"You don't like the position you're in, do you?" Carter asked.

"No, damn it, I don't." Cameron was angry.

"That, my friend, is the world of politics. When you ran for the Senate, you were the savior of the party in New York State because things were a mess and you liked that role. Well you can't play that role this time. You'll be the upstart challenging the seasoned veteran. You haven't paid your political dues and a lot of people aren't going to like that."

"So, how do we counter this image? Someone on the team must have some ideas? How about you, Franklin?"

Franklin was spending more of his time in Washington and Cameron seemed to think he had answer for everything that popped up.

"You have one option," Franklin said.

"And that is?" Cameron asked.

"The Vice Presidency."

"No way, Franklin. The Vice Presidency is not in my plans and never will be." Cameron felt himself growing angry with his advisors.

"You have no choice, Cam. Follow this. Enfield gets elected. He's a popular, successful President. His Vice-President is also well liked and inherits the office after eight years. You have two terms for Enfield and two for his Vice President. You cool your heels for sixteen years. Can you do that? I don't think so." Franklin had obviously made a decision.

"Carter—you don't go along with Franklin, do you?" Cameron asked.

"Suppose you challenge Enfield and you lose and in November Enfield loses. You, my friend, are the man who kept the Democrats out of the White House and no one in hell will touch you again," Carter said.

"How do we take Enfield out of the running?" Cameron asked.

"That is one hell of an unsolvable problem," Guy said.

"He must have a weak point. My God, can't you guys come up with something? That's what you're paid to do."

"You mean does he have a penchant for teenage girls—or something like that? I don't think so, Cam. Face reality. Christopher Enfield is a good man and he has garnered a hell of a lot of respect. He's got an attractive family and a very popular wife. They'll be the toast of Washington, Cam. It's the wrong time for you—face reality. Vice President. That's your goal. Go after it or lose everything." Franklin got up and started for the door. "Good night, gentlemen." He was gone.

"Shit. Is that how you see it, Guy? Are you a quitter, too?"

"Come on, Cam. You're being irrational. I know you're hell bent on always being a winner and we want to win, too. But, there is a big, cold picture out there. The team is right. We sit this one out or you shelve your ego and take second. It's your call. You need to know that I am not going down a political suicide path with you." Guy was angry.

Carter laughed. Cameron scowled and threw a book across the room. "Goddamn it to hell," he yelled.

tum tum tum ta tum...
tum tum tum ta tum...

It was time to go. The body bearers lifted the casket, moved in unison toward the door and stepped out into the cold sunlight. The caisson waited patiently as the bearers moved down the steps, slid the casket into place and secured it with straps. The drums began the beat—*tum tum tum ta tum*—softly as first and then louder—*tum tum tum ta tum*—with six white horses and three riders, the caisson creaked down the driveway, mourning in its own way for the still life it carried. They passed under an archway of dipped State flags—*tum tum tum ta tum*—out the gateway—onto Pennsylvania Avenue and toward the place where his dream had been born. Never again would he return to this house.

tum tum tum ta tum...

CHAPTER XIV

He smiled as he looked at the reporters in the pressroom. Sharon sat in a chair to his left. He had not informed Guy or Carter of his final decision, because, as he waited for the press conference to start, he was still not certain of the direction he would go. He knew they were angry every time he plunged blindly ahead without their advice. They would learn what he planned to do the same time the world did. He knew that they probably had a bet between them. Which of the two would be right? Which one would know his mind?

Cameron took a deep breath and stepped up to the bank of microphones. The early morning news shows had speculated that he was going to challenge Enfield. But they would be wrong, he finally decided. Guy was right; he had to swallow his ego and face reality.

"Ladies and gentlemen, I want to thank you for coming this morning. I know the speculation is that I will announce my challenge to the candidacy of Christopher Enfield. Governor Enfield is one of this Country's most respected Governors. He has a remarkable record of leadership in Michigan. He is a highly regarded family man with impeccable ethics and a determination to serve his Country. I believe he will be the next president of this great Nation and I believe that he will be a world leader who will be admired and respected by all nations. This morning, I pledge my total support to Governor Enfield. If it is his desire, I will campaign for him and serve him in any capacity that I can. Now, I will answer questions."

"Senator," the correspondent for CNN waved for attention. Cameron acknowledged him.

"Senator Marshall, up until today the word in Washington was that you would challenge Enfield—that you were determined to be the Democratic candidate. What changed your mind? Or have you made a deal with Enfield to serve as his Vice President?"

"I have not made any deals. I have spent a lot of time agonizing over this decision. Yes, I was considering a challenge to Enfield, but I realized a challenge would be counter productive to the goals of the Democratic Party to reclaim the White House in November. Party unity and party success are more important than my personal desire."

"Will you accept the Vice Presidency if it is offered?" It was Maxine Brighton, the ABC correspondent.

"I haven't given any thought to that, Maxine. And I doubt that Governor Enfield has either. In fact, Maxine I haven't even talked to Governor Enfield about my decision not to enter the primaries and to support him. He'll select the best person possible for his running mate; someone he'll feel comfortable with at his side. I don't know his thinking on that issue."

Carter moved close to Guy. "You owe me a hundred. I'm going to call Franklin and tell him to set up an appointment with Enfield's team. We've got to nail down this VP thing fast." Carter slipped out the back door.

"If it is offered, will you accept it?" Maxine was pushing for an answer that would give her a lead.

"Maxine, I can't answer that right now."

"Isn't your announcement today a smart political move to keep your own aspirations on track?" she continued.

God, Cameron thought, this woman is a goddamned pain. "You're right, Maxine, it is a smart political move—but not to benefit me—to benefit the party. I have no idea what Governor Enfield desires in a running mate. I am sure he has already given some thought to that. It's his decision, Maxine, not mine."

"And you expect us to believe that, Senator?"

Cameron turned his attention to others in the room. "Caroline." He nodded toward the New York Times Reporter.

"Will you run for re-election to the Senate?" Caroline Durant asked.

"Yes, Caroline, that is my intention. I am very happy in the Senate and I hope the people back home feel I have served them well."

"John," he said, pointing to a man in the back of the room.

"If Enfield offers you the vice presidency, will you accept it? Or, are you completely ruling that out?"

Shit, Cameron thought, *they're all alike. Fuckin' one-track minds. Hell, I just made up my own mind.*

"I think it is premature for us to speculate about what Governor Enfield has in mind."

Guy slipped in front of the microphone. "Ladies and Gentlemen, Senator Marshall has to get back to this office for a meeting. We thank you for your interest this morning."

Maxine Brighton turned to her friend from Newsweek. "He's after the VP spot. It's his only chance to stay viable on the national scene. I'll bet his people are setting up a meeting with Enfield's people right now. Well, I've got to file my story and then work the phones."

"I've learned not to question your insight, Max. We've both got contacts inside Enfield's camp. Let's go dig the dirt," Colleen Helmart laughed, put her note pad and pencil away and headed for the door.

Maxine smiled. *You're too obvious, Senator. Everyone in this room knows you'd do anything to have Enfield ask you to run with him. Maybe he's a real sharp politician and will tell you and your team to go to hell. I'd love to see that.* She turned and looked for her crew.

Guy followed Cameron and Sharon down the hall and into his office.

Helen looked up as they entered. "You looked great on TV this morning, Senator. We've had a lot of phone calls." She held up a handful of pink slips.

"Later, Helen, I have to talk to him first," Guy said, going into Cam's private office.

"So, Cam. What do we do now? Are you going to be Enfield's running mate? You sure as hell aren't consulting with any of us anymore. Maybe we should all go home."

"Calm down, Guy. Nothing has changed. I still want the Presidency in the worst way, but I think you, Carter and Franklin are right. It's not there for me now. You and the others figure out the VP thing. I'm going to spend my time with Sharon and the children and do my job here."

Sharon smiled at him. "I guess what will be, will be, Guy. Do you have time for lunch with me today, honey?"

"I always have time for you, Sharon. Sort out the phone calls, Guy. Figure out which ones I should return when I get back." He walked over, took Sharon's hand and left the office by the back entrance. Guy sat down at Cameron's desk and buzzed for Helen. "Order me a turkey sandwich, Helen, I'm going to play Senator for awhile." Guy released the intercom button and started sorting the messages.

Six blocks away, the private line in Carter's office rang. He picked up the phone and listened. "We have a plan," the voice said. The line clicked dead.

A week later, Guy and Franklin sat in Carter's living room and discussed strategy with him.

"I've had a couple of productive meetings with Enfield's team. I think we're close to an agreement," Franklin said. "There's a slight problem."

"Such as?" Carter asked.

"Maxine Brighton, from ABC, has a friend in the Enfield camp. She's dogging him for information and I gather he's pretty candid with her. The boys over there figure he's screwing Brighton and she gets some interesting pillow talk."

"That's a switch. I always thought girls were her thing," Carter said. "I remember she always seems to have some young, pretty rookie reporter under her wing. I guess it's true—a good reporter will do anything for a story—even switch-hit. What's Enfield going to do about the situation?"

"They're going to move the guy out of the picture. Going to send him on the road, I guess."

"They should send him to New Hampshire and let his ardor cool off." Carter laughed and winked at Guy.

"Yea, freeze his dick," Guy added.

Franklin, as usual, was not in the mood for humor. "I don't give a damn as long as they cut off the information flow. Enfield's camp wants this kept quiet, too, so we should be all right. The key to the deal is that Cameron stays out of the picture—no primaries, no talk about being Enfield's running mate, no comments on any of Enfield's policy statements. Enfield wants Cameron out of the spotlight. Just a Senator tending to his business."

"O.K.," Guy said. He sensed the tension in the room and wondered why.

"We'll need to arrange some hush-hush meetings," Franklin continued. "Enfield has to be certain he and Cameron will mesh on his major campaign points. We also have to make certain no one in our camp is screwing Brighton. How about it, Guy?"

"Jesus Christ, don't look at me. If I even think about another woman, Ann knows. My pants are zipped tighter than a drum."

The tension was finally snapped. Carter laughed and Franklin managed a smile. Guy realized it was a joke and laughed too.

#

Christopher Enfield had been the backup quarterback at Michigan State. He was blonde, tall, well muscled and flashed an electrifying smile. He had all the makings of a football hero, except for his fear of being tackled and his interception record was dismal. He knew he had absolutely no hope of a professional football career, so he went to law school.

He had literally married the girl next door. He and Emma started life together as playmates and grew into love during high school. They postponed marriage until after college. Neither of them ever considered anyone else.

Emma had been cute as a little girl and developed into a beauty by the time she was sixteen. She wore her sandy colored hair short and casual. Her green eyes sparkled and she was head-over-heels in love with Christopher.

They became lovers during their freshman year in college and were careful so that no accident would interrupt their career plans.

Christopher and Emma married during their first year in law school. Their wedding was the social event of the year and their fathers had great expectations for the charming couple. After graduation, Christopher joined his father-in-law's law firm.

Emma never practiced law. She willingly declined a career in order to devote herself to their children.

As the Enfields moved up the social and political ladder, friends began to see Christopher as a future Governor and eventually President.

In March, Christopher Enfield and Cameron met for the first time and discussed some mutual concerns. Enfield laid out his positions clearly and asked Cameron for reactions.

The deep Defense Department cuts that Enfield was proposing made Cameron angry, but he knew he had to control his temper and not tangle with the man who held all the cards. Cameron took a deep breath and told Enfield he could support him on all points. Enfield's aide handed him a briefing book, asked him to read it carefully and be prepared to discuss any concerns when they met again in a week.

Cameron agreed, shook hands with Enfield and started to leave the room. "Senator, when we meet again, bring your wife. I think it's important for the women to get along. My wife is very astute politically, so I'll be interested in her feelings. I'll have my people arrange a long weekend at our vacation home. Getting there without the press finding out will be half the fun."

"That sounds good, Governor. Sharon's anxious to get to know you and your family, too. Good bye." Cameron shook hands with Enfield, turned and left the room. One of Enfield's aides was waiting for him, guided him out the back door of the building and into a waiting car. The meeting had lasted less than an hour.

Enfield returned to the campaign trail and continued to chalk up delegate strength. A couple of relatively unknowns challenged him once or twice, but basically it was a walk in the park for the Governor.

In May, Cameron and Sharon were on their way to Lansing. It was almost midnight when the private jet touched down at the airport. A waiting car took them to the Governor's mansion. The late hour would hopefully keep reporters unaware of the visit.

Enfield and his wife were waiting in the living room. A light supper had been laid out on a table at the end of the room. They filled their plates and returned to comfortable chairs to eat. The conversation was polite chitchat. Serious discussions would begin when they moved on to the Governor's cottage north of the Capitol. Cameron knew that this was the crucial meeting. If all went as planned, he would go back home as Enfield's running mate.

As the early morning light appeared on the horizon, a helicopter took off from the lawn of the Governor's mansion and they were on their way to the Enfields' retreat. Sharon gripped the arms of her seat. This was only the second time she had been in a chopper and she was very uncomfortable. Emma Enfield smiled and over the roar of the motor, shouted, "I know how you feel."

They flew in silence for about twenty minutes and then the helicopter landed on a sandy beach beside a small lake. The engine shut down and quiet was restored. Enfield got up, helped his wife to her feet and then turned to Sharon. She accepted his hand and followed him down the aisle and out into the crisp morning air.

"If you can function without sleep, Cameron, we'll head out for some fishing. Are you a fisherman?" Enfield asked.

"I did a little a few summers ago."

"You've lived a sheltered life," Enfield laughed.

"I guess I'd better learn to enjoy it."

"It's a great way to relax. I'll get some gear ready for you while you change." Enfield kissed his wife and headed for a small building near the water. The others followed a stone walk to the main house.

Two aides carried their luggage into the house and upstairs to the bedrooms. Cameron changed into chinos and a flannel shirt and headed out to join Enfield.

The clear air felt good and Cameron was relaxed. He looked at Enfield as he sat in the boat, in a peaceful state of mind, waiting for a fish to bite. "We won't agree on everything," Cameron said.

"I know that," Enfield answered.

"All I ask is that you listen to my point of view."

"I will do that. I'm not locked into some of the positions I'm taking. Some things have to be said just for the good of the campaign. A lot of things change when you take over the office."

"I believe that and I can live with it. I only ask you to grant me the opportunity to express my opinions."

"I will, Cameron. You can count on that. You would have made a formidable opponent, my friend. I'm glad you'd rather be on my team."

I'd rather be on my own team, Cameron thought. "I'm being realistic, Chris. A fight could damage us both."

"You more than me, Cam."

Cameron looked at the man sitting in the stern of the boat wearing an old jacket and floppy hat. *Shit, I'm looking at the next President.* At that moment, he felt a tug on his line and he jerked the rod to set the hook. Too late— he had missed again.

"We'll try to steer clear of politics when we're with our wives this weekend, that way we won't bore them to death." Enfield said.

Cameron could feel a bond growing between Enfield and himself. Maybe they could make a team. It might not be such an ordeal to serve as his running mate. Together they could make a difference and in eight years, the prize would be his. He would wait.

That evening, the three Enfield children joined them for dinner. Sharon showed pictures of their family and she and Emma swapped stories. Emma was a delightful, intelligent hostess who successfully juggled the task of being the State's First Lady and a first class mother.

The Enfield youngsters were bright and articulate. Living in the spotlight had not spoiled them. They attended public schools and James, called Jamie, would soon graduate from high school as Valedictorian of his class. Like his parents before him, he was headed for Michigan State.

Ann Marie, sixteen, had her mother's beauty and charm. It was obvious that a lot of young hearts would be broken before she found the young man she would marry.

Charles, or Chip as he preferred to be called, was the youngest. He was a spirited sixth grader who cared more about baseball than he did about being the Governor's son. He was every bit as intelligent as his siblings, but he loved sports more than books. His body always bore a scrape or scratches because he gave his all in every game. His dream was to play first base for the Detroit Tigers and he would no doubt make it.

The Enfields were very much in love and also had great respect for each other. *God, they're a typical red-blooded American family. This guy is going to make a hell of a president. He's got me beat by a mile.*

The weekend behind them, Cameron and Sharon returned to Washington to wait for Enfield's decision. The call came an hour after they were home. Enfield would make the announcement a week before the Convention.

"The press will put two and two together long before that, but we'll wait," Enfield said before he hung up.

As expected, the press honed in on Cameron as Enfield's choice. Enfield gave in to the constant badgering, named Cameron and got back to the business of preparing for the Convention. Maxine Brighton collected $500 from her colleagues.

#

Carter was sound asleep when the phone rang. He grabbed it on the second ring. "It's done," a voice said and there was a click.

"Shit," Carter said.

His voice woke Renee. "What's the matter, honey?"

"Wrong number. Go back to sleep. I'm going to the bathroom."

He got out of bed and walked into the bathroom, urinated and went back to check Renee. She was asleep again. He walked into the living room and looked out at Washington. He stood for a long time without moving and then went into the kitchen and turned on television. He pressed mute so he wouldn't wake Renee again. He waited for the bulletin graphic to appear.

Sharon was sleeping soundly in Cameron's arms when the phone woke them. "What's wrong?" she asked.

"I don't know." He picked up the phone.

"Cameron, this is Carter. You'd better get up and turn on TV."

Cameron hung up and got out of bed, Sharon followed. He snapped on the TV in time to hear the reporter say, "Governor Enfield's plane went down about twenty miles from the Detroit airport some thirty-five minutes ago."

Sharon screamed and fainted. Cameron dropped to his knees beside her. "Oh, my God." He cradled her in his arms and tears streamed down his face.

Guy and Ann were the first to arrive at the house. He had called Bob Bumgardner, Sharon's doctor and he followed the Sheridans in the door. "She's on the sofa in the living room, Bob."

Ann threw her arms around Cameron. "This is horrible, Cam."

Carter and his wife arrived next and Carter said that reporters were arriving outside. Cameron waved Carter off. "You handle them. I'm not talking to anyone." He went into the living room to be with Sharon.

"Thanks for coming right over, Bob. This is a hell of a night."

"I've called an ambulance, Cam. She's having a miscarriage."

"Oh, God, no." Cameron he knelt beside his wife and whispered, "I'm so sorry, Sharon."

"I am, too, honey. We wanted this baby so much." Sharon was crying.

"I gave her a mild sedative, Cameron. It was the shock. She'll be fine, physically. You're going to have to give her a lot of support to help her get over what's happened."

"We've got some rough days ahead of us." Cameron started for the den. Bumgardner followed.

"I know, Cameron. The whole Country is going to be in a state of shock. Who was with Governor Enfield?"

Cameron kept his voice low, so Sharon wouldn't hear. "His wife and some aides were with him. Sharon doesn't know about Emma yet. Maybe you should tell her, Bob. I'm not sure I have the heart to do it."

"Let's wait until later in the day. Let me get her checked into the hospital. I don't think I'll have to do a D & C, so it'll just be some bed rest. I think the ambulance is here."

"Thanks, Bob. You're a good friend. I'm going with you to the hospital."

"Of course." Bumgardner stopped at the door and looked at Cameron. "Are you holding up all right?"

"I'm doing as good as can be expected, Bob." Cameron turned away and walked into the den where Carter and Guy were watching the news. "Sharon lost the baby. I'm going to the hospital with her now."

Guy got up and embraced Cameron. "I'm sorry, buddy. I'm so sorry."

Cameron struggled with his emotions. "I know you are, Guy. You and Carter handle everything here. What's the latest?"

Carter looked at a note pad in his hand. "There are apparently no survivors. They've got helicopters up and there's nothing but a black crater. It was Enfield, his wife, his campaign manager, two aides, two secret service men and the crew. Ten in all. What a damn mess. A witness said the plane went into a nose dive. I guess they never knew what hit them—I hope."

The week was a blur. Sharon insisted that she be allowed to accompany Cameron to Lansing for the funeral and her doctor reluctantly agreed, providing a nurse went with them. She was weak and wobbly as she got out of the car to go into the church.

"I keep seeing Emma talking about her children, Cam. This isn't right—it just isn't right."

Cameron slipped his arm around her waist and pulled her close as they settled in the pew and waited for the service to start.

The two identical caskets sat side by side in front of the altar. The State flag covered each one. Michigan State Police, members of the Company that guarded the Governor, stood a silent, grieving Honor Guard.

The children sat in the front row with their grandparents. All of them were devastated. The children looked pale and drawn and very frightened. There wasn't a dry eye in the house when Jamie spoke about his parents. Sharon squeezed Cameron's hand and laid her head on his shoulder.

That same day, other funerals were taking place in Washington, Lancing and two small Michigan towns.

The graveside service was beautiful and emotional and Sharon watched the grandparents holding back their own grief and helping the children through the final farewell to their parents. And everywhere there were reporters and cameramen.

After the service, they returned to the Governor's mansion with the family. Cameron took Jamie outside for a walk and they talked about the future and Cameron promised him that he would do everything he could to keep his father's dream alive.

When they returned to Washington, Cameron felt drained and angry. "It's all so damned unfair, Sharon."

"I know, honey." She leaned against him as their limousine pulled away from the airport. "I want to get out of this. Let's go home."

"We can't. It's too late."

Carter called him the next morning. "You'll be the nominee, if you want it, Cam. You were Enfield's choice and the Convention will honor that. You call it, Cam. We're already at work."

Cameron hung up the phone and walked back to the bedroom where Sharon was awake. She knew by the look on his face.

"Was that Carter?"

Cameron nodded yes.

"You're going after the nomination, aren't you?"

He nodded yes again.

"Is there anything I can say to change your mind?"

"No."

"What if I decide to leave you?"

"You won't, because you love me and God knows, I love you."

"I'm so damn scared, Cam. So much has happened. Why? Why did they have to die?"

"I don't know, honey. I just don't know."

tum tum tum ta tum…
tum tum tum ta tum…

The procession moved up Pennsylvania Avenue—slow step—each movement punctuated by the free-flowing tears of the thousands who watched the scene in stark disbelief. Less than four years ago, this man, now carried in death, had ridden down this same avenue full of life, waving, smiling, laughing—giving everyone hope and promise. They had held hands and shared their love with the world. For a moment she saw the love dance in his eyes again—heard him laugh—smelled him—felt the warmth of his touch—no, it was only his ring pressing into her flesh as she clinched her fist. She would never look into his eyes again. Oh, my darling, how much I long to hold you in my arms. Oh, God, I miss him so much.

tum tum tum ta tum…

CHAPTER XV

Politically the Country was in chaos. The Republican Convention turned into a free-for-all, with name-calling and accusations. It was well after midnight when Governor William Clifford Standard of Virginia, a virtual unknown, emerged as the nominee.

"How the hell did he ever get the nomination?" Cameron asked Carter, as they watched Standard's acceptance speech the next night. He looks like a deer caught in headlights. He's a nervous wreck."

"This race is over before it even started," Guy said. "The delegates look bored and exhausted."

"Speaking is certainly not his forte." Franklin grumbled.

"Does he have a forte?" Cameron asked.

"Well, we're looking for it. This is a hell of a surprise. We don't have a damn thing in our files on Standard. He's an unknown, who seems to have married a woman with political connections, which is how he got to be Lieutenant Governor of Virginia and then Governor when Hawkins took the Senate seat. He's never won an election on his own," Franklin explained.

"How did the party leaders let this happen?"

"Want to hear a crazy theory?" Brian Sheridan asked.

"The boy genius of politics is going to explain it to us," Guy teased.

"I could let you guys continue in blissful ignorance," Brian countered.

"I was just kidding, Brian. You've no doubt got it figured out. You've been right about a lot of things lately," Guy said.

"He looks like Cameron."

"What?" Cameron asked.

"You know, he just might be on to something," Carter said after a pause. "Look at him. Change the glasses and hair style and you two could pass for twins."

Franklin was staring at Cameron. "And he's Catholic, got some young children and a blonde wife. I think some misguided cretin convinced the party powerfuls that their one hope is to confuse the voters. Hence—a look alike."

"Brian may be right," Carter laughed. "Is he your evil twin, Cam?"

There was a great deal more concern in the Marshall camp about Standard's running mate, Vernon McIntyre, CEO of Alva Technologies.

"Interesting that they picked an business leader instead of someone with foreign affairs experience, given the state of world affairs," Franklin mused.

"With unemployment always an issue, this might be a shrewd move," Jacob said. "McIntyre did a hell of a job rescuing Alva. He's got the company back on its feet; they pulled off a couple of hostile takeovers and pushed their earnings through the ceiling. He looks damn good."

Lawrence looked at Jacob and then turned to Cameron. "We're going to go hard on the foreign issues. I don't think this Country wants two men who are totally in the dark about what is happening in the rest of the world in charge."

"I hope you're right," Guy said.

"I am!" Lawrence snapped. "And we are going to drive that point home again and again."

Plans for the Democratic Convention included a memorial service for the Enfields the first night. Cameron would deliver the eulogy and then he and Sharon would remain in seclusion at their hotel until the delegates made their decision. His speechwriters were already at work on his acceptance speech.

The Boys, Cameron's name for Carter, Franklin, Lawrence and Jacob, were wrestling with the question of a running mate. Jacob was running all types of scenarios through his computer.

Everyone was gearing up for the big run. Ryan, now an Air Force officer, would not be able to join the campaign. Guy vetoed his son taking a leave from law school. Brian had a natural aptitude and was proving valuable with his work with volunteers in the field.

Jay had no interest in politics and had decided to spend the summer in Europe, touring the continent with friends. David, Debbie and Nicholas would stay at home in Virginia with the housekeeper, under Gillian's watchful eye, until the last night of the Convention. Sharon's parents would not make the trip to Convention. Once again, Maggie ruled and Nick would be deprived of seeing the son-in-law he was so proud of, accept the nomination.

Sharon and Ann would work as a team. Cameron did not want Sharon, still struggling emotionally with the loss of the baby, to travel alone, so Ann had agreed to go out with her. Dates were already being booked with women's groups and community organizations around the Country.

Cameron was spending countless hours with his aides being briefed on foreign and domestic issues. Every evening they went through a mock press conference. Other aides were doing the same kind of drilling with Sharon.

A few weeks before the Convention opened, Arnold Orbaker, the former Governor of California, decided to challenge Cameron's nomination.

"What the hell does this guy think he's doing?" Cameron stormed.

"He's always wanted to be President, Cam. He tried to get the nomination twice before. He's an old party man and this looks like a good time to make his move again," Franklin explained.

"He was a decent enough Senator, he's got a lot of friends in the party, and he would have gone after the nomination if Enfield hadn't had a lock on it," Carter added.

"So, what do we do? We're not going to let him steal this from me!" Cameron felt his anger rising.

"He's not going to steal the nomination from you. You're the one who's going to appear before the delegates in the memorial service. You'll be seen as the one who is picking up the torch. Orbaker is going to be nothing more than a nuisance," Franklin said.

"I hope to hell you're right," Cameron snapped.

On the heels of Orbaker's announcement of his intention to seek the nomination, several Governors and the Mayor of Chicago jumped on his bandwagon with support. This put some early delegate votes into the Orbaker column.

Franklin called a quick meeting. "I've got some concerns that Orbaker might have more strength than we think."

"Jesus Christ, what do I pay you people for? You tell me there's no problem and I watch CNN's delegate count and I see it growing for Orbaker. There are commentators saying the Party is going to turn to this seasoned veteran. And what the hell is going on in Chicago?" Cameron demanded.

"Chicago is easy to explain. The mayor is Orbaker's brother-in-law. Evidently, the Governor of Illinois is in the Mayor's debt. That explains that." Franklin was casual with his explanation.

"I don't want any more excuses for people who are turning their backs on me. Find out what the hell Orbaker wants." Cameron realized he was yelling.

Carter was chewing on one of his ever-present cigars and he spit a piece of tobacco into the air. "He wants to be President, plain and simple."

"Well, he isn't going to be," Cameron countered. "Damn it, after all I've been through, I am not going to lose the ball game in the final inning. Now, you guys get your people out there and you get a lock on the votes and you do it fast."

"Want us to walk on water on the way?" Carter snapped.

Cameron looked as his friends. "I apologize, fellows. I'm so on edge with everything that has happened, I'm not thinking straight. I know you're working as hard as you can. I know you will handle this problem. I don't want to lose this thing now."

"We are not going to be defeated, Cameron. Trust me." Franklin's voice was cold and controlled.

Two hours before the opening ceremony at Convention Center, Arnold Orbaker was escorted to a service elevator and whisked to the twenty-fifth floor of the Royale Hotel. He was hurried down a deserted hall and into a room at the end of the corridor. The room was dimly lighted, but he could make out four men. He recognized Franklin, sitting at the end of the table. Another man was at each side. Another was at the bar. The unholy four—Carter, Franklin, Lawrence and Jacob, were waiting for him.

"Sit down, Governor, we need to have a little talk," Franklin said.

The group scared the hell out of Orbaker. He could not stand Franklin. There was something strange about him. He couldn't put a finger on it, but it was something that worried him. He's a cold son-of-a-bitch, Orbaker thought as he sat across from the man.

"We need to discuss how your decision to seek the nomination is hurting the Party," Franklin began.

Orbaker started to answer and then thought better of it and waited in silence for Franklin to continue.

"The Party can not afford to have a divisive fight at this time. Everyone is in shock over the Enfield accident. We need to heal the wounds with unity."

Lawrence took his turn. "We know that you are a man dedicated to serving your Country. We believe that you will answer any call that is given to you."

Orbaker did not like the tone of what he was hearing. Their intention was to prevent him from continuing his campaign for the nomination.

Lawrence opened a folder that was on the table in front of him. Orbaker froze when he saw the picture. "My, God, man, I was a boy. It was a private boy's school. Boys experiment," Orbaker pleaded when he regained his voice.

Lawrence moved the picture to one side and revealed another.

"What do you want from me?" Orbaker whispered.

"Ideally, we would like you out of the picture entirely, but it isn't an ideal world and the press might start asking questions we don't want asked," Lawrence said.

Orbaker was sweating.

"So," Lawrence explained, "the Vice Presidency. Neat, clean, no opposition."

"And if I have no desire to be the number two man?"

Lawrence picked up the photograph and smiled. "Then we'll have to discuss your retirement from public life."

"I don't want my family hurt. That was a long time ago." Orbaker was seeing the whole picture now.

"He's got a great ass, hasn't he, Jacob?" Lawrence slid the picture toward Jacob.

"No one will ever know of this visit. You will be in the Convention Center for the memorial service and for the first time, you will appear along side our candidate. You and Senator Marshall will appear friendly and cordial. Later tonight, you will call your supporters and tell them that for the good of the Party and the Country you will support Senator Marshall and you will tell them not to put your name in nomination. Is everything clear?" Lawrence asked.

"Yes," was all Orbaker could manage. A thought struck him, *Jesus Christ, I wonder if they had any thing to do with the Enfield crash?* Orbaker was scared. His mouth was dry. He knew that these men would stop at nothing to get the power they were seeking. *They are evil and I have no choice but to join them or go out that window.* His heart was beating fast. He took a deep breath.

"Perhaps you would like a drink before you return to the Convention?" Carter asked from the bar.

Orbaker was dying for a good stiff scotch, but he didn't dare have any alcohol in his system—it would be too easy for him to have an accident on his way to the Convention. "No thank you. I'd like to go now."

Lawrence stood up and walked over to a paper shredder. Orbaker watched as he fed the photograph into the machine. He knew full well that there were more copies. Lawrence returned and extended his hand across the table. "You'll make a good Vice President, Arnold. And someday, if you play your cards right, it may be your turn to be President."

Orbaker was weak kneed and pale when he joined his wife at the Convention. She took one look at him and almost panicked. He assured her it was the pressure of the evening and he was fine. Right after they took their seats, he saw Carter smiling at him from backstage.

My God, he thought, they're going to watch my every move.

The Convention opened on a somber, subdued note. Large photographs, draped in black, of Christopher and Emma Enfield dominated the scene. Most of the delegates wore black armbands and buttons with the Enfield's pictures on them. Arrangements had been made for the Enfield children and Mrs. Enfield's parents to sit with the Marshall family during the memorial service. Governor Enfield's parents had declined to attend the Convention.

Cameron had rehearsed and rehearsed his speech, wanting to be certain he would strike the right tone. When he finished, many of the delegates were in tears. A choir sang a hymn and then Jamie Enfield stepped forward to address the delegates. He spoke lovingly of his father and mother and then told the assembly that Cameron was the man to continue his father's work. Thus ended the Enfield Convention. The Marshall convention would begin the next day.

Orbaker and his wife retired to their hotel suite early. He called his campaign manager the next morning and told him he was dropping out of the race. By ten o'clock, Orbaker was standing before the press, pledging his support to Cameron Marshall. An hour later, Cameron was in front of the same reporters, praising Orbaker and asking the delegates to pick Orbaker as his running mate.

Orbaker was a pleasant man with beautifully coiffured white hair. He wore a moustache and trim goatee. Cameron thought he looked like Colonel Sanders and joked about running with the Chicken King. Franklin did not find that funny.

He was short and obviously in need of a good exercise program. He had a likable personality and would not be a detriment to the ticket. No one knew anything about his wife who had stayed out of the limelight to raise their six daughters.

The Convention went as scripted by the Marshall team. Cameron and

Arnold presented a united front in their acceptance speeches; their families held hands and enjoyed the adulation of the delegates.

Friday morning they began the campaign.

Guy's assignment was to meet with State and local Party Leaders around the Country. He had to keep the money flowing for the campaign. His responsibility was to hustle the big donors into cities where Cameron was so they could have their private moment with the candidate. Plans were discussed, carefully couched promises made, and checks gratefully received. Guy did not like his role, but it was necessary.

Brian Sheridan was coordinating campaign stops. His youthful energy appealed to young and old alike, and he had no trouble lining up volunteers who helped produce large, supportive crowds every where Cameron stopped. Brian was always gone to another city by the time the candidate arrived. He loved the excitement.

Sharon was becoming more comfortable with her role. A smart new wardrobe and new hairstyle caught the public's eye and she was becoming as popular as her husband. But she missed her family. She talked every evening to the children and to Cameron every night before they fell asleep, separated by many miles. How she missed cuddling in his arms. After the loss of the baby, she felt empty inside.

City by city—state by state—the days were a blur. The crowds were large and welcomed him with cheers and exuberance. He was using television well and the polls showed his popularity growing. It was almost as if he could say anything and the people would respond.

The early polls were showing Cameron well in the lead. He was surprised when he was called back to Washington for a late night strategy meeting. He was tired and wanted to get home to Virginia to be with the kids and Sharon, who had flown home earlier in the day.

"Look, guys, we're in good shape. Why this pow wow?" He looked at the four men seated around the table. "We're beyond the Convention bounce and the polls show me winning the election easily."

Jacob gave one of his rare smiles. "Standard is making a fool of himself every time he opens his mouth. We want to make sure we stay with the game plan, Cam."

"I thought you guys would be happy as hell. You look like doom and gloom."

"We have to be careful about being over-confident," Carter said, getting up and walking across the room to the bar.

"I don't think anyone is over-confident, Carter. But, at the same time, we can't behave like we're going to lose."

"Cam, if any of those crazy reporters start asking you questions about who's going to serve in your administration, don't speculate. Tell them the election has to be won first."

"Come off it, Carter. I sure as hell am not Tom Dewey. I'm not going to pretend to be president until I'm elected. Now, let's level, guys, something is up. What the hell is it?"

Guy and Brian slipped into the room and took seats near the bar.

"OK, let's get to the bad news. All of you haven't gotten together for a poker game. Spill it, Guy. What the hell has happened now?" Cameron demanded.

"McIntyre is getting a lot of mileage out of how he turned Alva Technologies around. They keep spreading the word about how the company was in the crapper until he took over. The stock is the highest in the Company's history. People like underdogs who are successful. We think there might be a shift in the polls coming," Franklin explained.

"He's running for the wrong office," Cameron countered.

"Let Brian tell you what he thinks, Cam," Carter said, taking a sip of his scotch.

Cameron walked over and sat at the table. Brian got up and stood at one end.

"This is going to sound like I'm smoking something funny, but hear me out, please."

Franklin nodded his head. Cameron scowled and shook his.

"Things are a shambles over at Standard's headquarters. Their boy can't do a damn thing right. He can't even read the speeches they prepare for him, always thinks he has to ad lib his own idea or put in some stupid joke. McIntyre is appearing stronger and stronger, but he's hampered by Standard. So, dear little Standard comes up with an illness, bows out, and McIntyre is the candidate."

Cameron laughed.

"Think about it for a moment, Cam," Carter said.

The room was silent for what seemed like an eternity. Cameron looked at Brian and then at the other men in the room. *Jesus Christ,* he thought, *this kid is better than all these other guys put together.*

"I think Brian is on to something, Cam," Carter said. "There's a lot of late night activity at Standard Headquarters. All of a sudden our sources are having a hard time coming up with anything."

"We have someone inside Standard's campaign?"

"McIntyre's too," Carter said. "Hell, they've got some one in ours. We use him well. Don't you, Jake?"

Jacob's face was red. He got up quickly and went to the bar. Carter laughed. Jacob was furious.

Cameron ignored the scene between his two aides and turned his attention to Brian. "Sit down, Brian, and let's talk this thing through," Cameron said.

Brian took a seat opposite Cam. Guy walked over to Jacob and tried to calm him down.

"You have keen insight, Brian. Standard is screwing up royally. The Party leaders have to be furious that they were hoodwinked into giving him the nomination," Cameron said.

Brian was excited that Cameron believed him and began his explanation. "I think McIntyre has a reasonable shot at beating us and he sure as hell will be a formidable opponent in four years. The question is, are they ready to write this election off? I don't think so. What they're ready to do is write Standard off and fast."

"I don't like what I'm hearing," Cameron said.

"None of us like what's going on either, but we can't call the shots for the other side. We'd like to, but…" Carter's voice trailed off.

"How the hell did you get so smart, Brian?" Cameron asked.

"I have good teachers." Everyone smiled and the tension in the room eased.

"OK how do we react? Let's hear the options." Cameron looked around the room.

"Well, Brian," Franklin said, "you called it, you give us your strategy."

"Obviously, we can't expose them for this political stunt because we don't have Standard's medical records and he could be a sick man, so we need to play it straight—you know, act surprised and concerned when the announcement is made. Cameron will call Standard, talk privately with him, express regrets, tell him how concerned he is about his health and the effect it will have on his family and offer any assistance we can give."

"Keep going, kid, this sounds good to me," Carter said, finishing his drink and heading to the bar for another. Franklin frowned his disapproval of Carter's drinking.

Brian continued. "Cameron publicly expresses concern for Standard and his family and extend bests wishes to McIntyre for the rest of the campaign. Basically, we say damn little and play this little gambit for real. We don't have any other choice."

"I agree with my son," Guy added. "McIntyre is going to get a lot of sympathy. He's almost become a folk hero out there, for what he has been enduring. We say little and continue the campaign."

"What do you see as McIntyre's new thrust?" Cameron asked.

"He'll continue his Putting America Back to Work theme," Franklin said. "He's done that at Alva and unemployment is always a strong campaign issue. This is where he has real strength against us, Cameron."

"With eight weeks to go, we're suddenly in a new ball game, aren't we?" Cameron asked.

Lawrence spoke for the first time. "Yes and a serious one. If they do what Brian thinks, the voters are going to be confused at first. The average person only half reads a newspaper. We have some columnist friends who will do some dirty work for us. When this happens, they'll explain Standard's withdrawal as a political ploy. But we don't know how much effect that will be with the man on the street. We're going to have to go after McIntyre."

"The debates are going to be crucial. Standard was such a nothing, we weren't the least bit concerned," Carter said. "McIntyre is going to come across strong. He's not going to put his foot in his mouth. And, Cam, he has a style much like yours."

"We've got to paint you as a solid, knowledgeable leader, who is totally in control." Jacob had over come his anger and was back to participating in the meeting. "I think we should continue with the foreign policy issues, which make you sound very Presidential, and call for summit meetings and disarmament talks."

"Suppose I went abroad and arranged a meeting with England, France and Germany, for November—right after the elections?" Guy suggested.

Cameron vetoed the idea. "It's isn't a political coup to arrange a meeting with our allies."

"But," Franklin offered, "how about a meeting with China's leaders? That would be a bold move."

"I think it's grandstanding," Carter said. "We have no reason to panic and McIntyre could use the move against us. China is a tricky situation. We'll keep it out of the campaign. Let's wait until they make their move. I don't think we should change a damn thing until then," Carter's tone told them the discussion was closed.

"Get me as much information on McIntyre's unemployment proposals as you can. We'll mix the speeches up, some on domestic issues, some on foreign policy. I'm in Chicago Monday—you know, my favorite city. I'd still like to pin the Mayor's ears back for jumping onto Orbaker's bandwagon. I know, Carter," Cameron added with a laugh, "no quarrels in the ranks."

"I'm catching an early morning flight to San Diego to meet Orbaker. I want to brief him on tonight's meeting. I think he should take the lead on domestic issues, you on foreign policy, Cam," Carter added.

"It is also time for you and Orbaker to start make appearances together. We have a team; something the Republicans no longer have. Let's make it very obvious to the public. Get Orbaker's wife—what the hell is her name?" Franklin asked.

"Linda," Lawrence said.

"Well, get Linda and Sharon on the road together. Christ! You guys have got to get along and do it damn fast."

Carter looked at his watch. "It's late and we're all tired and testy. Guy, take Brian upstairs and find him an office. I think it's time he came in off the road and worked here. Someone else can arrange for crowds. Pick somebody, Brian. As of now, you're an assistant campaign manager."

"Thanks," Brian stammered.

"Cam, there's a car waiting for you downstairs to take you home. Go see Sharon and the kids. Get some rest." Carter was barking orders and no one was going to argue.

Guy and Cameron got up and left. Brian lingered for a moment. The phone rang.

"Yes?" Carter turned to Brian.

"I want to thank all of you for your confidence in me."

"You're very valuable to us, Brian. Now go catch up with your father," Carter ordered.

As Brian went out the door, Carter punched the call onto the speakerphone. As he closed the door, Brian thought he heard a familiar voice. *Impossible*, he thought and headed for the elevator.

#

Vernon McIntyre was exhausted when he got to his hotel suite at two thirty in the morning. The speech had gone well and then he has mingled and shook hands with most of the business leaders. This would be the second night that he had had little sleep. The night before he and his advisors had worked until dawn preparing for Standard's withdrawal announcement.

He went to the bar, poured himself a stiff drink of scotch, shed his clothes and headed for the shower. He stood for a long time and let the warm water beat at the fatigue his body felt. Finally, he stepped out, toweled off, wrapped another towel around his waist and went back into the bedroom. He took a healthy drink of the scotch, picked up his briefcase and relaxed on the bed to do some reading.

When he awoke, sunlight was streaming in the windows. He had a headache and he was naked. He rubbed his temples and sat up. An empty bottle of scotch sat on the bedside table. There was a slight hint of a woman's perfume in the room. He remained motionless and tried to bring the night into focus. He knew he had come back to his room alone. He couldn't believe that he had consumed all the scotch. He was having trouble clearing his head.

McIntyre got up, got his robe out of the closet and went into the living room. He saw a brown envelope lying on the floor. It had been pushed under his door. He picked it up and tore it open quickly. Inside were eight by ten color photographs of him and a young girl in different sexual positions.

"Jesus Christ!" he yelled. The girl looked about fifteen. What the hell had happened last night? He tore the pictures into pieces and heaved them around the room. A note fluttered to the floor. He picked it up and read the poorly printed words: The Inquisitor will publish these in their next issue.

Everything was blurring before his eyes.

The maid was pushing her cart down the hallway when the sound of shattering glass broke the silence. She ran quickly back toward the elevators, yelling for security.

When the security guard opened the room, he saw a gaping hole where the glass window had been. The maid, following close behind him, screamed.

Twenty stories below a broken body lay on the sidewalk as a large rivulet of blood seeped toward the gutter.

The election was over.

tum tum tum ta tum...
tum tum tum ta tum...

A light rain began to fall as the march neared the Capitol. Here, such a short time ago it seems, he had been a young senator and they had sat in the freezing cold, holding hands, watching another man accept the reigns of government. They laughed and "what if'd" about it being them on the platform, and how they would live in the White House and travel the world. She didn't realize that it was not a dream but his destiny. He found triumph on the hill, earned the trust and respect of his Countrymen and became a statesman who symbolized hope and peace. Today, there was no laughter, no dream, no triumph. Today, he returned in tragedy and the heavens poured forth tears of sorrow on the mortals below.

tum tum tum ta tum...

CHAPTER XVI

The polls gave the Marshall-Orbaker team a commanding lead with both the popular and electoral votes. Standard's new running mate was a lackluster Congressman from the Midwest who had been given his fleeting moments of glory and didn't know any better than, out of misguided, blind loyalty, to let his party use him.

"This will give him some great memories to tell his grandchildren when he retires. Hopefully, they won't figure out that grandpa had no idea what the hell he was doing," Carter remarked as he watched the two Republican candidates make a last minute pitch to the voters of the Country.

"Are you planning to have me say anything to the press when I leave Washington tonight?" Cameron asked.

"Actually, we'd like to talk you out of leaving Washington, Cameron," Franklin said. "If you're here, it could give people the idea that you are taking charge immediately."

"Sharon and I want to be home—where this all started to take shape. It's important to her—and to me. I want to be alone with my family tomorrow."

Carter started to tell him that he would never again be alone, but he thought better of it. He had decided not to argue with Cameron on the decision.

"I hear you, Cam," Carter said. "The Secret Service has secured your home in Seward. There won't be any problems."

"You know, I've wanted this to happen for so long and now, when it's all in my grasp, I'm scared."

Lawrence gave one of his rare smiles. "We all are, Cam."

Franklin stood up and raised his glass. "To President Marshall, a man of the people."

He heard the others in the room mutter, "here, here" and he smiled. For the first time, Cameron thought, a dream of mine is coming true.

"Here's your itinerary and some remarks for the press before you board

187

the plane. A car will bring Sharon and the kids in from Virginia. So," Carter said, patting Cameron on the shoulder, "Why don't you review your remarks while we tend to some last minute details before we head to the airport."

"Sounds like a good idea. How soon do we leave?" Cameron asked.

"In about forty minutes. Let's head for our offices fellows and pack our papers. We're going to be damn busy after tomorrow."

Cameron sat alone and rubbed his eyes. The weeks of endless campaigning had taken their toll—he was exhausted. He moved over to the sofa, stretched out and fell into a deep sleep. For the first time in months, he did not dream.

Carter roused him. "It's time to leave for the airport, Cameron."

Cameron had trouble clearing his head. His eyes ached. He wanted to keep sleeping. He got to his feet and was disoriented for a moment.

Carter grabbed his arm. "Are you all right?"

"Yes, I'm just exhausted. And my leg is killing me. Damn plates."

Cameron winced as he took a step. He was limping, trying to favor his sore hip.

"What a hell of a time to have this flare up. Is there time for a hot bath?" Cameron asked.

"I'm sorry, Cam. The limo is waiting," Carter replied.

"Get me a couple of pain pills and a glass of water. I'll make it to the plane. Call ahead and tell them to have some hot packs for me, Carter."

"Right."

Sharon and the children were waiting in the VIP lounge when Cameron arrived at Washington National. She could tell at a glance that he was in pain.

"Your leg is getting worse, isn't it?" she whispered as she hugged him.

"I took some medicine, but it hasn't kicked in yet." He walked over and hugged the children. "Are you ready to go home?"

David was his usual withdrawn self and stood back, watching the others. The public life his family was living was raising havoc with his teenage years and he resented his lack of privacy.

Cameron went over to him and extended his hand for a handshake. David had let him know some time ago that he was too old for hugging. David reluctantly took his hand. Cameron wished he could reach the young man and help him with his pain.

"Stand beside me when I talk to the press, David. Maybe they'd like to hear from you, too."

"Why the hell would anyone care about what I think?" he shot back.

"Give it a try, OK?"

David nodded yes and they headed out the door to face the reporters. Sharon and Nicky, as bouncy and care free as usual, followed.

Cameron stood with his arm around his stepson's shoulder when he spoke. "Tomorrow, there will be a free election in a free land. A day when you, as American citizens, will make your decision in privacy, with no one coercing you."

"Remember," he continued, "that the decision you make tomorrow is a decision that this Nation must live with for the next four years. It will effect you as individuals and the Nation as a whole."

"I am going to ask you to show the world that we are proud of this privilege of a free election. Regardless of how you have decided to vote, please do one more important act for your Country. Fly the American flag tomorrow as a symbol to all the oppressed people in the world that freedom is alive and democracy can work for everyone. Thank you and God bless you."

Carter turned to Guy. "Where the hell did that American flag thing come from?"

"I have no idea, Carter. He keeps coming up with these ideas on his own. He never mentioned it to me," Guy responded.

"Well he sure as hell didn't use the remarks we prepared for him. I don't like he way he keeps going off in his own little direction. We've got to watch that. It could be dangerous," Carter snapped.

Guy was startled by Carter's anger.

A couple of reporters asked David some questions and for a moment he forgot to be sullen. Cameron smiled and they waved and headed for the plane. Photographers and reporters hurried ahead of them and there were cries of "one more picture, Senator," and then a flash would explode in their faces. The Secret Service and airport security shoved at the crowd, but it was a losing battle. It was too few against too many.

Finally, the Marshalls slipped through the door and onto the plane. Cameron stopped and leaned against the first seat. He was in throbbing pain. Sharon grabbed Cameron's arm. "Sit down, right here," she ordered.

Cameron dropped into a seat. He was sweating. He leaned back and took a deep breath. Others in their party were filing in behind them. Sharon moved so that her body shielded Cameron from their eyes. Some knew something was wrong, but they continued back into the plane.

Guy stopped. "Do we need a doctor?"

"No!" Cameron snapped. "I'll be fine."

"Yes, we do, Guy. See if you can find someone to see him when we land," Sharon said.

"Sneak him in so the press won't notice," Cameron added, handing Sharon a pill bottle.

Sharon opened the bottle and gave Cameron two pills. A stewardess handed her a glass of water. Cameron gulped the pills.

"You're taking too many of these," Sharon whispered.

"I know. But, we have to get through this. I'll take care of it after tomorrow—I promise."

"I hope you know what you're doing, Cam."

"It'll be all right, Sharon. I promise you."

"It'll be so good to be home," Sharon sighed as she settled herself in the seat by the window. "I can't seem to get used to all the reporters and their questions."

"If we're successful tomorrow, they will be with us for a long time."

"I don't know, Cam. I'm numb. I can't imagine being married to the President of the United States."

The engines of the plane roared and they began to taxi down the runway. Cameron reached up, snapped off his light and fastened his seat belt.

"I wish I could promise you that your husband was going to be president. We'll have to wait and see."

"I'll never make it through tomorrow, all day—not knowing. Isn't there some way we can find out early?"

By the time the plane climbed into the sky, the pills were easing the pain. Cameron tipped his seat back and settled down for a nap. Sharon felt her own fatigue. She looked out the window at the lights of Washington, the city they had both grown to love in a short time. Washington was quiet. The Senators and Congressmen were home now, working for their own reelections or the election of friends.

Soon construction would begin at the Capitol and the White House and the city would prepare to welcome a new administration. There would be some who would return to Washington to finish up business, clean out their offices and head home to private careers or retirement. Nothing was permanent in the city. New, young faces would move in, all eager to earn their own reputations and make their own contributions to the government.

Cameron's Senate seat would go to someone else. Sharon hoped it would be Stanley Striker, but Cameron said he was not in favor with the party. He's a good man, too, like my husband, Sharon thought.

Sharon unfastened her seat belt and leaned toward Cameron, resting her head on his shoulder. She closed her eyes, but sleep refused to come. Her mind was too busy and she had a strange, foreboding feeling. She got up and walked back a few rows to see the children. David had been allowed to go forward to the cockpit and sit with the pilots. The other children were in the back of the plane, eating pizza with some of the staff.

Helen saw Sharon and came forward. "Is he all right?"

"He's having a lot of pain from his hip. You know what it's like when he gets exhausted. We think he's just developing arthritis, Helen. He has been on the go so much."

"Maybe he can get some rest after tomorrow."

"We're supposed to have a two week vacation, but somehow I don't think we'll be alone. Are you going with us?"

"Yes, Sharon. He said if he won the election he would have to take a lot of work with him on the trip. I'm sorry."

"Don't be sorry, Helen," Sharon said. "It's not your fault. You're only doing your job." Sharon smiled and lightened up. "Anyway, you're part of the family." Sharon hugged Helen and walked back to her seat and sat deep in thought, looking off into space, as they flew north.

The big silver and red bird swooped down from the darkened sky, touched the earth and rolled to the main terminal at Lakeland Regional Airport.

Sharon knew the procedure well. No one would leave the plane until the press plane had landed and the reporters were ready to cover their arrival.

As soon as Cameron's plane stopped, the door opened and a doctor, dressed like a member of the flight crew, slipped onto the plane to examine Cameron's leg.

"You need to be off your feet—now."

"I can't, doc—not tonight. Can you give me some cortisone or something? I promise I'll see my physician Wednesday," Cameron said.

"I have to look strong. There have been so many problems with this election; I can't let the American people down. Get me through tonight and tomorrow, doc—please."

Without a word, the doctor gave Cameron a shot of cortisone and another painkiller. He turned, walked back to the door and left the plane. Clearly, he was not happy with how he had been forced to treat his patient.

"It'll be all right, Sharon. I promise you," Cameron said, squeezing her hand.

Several thousand people were gathered in the terminal. Some had waited all afternoon to greet the candidate. Guy stepped off the plane and returned with the Mayor and his wife. Cameron would spend a few minutes in private with them and then they would leave the plane together. Calvin Blackworth was a Republican, but on Carter's advice, Cameron was going to show him the courtesy of a joint appearance.

They walked down the ramp and into the terminal waiting room, Cameron and Blackworth first, followed by Sharon and Elaine Blackworth. Sharon carried the bouquet of yellow roses Elaine had given her. Microphones and reporters waited for them.

"I'm glad to be home," Cameron said. "And I would say from this enthusiastic greeting tonight, that tomorrow, I should carry your fair city, Mr. Mayor."

The crowd cheered and even Blackworth, plainly uncomfortable with Cameron, managed a smile.

Cameron and Sharon moved forward, shaking as many hands as they could reach, being touched by people on both sides of the walkway that the Secret Service and airport security had cleared for them. The Secret Service men were beside themselves with concern, but they acceded to the candidate's wishes. After tomorrow, it would be different.

Guy was waiting for them at the car. "Listen, Cameron, they want a motorcade through the city," Guy shouted into Cameron's ear, over the sound of the crowd and airplanes landing and taking off.

Cameron nodded all right and stepped aside so Sharon could precede him into the car. Guy leaped into the front seat as the car started to move.

"I understand we've got people waiting on the streets in every town from here to Seward. We were going to hit the expressway and make a bee line for home, but I think it's impossible," Guy said.

"We'll take as much time as we need, Guy. If there are large groups, tell the Secret Service we'll stop and get out."

The look on Sharon's face told Cameron and Guy she was angry.

"The Secret Service won't like this one damn bit. They can't guarantee your safety if you keep moving into the crowds."

"We're home, Guy. No one is going to hurt us here." Cameron turned his attention to the people on the streets.

"If he were president, he would have to listen to his guards," Guy said to the driver.

"Tonight, we stop and I shake hands, all the way home. End of discussion."

"You're the boss," Guy shot back.

Seward was all decked out in red, white and blue for their candidate's arrival. A colorful billboard at the city limits welcomed him and Sharon home. The Seward High School band stood in formation on Main Street, waiting for his car to pull up behind them, so they could lead the parade to the Civic Center. It didn't matter that it was almost two o'clock in the morning. No one was going home until they welcomed Cameron and Sharon Marshall home.

"Damn, this is going to go on until dawn," Guy grumbled.

"Yes, but the press is going to be beautiful. I'll bet Carter and your son are behind this welcome, so stop grousing, Guy. Enjoy the moment," Cameron said.

When they pulled up in front of the flag festooned Civic Center, the Mayor and her husband, along with a host of local politicians, were waiting. "Everyone gets their moment in the spotlight," Guy mumbled.

As he stepped from the car, Cameron shook the Mayor's hand and kissed her cheek. Sharon accepted another bouquet of roses and a kiss from the Mayor's husband.

"You certainly have to say that Seward loves its favorite son, Senator," Mayor Sylvia Van Kiel gushed, waving enthusiastically to the cheering crowd.

Cameron and Sharon followed the Mayor up onto a temporary stage and Cameron held up his hand for quiet. "Friends—my family and I are overwhelmed with this welcome. It is wonderful to come home and be met with so much love. Thank you for tonight and for your faith in me. I've come to know many of you personally and, win or lose tomorrow, I feel like I am the richest man in the world because I have so many friends. I've been away from home a long time and if the vote goes the way we expect it to, I will be away from home for a long time again, but my heart will be with you always."

"It seems like only yesterday that we were all here—when it all began. I pray that we will meet here again tomorrow night—in victory." Despite his best intentions, Cameron's voice was choking with emotion.

The crowd went wild and began chanting for Sharon and she stepped to the microphone, fighting to hold back her own tears. She was unsuccessful and big tears flowed down her cheeks.

"We're so happy tonight, you are so wonderful to come out and meet us. The Senator and I can't thank you enough for making this a special homecoming. And, I promise you, my husband is going to be the best President this Country has ever had."

The crowd roared approval as Cameron and Sharon shook hands with all the people on the stage. Cameron had a word or two for each one and Sharon accepted kisses on the cheek from the men.

Ann Sheridan had returned home a week earlier and turned their house over to the press. She moved into Cameron and Sharon's house and had been busy overseeing all the preparations for their arrivals. The telephone company and Secret Service had been busy installing additional phone lines and high-tech security devises. They would be linked electronically with the world from their private fortress.

Ann greeted them at the front door. She kissed Cameron, Sharon and her husband, who was bringing up the rear.

"I'm so excited. I've been watching it all on television. I don't even know what I'm doing. I can't remember when I've cried this much," Ann said, wiping her eyes and blowing her nose.

Cameron smiled and hugged her close.

"Did the children get settled?" Sharon asked.

"I think they're all in bed and sound asleep. They looked really tired," Ann said.

The children had been brought straight from the airport to the house.

Cameron pulled off his coat and tie and dropped them over a chair. "It's been quite a day." He kicked off his loafers and eased himself into a chair.

Guy came in carrying two briefcases, which he dropped on the table. "Why don't you two call it a night? Ann and I are to go over to our house and check on the chaos before we turn in."

"You should see the house since the press took over. They're everywhere," Ann said.

"Brace yourself, honey. It's worse now. A plane load came up from Washington with us."

"Where will they all sleep?"

"Anywhere they can find a spot," Guy said. "Most of them won't sleep much tonight. They'll be watching this house and grabbing for any scraps of news they can find—or make up. I want to keep them at bay until dawn. He's had a damn hard day."

Guy was no sooner gone when Carter and Lawrence arrived to give Cameron a final run down on the polls and their projections, State by State, on how they expected the voting to go.

It was after four in the morning before Sharon and Cameron were alone in their bedroom.

"Oh," Sharon sighed, "It's so good to be home. I'm too tired to think." Cameron unzipped the back of her dress and kissed her on the neck as he finished.

"I feel pretty good now," he said.

"I'm glad. I was worried about you when we left Washington." Sharon said as she went into the bathroom.

"I guess that nap on the plane did the trick."

"I'd give anything if I could sleep like you do, Cam."

Cameron took a quick shower, put on fresh pajamas and slipped into bed. He waited for Sharon to get settled and then turned off the light.

"Ummm," Sharon whispered. "Why does your own bed always feel so much better than the others?"

Cameron slipped his arm around Sharon, kissed her cheek and quickly fell into a dreamless sleep.

Cameron woke as light was appearing in the window. He turned his head and for a few moments watched Sharon sleep. Her blonde hair spilled across the pillow and he wanted to caress her and arouse her passion, but he held back, knowing how tired she was and how she needed the sleep.

He slipped out of bed, grabbed some clothes and dressed. He looked anything but like a man about to be elected President of the United States. His light gray slacks needed pressing. His black loafers were scuffed and dusty. Under a navy blue windbreaker he wore a blue plaid shirt. He ran a comb though his hair and then tried to finish the job with his fingers.

His eyes cried for sleep, but his mind, racing over and over the events of the past few months, would not let him rest. He was uneasy, nervous and his stomach was tied in a knot. He was afraid when he should be confident. He wanted to be alone, yet he needed someone to talk to, someone to listen to him, someone to be with him.

He stood, like a forlorn little boy, blew a kiss to his sleeping wife and left the bedroom, easing the door shut behind him.

He was surprised to find Guy in the living room.

"I thought you'd sleep until noon," Guy muttered.

"I've been awake for a long time." He sat on the edge of the sofa and fumbled in his pockets for his pipe. Without getting up, Guy picked it up from the table and tossed it to him.

"Thanks," Cameron looked around for his tobacco pouch. "Well, this is it."

Guy nodded a response and continued reading the paper.

Cameron stood up, stretched, and walked over to the fireplace. "Think we should start a fire? The house feel chilly."

Guy shrugged, but Cameron paid no attention.

"I always have trouble starting the fire. I've bought every conceivable gadget and none of them work for me. Sharon wads up a piece of newspaper, tosses in a match and presto—one roaring fire. I wonder what I do wrong? At least I'll never be guilty of arson."

He wandered back to the sofa and put his pipe on the table. "I like a fire on a cold day. I'd like to sit in that chair today and read and be warm."

He moved again, toward the window. "It'll never be like this again, will it? I bet it snows before the day ends. Do you think we should check the weather across the country, so we can predict the voter turnout today?"

"All the news services moved that story hours ago." Guy folded his newspaper and tossing it on the table.

"We can't do anything about the weather anyway." Cameron turned away from the window. "Sharon's still asleep. Or did I already tell you that?"

"I hope to hell she sleeps all day, or at least until you get out of this fuckin' mood. What the hell is wrong with you?"

Cameron drew a deep breath. "I'm scared. I'm so goddamned scared, Guy."

"We all are, Cam. None of us have been where we're about to go. We've worked our asses off and now the moment is near and we're waiting. Waiting for the people to decide—the voting American public with a hundred million reasons for choosing a man. Voting Democrat or Republican because that's what their grandfather did—voting for a man because he's handsome, or wears nice clothes, or has curly hair. Think of the damnedest, most obscure point and some damn fool will vote for you. But, never because you're the best-qualified candidate or because you present a logical, plausible answer to the problems of the day. It's a hell of a system, but by God, somehow it works."

Cameron shook his head in agreement. "The men who drew up our system of government knew it wasn't perfect, but it's the best thing around so far. Wouldn't it be nice, Guy, if we could have a system where the candidates could appear in national debates, watched by everyone in the Country? And on the basis of these debates, and I don't mean staged media events but true issue discussions, the public would decide who was best qualified. Imagine, no more expensive advertising campaigns with the so-called subliminal messages no one understands and no more running around the Country shaking hands with mobs, being shoved by photographers and having microphones poked into your face by some reporter who prays you miss-speak. I'm so goddammed sick of phony sound bites I could scream."

"I'm not going back to Washington with you, Cameron."

The words caught him off guard. "What?" Cameron was not certain if he had heard right or not.

"This is the end of the road for me, Cam. I get off here."

"Quit the crap, Guy. You can't tell me that you would work this hard to get me into the White House and then sit back here, watching. You're as primed for this thing as I am. Where did this crazy idea come from? It better not be from Carter or Franklin and his boys. I'm getting tired of being intimidated by them. You're my closest friend. We're in this together. You sure as hell are not going to let me face this alone."

"I made the decision myself, Cam. For personal reasons."

"Look, Guy, I can understand how you feel right now. I'm overwhelmed, too." Cameron moved over and sat on the sofa. "If everything goes as we expect today, in two months, you and I are going to be two of the most powerful men in the world. That's enough to scare the shit out of anyone. We've come this far together and we're going all the way together. I have to have you with me, Guy. You're my balance wheel. I need someone close to me whom I can trust. You're it. Period."

"I can't, Cam. It wouldn't be fair to you."

"Let's level here, Guy. What the hell is really going on with you?"

"Ann isn't my first wife," Guy said.

"I know."

Guy was startled. "How?"

"It's in your security clearance."

"And you never said anything?"

"Why should I? You're not the first man who's been divorced. Sharon is my second wife. I figured someday, if you wanted to, you'd tell me all about it. Not that it's any of my business."

"How much do you know?"

"I know you have a son—somewhere."

"Does the report tell you that he's not mine? That he's the son of a black man?"

"Yes."

Guy buried his head in his hands as he talked. "I didn't know, Cam. Honestly, I didn't know. She was so beautiful—I can still see her light brown hair and blue-green eyes that danced when she smiled. God how I loved her. We were high school sweethearts—went together for four years—our families approved and everything. Goddamn it, Cam, it was a living fairy tale and we loved each other so much. Or at least I thought we did."

"We were planning to go to college first and then get married. Then she told me she was pregnant. We were married two weeks after graduation and I went to work for her father as a salesman in his furniture store. We figured we'd have the baby and when it was a couple of years old I could go to college. Jesus, we were happy—we were so goddammed happy."

"We wanted that baby more than anything else in the world, Cam. Her parents were really supportive and looking forward to their first grandchild. I never had any idea she had been with someone else."

"God, I've never seen such a look on a man's face. At first, I thought the baby was dead. The doctor was so pale. He told me I had a son. And then I saw him. He was black, Cam—he was black."

"Her parents didn't know. I don't think she even suspected. I think she thought it was my baby she was carrying. It was pure Hell. Her father was yelling at Alicia and her mother. Everyone was staring at us. I wanted to get out of the hospital as fast as I could and run away. The whole damn world had collapsed around me. I ran out to my car and I stood there, swearing and throwing up." Guy's hands were shaking and he was pale as a ghost.

Cameron wanted to reach out and comfort his friend, but he remained motionless.

"It was a fuckin' nightmare. That poor damn kid came into a world of people who were screaming at one another. You know what her father did? He hung himself. He went back to his goddamned store, found a rope and hung himself. I enlisted in the Marine Corps the next day. I never saw the baby or Alicia again."

"Have you told Ann?"

Guy nodded no.

"You should. You're killing yourself with a guilt that isn't yours. Tell her. She loves you. She'll understand."

"What do I do, Cam, if Alicia turns up and decides to sell her story to one of the tabloids? It'll be an embarrassment to you and it'll destroy my family."

"I don't think that will happen, Guy." Cameron did not explain that the security report had included a news clipping of Alicia's death in Chicago at the hands of a rapist. The suspect had never been caught. No mention had been made of a survivor.

tum tum tum ta tum…
tum tum tum ta tum…

The stately, sad catafalque seemed dwarfed in the center of the towering rotunda, mute in black bunting, waiting to cradle the fallen leader. Carefully, the body bearers placed the flag covered casket on the platform. Relieved of their burden, they moved away. With well-rehearsed precision, the honor guard slipped into position, came to attention and stood, not moving a muscle, like a silent chorus in a Greek tragedy. These modern-day witnesses would watch over him through the hours of the night while thousands inched by in an attempt to assuage their shattered hearts.

tum tum tum ta tum…

CHAPTER XVII

It would be very late New York time, before the election would be declared officially over. Not because of a close vote, but because the networks had agreed that no winner would be declared until all the polling places in the Country were closed. Never the less, there was tension in the room as they watched the early returns. Polls had been wrong before—just ask Tom Dewey.

To their surprise and shock, Senator Standard had made inroads in the industrial states. The loss of Pennsylvania came out of the blue and the Marshall forces were rocked for a moment.

"What the hell is going on?" Franklin bellowed.

"Relax, everyone, its a fluke," Carter said. It's the unemployment and a lot of people were getting on McIntyre's bandwagon. His suicide came so close to the election that I don't think some people realize he's gone."

"Maybe we should have worked harder on the domestic issues. At least in the Northeast," Guy said.

"You didn't think we'd carry every state, did you?" Cameron asked. "That's a little too much to hope for, guys."

"I don't like to make fuckin' basic mistakes," Franklin said.

"If it makes you feel any better, when I make my acceptance speech tonight, I'll wear a sign that says 'I lost Pennsylvania.' I'll take full responsibility and when I get into office, I'll close all the coal mines to teach then a lesson."

Franklin never enjoyed Cameron's humor. He grunted something unintelligible, got up and started out of the room. "I don't accept any goddamned mistakes."

Cameron shook his head, got up and extended his hand to Sharon. "Everybody's a little tense. Let's go for a walk."

They slipped out the side door and headed toward the lake. Cameron saw the shadows of the Secret Service men keeping a discreet distance away from them. They would always be there now, ever watchful and alert.

Sharon pulled her coat tighter to her body. The November nip was in the air and snow was not far away. Cameron slipped his arm around his wife's waist and pulled her close.

"This is where it all began," he said as they descended the steps to the beach. "I wonder what would have happened if I hadn't followed you that night?"

Sharon laughed. "It wasn't the following—it was what we did on the beach."

"God, we were horny."

"We had no idea what was ahead of us, did we?" Sharon asked.

"Would it have made a difference if we had known?"

"No—I suppose not. I'm a big believer in what will be will be. I guess we're just along for the ride."

"My, my, the evening has turned you philosophical, my dear."

They stopped and he kissed her gently.

"Do that again," Sharon whispered.

"With pleasure, my love."

The next kiss lasted longer. They pulled apart and he caressed her face.

"Oh, Cam." The tears started.

They stood locked in each other's arms, both crying—crying for the baby that was lost—for the Enrights—for the first loves of their lives. They did not hear Guy come up behind them.

"I think it's about to be official, Mr. President," Guy managed between gulps of air. "More Secret Service men have arrived. Senator Standard is scheduled to make an appearance in a few minutes."

"We'd better head back to the house, Sharon. Give us a minute, Guy and we'll be there."

Guy turned and ran back toward the house. Cameron took a handkerchief out of his pocket and handed it to Sharon. She wiped her eyes and blew her nose. He ran his hand over his eyes and smoothed his hair.

The television networks were already well into their prepared material on the President-elect when Cameron and Sharon returned. Tears of happiness flowed this time for Sharon when she saw Ann and they collapsed into each other's arms. Cameron fought to control his own emotions and concentrated on the television screens.

"Mr. President," Guy said, extending his hand. Cameron pulled him into an embrace.

"Thank you, my friend," Cam said.

Bedlam broke loose as a group of reporters and photographers pushed their way into the house, taking pictures of anyone and everyone and shouting questions.

"I gave them pool privileges," Guy explained as he moved across the room to take up his vigil by the phone. He glanced at his watch and then at the phone. He was muttering to himself, "ring, damn it, ring."

It seemed like an eternity, but it was less than ten minutes before the call came. The room hushed as Guy answered and then extend the receiver to Cameron. Cameron took a deep breath and walked to the phone. He smiled at Guy and Sharon and then said, "hello."

Standard's remarks were brief and Cameron said thank you, wished the Senator well and hung up. Then he pulled a crumpled piece of paper out of his pocket, looked at it, smiled, tore it into pieces and handed the pieces to Guy.

He turned to the press. "Ladies and gentlemen, my wife and I need to get ready to make our official appearance. If you will give us a few minutes, I need to shower and shave, and then you can accompany us to the armory, where our friends and neighbors are waiting to begin a victory celebration."

Carter, Franklin, Jacob and Lawrence stayed behind while Guy and other aides accompanied Cameron and his family into Seward to thank the Nation.

As soon as the house was empty, Franklin took control of the meeting. "We've finalized the key cabinet positions. To make things look good, we'll leak a few names that won't make the final list."

"You don't think he has some people in mind?" Jacob asked.

"He probably does, so we'll let him pick two or three of the lesser positions. He can do HUD, Interior, and Agriculture—but we control the big ones. Our friends have been waiting a long time for this and we're not going to screw up." Carter was emphatic when he spoke.

"I hope you guys have him under control. Let's see the list," Jacob said, extending his hand toward Carter.

"It'll be best if you don't know right now. You're the one who's got to take the lead in convincing him that the choices we propose are the best ones. He loves your book long assessments. You'll have to get some suggestions from him and then work him around our way," Franklin said. He could tell that Jacob did not like being denied information that the others had.

Cameron did not remember much of the night. He was drained. He had always thought he would feel exhilarated, but after returning home from celebrating with his supporters, he was exhausted. But sleep did not come. He lay awake most of the night thinking and wondering what was ahead of him. Sometime around dawn he drifted into a restless nap. Sharon had been sleeping like a baby all night.

The days were overwhelming. There were a myriad of details and each one seemed to demand his attention. He was scheduled to spend two weeks on a private estate in Florida with his family. It wouldn't be much of a vacation for him—he had to assemble an administration—build a cabinet—find people he could work with and trust. The nanny and Secret Service men would take his children to Disney World.

"You know what the damn problem is?" Cam said to Carter and Franklin over breakfast. "We don't pay enough to get the best people. You can't expect sharp people to give up private jobs for what the government pays and demands. And there are the damned inquisitions by the press. I agree with them that government officials should be above reproach, but they poke into every goddammed corner of their lives. I want the best people we can find and I'm not going to get them."

"No one will argue with you, Cam. You're right on target." Carter stabbed his fork into the stack of pancakes in the center of the table. "But what the hell can we do about it? Our nominees have to be approved by Congress."

"We can't do a damned thing, and that's what's so frustrating. OK, let's hear that preliminary wish list."

"Well, I know you don't want to hear this, but we owe some political debts," Franklin kept his voice low and hoped Cameron would do the same.

"I hate that and you know it, Franklin." Cameron could feel his blood pressure rising.

"Come on, Cam, you're not that damned naive. You don't think we could engineer your election without owing some people, do you?" Guy asked, as he joined them at the table.

"No, I know damn well how the game is played. I just don't like it."

"I'll have Jacob prepare some evaluations of potential cabinet members, Cam. You can look over the information and give us your feedback. Give us any suggestions you have soon, OK?" Carter said, closing the discussion.

It was the briefings by Richardson's advisors, the State Department and Defense Department that bothered Cameron the most. The world situation and position of the United States on many issues was much more tenuous than he had dreamed. He was inheriting a hell of a mess and he didn't have the slightest idea how he was going to untangle the web and solve the problems. The thought of what was ahead scared the hell out of him.

The time in Florida went quickly and they returned to their Seward home to spend the holidays quietly and alone.

He remembered, just before they left for vacation, watching with a heavy heart as the workmen started erecting a high wooden fence that would forever seal his home from the eyes of the prying public. Guy had at first been reluctant to have his home included in the isolated compound, but faced the inevitable and relented, knowing the necessity of having quick and private access to the President-elect.

"Nothing will ever be the same again," Cameron said half-aloud to Guy.

"I know what you mean. I pray it all hasn't been a mistake."

"Sharon and I were so full dreams when we built this house. It'll be a long time before we can live here again. I guess our dreams weren't as great as what has come to pass."

"You dream your dreams, but in the end, it is destiny that charts your course. Would we have changed anything if we had known this was going to be ahead of us when we used to bullshit about our futures when we were in 'Nam?" Guy asked

"I don't know, Guy. I still am not sure how the hell all of this happened. Something beyond our comprehension took charge and all we can do is accept the results, graciously, I guess."

"And, rising to the occasion, a man does what has to do, even if it means his death," Guy added.

Cam turned and looked at his friend. "When the hell did you come up with that line? Are you smoking something funny?"

"No, but I've been thinking about it. I'm just scared shitless, Cam. I'm in so far over my head, I wake up in a cold sweat every night. I'm a small town attorney and you got come crazy idea I could be the chief-of-staff to the President. You're the one smoking something."

Cameron laughed. "You're not alone, Guy. I bet every newly elected president is scared to death as the big day draws closer. Hell, in six months, it'll be old hat."

"Keep telling yourself that, buddy. I'll remind you of the comment in six months."

"It's a deal, Guy."

#

It was a relatively quiet Christmas Day with all of the family together, including, surprisingly enough, Sharon's parents. There was a noisy exchange of presents and a delicious turkey dinner that Sharon and Ann insisted upon cooking themselves.

On New Year's Day, Cameron, Guy and their sons took over the living room and watched bowl games all day.

Sooner than they expected, it was time to get ready to leave their home and return to Washington and begin a life none of them had ever known.

#

Cameron stirred in his sleep, turned and slipped his arm around his wife as she lay beside him. Sharon was awake, her mind racing over all the details that needed taken care of before they left. She and Ann had returned from New York City late the day before, after final fittings for their ball gowns and ceremony outfits. Sharon had selected a blue wool dress, light blue cashmere coat and much to her dislike, a hat for the swearing in at noon. Ann's choice had been a light green suit. She, too, had agreed to wear a hat.

Cameron and Guy had enjoyed the stories of their experiences with the designers and teased their wives about their extravagances. Cameron advised them to pack the clothes carefully after the inauguration, so they could be worn again in four years.

"Come now, Mr. President," Ann had teased, "You can't have your wife appearing on the cover of all the major magazines twice in the same outfit."

#

"A penny for your thoughts," Cameron said nuzzling his wife's neck.

"I'm thinking about the changes that are coming. I hate to leave this house. It has so many good memories." She snuggled closer to her husband.

"We'll have good memories in our new house. And, you'll see a lot more of me. We can arrange to have lunch together—every day."

"Cam—I'm worried about the children. They're starting to enjoy having their pictures taken all the time. They're becoming overbearing about their 'press coverage,' as Debbie puts it. I wish you'd talk to them," Sharon said.

"Tomorrow—not today." He kissed Sharon and pulled her tight against him. "We can talk about a lot of things tomorrow."

"Cam—I love you so much." Sharon returned her husband's kiss with an intensity that surprised him for a moment. Then he responded, probing his tongue deep into her mouth. A deep sigh escaped from Sharon as her hands reached down to fondle him.

At that moment, their bedroom door flew open and Debbie and Nicky came charging into the room.

"Don't you two ever knock?" Cameron demanded.

"Come on, Dad, you and Mom are too old for that love stuff." Debbie laughed and flopped on the end of the bed. Cameron pulled away from Sharon as Nicky landed between them.

"It's times like this, when I wish we didn't have any children," Cameron teased.

"Dad, this is a serious visit. Mother, I can't decide what to wear when we leave today," Debbie said in a very serious voice. "I know I'm going to have my picture taken when we arrive in Washington and I have to look my best."

"Me, too," Nicky added.

"What did I tell you, Cam," Sharon said with a laugh.

Before Cameron could respond, the phone rang. It was Guy telling them that the schedule had changed and they would be leaving in an hour. Cameron jumped out of bed and headed for the bathroom, leaving Sharon to settle the fashion crisis.

#

Washington was filled with people and excitement. There was a feeling of hope in the air—the exhilarating sense of a fresh start—expectations to be met—promises to keep. Sharon knew it was like this every four years, but this

206

time it was for them—for him—the man she fell in love with one night on a deserted lakeshore.

In the two days prior to the inauguration, they were caught up in a whirlwind of activities, that culminated with a Hollywood-style gala. The kids loved meeting their favorite performers. Sharon was overwhelmed by all of the celebrities and the unabashed adoration they heaped on her husband. They were welcomed back to Washington in a grand and glorious style. The Country was in a partying mood, buoyed by their belief that Cameron Marshall would be a dynamic, successful leader.

They awoke on inaugural morning to find snow transforming the Washington landscape into a panorama of virgin white. It had started falling before dawn and forecasters predicted that it would continue to snow lightly all day. The temperature was not expected to rise above thirty degrees.

The Marshall family started the day privately with a special mass, said by Cameron's long time friend, Father Joseph O'Connor. Then they joined the Orbakers for a public prayer service in the National Cathedral. The limousines were in front when they stepped outside, waiting to hurry them to the White House for the traditional coffee with the outgoing President, Vice President, their families and Congressional leaders.

Soon it would be noon. Sharon was determined to try to take in everything and remember every moment, but there seemed to be so much confusion that before she knew it, she was being escorted to her seat on the platform. She looked over and saw all of the children already in place.

It's time, she thought. *All this is real. This is really happening to us.*

Sharon held the bible with shaking hands. She could hardly see her husband's face as he took the oath. When the Chief Justice spoke the first words, tears welled up in her eyes and she fought to keep control. She remembered his hug and then she heard the first strain of *Hail to the Chief* and the tears flowed. Even Cameron found himself blinking and trying to keep control as he turned and faced the cheering thousands that had braved the cold. He stood at attention, stunned by the accord being shown him. He knew the ceremony well, but it was so different when all the pomp was for him.

As the tumult died away he looked at his notes, then up at the people, still standing and cheering. He drew in a deep breath at the sight of thousands before him, waiting for his words. He prayed silently that his voice would be firm and strong.

"We stand together, today, on the threshold of a new era—a time when the actions we take in the next few years will determine the future of the entire world. We have the duty of laying the groundwork for what will surely be the most exciting time in the history of mankind—a time when no one will go to bed hungry at night—when no one will cry in the dark afraid there will be no morning light—a time when disease after disease will be eradicated—a time of unprecedented technological progress beyond our imagination and, most importantly, a time when we must strive to accomplish the end of the most devastating diseases of all—hate and war."

Sharon knew the words of his speech by heart. He had practiced and polished phrase after phrase for more than a week. He had not been happy with the speech his writers had prepared, so he turned to other Presidents' speeches and tried to glean some insight into their thoughts at the awesome moment when they assumed power.

"Strong," he said to her late one night, "I have to be strong. That's what they want, someone they believe is capable of protecting them."

"Today, members of our armed forces are gathered at military installations around the globe to hear the first words of their new Commander-in-Chief. Like every American and every citizen of the world, they want this to be a message of peace—a promise that fighting and dying will cease forever. Peace is an intangible property, never casually bargained for and never easily won. It is sought by every freedom loving man, woman and child on this earth; it is destroyed by every man who hungers for power and conquest and by every individual who seeks to enslave another."

Sharon's attention wandered and she looked out at the thousands of people gather before her. She remembered how, four years ago, she and Cameron had been part of the crowd.

Cameron continued, "It is for us, in this powerful, free Nation, where power is transferred by free election, to be the leaders in the never ending search for peace."

"Oh, God," Sharon whispered silently, "Please let us be doing the right thing. Please don't let this all be a mistake."

"Together we must forge the swords of war into torches of peace. We must hold high the light from the eternal flame so that every dark corner of the world is forever illuminated. Let America continue to be what our forefathers ordained—the home of the free and the land of the brave."

Sharon shifted her attention back to her husband and smiled. At that moment, a television camera was focused on her face and her loving smile was flashed around the world.

"America stands ready, at this moment, to work with all nations who honor human rights. But, we will not cooperate in any way with governments that deprive citizens of their homes, their lives, their innate freedoms. We will never abandon innocent men, women or children, no matter what their nationality."

Sharon wondered what her mother was feeling at this moment as she watched her son-in-law address the world. Maggie was seated on the platform with all her grandchildren, but she would not allow herself to enjoy the day. Deep inside, she would always hate Cameron Marshall for marrying her daughter and taking her to Washington.

"A hundred years ago, the election of a man to lead this Nation was not crucial to the security and well being of the entire world. A hundred years ago it was not possible to devastate a country simply by pushing a button. Today your President is not only the leader of the greatest free Nation in the world, he is a statesman charged with keeping the peace on this planet."

Gillian clutched her husband's hand as she listened proudly to her father. *I wish I had known you sooner Dad. It took me a long time to realize that you are a special person.* She slipped her hand free and dabbed at her eyes with a tissue. "I love you, Daddy," she whispered aloud. Young Guy slipped his arm around his wife's shoulders.

"Let our friends and foes alike know that we will stand strong and united in the face of every challenge. We will support our allies in the preservation of freedom around the world. We will make no promises that cannot and will not be honored and kept."

Ryan looked at the man who was now his Commander-in-Chief. *I wish we could have been close, Dad. I wish you hadn't kept us out of your life for so long. I wish I could have known you through a child's eyes.*

"Let those members of Congress gathered here today, listening to the first words of this new Administration, be thus informed: we have not come to Washington to engage in the game of politics. We have been sent to Washington by the citizens of these United States to lead this Nation, and lead it we shall, by the Grace of God, to be best of our ability."

Franklin looked at Guy and shook his head. "I'd say our boy is deviating from the script a little, wouldn't you?"

"What the hell do you want me to do, Franklin, break his fingers so he can't make changes?" Guy snapped.

"That might be a solution, Guy." Franklin stomped off in a huff.

Guy looked at Carter, who shrugged. "What's done is done, Guy. So, he deviated from the text. Let him have his moment. Franklin's got a lot on his mind right now."

Deep inside, Carter knew Cameron was becoming more and more of a problem.

tum tum tum ta tum
tum tum tum to tum

"O hear us when we cry to thee
For those in peril on the sea"

As the hymn played, her mind was filled with memories of the son and of the day, not so long ago, when they had taken him home to lie on a hillside, near his father. It had been cold that day, too, and he had reached out to comfort her and she had refused his touch—in her heart, blaming him for what had happened. Today, nameless thousands were reaching out to her—seeking her comfort—she had to be the comforter now—he would reach out no more—except through her. We are all in peril, left to wonder what might have been or does true greatness lie in sacrifice? Will he now be larger than he ever could have been in life?

tum tum tum ta tum

CHAPTER XVIII

The President's first overseas trip was, without question, a resounding success. The summit meeting with the Prime Minister of England, the President of France and the Chancellor of Germany had gone exceptionally well. They had warmed to Cameron and he to them. The press reports from the meetings on the economic and defense accords they had reached showed Cameron as a capable, respected World Leader.

When a last minute change in his itinerary was made to include the tiny Asian country of Tsinguan as a final stop, Cameron was upset and argued against the visit.

"Why in the hell do you want me to visit that shit ass country?" he raged at his Secretary of State, Dwight Patterson. "We've scored big time in Europe. Why risk tainting our success with attention to that ignorant bastard Koussi?"

Cameron's aides had never seen his so angry.

The Secretary argued that the visit and talks with the Prince were essential to the State Department's goals in South East Asia. Prince Koussi was wavering between Communism and Democracy and the State Department hoped a personal visit from the President would flatter the Prince and strengthen his position with his people.

"It will be a great embarrassment to the United States if the Prince changes his allegiance, as he always threatens to do." Patterson spoke in his usual whiney manner. Cameron was amazing that Patterson was able to keep his composure in the wake of his fury.

"If we lose Koussi, Congress will be screaming about the millions in aid that we send his Country and the press will have a field day" Patterson concluded.

"You know, Dwight," Cameron said in a calmer voice, "It's a damn pricey base for CIA operations. But, you're the foreign affairs expert. So, against my better judgment, we'll go. Don't ever pull a surprise like this on me again, do you understand?"

Patterson glared at Cameron and remained silent.

\#

From Paris they were flying directly to Tsinguan. Cameron glanced at Sharon, seated beside him, reading a book. She was enjoying their first official trip and was looking forward to their visit to Tsinguan.

"Have you ever seen a picture of the Prince?" Cameron asked.

"No," Sharon replied, shifting her eyes from the book.

"He's not very attractive. He's heavy, short and his face is pox marked. He's also given to childish tantrums. I find it hard to believe that Gloria married him, but I guess it was the status of being a Princess. He does have great personal wealth—all stolen from his people."

Sharon closed her book and looked at her husband. "I think you're jealous."

"Don't be silly."

Sharon laughed and took his hand. "Yes, you are. Old loves die hard, they say. Do you think she's still carrying a torch for you?"

"Come on Sharon, it was over years ago. I hadn't even thought about her until Dwight insisted on this visit."

"Me thinks thou dost protest too much, Mr. President."

As the plane banked to the left and started to descend, he closed his eyes and her face was before him, laughing, smiling, beckoning to him. He smelled her perfume and felt the warmth of her lips on his. Deep in his soul the flame of their love had never completely died and he ached to hold her close and hear her whispers in his ear.

"Well, honey, we'll soon know," Sharon continued. "We're landing."

Air Force One settled gently onto the tarmac at Hungnang International Airport. An Honor Guard, resplendent in bright scarlet uniforms accented with gold braid and high black babushkas, greeted them. The men wearing the uniforms were sweating and uncomfortable in their hot, out-of-place costumes.

Men scurried to unroll a red carpet as the plane rolled to a stop. As the President and First Lady descended the steps, the military band, also dressed in the ridiculous uniforms, played Ruffles and Flourishes and the National Anthem. They were off-key, but Cameron kept a straight face.

The Prince and Princess waited at the bottom of the steps.

"Welcome to my Country, Mr. President," the Prince snapped a salute and extended his hand. Cameron ignored the salute and shook the Princes' hand politely. He then introduced the Prince to Sharon.

The Prince kissed her hand and then turned to his wife.

"May I present Her Most Royal Highness, Princess Alylania."

Sharon smiled and took the Princess' outstretched hand.

She's even more beautiful than the last time I saw her, Cameron thought.

Their eyes met and a silent hello passed between them. For an instant his heart lurched and he almost forgot that he could no longer love this woman.

Cameron and the Prince left their wives and moved off to review the troops. Cameron moved at his usual fast pace, outdistancing the slower, much heavier Prince. At the end of the line, they were met by his security team's worst nightmare—an open car.

The Prince followed Cameron into the back seat. As soon as they were seated, the driver pushed a button and the back seat was elevated.

"How do you like my little innovation? This permits me to ride in complete comfort and still give my people a full view of their beloved leader."

Shit, now I'm going to get my goddammed head blown off.

He could see the panicked look on the faces of his Secret Service agents. They would be in mortal fear for the entire five-mile trip to the palace.

Along the route the people cheered both the Prince and the President.

"You see, Mr. President, you are as popular in my Country as you are in your own."

"It pleases me, Prince Koussi. I have looked forward to this visit to your charming land for some time," Cameron lied.

"To see Tsinguan? Or, to see the Princess?"

Cameron glanced at the Prince.

"She told me before we were married. Not that it was you, but that she had fallen very much in love with someone—a soldier. You were jealous of her career so you did not marry her. What a pity. You were very foolish. She is a beautiful woman—and she knows how to make a man happy in bed. I didn't know it was you until you were elected President. Then I knew that you were her soldier." The Prince made his last statement sound cold and harsh.

"She needn't have told you. It was over long before she met you," Cameron said, trying to head off an awkward situation.

"Oh, she never told me. But, a husband knows. The night you were elected,

I found her in her bedroom, crying. Tears of joy, I believe you call them. She was happy for you, Mr. President—or perhaps she was unhappy for herself. You'd know if your wife were in love with another man, wouldn't you?"

Cameron wanted to answer the Prince, but knew nothing could be gained.

Goddamned you, Patterson. When I get home I'm going to kick your sorry ass out of Washington.

Cameron kept his attention focused on the crowds. He and the Prince did not speak for the rest of the trip.

The palace was a huge, stone building that glittered like gold in the later afternoon sun. It was built beside a tranquil, blue lake that reflected the towers and flags. They passed through the ornate main gate and drove past rows and rows of red, yellow and white roses. Along the driveway, more troops, members of the Prince's elite Palace Guard, stood at attention.

A servant showed Sharon and Cameron upstairs to a private apartment. Their luggage was taken to separate bedrooms and unpacked by maids. When they were alone, Cameron opened the door to Sharon's bedroom.

"Somehow, these people seem to have the idea that American husbands and wives do not share the same bedroom."

Sharon laughed at the remark. She was reclining on the bed with her shoes off.

"Let's slip out to a good motel, honey," he whispered as he ran his hand up her leg to her thigh. He leaned over and kissed her on the lips.

"Now, Cameron, what would the Prince think?"

"To hell with the Prince. I love you and I'm half hard at the thought of getting on top of you." He sat down and ran his hand over her breasts.

"What's wrong?"

Cameron sat up in mock disgust. "Well, I guess the romance has gone out of our marriage. It's over when the husband says I love you with a bulge in his pants and the wife asks what wrong."

"I didn't mean it that way, honey. You can say I love you to me a thousand times a day." She pulled his head down and kissed him. "I'll never get tired of hearing those words—never—ever."

They were silent for a few moments.

"She's very lovely," Sharon whispered.

Cameron sat up and looked away from her.

"She still loves you and I'm jealous," Sharon said.

Cameron got up and walked over to the window and looked out at the courtyard. "I hadn't thought about her in a long time, Sharon. If I had had my way, we wouldn't be here. But, Dwight was having apoplexy. Damn, but my dislike for that man is growing."

"Relax, honey. You don't have to explain. I was only teasing you a little. Come on, stretch out beside me and relax." She patted the space beside her on the bed and Cameron walked over and joined her. She turned and put her head on his chest.

"I'm not worried about the Princess—or you. But, it is a wife's prerogative to be a little jealous of a woman who loves her husband."

"You and the Prince share the same sentiments."

"It must have been an interesting ride."

"It was. He let me know how he felt in the car. Not in so many words, but the subtext was obvious."

"That's ridiculous, Cam. You're not an ordinary man. You can't come here and rekindle an old romance with his wife. You're the President of the United States and very much married. Besides, I'd create an international incident by scratching her eyes out."

"Gloria doesn't mean a damn thing to me anymore." He propped himself up on a pillow and mused half-aloud to himself, "Seeing her did stir up some memories…"

"We've got a formal dinner soon. Shouldn't you be getting ready?" Sharon asked, changing the subject.

He followed her into the bathroom and watched in the mirror as she drew a tub of water, poured in bubble bath and slipped her body beneath the foamy surface. He lathered his face and began shaving.

"We have to be careful tonight, honey. The Prince is a dangerous man. He's been playing both sides for so long he doesn't even know where he is. He's our friend as long as the money rolls in. If we cut off his paycheck, he'll be red by morning."

"I had no idea this was such a serious visit."

"It's only now dawning on me how serious it is. And I have been stupid to get us into this. Right now, I am very much concerned. You can believe that our rooms are bugged."

"Oh, no," Sharon gasped, remembering their conversation.

Cameron walked over to the shower and turned the water on full blast. He did the same at the sink. He crossed back to Sharon and got down on his knees so he could talk to her and be heard.

"The Prince has known for some time that I was involved with his wife. Patterson is the real snake and when I get back to Washington, I am going to hang the bastard out to dry. This, my love, is a blackmail set up. Our people know what kind of arrangements to make for us. We never have separate rooms. Only here? Why? The Prince ignites some old feelings about Gloria in me this afternoon, so that I'll be happy to be away from you tonight. When we drink the final toast this evening, you'll have a little something extra in yours, to help you sleep very soundly. Later, dear Gloria comes calling to renew old acquaintances. By morning, the Prince has the United States by the balls."

Sharon laughed. "You sound like a fiction writer."

"I know it sounds preposterous. Maybe I'm filling in a lot of sordid details between the lines, but something is in the wind. I've never had a good feeling about this part of the trip. I sense something. Goddamn it, Sharon, this piss-ant country is not important to the United States. Patterson wants my ass."

"Maybe the Prince wants to test his wife's fidelity," Sharon joked, trying to lighten the mood.

"He should be watching the servants."

"That was cruel, Cameron."

"But true. I found out that our little princess had quite a reputation before she was reinvented as Gloria Kenwood."

"Did you ever…?"

"Sleep with her? No, darn it."

"That's an interesting way to put it."

"I still had a hole in my pelvis and wires running here and there. Some things didn't function quite right under those circumstances."

"Poor, baby." Sharon patted his cheek.

"Don't get funny."

"My, my, we do get testy when we talk about not performing."

"And you my dear, are hogging the bathroom. Would you mind speeding it up, so I can shower and dress."

"All right, if you insist." Sharon stepped from the tub and Cameron held out a bath towel, which she wrapped around herself. He kissed her on the back of the neck.

"Sharon?"

"Yes?"

"If anything should happen tonight, go with Guy. Don't ask any questions, just go. Don't worry about me. Do you understand?"

"Sharon was taken aback by his tone. "Are you in danger?"

"I don't think so. Please, do what ever Guy tells you, OK?"

"Of course, Cam. But, honey, be careful. Please."

"I will, Sharon."

The sight of the dining room dancing in the flickering lights of a thousand candles took Sharon's breath away. She could not recall ever having seen anything so beautiful. Again, the band struggled through the musical tributes to the President and the guests applauded as the Royal Party moved to their seats at an elevated head table.

The china was elegant, edged in thin bands of gold. Wine glasses were set for every course and they too, were rimmed in gold. A servant stood behind each of them, eager to attend their needs. Each, except for the one who would serve the President, held bottles of champagne. Cameron's servant would pour soda water for him. Following the obligatory, flattering toasts, they were treated to French cuisine, which surprised Sharon. The Prince had an excellent chef in his kitchen.

Cameron and the Prince made polite conversation throughout dinner, but there was an obvious tension in the air. Sharon felt uncomfortable and kept trying to think of things to say to the Princess, while her mind raced ahead to what might happen before the evening was over.

When the meal ended, the four of them led the guests into the grand ballroom for dancing.

"In my Country, Mr. President, it is traditional for the Princess to have the first dance with the visiting Head of State. I'm sure you will honor our tradition," the Prince said.

"It will be my pleasure, Your Highness." Cameron bowed to Gloria and offered his arm. Sharon turned to the Prince, expecting him to offer her his arm and lead her to the dance floor.

"Your wife and I will watch." Prince Koussi took Sharon's arm and escorted her to a high backed chair, covered in gold cloth and decorated with jewels. Sharon knew exactly where the foreign aid had been going. She forced a smile at the Prince and sat looking out over the dance floor. For the first time, she felt afraid.

Cameron led Princess Alylania to the center of the dance floor, bowed to her and slipped his arm around her waist as the music began. The other guests stood and watched. They applauded politely as the couple started moving to the rhythm of the orchestra.

"It's good to feel your arms around me again. It has been a long time," the Princess whispered.

"I'm very happy to see you again. You are even lovelier than the last time I saw you. Life here seems to have been good to you."

"You are very formal tonight, Mr. President."

"The occasion is very formal."

"Not for us. Not being together again after all this time. Oh, Cameron, I've dreamed of this moment, day and night. I've never stopped loving you, Cameron, not for a moment. I should never have let you walk away from me that night. Thank God we have been given another chance."

The floor was becoming crowded now as the guests were joining them, but they kept a respectful distance. Cameron glanced over the Princess' shoulder and could see that the Prince and Sharon had not moved. The Prince was standing beside Sharon's chair, staring at them.

"What do you mean a second chance?" Cameron asked.

"Come." Gloria stopped dancing and took his hand. "Let's go outside where we can be alone." He followed as she led him through the French doors and out onto the dimly lighted balcony.

"Kiss me, Cameron," she cried, throwing her arms around his neck.

Cameron pulled away. "There is nothing between us any more."

"You can't mean that." She wrapped her arms around his waist.

Cameron could see figures standing in the shadows. *God, I hope those are my people,* he prayed silently.

"Of course, it will look bad for you at first, dear," she continued, "but the American people have a great capacity to forget and forgive. It will probably be the end of your career as President. We can be a royal couple, living in exile." Her hand was rubbing his crotch and he was afraid he was going to respond.

Cameron pulled free and walked a few steps away. "Being President is not a career, but you wouldn't understand that. It is a privilege. And I take that privilege very seriously."

She clapped her hands in mock applause. "Bravo, darling, what a noble thing to say."

She moved behind him and put her hands on his shoulders.

Cameron turned and put her hands down. "I also happen to be in love with my wife."

"Oh, Cameron, you are rising to great heights tonight. How kind you are. She is such a plain woman, but I suppose she has her points."

Cameron was furious, but determined to keep his composure. Damn, I wish I knew who was standing in the shadows. He strained to make out the faces on the shadowy figures.

The Princess moved back against him. "She's not for you, Cameron. I'm your woman. I can feel how much you want me."

Cameron pulled back from her touch. "There's a little problem with your plan. I don't love you and I don't want you."

She slapped him hard across the face. "You're saying that because you are a weak man. You never did have any balls."

Cameron forgot about protocol and grabbed her by the arm. "Listen, Gloria, if I loved you, nothing else in the world would matter. Hell, the King of England abdicated his throne for the woman he loved. I'd do the same thing. I'd give up everything for the woman I love and Sharon knows that. I did love you once—at least, I thought I did. I'm not so sure right now. You wanted power and I was a wounded, lonely Marine. And I was feeling sorry as hell for myself. You couldn't see any future with me—and then you met your prince. Only now, you want me to believe that you want out of your deal because the man you married has turned out to be a tyrant and the head of a Country that may not exist tomorrow. I figured everything out this afternoon. I guess life has always dealt you a short hand. I'm sorry. I'm truly sorry for you and the mess that you are in, but I'm not going to fall into your little trap. Excuse me."

Cameron turned and went toward what he hoped were his Secret Service men standing in the shadows. He was relieved to see familiar faces. He whispered to them for a moment and then went back to the Princess.

"You can't talk to me this way. If the Prince knew..." she sputtered.

"What would he do? Have me arrested? You're forgetting who I am now. I am protected wherever I go. Some of those men sanding in the shadows are my guards. Like you, I was followed the minute we moved onto the balcony."

Her voice changed and she was softly begging him again. "This is foolish for us to quarrel, Cameron. I still have your telegram. You said if I ever needed you, you'd be there. I need you, Cameron—now."

Damn, she's good. No wonder she won the Academy Award.

"If you truly needed me, I'd be here to protect you. But, you're lying again. This is your poorest performance. This is good-bye, Gloria—forever. I will not see you again."

"Please, one kiss—a good-bye kiss, Cameron? Please?" She grabbed hold of him again.

Cameron pulled her hands free. "No kiss, no handshake, no touch. You're a woman I never met. I'm sorry." Cameron left her standing alone. He hesitated for a moment and went inside, followed by two Secret Service agents.

Sharon was nervous sitting beside the Prince. She had seen Cameron and the Princess disappear onto the balcony and she was afraid of what might happen at any moment.

"You husband and the Princess have been gone for sometime. Are you concerned about your husband's fidelity?" the Prince whispered to Sharon, "Or, his safety." Then he laughed.

"I never worry about my husband, Your Highness," Sharon lied, felling the rapid beating of her heart.

"My wife is a very beautiful woman and they were once lovers. And old love dies hard."

Sharon was angry. "They may have been in love, but they were not lovers!"

"Do you believe everything your husband tells you? You American women are stupid."

Sharon felt her face flush. She fought to conceal her anxiety. For a moment, she thought she was going to burst into tears. She didn't like the grin on the Prince's face. He seemed to reflect the confidence of a man whose plan was working perfectly. Sharon was cold with fear when she saw Cameron reappear. Then she felt Guy touch her arm.

As Cameron approached the Prince, Guy whispered in her ear, "We're leaving for the airport now."

As she moved away with Guy, she heard Cameron's voice. "Prince Koussi, I would like to see you in your office." His tone was cold and harsh.

The Prince shot to his feet. "What is the meaning of this rude interruption of my party? First you go off alone with my wife and now return and demand to see me in my office. I would like to remind you that this is my Country, Mr. President. You cannot order me around like you do your servants."

Cameron looked the Prince in the eyes and smiled. He leaned forward and said in a low, deliberate tone, "Get your ass into your office—now!"

The Prince moved quickly and Cameron followed. Behind them, their respective bodyguards eyed each other with suspicion and followed.

The office was large and ornate, with over-stuffed leather furniture. Pictures of the Prince and world leaders smiled from the walls. Cameron shut the door and stood, with his back against it. The Prince seated himself behind his large, mahogany desk.

"I will do the talking and you will listen, Prince Koussi. The United States has given your country billions of dollars in aid. I see that we have furnished you with a magnificent office. Very nice carpeting."

Cameron ran his foot back and forth over the deep pile of the wine red floor covering. "Your office is more luxurious than mine."

"I cannot be held responsible for the fact that you are a fool."

Cameron kept his composure. "My Country is tired of seeing this aid money misused. We send you aid for your starving people, not to maintain your palace. Your people wander the streets in search of food while you rot in luxury." Cameron watched the Prince's face grow red with rage and anger.

"Prince Koussi, there will be no further aid from the United States."

Prince Koussi jumped to his feet and screamed, "I have other friends!" He banged his fist on the desk and sent papers and pens flying.

"I'll bet that you do. But your friends don't trust you, do they? They aren't going to let you run your Country when they take over. That's why you hatched a little blackmail scheme to keep me in line. I still haven't figured out how you got to my Secretary of State, but you can bet I'll cut his balls off when I get home. You're a pathetic little man, caught in the middle. I feel sorry for you, because in the end you are going to lose it all."

"You are a lying bastard!" The Prince spit the words at Cameron. "They are my true friends. They promised I could keep my country."

"You should be a student of history, Koussi. You'd find the pages full of broken promises from Cuba to Vietnam."

"The CIA killed Castro."

Cameron laughed. "We had no desire or need to assassinate Castro. He died of a heart attack. Ironic, isn't it? All the years that he played one against the other, and in the end, it was simply God's hand."

"You are a liar."

"Believe what ever you want to believe, Koussi."

Koussi was begging. "If you do not discontinue my money—I mean the aid to my people, I will promise you my loyalty."

"You will guarantee free elections? You will let the people decide who will lead them? You will resign at once?"

In a flash, Koussi flew into a rage. He heaved a large paperweight at Cameron. It smashed a vase beside the door. "Never!" he screamed, at the top of his lungs.

"Those are my Government's terms. You may accept or reject them. They are not negotiable."

Koussi had regained some control. "I will never accept your terms. You capitalist dogs think you can buy my Country, but you're wrong. Go back to your rich life and ugly women. I understand now why my wife rejected you. She is a very wise woman. Go on—go home—let my people starve. There is no compassion in your heart."

For an instant, Cameron let himself be angry. "Your people would not be starving if you did not steal from them."

"Get out of my office, you self-righteous son-of-a-bitch."

Cameron moved forward, leaned across the desk and grabbed the Prince by the front of his robe. "Make one move toward me before I leave your Country and you will be ruling a pile of sand in the morning."

He shoved the Prince backward into his chair and headed to the door. He paused and looked back. "Good-bye, Prince Koussi. May your God be merciful to you."

Cameron exited the office and followed four Secret Service agents down the hall and outside to a waiting car. They apologized as two climbed into the back seat with him. The car took off with tires screeching.

The short ride to the airport was fast and uneventful. Cameron saw that the back door to the plane was already closed as he hurried up the front steps, followed by the Agents. The car shot forward with a squeal of tires, on its way to the waiting cargo plane. As Cameron stepped through the door, the engines began to roar to life. His crew was wasting no time.

They were quickly down the runway and into the sky. All lights were out on the plane. Cameron peered out the window and held his breath. A missile would be quick. Air Force One had a missile defense system. God, he hoped the damn thing would work. He knew that they would not be in Tsinguan air space long and he was holding his breath. The plane banked sharply and Cameron knew his pilots were having the same thoughts.

Sharon clutched his hand and looked out the window. "Whose planes are those?"

Cameron was relieved. "They're ours."

The Air Force had said the hell with sovereign air space and was waiting to escort them home. Cameron sighed and settled back in his seat.

"It was a close call, wasn't it?" Sharon asked.

"The world will never know how close."

Two nights later, the phone in Cameron's bedroom rang in the middle of the night. He grabbed it on the first ring, hoping it would not disturb Sharon.

Cameron listened to the Secretary of Defense's words. "Thank you," was all he said as he hung up.

"Sharon was awake. "Something serious?"

"The government of Prince Koussi has been overthrown. The Prince and Princess are dead."

"Oh, Cam, I'm so sorry," Sharon put her arms around him and pulled him close.

"So am I—so am I."

"Did you know this was going to happen?" Sharon asked.

"I gave the order." Tears slid down his face and he tasted salt as he bit his lip.

tum tum tum ta tum
tum tum tum ta tum

Sail on, oh ship of State,
Sail on, oh Union strong and great.
Humanity with all its fears,
With all the hopes of future years
Is hanging on thy fate.

It is easy to lose grief in the tradition and dignity of the ceremony. The somber beauty of the pageantry somehow seems to dull the senses, but what will happen when there is only a terrible void? What is life going to be like when the silence and loneliness remain? How much comfort can be found in memories? How much can you relive in dreams? How bright will the day be when the sun comes up again and all this is merely pages of the past? Sail on, oh Ship of State…Sail on—alone—without him.

tum tum tum ta tum

CHAPTER XIX

Peter Stuyvesant Culwell—born in a two-room sharecropper's shack outside Reidsville, Georgia—was the third born of nine children and the most intelligent and toughest. There had been more than nine—there was a little girl who died at birth and a brother, a year older than Peter, who died one rainy morning in March, a month after Peter's birth. He was buried under a scrawny tree in the Negro Cemetery, three miles from home. Sometimes, when the weather was good, Peter would visit the brother and sister he never knew.

His earliest memories were filled with hunger and hand-me-down clothes that were patched and never fit—cold feet, because he had no socks and sometimes, no shoes—a one room school—a two mile walk each way—and the taunts of 'nigger'—and a mother, who in her own way loved him and all of her children.

Peter did not know his father. He had been a white man who passed through one summer and left his seed to grow. His mother had given him his father's name—or at least, the name the man had used. As he grew older, he became aware of the many visitors to the house—the nights when the rusty springs of his mother's bed creaked as the man took his pleasure. Sometimes, the man would leave money and for a few days, there would be plenty of food in the house.

Peter hated to see his mother's body growing heavy with a child. His mother told him that children were a gift from God and that they filled a need deep inside of her. When he was thirteen, Peter understood better. Children meant more relief money and the only need they fulfilled was his mother's lust for a man's body.

Peter quit school when he was fourteen and for a while, he farmed and scratched a few pennies from the dry, raped soil. He tried to take care of his bothers and sisters, the best he could. That was the summer Culwell came to live with them. He liked Culwell and took his name. He was the only father Peter had ever known.

#

"A bunch of nonsense, gettin' married. Don't ever do it, Peter," Culwell explained to him one evening when they were sitting side-by-side, fishing in the river. "Ain't smart to let some damn woman own ya."

Peter didn't care whether the man married his mother or not. It was better than having strangers in the house all the time. He admired Culwell, a gangling, six-footer who smiled and sang around the house—and told wonderful stories. He was a happy man and he taught Peter that fishing was more important than working. Peter couldn't remember his first name, so he called him Papa Culwell.

His love for Papa Culwell was shattered one afternoon when he entered the house and found him moving heavily on his sister's body. Peter stared wide-eyed in horror at his sister's naked form beneath the thrusting, dark body of the man he idolized. He stood like a stone in the doorway, listening to the groans and watching his sister lunge upward with her arms and legs wrapped around the man he considered his father. He was sick at his stomach. He spun around and ran from the house, letting the door slam behind him.

"Goddamn you, you nigger," he cried. "Goddamn you!!"

He never mentioned what he had seen to his mother. But she knew. His sister knew, too, and she stopped talking to him. By the time fall slipped into winter, his sister's body was growing heavy like his mother's had so many times. He hated them—all of them. Culwell made one feeble attempt to explain how it had happened—how a man had certain needs—how Peter would understand soon—how Benita had been willing—how it was time she knew the pleasures of life. Peter wanted to kill them all.

He ran away. For a while, he lived in alleys in Atlanta. He kept moving around so the drug dealers wouldn't find him and force him to sell their goods. He returned empty bottles and cans and found a few odd jobs and finally had enough money to buy a bus ticket, get on the dog and head to Pittsburgh. He didn't know why he had picked Pittsburgh. He didn't know anyone there, but the fare had been right and he went. He was a lonely sixteen year old boy and determined not to let on to anyone for fear they would turn him over to the police. He kept his cap pulled down and his collar turned up so no one could get a good look at his face. It wasn't necessary. No one on the bus gave a damn about him.

As the bus traveled north, he realized that he had made a big mistake. He should not be heading north. He saw the snow and he shivered more and more in his thin coat. What a dumb nigger I am, he thought.

He got off the bus in Pittsburgh and started walking down the street. He had gone three blocks when he was jumped by a gang, who beat him up and stole his hat and coat. An old black man found him and helped him to his feet. They found a grate where steam was rising and the old man put a tattered blanket around him. For a while, Peter was warm and he slept. When he woke, the old man was gone and he was alone again.

Peter pulled the old blanket around his shoulders and started down the street. He stayed close to the wall and looked fearfully at any one who approached him. He was hungry. What little money he had in his shoe was gone. The old man had robbed him.

Across the street, Peter saw a Marine Corps recruiting office. He drew a deep breath and made his decision. He hid the blanket in a doorway, smoothed his clothes and crossed the street. A bored, disinterested recruiter wanted to make his quota, so he paid little attention to Peter as he filled out the papers.

Before the day ended, Peter found himself on a bus, headed back for the south he hated. He shared his seat with another frightened black boy who did not look much older than him. They didn't talk much on the trip, just sat side by side, scared to death at what they had done out of desperation.

Peter loved boot camp. Everyone else bitched and moaned and damned the Drill Sergeant, but Peter loved every minute of it. With the improved diet, he grew three inches and put on twenty pounds of muscle. He spent all his free time working out in the gym and his physique responded to the hard work. He was now a handsome, well-built, almost six-foot marine. He was still a loner, but at least he had a roof over his head and he was warm. He had no idea what had happened to the boy who had shared his seat on the bus.

He went home once, in his spotless uniform with his head held high. He was proud of something for the first time in his life and he wanted his family to be proud of him.

He looked in disbelief at the squalor his brothers and sisters were living in. His sister had a little boy and her bulging stomach told Peter that another was on the way. *The circle will never end.* His mother looked old and worn as she sat in her favorite chair, sipping whiskey.

"Mama has a lot of pain," Benita explained as she refilled her mother's glass.

Papa Culwell was gone and in his place was another slick-haired black man. They called him Benita's husband, but Culwell knew better. He would like to have seen Papa Culwell again, to show him that he had become a man.

Peter spoke politely to his mama and sister, fighting to keep the bitter taste of hate from his mouth. He lied about his leave because he could not bring himself to stay in the house and eat at the table where flies crawled over everything. He could not believe that he had once been a part of all this. Tears dripped from his eyes as he walked across the front yard to the dirt road. He knew that he would never see his mama or brothers and sisters again.

Peter returned to camp and the new life he had made for himself. He vowed that he would never again open the door to his past.

Vietnam erupted and Peter found himself in the thick of the war. He was a fighting machine and he watched every move that the white men around him made. He did not trust them. He had heard stories of what they did to the poor black boys. Hell, he could break one of their necks with his bare hands and they wouldn't even know what had happened.

He resented the young Lieutenant, who never seemed to get his uniform dirty. He was a rich kid who had learned the techniques of war in the antiseptic rooms of Annapolis. Peter wondered why his old man had not been able to keep him out of the war.

Somebody fucked up—big time, letting this pussy into the Marines.

Peter fought his feelings, but the hate was deep and festering. He kept his gun clean and tried to keep the mud scraped off his boots. IT was a hopeless task. It was cold in 'Nam, colder than it had been in Pittsburgh. "Goddamn it," he muttered, "I'm always cold."

Peter remembered the god-awful fear that gripped his body when the shells starting exploding around him. He crouched lower in his muddy foxhole and held his breath. Suddenly, there was the searing, excruciating pain. He could hear himself screaming and he remembered the man crawling through the mud and finally reaching him—then, the blinding flashes as though the heavens were trying to consume them—and the man—shielding his broken body with his own.

He spent a few weeks in the hospital—he never saw his commanding officer again—perhaps he died—and then he went back to the line—back to fight and perhaps to die this time. He had volunteered to go back because there was nowhere else to go.

He could vaguely remember the night they had been captured. It had been shortly after he had been relieved from guard duty. The gooks overran their camp and took them prisoner. For a moment, Peter had expected to be shot. Instead, they were marched north.

There were about thirty men when they started out. They walked for days, tired, wet, cold and hungry. Many men died during the walk, but he survived. In prison he listened to the talk and began to wonder and question. They were right. His country had never done a fuckin' thing for him.

When the war ended, Peter was one of twenty-two Americans who refused repatriation. He went further north into China, where no one called him nigger.

He married a young peasant girl and they had two sons. They lived in a tiny house that had a nice floor and his children had clothes and they had food on the table, all supplied by the government. The government taught him the Chinese language and now he worked as a translator and interpreter. Nothing of great importance ever came across his workspace; mostly he worked on English language newspapers.

Days, weeks and years dragged by. He felt like he was existing in some sort of vacuum. His unhappiness grew.

Peter and his wife were treated with cautious respect. They had no friends and the high-level government job he had been promised when he had agreed not to return home never materialized. He knew better than to complain and so he set off every morning, on his bicycle, for his boring job.

And the years passed.

He still missed the afternoons when he and Papa Culwell would wander off and fish. Most of all, he missed the chance to own land. Ever since he had been a little boy, his dream had been to own a farm. Not a big farm, just something that would be his. "It was a foolish dream," he told himself and pushed it into the back of his mind and concentrated on his work.

In the course of his daily reading, he learned of the race riots and the marches and the sit-ins in the United States. He did not fully understand Civil Rights, but he came to admire Martin Luther King, Jr. His Chinese co-workers told him he was lucky to be free of a country that treated people like dogs. He agreed with them, but deep inside, he was bothered by something.

Peter sensed that things back home were changing. Progress of some sort was being made but his life was not changing. He was nagged by the thought that his black brothers were free to march while he was not any better off in China than he had been in Georgia.

"You will never get home to America, but you can die with the knowledge that you served your Country honorably in the end."

Peter had not heard the man come up beside him and was startled by the voice. The man talked softly as they rode together.

"No one will ever know what you have done and your name will probably always be listed as a traitor. In your heart, you will know the truth."

The man was Chinese. Peter had never seen him before. He knew that he should ride away. He should turn this man over to the authorities. Instead he decided to get more information.

"What do you want with me?"

"We need a little help. All you have to do is provide us with a little information."

"What kind of information?" Peter asked.

"All that will be made clear to you in time, if you agree to help us."

"Why should I help a Country that has turned its back on me?"

"Because of the man," the stranger said.

Peter had no idea what the stranger meant.

"What about my wife and children?"

The stranger ignored Peter's question. "You will be a spy. We will ask you to get us some secret information. A lot of men lose their lives doing that. We would not ask you if it were not essential to the security of the United States."

The stranger rode off quickly, leaving Peter to wonder what had happened. *Maybe it is a test. Maybe the government wants to give me more responsibility and they want to be sure of my loyalty.* He decided he would report the encounter to his superior the next day.

Peter slept little that night as he replayed the man's words again and again in his mind. *The man. Who the hell is the man?*

He did not talk to his superior the next morning. He decided to see if the man would appear again. If he did, he would turn the mysterious man in to the authorities.

Two weeks went by and Peter heard nothing from the stranger. He looked for him everyday as he rode home, but he wasn't anywhere along the route. Peter was beginning to think he had dreamed the whole thing up when, as sudden as the first time, the man was peddling beside him again.

"We're offering you the opportunity to repay an obligation," the man said.

"I don't have any obligations," Peter said.

"Yes you do. Think about it for a moment?"

What am I suppose to know? What is this man talking about? I have done nothing to owe someone something. It is a trick and I have fallen for it. Peter was scared.

Peter was surprised to hear his own voice ask, "If I do what you ask of me, will you get me out of here and safely back to the United States. My wife and sons, too."

"I'm sorry, Peter. We can do nothing for you. If you are caught, we will deny that we know you."

"You sure as hell ask an awful lot. No deal."

"We're offering you the opportunity to repay a debt."

"I don't owe no fuckin' debt."

This time it was Peter who rode off alone. He hadn't meant to get so angry, but there was no reason for him to help anyone. China was his country now— not America. What respect could he have for a society that let his family live in a house that wasn't fit for pigs? What love could he have for a Country that denied him an education because of the color of his skin? He had a good home and a family and a job because he had turned his back on that Country. So what if he was a traitor, he was alive and well. He sure as hell didn't have any goddammed obligation to the United States.

He was still afraid. It was a deep fear that he had felt as a child when he saw white men and the Klan and the fat, sadistic Sheriff and his men. Here he was afraid of his own family. He dared not even share his deepest thoughts and fears with his wife. She was a Communist and would turn him over to the authorities if he dared mention anything about the man on the bicycle.

He spent another sleepless night. His world was falling apart and he did not know why. He sat in the blackness of his kitchen and thought.

At least back home I could speak my peace now. I could call the President a bastard if I wanted to and no one would beat me. Things are different there now. Blacks are winning new rights every day. This new President even had a black man in his cabinet.

\#

He eyes ached and his back pained him as he sat at his desk, rereading the article he had finished translating. "Why the hell did you have to be elected President?" he whispered under his breath.

He started passing information to the man as they rode home together. Most of the information did not seem important to Peter. He wondered why they were so damn interested in tripe. Then he was given a promotion and moved to another building. He was informed that he would be handling secret documents.

This must be what they are waiting for, now I will learn what they really want.

He was on the alert now, always looking for information. Two weeks passed before he hit pay dirt. When he took his reports into his superior's office, he saw some papers stamped confidential on the desk. His superior was not there, so he took a chance and read them.

"Oh, my God, now I know!" he whispered to himself.

He was anxious to pass the information on to his contact. As he was leaving the building, he saw the man in the distance, talking to an official. Peter broke into a cold sweat and pain gripped his chest. He took a gulp of air and fought to control his panic.

He could not tell his wife or sons that he had to leave. They would not understand why he had done what he had done and why he must go to the United States. They would see him as a traitor. His oldest son had joined the army and it would be his responsibility to turn his father in as an enemy of the people. He would have to do this alone. Somehow, he would have to make his way back to the United States. He had to warn the man. He knew what they were going to do.

He saw his youngest son off for school, kissed his wife, got his bicycle and started down the road. He had his life savings taped to his chest, an extra sweater under his shirt and a meager lunch. He did not know how long it would be before they started looking for him, so he took a narrow road out of his village.

No one paid any attention to him. He had to ride about fifteen miles north to a village where he could catch a train. About a mile from the village, he crossed a small river. He stopped for a moment, looked around and saw that no one was in sight. He picked up his bicycle and tossed it over the bridge and into the water below. He began walking.

He would get as close to the North Korean border as possible and then he would have to continue on foot. When darkness came his wife would know that he was gone. He knew that if he were caught, he would be shot. He sat alone on the train, thinking of the day so long ago when he had huddled in the cold bus on the ride to Pittsburgh.

He slipped across the border at night and found a small village where he paid a farmer to give him a ride to Chungsan. There he found a young fisherman who was willing to take him to Inchon in a small boat. He felt a little safer when he landed in Inchon and he took a chance on a train to Seoul. Once there, he found someone who provided him with papers so he could go to South Korea. He hoped his savings would hold out. He had more bribes to pay and tickets to buy.

He was sorry that he had left his family with nothing. He hoped that they would not be punished by the authorities for what he was doing.

His trip across the border into South Korea was uneventful. The guards seemed disinterested as they boarded the over-crowded bus and looked at the faces. He was near the back and he kept his head low.

He bought a used suit and shoes in Seoul. He needed to look more like a westerner. No one paid any attention to him when he boarded the plane for Hong Kong. He had bought his ticket on the black-market—paying more than it was worth, but he didn't have to explain his Chinese currency that way.

In Hong Kong he would be able to exchange his money, buy a ticket for New York City and be on his way. He began to feel now that he was not important enough for anyone to care that he was gone. He was confident that they did not know he had read the secret report.

It took him a few hours of searching to make contact with a man who furnished him with a new passport and a ticket to New York City. Very little of his money was left, but he would worry about that when he knew he was safe. It seemed strange to him to be thinking about going home and for the first time in years, he wondered about his mama, brothers and sisters.

Despite the fatigue gripping his body, he was afraid to sleep on the plane. His kept his mind busy trying to figure how he would get to the man. He knew he would not be able to get an appointment to see him, nor would the man recognize his name and take a phone call. He would have to find someone who could help him. His old Sergeant was now the President's aide—would he be as hard to reach as the man?

Jesus! What a hell of a problem this is. I travel half way around the world with information that is vital to the safety of the United States and there won't be a goddammed person I can get to who will listen to me.

Peter starred out the window in frustration. "Think," he muttered to himself in Chinese, "think."

He asked the stewardess for some stationery and an envelope. While the man beside him slept, Peter sat hunched over the lap tray, writing a letter to the President. He detailed everything. When he finished, he had six pages. He folded the letter and placed it in the envelope, which he addressed simply: To the President. He put the envelope in his inside jacket pocket and allowed himself to doze.

He felt relief and free when he got off the plane at JFK. He knew it was easy for a black man to get lost in New York City. No one would find him now. This would give him time to work out a plan. He had no luggage to claim, so he hurried outside the terminal and into a waiting taxi. "I need an inexpensive hotel in Manhattan," he said to the driver. The driver nodded and they raced off into traffic.

It looks damned inexpensive, Peter thought as he paid the driver. *I haven't got much money left, so this will have to do.*

He went inside and registered under his own name. *Who the hell will know,* he thought as he signed his name. He paid in advance for two nights and took the elevator to the sixth floor. He unlocked the door of his room and looked around. It wasn't too bad. The carpet was stained and worn and the windows hadn't been washed for years, but the bed looked clean. There was a lot of noise in the hall from kids running around, but he wasn't going to let that bother him. He went to the window and looked out at the dirty brick building next door and down at the trash in the alley.

Peter did not hear the sound of his hotel door opening. He almost heard the sound of the silencer before the bullet tore through the back of his head. The impact knocked him forward into the window, shattering the glass and panes. His body tumbled out into space and down into the maggot covered garbage of an open dumpster.

The man took a brief glance, pulled the curtains shut and left the room, locking the door behind him.

tum tum tum ta tum…
tum tum tum ta tum…

They were old, young, rich, poor, unloved, forgotten, confused and frightened. They were from near and from far. Somehow coming here and seeing with their own eyes would enable them to grasp the reality of what had happened. They came throughout the night and into the morning light, moving slowly and patiently, waiting to have a few moments with him. From time to time, members of the family slipped in and out, unnoticed or at least unacknowledged. He was not alone—yet—he was still with those who loved him.

tum tum tum ta tum…

CHAPTER XX

"His information has always been accurate. I see no reason why we should not believe him this time. In fact, it is a fairly safe bet that the man is now dead." Air Force Chief of Staff General Sidney Mauer spoke in a matter of fact tone, assuming he would have the final word.

help me—God—somebody help me—please help me—don't let me die—mama—mama—help me...

The President tapped the fingers of his right hand on the desk and looked around the room at his Cabinet seated in his office. They were all reading a report in a light blue cover that was clearly marked Top Secret. He watched for reactions.

According to the report, at dawn, Red China had launched four low-orbiting satellites, each carrying a new deadly nerve gas. The Chinese had developed a way to deliver that gas to a target on earth. An attack on the United States was imminent.

It would be a quick and silent death for the Country. An invisible, odorless gas would spread across the North and South American continents. In seconds, men, women, children and animals would drown in their own fluids as their lungs filled. In a few days, the gas would be gone and the enemy would come, gather up and dispose of the decaying bodies and claim the land. In time, all traces of the gas and its victims would be gone and the land would be inhabitable once again.

"Do we really believe they have the technology and are prepared to carry out this attack or is this simply an attempt to bluff us into surrender?" Cameron asked to no one in particular.

Secretary of State Dwight Patterson rose. He cleared his throat—a nervous habit that never failed to annoy Cameron. "Mr. President," he began, in his irritating high pitched voice, "I firmly believe, and I have substantial evidence, which I propose to present at a later time, to support my opinion in this matter, that China will attack the United States in less that twelve hours."

Cameron hated the Secretary's bullshit diplomatic answers. *Just once,* he thought, *I wish this son-of-a-bitch would give me a straight, yes or no answer.*

"This attack will result in the destruction of the population of the entire continent. I don't see how a vast wasteland will further their ultimate aim of total world domination. If any thing, they need our farmland and crop production. Previous information has indicated that they were concentrating their efforts on ways of feeding and sustaining their increasing population," Cameron said.

"You are right, Mr. President," Secretary of Interior Jocelyn Tyler added. "The use of this chemical could leave the United States, Canada and South America uninhabitable for generations. No one knows how long the effect will last, because there is no real way to test for long range, residual effects. We, unfortunately, will be the guinea pigs."

"They must also be aware, Dwight," Cameron continued, looking straight at his Secretary of State, "that we will be successful with immediate retaliation. I'm sure their intelligence reports have made an accurate assessment of our nuclear arsenal and ability to deliver same."

They also know that I am the only one with the authority to launch an attack. So, what are they planning to do with the Vice President and me? This may get dicey before we're finished.

"I believe, Mr. President, that we will receive a surrender-or-else ultimatum and that we must reach our decision in less that twelve hours." Patterson looked around the room for approval from his colleagues. Most of them were deeply engrossed in the report and not paying any attention to him. Patterson sat down with a disgusted look on his face.

Cameron looked at his watch. 9:45 AM. *By ten tonight, life could be over for us, if I am to believe my advisors.*

"Why twelve hours?" Cameron asked. He was enjoying the drama unfolding before him.

General Mauer rose and walked toward a map he had set up earlier. "In twelve hours, all their satellites will be in the optimum position for firing the missiles."

"Are they aware that we know what the situation is right now?" Cameron asked.

CIA Chief Gunther was next to his feet. "I don't believe so. They have been launching a great number of satellites in the past few months. Up to now, they have all been for reconnaissance and weather information. To the best of our knowledge, none of them have been armed. The four in orbit now appear to be harmless weather satellites."

"And you are confident that the information received from this unnamed agent, confirms that China has this new technology and the satellites are armed?" Cameron asked.

Gunther continued in his same, calm efficient voice. "I believe you have all read the report in front of you."

Each person had the complete intelligence report, meticulously prepared personally by Gunther. But all the reports were not the same. The information given to the President, Vice President, Secretary of Interior Tyler and Chairman of the Joint Chiefs General Mitchell Hartwell contained extra pages, giving the name and background of the agent making the report and information that Red China had failed in developing the technology to deliver missiles from outer space. There was also a copy of the hand written letter found on the body of Peter Culwell by a New York City detective.

Cameron looked around the room, considering each person. This was his Cabinet—trusted advisors he had asked to serve with him in Washington. Honorable people who were expected to help him make important decisions— help him protect the people. He had picked their brains, used their ideas, followed their advice, and shared confidential information with them. Now, he did not know whom in this room he could trust.

Now, Cameron was faced with a conspiracy in his own cabinet. Three men were definitely involved: Patterson, Mauer and Secretary of Defense William Clarke.

Cameron let his gaze linger on Clarke. *You have served your country so honorably in the past, Will, why have you changed? Why are you involved with these people? Are there others I don't know about? Do you hunger for power so much you would sell out your Country?*

Cameron shook his head and let his eyes look at the others in the room. He knew he could rely with certainty on only four people: Gunther, Orbaker, Tyler and Hartwell.

It was Gunther who had called him in the middle of the night.

#

"Mr. President, Milo, I need to see you without anyone knowing I'm there."

"I'll arrange it. Use the side door."

When Gunther entered the living quarters he handed Cameron an envelope without saying a word. Cameron sat on the sofa and read the hand written pages. He looked up at Gunther in disbelief, got up and motioned for Gunther to follow him. The two men went into the bathroom, where Cameron turned on the shower and the water in the bathtub. The two men sat on the edge of the tub.

"My God, Milo, what do I do? How did you get this?" Cameron asked.

"A New York City detective gave it to one of my agents. They're friends and both men had enough sense to keep their mouths shut and get the information to us."

"How did Culwell die?"

"He was shot. The impact of the bullet knocked him against a window and he fell into the alley. Whoever did the job was sloppy and didn't check his pockets."

"How wide spread is the conspiracy?"

"I have no idea, Cameron. And, after reading this, I don't know who I can trust to investigate."

"Jesus Christ. What are we going to do?"

The two men decided they would inform no one else until they had a time to consider all the ramifications.

Cameron stood up and shook Milo's hand. "Thank God I can trust you, my friend." Cameron remembered how angry Franklin and Lawrence had been when he had insisted on Gunther as his CIA chief.

"I will not call you again, Cameron. I will get written messages to you some way. Destroy them after they're read."

"I understand." Cameron handed Culwell's letter back to Gunther. "Good night, Milo."

#

Cameron snapped back to the present and looked at the men and women seated in his office. *How many of you are after my ass? How many of you*

*are willing to risk the lives of millions of innocent people to further your
own ambitions?*

Cameron glanced at his watch. "Ladies and Gentlemen, you must excuse
me." Cameron got to his feet. "My family has returned to Washington. I must
greet them. I'll return as quickly as I can. Arnold, will you join me please?"

Patterson jumped to his feet, overturning his chair. "You can't walk out of
here like this! We are facing the end of the world. Key Congressional leaders
must be summoned so we can decide surrender terms."

Several people in the room were shocked at Patterson's outburst and
statement.

The President's eyes were pure ice. "No member of Congress will be
summoned at this time, Mr. Secretary." He saw a faint smile cross Gunther's
face. "You will all remain in this room until I return. Is that clear?"

The President was out the door before anyone could speak. He stopped at
his secretary's desk, leaned over and spoke softly. "There is to be an
immediate breakdown in communications to and from the White House. Have
the lines shut down, now."

Mrs. Grenadier's hand was already on the phone.

He moved to the Marine standing beside his office door. "No one is to leave
or enter my office. You will place under arrest, or shoot if necessary, anyone
who defies my order. Do you understand?"

"Yes, sir," the Marine answered, his hand already on his side arm.

Cameron turned to his Vice President. "Take Linda and the girls and leave
for West Virginia at once, Arnold."

"They're in California, Cameron." Arnold spoke with a quiet resignation.

"I'm sorry, Arnold."

"I know you are—so am I."

"You and Hartwell have to go, you know, on the off chance the threat is
real," Cameron said.

"Yes." Arnold turned and walked away, his shoulders sagging and his eyes
looking at the floor as he disappeared down the hall.

In the oval office, the Cabinet members sat in stunned silence.

Patterson spoke first. "Gentlemen, I feel it is imperative that we contact
Congressional leaders at once. It is obvious that the President is unable and
unwilling to act."

Attorney General Mead Knapp, a close personal friend of the Vice

President, had remained silent through most of the meeting. He was a soft-spoken man, who always considered every remark he made.

"I believe you are mistaken, Dwight." Knapp's gentle southern drawl had an almost soothing effect on the others. "The President is faced with a decision between two alternatives, either of which could result in the end of this Nation—one by submission and the other by surrender. Do you expect him to..."

Patterson cut him off. "The decision is obvious to me."

"Surrender? I expected that of you and so does he." Knapp's remark hit home. "They criticize him for being soft on Communism when all the time, it's you. Do you know what they call aiding and abetting the enemy?"

"This is no time to be arguing among ourselves," Mauer interrupted. "We have only a few hours in which to decide our strategy."

"As ranking Cabinet member, I will decide the strategy," Patterson snapped.

"The President will make the final decision," Gunther said.

Patterson was not about to be silenced. "I intend to summon several key members of Congress. We cannot permit this mad man to destroy the world!"

"Who are you talking about, Dwight. The President or yourself?" Knapp asked.

Patterson hurled a coffee cup across the room.

"Are you all too goddamned blind to see that the President cannot face the fact that he has to surrender this Country in order to keep us from being destroyed? He is impotent in the face of disaster. He must be replaced at once." Patterson crossed the room and sat at the President's desk. A faint, twisted smile touched his lips as his hands caressed the polished wood.

Soon all of this will be mine.

Gunther was looking around the room, studying faces. *How many of you are on Patterson side? Come on, show yourselves. You bastards have underestimated the President, you know.*

It was obvious some knew nothing about the conspiracy and if they did, they were now backing away from Patterson to save their own skins.

Patterson pressed the intercom button and ordered Mrs. Grenadier to summon Senate Majority Leader Maxwell LaSalle and Speaker of the House Luther Banks to the White House at once.

Mrs. Grenadier's voice was calm as she replied. "I'm sorry, Mr. Secretary, but we are experiencing some difficulty with our telephone lines at the moment. It is impossible to complete any out-going calls."

"Send a messenger," Patterson screamed.

"I'm sorry, Mr. Secretary, but the President left orders that no one is to leave the office."

Patterson crashed his fist into the intercom and sent it hurtling to the floor. "He's gone mad. Knapp—you're Attorney General—do something. That goddammed asshole can't legally keep us prisoners in this office."

Knapp rubbed his hand over his lips. "I'll have to check into the matter before I render a legal opinion. This is a National Security issue that gives the President certain powers. If you wish to make a formal complaint, you can come to my office tomorrow morning and I'll check the law."

Gunther turned his head so Patterson would not see his smile.

Patterson made a fast move around the desk and grabbed Knapp by his tie and pulled him to his feet. "Listen, you goddamned little weasel, there won't be any tomorrow unless you get me out of this office—now!"

Knapp's face was turning red from the force Patterson was using.

Elaine Meeker, Secretary of Transportation, a hundred pound, five-foot dynamo from Maine, jumped to her feet and hit Patterson in the back of his head with her fist. "Let him go before you choke him to death."

Patterson whirled and pulled back his hand to strike Meeker when General Hartwell's deep, authoritative voice was heard.

"Stop. This has gone far enough." Knapp fell to the floor, gasping for breath.

"I'll tell you right now, Secretary Patterson, the President is not going to sell this Country out to anyone. Sit down! Right now." Hartwell moved toward Patterson, who was so surprised by Hartwell's commanding tone that he followed the order.

"If I had my way, Patterson, you'd be tried for treason and I would personally shoot you on the front lawn of the White House. I'm afraid the President will be much more Christian like with you."

The color drained from Patterson's face and he was sweating when the President reentered the room, went to his desk and picked up the hot line.

"Premier Choi," Cameron ordered. The connection was completed without delay.

He heard an interpreter and was angered. "There is no need for an interpreter, you speak and understand English as well as I do," Cameron snapped.

Everyone in the room was concentrating on what the President was saying. Patterson was wiping perspiration from his face.

"Listen carefully, Premier Choi. The decision you make in the next few minutes will determine whether or not this world is going to continue to exist. Do you understand me?" Cameron flipped a button on the phone and put the Premier's reply on the speaker so everyone could hear.

The Premier's heavily accented voice crackled over the miles. "You sound angry, Mr. President."

"Angry does not adequately describe my feelings at this moment. There isn't any time to play games. I serve you official notice that at 12:28 PM, Washington time, exactly thirty minutes from now, the United States will launch a full scale, nuclear attack on your Country. Such an attack will destroy your cities and annihilate most of your population."

"My God, he's insane," Patterson gasped.

"Shut up," Secretary Meeker snapped.

Gunther and Hartwell moved in front of the President's desk. Each man held a revolver. Cameron looked up with a smile and continued his conversation.

"Our forces are at this moment at DEFCON TWO. You have the intelligence to verify this. You are to move the four satellites that were launched by your Country this morning into orbits that take them away from the United States. Then, they are to be destroyed."

"You are going to war over weather satellites, Mr. President?" Choi asked.

God, I hope Culwell was right. Cameron thought. "I have information that indicates you intend to launch a chemical warfare attack on the United States."

There had better be nothing on those satellites, he prayed silently. "If those satellites do not change orbit within thirty minutes I will blow you and your goddamned Country off the face of the earth."

"You will attack an innocent Nation, Mr. President?"

"Act fast before I decide that thirty minutes is too long for you to live." Cameron slammed down the phone before Choi had a chance to respond

"Ladies and gentlemen, we will now sit here and see if the information I received from a brave man, is right." If he's wrong, I have doomed us all. Several of you may want to spend the time drafting letters of resignation."

"Mr. President, I think you and your family should evacuate now, in case there is an attack," Hartwell said.

"No, we'll remain here. If we rush out of Washington, in a matter of minutes the media will be broadcasting news of some crisis and the entire Nation will be on the verge of panic. My family and I will remain here. For the sake of government continuity, you and the Vice President should leave now," Cameron said. "It's a nice day for a flight."

Twenty-five minutes remained.

The President thought of Sharon, with whom he had had so little time. Most people have forty or fifty years. They grow old together. He and Sharon had missed the young carefree days of newly weds. They started life together with a family and in the public eye. There had been so little time alone.

The children mattered the most. For a minute he was tempted to change his mind and send Sharon and the children away to safety. He could go, too. An office awaited him. He could control everything from an abandoned coal mine that had been converted into his emergency headquarters.

Cameron stood up and looked out the window. *Culwell came half way around the world to warn me and wound up dead for his effort. Who killed him? Could his death have been planned from the beginning to make his story more plausible? Maybe the killer threw his body out the window. Maybe the letter is a fake. Jesus, what if I'm wrong?*

No one spoke, but Cameron could hear nervous shifting. Patterson was the first to break the silence.

"You're serious about the attack, aren't you? What will the world think of us?"

Cameron turned and looked at his Secretary of State. "Unless that phone rings damned soon, Mr. Secretary, there may be no world to care about what we do. I did not make an idle threat. If my terms are not met by the deadline, the United States will, with deliberate forethought, launch a nuclear attack. You didn't think it would come to this, did you?"

"Suppose the satellites aren't armed? Suppose they couldn't develop the technology? Patterson asked.

"I'm not supposed to know that am I?" *Thank God, Culwell was on the level.*

Cameron felt the tension in the room ease. "I've called Choi's bluff, which you assured them I would not do." Cameron reached into his desk drawer for a pipe and some tobacco. He had almost stopped smoking, but now seemed like a good moment to take in some nicotine. As he packed the tobacco, the phone rang. He picked it up, listened for a moment, smiled and hung up. He struck a match and lighted the tobacco. He was exhausted.

"The satellites are changing orbit. General Hartwell will cancel our attack plans. You know, Dwight, I think I will hold off accepting your resignation. I think I'll send you to China tomorrow, so you can explain to your friends personally how your little plan failed. Now, get your fuckin' ass out of my office."

As the Cabinet Members filed out, talking among themselves, a furious Senate Minority leader Maxwell LaSalle rushed into the office.

"How the hell can you pull something like this without consulting with us first?" LaSalle screamed. His face was as red as a beet.

A friend on the White House staff had alerted him, no doubt. Cameron had no idea how much information LaSalle had received, but he did know that his anger was justified. It was a breech of political etiquette to have excluded key Congressional leaders.

"Calm down, Senator. I haven't had time to even consult with members of my own party."

"That's no excuse," LaSalle snapped.

"Damn it! There wasn't time," Cameron shouted, slamming his fist down on the desk. His head was suddenly beginning to pound.

"The security of this Nation was threatened and there wasn't any time to be involved in a debating society. Action was necessary! Swift, decisive action!"

"You're damned arrogant for a man who faces reelection next year," LaSalle countered.

"I'm not concerned about reelection. I am concerned with the safety and future of this Country. I'm not going to sit here and see the United States delivered into the hands of the Communists. If the people don't like what I did today, they can put someone else in office. That's their choice. I protected a society and system of government that lets them make that choice. If you feel that you need to nail my hide to some political wall, go ahead. I don't give a damned. I am President and will be until the people vote me out of office. So, don't come whimpering and whining into my office because your ego is hurt."

LaSalle made a hasty retreat from the office, almost knocking over Carter, who was standing in the doorway, listening to the conversation.

#

Father Joseph O'Conner always remembered Cameron in his prayers. He prayed that God would bless the President and grant him wisdom in his decisions. He prayed for the man he had met a long time ago in Viet Nam. Father O'Conner had been a Marine Corps Chaplain and to him had fallen the duty of informing the young Marine that his wife had died in childbirth.

The now gray-haired priest was sitting at his desk, working and reworking his Sunday sermon when the phone rang. He picked it up and heard the familiar voice of the President say, "Father Joe, this is Cameron." It always pleased him to hear the voice, but he sensed distress.

"What's wrong, my son?"

"You're very perceptive, Father. This trouble has passed, for this time. I'll be explaining it to the Nation later this evening. Can you come to Washington?"

"When?"

"Now."

Father O'Conner thought for a moment, his eyes focusing on the picture of the President and his family. He had been given the picture on Inauguration Day and kept it on his cadenza as a constant reminder that he was a special friend to a special man.

"I have taken the liberty of sending a plane for you," Cameron continued.

"Yes. I'll come. You sound very troubled."

"We'll talk when you arrive, Father."

Father O'Conner was puzzled. There seemed to be no threat of a world crisis. There had been some crazy rumors that there was trouble between the President and First Lady, but he did not believe the stories for a minute. Yet, the President was clearly troubled. He would have to hurry. It would not take long for the plane to arrive from Washington.

The parish secretary stuck her head into his office. "Excuse me, Father, but there is a car here for you. Are you going some place?"

"I have to go to Washington, Felicia. There is some sort of emergency. I don't know when I will be back." He hurried to his room to pack a bag.

#

Washington was in a state of high anxiety. Reporters were hurrying into the White House as camera crews set up on the lawn. Long, black limousines, bearing Congressional leaders, were moving in and out of the White House driveway.

When Father O'Conner's car stopped, he asked the young aide who opened the door what the problem was.

"No one seems to know, Father. The President summoned key member of Congress two hours ago. He also requested television time so that he can address the Nation at eight o'clock. It has to be something big."

The Priest was escorted straight to the President's office.

"Father Joe." The President extended his hand. "Thank you for coming on such short notice."

"Mr. President," he said, holding the hand for a moment. "There seems to be a lot of activity here this evening."

"Come. Walk with me in the garden. I'll try to explain what has happened."

As they stepped outside, two young marines, carrying rifles moved into position behind them. My, God, we're at war, Father Joseph thought.

He listened intently as Cameron recounted the day's events.

"Your Country will be proud of you, Mr. President, and rightly so."

"But, Father, I played a very dangerous game with their lives. I could have set us on a path that might have destroyed the world."

"You didn't. You averted that. Could you have delivered your people into the hands of the enemy?"

"Of course not."

The two men walked in silence for a few minutes. Then the President spoke again.

"In my campaign for this office, I was critical of the previous administration, which I felt did not always act in the best interest of the Country. It's easier to read history and look back and consider what I would have done differently. I don't believe we should have capitulated in Korea. I believe that MacArthur was right about moving into China. I pledged that I would not make that same mistake, yet I may have made it...today."

"What do you mean?"

"Our forces were prepared to strike a blow that would have eliminated any future threats from China."

"Why didn't you?"

"Such an attack would have caused the death of millions of innocent people. I couldn't issue that order, Father."

"Nor could any American President, Sir. We are not conquerors. We are not destroyers. There is too much love in the hearts of the American citizens to start such a swift and terrible war. We are not afraid to die for what we believe, but we're not cruel enough to destroy another nation. We defeated Germany and Japan and then turned around and spent billions rehabilitating them. America is not destined to kill innocent women and children."

"I won us some time today, Father, that's all. Perhaps a year, perhaps five years, perhaps only hours. I acted on information that we could not confirm was accurate with any degree of certainty. That was one hell of a gamble."

"It will be long enough, Mr. President. We must never stop believing that the next hour may bring a lasting peace to all nations."

The President sighed. "It's been a hell of a day. I've even ruined my cabinet."

"You, in good faith, asked those men to serve this Country, but ambition destroyed their loyalty. Perhaps, in their agonizing retrospect, they will realize their mistakes."

"I have to face the Nation now, Father."

"And they will accept your decision and their respect for you will be greater. Will you also tell them of your problems with your cabinet?"

"No. I've given Patterson and his cohorts a graceful out. There will be speculation in the press when the resignations are announced, but I plan to divulge no details. That I leave to history."

"This world will thank God for you tonight, Mr. President."

"Why aren't you a Cardinal, Father Joe?"

"Because I am simply an old priest who's never done anything more than teach the word of God as he believes it. It is very presumptuous of me to be here tonight, listening to your problems."

"Father Joe, you are much too humble and the Church will never know how great a leader they have missed. Will you pray with me before I face the cameras?"

"Of course, my son." The walked back into the office and knelt beside the President's desk. When they finished, Cameron stood and embraced him.

"You give me great comfort, my friend. I am thankful for someone with whom I can share my thoughts and problems."

"I will always be here for you, my son."
Father Joe shook hands with Cameron and left the office.
"He knows nothing further," he said as he passed Carter in the hall.

tum tum tum ta tum…
tum tum tum ta tum…

The centuries old pageantry was meant to help those left behind find strength, comfort and closure. The rehearsed rituals would elevate him beyond mortality and into the annals of history, where his words and deeds would remain for all who came after, as a reminder that once, long ago, a man with a dream for the world walked the earth. Unknown forces propelled him beyond his control. It was destined to end in a blinding flash of misguided lust for power. It would be decades before the threads would be untangled and the betrayals revealed. But even then, who could be certain of the answers found?
tum tum tum ta tum…

CHAPTER XXI

The furor over the confrontation with China was the topic of debate in Congress for almost three months. Cameron knew he should have had the leaders involved and it was his own headstrong brashness that had gotten his administration into the time consuming debate with the Republicans. His approval rating with the people was at an all time high and the longer Congress moaned and groaned, the higher it went.

When Congress finally woke up and realized that the American public and media were no longer paying any attention, they put it behind them and got the confirmation hearings going on the new cabinet members the President needed. It was six months before everyone was in office and the administration was back on track with time to concentrate on Cameron's domestic programs.

Without warning, the Middle East erupted. In the middle of the night, a crazed dictator believing that Allah had spoken to him in a dream and commanded him to attacked Kuwait, seize the oil fields and kill thousands of innocent civilians. The world's reaction was swift and decisive and once again it was American troops charged with saving the oil supplies and desperate civilians.

The President was at his desk before six, which was not unusual. He liked the quiet time of early mornings and today he wanted to work on the short speech he would deliver when he lighted the Nation's Christmas tree. He knew in his heart what he wanted to say about the Christmas season, but he was having trouble transferring those feelings into words.

Cameron was especially troubled because he would light the tree in a time, once again, when the Nation was involved in a costly conflict half way around the world. As the very moment he touched the switch that would turn the tall tree into a glowing symbol of peace and hope, young American men and women would be risking their lives.

The buzzer on his desk startled him. He glanced at his watch and realized that his secretary had arrived at her desk. She frequently joined him before the official day started and they would steal a few private moments over coffee.

"Good morning, Helen," he said as he pushed the intercom button.

"Good morning, Mr. President. I'm sorry to disturb you, sir, but Secretary of Defense Woods is here to see you."

Casey Woods, a classmate of Cameron's at Annapolis, had replaced William Clarke. Actually, Casey had been Cameron's first choice for the position, but his advisors had found too many problems with the outspoken former Marine. Cameron liked and trusted Casey and had appointed him without consulting Franklin and company.

Cameron paused for a second. It was still too early for his first appointment. Trouble. His heart lurched. "Send him in."

Cameron stood up and extended his hand. "Good morning, Casey. What brings you here so early?"

"I'm afraid I've brought you some very bad news, Cameron."

Cameron walked around his desk, took the Secretary's arm and guided him to the sofa. "Let's sit here."

As he sat down, Cameron reached for his pipe. The Secretary remained standing.

"Cameron, there is no easy way I can say this—I have received word that your son's plane is missing. It was apparently shot down by a missile over enemy territory."

Cameron's hand froze in mid-air as he heard the words. He was stunned. Tears flooded his eyes. He jumped up and walked across the room and looked out the window.

"They're searching for him," Secretary Woods continued.

"Then he hasn't been killed?" Cameron asked, still staring at a spot on the lawn.

"We don't know. His wingman reported that he did not see him eject. Until we find the wreckage and a body, of course, there is hope. We will do everything we can."

Jay…my God, Jay. He remembered so plainly the day—how long ago was it—it was his first year in the Senate—and Jay had visited him in his office and told him of his plans.

#

251

Cameron was surprised and curious when he looked at his day's appointments and saw Jay listed for three o'clock. He appeared right on time.

"Why the formality of an appointment? Have I done something wrong?"

"No, sir," Jay said. "I wanted to talk to you alone."

Cameron moved across the room to sit in the conversation area of his office. Jay sat in a chair facing him. Jay was about to start his senior year in high school and was still wrestling with a decision about college.

"What's on your mind, son?"

Jay got up suddenly and started pacing the floor.

Cameron hesitated for a moment and then dared to ask, "Is it a girl?"

"What?" Jay looked at his stepfather and started laughing. "A girl? No, it's nothing like that. I've made up my mind about college."

Cameron smiled with relief. Then it dawned on him that perhaps Jay had changed his mind and was not planning to go to college.

"I would like an appointment to the Air Force Academy."

Cameron was surprised. "That's a very admirable decision, Jay."

"You're not angry?"

"Why should I be angry?"

"I know how proud you were when Ryan graduated from Annapolis." Jay moved closer. "I don't want to follow in his footsteps—or yours."

"I would never force you to follow in my footsteps. You have to make your own decisions about your future. Sit down and relax, Jay. Let's talk for a minute. We never seem to find time to talk, do we?"

"No, you're always in the office."

"I know and there really isn't much I can do about that. The Senate demands a great deal. Tell me more about why you picked the Air Force."

Jay sat on the edge of his chair and spoke with enthusiasm. "I want to be part of the space program. I love to fly and someday, I want to go into space."

Cameron could see a sparkle in Jay's eyes that he had never seen before. "I don't blame you a bit, Jay. It's an exciting time with our first space station about to be launched. I think if I were your age, I would want to do the same thing."

"Then you're not upset because I picked the Air Force instead of the Naval Academy?"

"No. I'm proud of you. I love you very much, Jay. I've always considered you my son. You know that, don't you?"

Jay nodded yes.

"I'm proud of all my children and so is your mother. The strength of this Nation lies in dedicated young men and women like you. Ryan picked Annapolis because he wanted to land airplanes on aircraft carriers. It was his decision and it still scares the hell out of me."

Cameron remembered when Ryan had talked him into going along for a ride to see what it felt like to find a floating island in the ocean. He had almost crapped his pants when they landed. *God, what a sight that would have been in the press.* He smiled and brought his attention back to Jay.

"You're a responsible young man and you're taking a very important step.
"

"Thank you, Dad. I was worried you'd be angry."

Cameron stood up and looked down at Jay. "Stand up."

"Yes, sir." Jay stood as Cameron asked and as he got to his feet, Cameron hugged him.

"I know you're a man now and you would prefer a handshake, but I'm your father and you get a hug." Cameron felt Jay's arms grip him.

"Dad, will you help me tell Mother?"

"She probably isn't going to be as understanding about this as I am—you know how Mothers are. I tell you what, let's go to Camp David this weekend. I'll have the chef prepare her favorite dinner and we'll break the news to her then."

"Sounds like a good idea," Dad."

"If she throws us both out of the house, the press won't be there to watch."

Cameron felt a surge of pride as he watched Jay leave his office.

#

"Is there much chance he's alive?" he asked Woods.

"I doubt it, Cameron."

"Does the press know?"

"No. This will remain classified information until you release it."

"Thank you for that, Casey. I'd like to wait until we're certain before I tell his mother. Oh, God, Casey, he didn't have to go over there. He didn't want to go, but he wouldn't accept special treatment. I promised his mother he would be all right."

"I wish I could take this pain away, Cameron." Casey moved over and let his arm rest on his friend's shoulder for a moment before he left the oval office.

#

Jay was storming around the office. "We were there once before and we didn't finish our job. Now we're back again—where we don't belong, Dad. We can't be responsible for all the god damned problems in the world. How could you do it? You lived through a mistake like this yourself. You're listening to those damn crybaby oil barons, Dad."

"Jay, you don't have all the facts. I can't share classified information with you. It's feeble of me to ask for your trust, but that's all I can do."

"How can you sleep at night? Doesn't your conscience bother you?"

"Jay, come, walk outside with me. Let me try to tell you how I feel." Reluctantly, Jay went with him. The sun was beginning to dip below the horizon.

"I find that evening, as the sun begins to fade, is the best time to be close to God. I like to walk in the rose garden and talk with him. You know, there's one thing about God, I don't have to worry about security clearance or that I might read what I say in tomorrow's newspapers. I can open my heart and somehow my problems don't seem so heavy."

"You're trained to believe that way."

"No one can be trained to believe in God, Jay. You can be trained in rituals and for some people that are all there is—a ritual. God loves all people— Catholics, Jews, Protestants, Hindus—even atheists—and I know he loves me and my family."

"I don't believe the way you do."

"You don't have to, son. Someday, you will find God in your own way. It takes time. I was a pretty tough fellow when I went into the Marine Corps. When I lost my first wife and got a hole blown through me, there wasn't a power on this earth that could have convinced me that there was a God. But, a miracle happened to me."

Cameron stopped walking and faced Jay.

"I found the love of a wonderful, caring woman. And I knew from the moment I met your mother that I would love her forever. Suddenly, there was something wonderful in my life. Just touching her hand made me feel that everything was all right. You'll know that moment, too—when you fall in love—when you hold your first-born child in your arms. Or, perhaps, when you're in some strange land, it will come to you. You'll realize that there is a purpose to your life. And, son, God will enter your heart and from that moment on, you will understand all the things that have happened to you."

"You always make things sound so simple."

"Nothing is simple and certainly life is never simple. Some people find it so hard they give up. But, it's worth working for, every minute, even when you don't understand why things happen the way they do. I know it's been difficult for you and your brothers and sisters. There is nothing I can do about our lives, Jay. It's a hell of a responsibility to be the President's son and I know the decision you are struggling with right now. As my son, Jay, you don't have to go into the combat zone."

"I can't have it that way," Jay said.

"I know you can't. And in my heart, I don't want you to. I don't want any of our young men and women dying in a war I got us involved in, Jay. I want peace more than anything—but I have no magical powers I'm only a man and I make the best decision I can in the interest of this Country and the world. I'm sorry it's taking you away from us."

"So am I, but I will not have someone else go in my place."

"When you do leave?"

"Tomorrow."

"Have you seen your mother?"

"No."

"Do you want me to go with you, when you tell her?

"I'll face her alone."

"This is going to be very hard on her."

"I know. Just remember, Dad, I don't approve of what we are doing. We should have finished the job the first time and we sure as hell better finish it this time."

"I understand your feelings, Jay. I will do everything in my power to end it quickly." Cameron extended his hand.

Jay hesitated for a moment and then took it. Cameron pulled him close into an embrace. Jay seemed stiff, but accepted the affection.

#

Woods' voice brought Cameron back to reality. "I'll be in my office, Cameron. I'll let you know the moment we have any further news."

"Yes. Thank you, Casey. Please—have my secretary find Mr. Sheridan."

"Of course."

Guy raced to the President's office. He was shocked when he opened the door and saw Cameron, crumpled in a chair, holding his head and sobbing.

"Guy—Jay's missing. I've killed my son." The words were a pitiful cry. Guy walked over to Cameron and let his hand rest on his shoulder. He knew that there was nothing he could say to ease the agony. He also knew that Cameron would have to tell Sharon and knowing Cameron, he would do that alone.

Jay came home to them on a snowy day in late November. Cameron, Sharon and the children stood shivering and trembling as they waited for the proceedings to begin. The Air Force band began a hymn and slowly the honor guard emerged from the back of the plane, carrying the flag covered casket. Sharon gasped and sagged against Cameron when she saw it for the first time. Cameron tightened his arm around her.

"Oh, God, Cam," she whispered. "It's real. He's gone."

Tears flowed down the President's face. Debbie gripped his free hand and he saw Gillian turn into her husband's arms and sob. A saddened Nation watched the agony of the First Family.

The consequences of his actions as President hit Cameron like a fist in his solar plexus. For a moment, he thought he was going to throw up. *I sent him to die,* was the only thought running through Cameron's mind. He clung to his wife and stared off into the distance.

"Excuse me, Mr. President."

Cameron focused his attention on the young Air Force Officer saluting him. He returned the salute.

"This is a letter addressed to you, Sir."

"Thank you," Cameron accepted the envelope and put it into his pocket.

When they returned to the White House, Cameron slipped away from his family, went to his office and opened the envelope.

Dear Dad—

I've done a lot of growing up since I got here. I've come to realize a lot of things you tried to tell me, but I was too stubborn to listen.

I was never happy with the changes in our lives since you came to us. Perhaps it was because I imagined myself the man of the family and you replaced me. I hated the public spectacle we became when you got involved in politics. And, God, it was hell for me, once you became President. I pretended it didn't matter, but you knew the truth, didn't you?

We were not cut out to lead the life you chose for us and I resented you for that. I resented the loss of my childhood, the prying photographers, the Secret Service, everything that kept us in the public eye. I resenting you placing the Country's needs before our own.

I've had a lot of time to think lately. What else can you do when you have only a lot of sand to look at? I know now that you became President because the Nation needed a strong leader and you are that man.

I really went into the Air Force to spite you. I'm sure you knew it, but you didn't say anything. I'm proud now that I am a member of the Air Force and flying support for our brave ground troops.

My problems and struggles with my boyish pride and myself are dwarfed by the magnitude of the decisions you make every day. I need to beg your forgiveness, but I know now, that it is not necessary—you always loved me, unconditionally. I am truly proud that you became my father and that you are my President.

We must continue the struggle for freedom in this world. Too many innocent women and children are suffering needlessly because of vicious dictators who seek to control the world.

I need to have you help me tell Mother something. I have met someone very special. She is a local girl. Her family was killed in a bombing raid about a year ago. She works on our base. You, Dad, will understand how I feel, because I know how much you love Mother.

I think Mother will, too, once she gets over the shock of losing her little boy. Her name is Shala. We were married three months ago.

I must close now. Twilight is approaching. You would love it here at this time of the day. When the sun is about to disappear beyond the horizon there is an almost overwhelming feeling of peace. You would find it very easy to have your talks with God.

Give my love to Mother and the family.

Jay

Cameron looked into the envelope and found a small picture of Jay and his bride, laughing and happy. Cameron looked at it for a moment, got up, went to the phone and asked Mrs. Grenadier to get the Secretary of Defense. He had to get Jay's wife home as quickly as possible.

After his call, he folded the letter, put it back in his pocket and stood looking at the picture. He had a daughter-in-law he didn't know, who was about to be flown halfway around the world for a final good-bye to her husband.

"Oh, Jay, I am so sorry," he whispered.

He went upstairs and found Sharon lying on the bed. The doctor had given her a sedative and she was almost asleep. He handed her the picture, without a word.

"Jay's girl?" she whispered.

"His wife."

"Oh, Cam, no. The poor thing."

"She'll be here by morning. I don't know how she got left behind, unless they hadn't told anyone they were married."

"She's so young—and beautiful, Cam. What do we do now?"

"She'll be her tomorrow. I knew you'd want her to be here with us when we take Jay home."

Sharon clutched the photograph to her breast. "My poor baby. I miss him, Cam," and a flood of tears came.

It was around midnight when Secretary Woods called to report that Jay's wife was on a plane and would land at Edwards Air Force Base around 11:30 in the morning. Cameron hung up, got out of bed and went out into the living room. He found Ryan dozing in a chair.

"What are you doing out here?" Cameron asked.

"I didn't want to go to one of the guest rooms. I felt like staying close, I guess."

Cameron smiled at his son. "Want something to eat? We can raid the refrigerator or I can send someone out to an all night pizza place."

"I'll take my chances with the refrigerator."

There was a small kitchen in the living quarters and Cameron and Ryan took inventory of the contents. All they found was some cheese, cold beer and a quart of milk. Ryan picked up a can of beer and looked as his father.

Cameron shook his head no.

"Grab the cheese, we've got some crackers. You know, Dad, it's pitiful, to live in the most famous house in the world and not even be able to make a good sandwich at midnight."

"And they think the President has all the perks in the world."

The two men laughed and for a few minutes the pain was forgotten.

"You loved Jay like your own son, didn't you?" Ryan asked.

"I never thought of him as anything but my son. When Sharon and I married our families became one. All of you children are ours."

"He's my brother." Ryan's eyes filled with tears.

"I know." Cam put his arm around Ryan's shoulders.

"His wife is coming home in the morning." Cameron choked back a sob.

"It's going to seem strange meeting her, you know, this way."

"This must be terrible for her, Ryan—losing Jay and now being hurried off to meet some people she doesn't know. I think we'll take a car to the airport instead of the chopper."

"Good idea. She doesn't need to be any more frightened than she must be right now," Sharon said from the doorway.

Cameron was quickly on his feet. "I'm sorry if we woke you."

"The phone did, but it's all right. I think I'd like to be with you and Ryan." Sharon sat at the table and took a sip of Ryan's beer.

Cameron sat down and took her hand. For a while they were silent, each lost in their own thoughts.

Ryan stood up. "Will I give the Secret Service fits if I go down to the main kitchen and get some stuff for omelets? I make a mean cheese and mushroom omelet and I'm starved."

"Get enough for me," Debbie said, joining the group.

Debbie made coffee, Sharon made toast and Ryan cooked the omelets. They sat and ate and shared their memories of Jay.

"Sharon, the decision is yours, but I would like to have Jay brought here to lie in State before we take him home. I think he deserves the honor. Our friends can call here and then we'll have a private service in Seward."

Sharon thought for a moment and then nodded yes. "Can we keep the press away?"

"Probably not here, but I'll ask Carter to do his best when we get home. OK?"

"Yes."

Cameron conveyed his wishes to Guy and left the details to him and other aides. The protocol officers would know how things should be handled. Condolence messages were already arriving from around the world and Cameron and Sharon took time to read some of them before heading to the airport to meet their new daughter-in-law.

Sharon gripped Cameron's hand as they sat on the tarmac, waiting for the flight to arrive. Sharon kept looking at the picture of Jay and Shala.

"She must be scared to death, Cameron. What do I say to her?"

"I don't know, Sharon. Every thing is happening so fast. Let's wait and see."

They saw the plane land, travel down the runway and disappear from of sight. It seemed like an eternity before it reappeared again, moving toward them. The Secret Service agent opened the door of the car. Cameron stepped out and reached back to help Sharon. Because of the television cameras, Cameron had indicated that he and Sharon would board the plane and have a private meeting with Shala.

An Air Force Colonel approached, saluted the President, offered his arm to the First Lady and escorted them up the stairs. Cam heard Sharon's deep intake of breath as they entered the plane. There, seated beside a female Air Force Lieutenant sat Jay's wife.

"She's tiny," Sharon whispered.

The Lieutenant rose, saluted her Commander-in-Chief and moved toward the back of the plane. Shala got up slowly.

Sharon stepped forward and wrapped the girl in her arms. A low, animal like moan erupted from Shala. Sharon hugged her tight and rocked back and forth, comforting her like the child she was. Cameron let his hand rest on Sharon's shoulder and stared at the floor.

"Shala," Sharon whispered. "It's all right. You're safe. You don't have to be frightened anymore. We will protect you."

The moaning stopped. Sharon stroked the girl's hair.

"Honey, I want you to meet Jay's father—the President."

Shala peeked at him from Sharon's arms and then shyly extended her hand. "Mr. President," she said in a small voice.

Cameron smiled and reached for her hand. The girl pulled back and clutched Sharon tighter. Cameron stepped back.

"I am so sorry that we have to meet this way, Shala. Were you treated well on your trip?" Cameron asked.

"Yes. Everyone has been very kind to me. I was so scared when they told me I had to come here."

"You have nothing to worry about. Cameron and I will take care of you now. You're part of our family, forever," Sharon said.

"Thank you. Where is Jay?"

"Jay will be coming to the White House shortly after we get there," Cameron explained.

"May I see him?"

"Yes. You will have all the time alone with him you need."

"Thank you, Mr. President."

"Please, Shala, you don't have to call me Mr. President. Call me Cameron or if you feel like it, Dad."

"Thank you."

The rest of the day was a blur. The pain was almost overwhelming as they stood on the porch and watched Jay's flag draped casket carried inside by the Air Force Honor Guard. They let Shala be alone with him first and then they all gathered to stand in silence and remember him. As night fell, Cameron had an official duty to perform. He had declined the offer of the Vice President to appear in his place. He had something he had to say to the Nation.

The President moved slowly onto the portico of the White House to light the Nation's Christmas tree. Sharon stood at his side.

"Mrs. Marshall and I face this season of hope and good will, with heavy hearts as we prepare to bury our beloved son, Jay. Like too many of you, we have come to know the true price of the responsibility of maintaining peace in the world. Tonight, as we are gathered here and at home, many of our young men and women find themselves involved in a peace mission far from the love and warmth of their families. These brave young patriots know, deep inside, that this nation, inherent in strength, faith in God and dedication to freedom, is the bulwark upon which the salvation of this troubled world rests.

"We are one Nation—under God—one cohesive unit, bound together unto eternity, in the pursuit of peace and happiness, freedom and equality, for every man, woman and child who walks this earth. It is an awesome responsibility and the price we pay dear. But, as our son Jay came to learn, we cannot turn our backs on those innocents who are subject to the hate and tyranny of dictators."

"Jay wrote me a letter shortly before he was killed and in that letter was a message he asked me to share with all of you tonight.

"I serve because I believe in a merciful God,
Who promises peace on earth to all men.
They fight because they believe only in
Power, control and destruction.
I serve a Country that believes all men are
Free and equal. They fight because they fear most
the minds of free men.
I serve because I believe in tomorrow,
A new dawning of sunlight and hope.
For the victims of war there is only a
Sad memory of yesterday's tyranny.
I serve for a brown-eyed, dark haired woman,
Whom I love and cherish with all my heart.
I serve so that the children, born of our love,
Will face a future of peace and prosperity.
I serve for a dedicated, lonely man,
Who sits in an oval office
And makes the decisions that guide
The mightiest Nation on the earth.
I serve because this man is rich in
wisdom and compassion for his fellowman.
I serve because he is my President and most of
all, because he is my father."

Cameron's voice was choking as he finished Jay's words. Sharon held her head high and let the tears slide down her cheeks. She made no effort to wipe them away. She felt drained and was damn tired of being on public display.

Cameron reached for the switch to the light the tree.

"This is for you, Jay and all the men and women who have paid the ultimate price to keep the torch of freedom bright."

The crowd gasped as the tree came alive with lights, but there was no applause or cheers.

The sky was gray and dismal the next morning, matching the mood of the people in the White House. A gray hearse carried Jay's flag draped casket to the church for the Funeral Mass. Reporters waited outside in the cold for the First Family to emerge.

Following the Mass, Jay's body was transported to Edwards Air Force

Base and placed aboard Air Force One for his final journey home. Carter had done his job well. Only three pool reporters were accompanying the family.

It was a forty-five minute ride from the airport to Seward. A few hundred people gathered to watch the plane arrive, but they were quiet and orderly. Others were standing along the route the small motorcade traveled. For the most part, the Marshalls were being granted privacy.

Cameron stood at the gravesite with one arm around Sharon and the other around Shala as the Priest led the prayers. Each clutched a red rose they would place on the casket. Cameron glanced over to the left and saw the headstone of Jay's father.

He became a brave man, David, you would have been proud of him. And I loved him like my own son.

He felt Sharon take a deep breath and he tightened his arm. He let his left hand move to Shala's elbow, as they moved forward. They placed the flowers and turned away. Secret Service men held the doors of the limousine open. When the car started moving, Sharon spoke.

"Shala and I are going to stay in Seward for awhile, Cam. It's peaceful near the lake and I need time alone."

"I'm sorry, Sharon. I am so sorry this happened."

"So am I." Sharon turned away from him.

"Don't shut me out, Sharon, please."

She turned and looked at him. He dropped his head so he wouldn't have to look into her eyes. The pain in his hip was growing worse. He had taken a pain pill an hour ago and the effect was already wearing off. He wanted to pull Sharon close and let the warmth of her body block out everything.

"Go back to Washington, Cameron. That's where you belong. I need to have some time here, with my family and friends, to grieve for my son."

Cameron wanted to tell her that he hurt, too, and needed love and support but the look on her face told him to keep his thoughts to himself. She was not ready to face official duties. She needed to be a mother with a broken heart.

This way is best. Maybe we both need some space right now.

When the car pulled up in front of their home where friends and relatives were gathering, Cameron stayed seated. Shala exited first.

Sharon looked at Cameron. "She's pregnant."

Before Cameron could react, Sharon was hurrying into the house.

"I'm returning to Washington now," he instructed his driver.

He had caught the press off-guard, so no one was at the airport. The plane was ready. Cameron glanced around and started climbing the stairs. He bit his lip and fought the pain every time he lifted his right leg. He staggered and almost fell as he entered the plane. He gave in to the pain and leaned against the side of a seat. A crewmember stepped up and took his arm.

"Let me help you to your seat, Mr. President," the young Lieutenant said quietly.

Cameron did not resist.

tum tum tum ta tum…
tum tum tum ta tum…

It was the silence…the damn silence…it permeated everything…invaded the very soul of everyone present. There was the whispered shuffling of people moving into position…a muffled cough…a sigh-like sob…but no voices…there was no need to speak because there were no words to be added. The stark reality of the act about to be concluded said everything in the silence of a tragedy far greater than any conceived by the poets of ancient civilizations. A life was silenced. *It isn't fair,* the woman thought. *His life had never been lived in silence.*
tum tum tum ta tum…

CHAPTER XXII

Cameron was stretched out on the examining table, waiting for his doctor to finish studying the X-rays.

Finally, he could wait no longer. "Well?"

"Well, Cameron," Rafe Martin said, pulling a stool close to the table and sitting down, "Things don't look too good. The reason you've been having so much pain is bone deterioration. The metal plates are slipping some. That rocket blew a hell of a hole in you. It's remarkable how well they patched you up."

"You know, Rafe, when I get in the tub, I swear I can feel those damn plates. What do we do about the situation?"

"There isn't much we can do now. You need to take things easier."

"You tell me that all the time."

"You need to start listening, my friend. You've got to get off your feet more—period. About all we can do is give you pain medicine to keep you comfortable. An operation won't gain us a thing. You've go to ease the strain on that leg," Jake explained.

Commander Raford Martin had been Cameron's personal physician since his days in the Senate. Cameron liked the guy, with his shiny baldhead and dark-rimmed glasses, usually dangling on a cord around his neck. He was one of the few people who felt comfortable calling him by his first name and Cameron liked that. He was a highly skilled physician. Cameron trusted Rafe and knew that he could always see him in private and not read it about the next day.

"What about the campaign, Rafe?"

"It's going to raise hell with your condition. You are not going to be able to do sixteen-hour days. You'll be in pain that will require heavy medication to control."

"What about crutches?"

"Cameron, you're headed for a wheel chair. You don't know how I hate to say those words, but that's the bottom line."

"Roosevelt did it."

Rafe looked at him for a moment in silence. Then he got up, went across the room and looked in a cabinet for some medication. "I want to have a couple of colleagues look at your X-rays. I think you should talk to Sharon and discuss your future plans together. How is she doing?"

"Better, I guess. Jay's death took a hell of a toll on her."

"Things still strained between you two?"

"Some. But, we're working through it. I think we're strong enough to survive."

"I'm not so sure. You look worn out. You've got to take some time off and recharge your batteries.

"Easier said than done, Rafe."

Rafe moved close to him. "If I were you, I'd think long and hard about another four years." He took Cameron's left hand, opened it and slapped a bottle against the palm. "These should help—at least for awhile."

"Thanks, Rafe. I'll talk to Sharon—I promise."

Rafe smiled and shook his head. "You'd better get dressed and back to your office before the press tracks you down—Mr. President."

Cameron sat on the edge of the table for a few minutes. He glanced at his watch and remembered he had a Rose Garden ceremony at 2:30. Time to get back to work. He winced in pain as his foot touched the floor.

#

Air Force One picked up speed and roared down the runway. There was a slight bump and the huge plane was on its way into the sky. Cameron reached over and took Sharon's hand. She looked at him, smiled and leaned her head over on his shoulder. Each was lost in their own thoughts.

The engines on the plane grew quieter as they reached cruising speed. A young Air Force officer brought them coffee and fresh cookies.

Sharon unfastened her seat belt and turned toward the window.

"It's a beautiful day, Cam," she whispered as her mind filled with the memory of last night, when she and Cameron had finally buried the grief of Jay's death in a passion they thought they had lost.

"I think it's time for us to go home," Cameron whispered.

"Yes. There's too much pain here."

"We had such great hopes and dreams when we first came to Washington. Remember?"

"How could I forget? My handsome Senator who wanted to save the world." She looked into Cameron's eyes. She saw a pain she had never seen before.

"It wasn't supposed to be like this Sharon. How did I let it happen? How did I let disloyal people get into my Cabinet? How did I lose control? My God, I don't even know who to trust anymore."

Sharon remembered the night before, when he sat on her side of the bed caressing her face. His hand felt soft and gentle as the fingertips brushed lightly over her cheek.

Without warning, Cam had jumped up and rushed into the bathroom. Sharon had heard him vomiting. She had squeezed her eyes tight to hold back the tears and fought the urge to go to him. She remembered him coming back into the room and she had felt him get into bed beside her. For a few moments, she hadn't moved. Unable to think of anything to say to him, she had turned until she was facing his back. Slowly she had extended her hand and touched his side. She remembered feeling his body tremble.

#

"Would you like more coffee?" The voice brought Sharon back to the moment. She smiled and held up her cup for a refill. She picked up a cookie and took a bite. "I'll miss the fresh cookies."

Cameron laughed. "We hob knob with the most powerful people in the world, and you're going to miss cookies."

"Are you still comfortable with your decision?"

"Yes. A part of me hates the thought of running away but…" his voice trailed off and he shifted in his seat to get more comfortable.

"I keep thinking you'll get in front of that crowd in Portland, hear the music and the cheers and wild horses won't keep you from running again. Please believe me, Cam, I can't go through another campaign."

"Why do I get the feeling you don't trust me?" He leaned over and kissed her. "Umm, you taste of chocolate chip cookies."

#

The Governor of the State of Oregon rose, moved to the podium and began her introduction. Cameron sat patiently, realizing that the Governor's speech was probably going to be longer than his.

His attention picked up when he heard, "Ladies and Gentlemen, the President of the United States."

The combined bands of Portland's Junior and Senior High Schools struck up *Hail to the Chief* and Cameron got to his feet. His heart still beat a little faster when he heard the music. He walked forward to accept the cheers of the crowd.

Guy leaned over and whispered in Sharon's ear, "They love him. He won't have any trouble getting reelected."

Sharon looked at Guy and shook her head. *We're in this for four more years.*

She took a deep breath and stood up to join the crowd in applauding her husband.

Cameron stood on the edge of the stage, waiting for the tumult to subside before he moved behind the podium to begin his speech. He never saw the young man in the front row rise holding what appeared to be a crutch.

The sound of the shot was lost in the ovation.

Sharon heard a scream but didn't recognize the sound of her own voice. *It's a dream and that's why there's no sound.*

The force propelled the President backward into the people standing behind him. Hands reached out to grab him, as his body crumpled to the floor. Sharon gasped as she saw the spreading red stain on his pale blue shirt. A few seconds had elapsed. Somehow she got through the tangle of bodies and dropped to her knees beside him. She felt the weak grasp of his fingers as she clutched his hand.

"Noooo," she screamed. "Noooooo! Cameron!"

He opened his eyes and she knew that for a moment, at least, he still saw her. She leaned her face close to his lips and thought she heard him whisper I love you.

Sharon pulled his head against her breast. "Oh, God, please don't let him die," she begged.

The President moved his left arm slightly.

268

"He's alive," Guy screamed.

The blast had almost cut the President in half. The force had knocked him into two rows of people, who were unable to stop his momentum and they had all wound up in a bloody heap. For the moment, it was impossible to tell whether or not others had been shot.

The air was filled with the gut-wrenching stench of blood and urine and feces. The President and others had soiled themselves.

The President's Secret Service Agents reacted instantly, brandishing automatic weapons, but the surging mass of horrified, screaming people made it impossible to single out any individual.

"Where the fuckin' hell is the bastard?" one agent screamed.

Rafe Martin shoved Guy and Sharon aside and ripped Cameron's shirt open. Two Secret Service men tried to get others who had been knocked down, out of the way.

"Son of a bitch," Rafe muttered. "They blew a goddamned hole through him."

Guy pulled Sharon up and into his arms, turning so she would not see the blood pouring from the gaping hole in Cameron's chest. Two more doctors joined Rafe and they were trying to stop the bleeding.

Scenes from Vietnam flashed through Guy's mind and he knew all too well what the outcome was going to be—it was too goddamned late.

Paramedics arrived with a stretcher and Cameron's body was lifted, covered and hurried across the stage and out the door to a waiting helicopter.

Guy was numb. He had no idea what to do or where to go. He hugged Sharon closer and tried to force his mind to work. *Think man—don't panic— think—get her out of here—get her to him—now—don't stand here— move—move...*

"Move! Now! Don't stand there, goddamned it. Move!" It was a terse command from a Secret Service Agent. Guy let the man lead them from the stage and outside to a waiting car. The door was slammed shut and with a lurch they shot forward, siren screaming, lights flashing.

"Where are we going?" Sharon asked.

"To the hospital." Guy pressed his fingers to his eyes, trying to blot out the horror of the scene he had witnessed. He was drenched with perspiration, but shivering with cold. Again and again, the scene flashed before his eyes. He heard the noise, saw the startled look on the President's face as he hurtled backward, clutching his chest.

"They shot him." Sharon's voice was flat and emotionless. "They shot him, Guy. Why? Why did they shoot him? He was a good man."

Guy bit hard on his knuckles to keep from crying out. He couldn't break down. There were things he had to do now.

But what? My, God, what do I do? My President is dead. I know that— I've seen that look before—he's dead—the Vice President—I have to get to him.

Guy covered his eyes with his hand and the memory of a conversation he had had with Cameron a few weeks ago came flooding back. It was a week after the show down with China and the shakeup in the Cabinet. They were having coffee in the oval office—two old friends, comfortable with each other, kicking back and talking.

#

"Remember, Guy, you serve the President. If anything happens to me, Arnold will need your help. Don't let our friendship stop you from doing your job." Cameron had pulled his shoes off and he sat with his feet propped on the coffee table.

"I don't like Orbaker." Guy stirred his coffee and took a taste from the spoon.

"He's not too bad a person, once you get to know him. He's been loyal to me and I appreciate that. If there is a sudden change in government personal feelings must be set aside. That's the price you pay for being here, Guy."

"Where the hell did you get this crazy notion that something is going to happen to you?"

Unconsciously, Cameron rubbed his hip. "Guy, this is a world we don't understand anymore and anything can happen at any time. Promise me you won't cut your own career short because of loyalty to me."

#

Eight doctors labored under the stark white lights of the trauma room, using all their skills and knowledge and the best equipment available to perform a miracle. There was to be no miracle on this day. They had all known from the moment he had arrived that their efforts would not be successful, but they had

270

to try. The miracle would be reserved for someone else, on another day—someone less important than the man whose life ebbed before them.

The sixth sense that all good reporters have told the press traveling with the President this was the big story even before it played out. For most, the official announcement would be an expected formality. They had started working on how they would inform the world of the President's death on their way to the hospital.

One reporter had stepped down a hall to be alone for a moment and found Guy Sheridan, beating his fist against the wall and sobbing. The man who had helped Cameron Marshall become President was writhing in agony. The reporter started to reach out and offer comfort, changed his mind and returned to his colleagues. He did not report what he had seen.

Carter kept his composure and strained to read his hastily scrawled notes to the waiting world. He forced himself to keep his voice low and calm as he began the official announcement. He stood alone in the room for some time after the reporters had run for the telephones and the television cameras had been turned off.

A Secret Service man moved quietly to Helen's desk and in a low, solemn tone, gave her the news. She got up and walked into the Oval Office, ran her hand across the polished mahogany, then moved to a chair. She sat down and began keening like an Irish Fisherman's wife. They found her in a semi-catatonic state an hour later.

Sharon was calm. She asked for a few minutes alone with Cameron after the nurses cleaned his body. She lifted his cold hand to her lips and kissed it. She caressed his face and smoothed his hair. She bent down and kissed his lips softly. "Good-bye, darling. I really loved you. From the first moment we met, I knew I would always love you."

Sharon moved away from his body and never looked back. She walked out of the room and saw Guy waiting beside the door. "Let's go home," she said, extending her hand toward him.

Twilight engulfed the city as the black hearse moved silently through the streets of Portland, toward the airport and Air Force One. Church bells tolled mournfully, echoed by bells in Washington and other cities. Across the land, bells would toll until the final act of this tragedy was completed and he was passed to the ages.

In was an interminable flight back to Washington. The power that the

Marshall people had when they arrived in Portland was gone—passed to Arnold Orbaker and his staff in a short, quiet ceremony conducted in the Oval Office ten minutes before Carter announced Cameron's death. To everyone it seemed, somehow, that as long as they were airborne, nothing would be final. They were in between—in a void—beyond reality—in a sort of, what did Rod Serling call it—a twilight zone. Once back in Washington, law and tradition and protocol would take control. Here, in the cloudless sky, they could relive their personal memories.

Carter walked to the back of the plane and looked at the casket, flag covered and strapped in place. He eased closer and whispered, 'It was never meant to end this way, I swear, Cameron. We couldn't stop what was happening."

Carter turned to leave and then changed his mind. He walked over to a seat and sat down. A vision of the President, sitting in his usual place, shoes off, feet propped up, chewing on his pipe, relaxed and full of snappy remarks, popped into his mind. Carter drew a deep breath. His hands were shaking.

Carter felt a presence and he jumped up and whirled, expecting to find someone standing behind him. There was no one there. "Jesus," he said, "this is damn spooky." His pulse was racing. He moved toward the front of the plane, as though he was being chased by something.

He saw Sharon, sitting alone beside the President's empty seat, looking out the window, her mind filled with her own memories and horrors. She had not been back to visit him yet, but he knew she would want a few minutes alone with him before she stood in the world's spotlight and let millions of eyes watch the arrival in Washington. Carter started to join her, thought better of it, and slipped into the seat beside Guy.

Guy was taking the President's death hard. His right hand was bandaged, a stark reminder of the futility that had overwhelmed him at the hospital.

"Damn lousy day."

"Look at the stars, Carter. Gleaming as if nothing had happened. We'd be better off if this is damn plane crashed into a mountain."

"Get a grip on yourself, Guy. We've got a long, hard job ahead of us. We can't let the President down now. Here's his speech. I took it out of his coat pocket at the hospital. You can destroy it."

"And replace it with one you'll write before we get back to Washington? This stinks, Carter. And there's a new President sitting in his office right now—right in his goddamned chair. God, why did we have to go to Portland? Why the hell were you so insistent that he make his announcement there? We don't owe that shit-ass governor that much." Tears streamed down Guy's face.

Carter laid his hand on Guy's arm. "We lost him and that's the way it had to be."

Carter went back to the bar and poured himself a double scotch and downed it quickly. He felt the warmth spread through his body. He refilled the glass and went to his own seat.

The plane was filled with Cameron's spirit. It seemed as if any moment he would call for one of them to discuss a new idea, a plan. The call would never come. The big jet would soon be starting its descent into Edwards Air Force Base.

#

Ann Sheridan generally accompanied her husband when he traveled with the President, but this time she had remained behind to get things ready for the vacation they were planning. Ann had aged gracefully. She had kept her figure and you had to look hard to find any gray hairs. She was pleased with her looks and loved to surprise people with the news that she had two grandchildren.

Ann was at home, in the kitchen, singing along with the radio when the news came—the flash—so seldom heard—the excited voice—"Ladies and Gentlemen, the President of the United States is dead."

Her knees buckled and she clutched the counter.

Ryan was at this desk in the Pentagon when the word reached him, and like all members of the armed forces, he was placed on alert.

Gillian was examining a patient when one of her colleagues came into the room, apologized for the interruption and asked her to step outside.

"We're here to escort you to the White House, Dr. Sheridan. There's been a problem in Portland."

They hurried down the hall together and when she reached the car, she knew. Agents only cry when they've lost a President.

Debbie was at home, breastfeeding her new baby, when the Secret Service man who watched the house tapped on the front door and came inside. He didn't have to speak a word—his face said it all.

David was at basketball practice when the coach blew the whistle and the agent came over to him and put his arm around his shoulder.

Nicky had been picked up at school and taken home quickly, with no explanation. No one was certain who would tell him about his father.

As dusk settled over the city of Washington, the bells continued to tell the world, in low, mournful tones, that a leader had fallen—Cameron Jason Marshall—a man filled with hopes and dreams—had been the victim of an assassin's attack. A great sadness spread upon the earth and tears flowed for him.

Tears flowed from the son, who came to know and love his father late. He was the image of his father and he would bear his grief in stoic silence, giving his strength to his stepmother and siblings. Someday, he would pick up the fallen sword and continue the battle.

Tears flowed from the stepson, who had lost one father and then found the love of another, who would once again see a person he loved lowered into the ground.

Tears flowed from the daughter, who would remember all her days the smiling man who would slip his arm around her and listen to her problems, even when he was dealing with a world crisis. She would keep him alive for her children, tell them about their grandfather—share things the history books would never know.

Tears flowed from the stepdaughter, clutching her first-born babe to her breast and wondering what kind of a world her child had entered.

Tears flowed from the friend who helped make him what he was, never knowing, never suspecting how it was all going to end.

Tears flowed from the elderly couple, huddled in their living room, remembering the little boy they had nurtured and loved when his parents had been so consumed by their own problems that they had no time for their son. They remembered a friendly little boy who liked sugar cookies and Christmas. In his own children, they saw him live again, but it would never be the same.

Tears flowed from the woman, who sat at the paint-chipped wooden kitchen table and held a dog-eared high school yearbook in her lap. She gazed at his young face and then at the picture of her son—his son—the son he never knew he had.

Tears flowed from the Citizens of the Nation, who, believing him to be a man who could be trusted, selected him to be their leader. It would be a long time before they would ever find such trust again.

Tears flowed from the world that had tested and tempered him. It was a better place because he had lived and now worse, because of the way he had died.

Tears flowed from the angels, while knowing that for everything, God has a reason, they could not quite understand this and so they let great tears of sorrow wash the earth. The eternal stars glittered—but were they as bright as the night before?

#

"Sharon—you've got to make a decision about where he is to be buried." Carter's voice snapped her out of her reverie and back to reality.

"I know where his grave must be," Sharon whispered. She was sitting in the Presidential Suite at Bethesda Naval Hospital, waiting for the autopsy to be finished. Someone had brought her coffee, but it sat, untouched on the table. She held her head in her hands and fought back the tears.

My fellow Americans, I stand here today somewhat in awe of the task before me, but let me assure you, I do not stand here in fear.

"Let him lie in Arlington."

You have sent me to Washington to keep the watch and protect, for every man, woman and child, the tenets held so dear—freedom and equality.

"Are you certain you want to leave him here?" he asked.

*I have not come to Washington to engage in the
game of politics, but rather, I have been sent to
Washington to lead this Nation, and lead it I
shall, by the grace of God, to the best of my ability.*

"Bury him where his people can come and honor him," she said.

*We shall not be intimidated into a compromise in
the name of peace, for peace on earth can never
be compromised, nor must we act in haste,
without deliberation and forethought to the
consequences.*

"After we take him back to the White House, I'll show you."

Sharon drew a long breath and looked up at the people standing around her. "We went there one evening—it seems so long ago now. He loved to look at the City at night. He was a new Senator—but it was the beginning. I know now, but how could we have known then? We couldn't know it was going to end this way, could we, Carter?"

Carter turned and moved away. His stood with his back to Sharon, looking out the window. Sharon kept talking. She was seeing Cameron again, young and full of dreams, making a decision that is offered to few men.

"He told me that someday he would run for President. I didn't believe him—maybe I didn't want to believe him. I was frightened and he took my hand and gave me that reassuring smile of his…" Sharon's voice trailed off.

An officer approached Sharon and told her that they would be ready to return to the White House in a half hour.

For a moment, Sharon didn't recognize General Mitchell Hartwell. Everyone around them seemed to be out of place, moving stiffly and quietly. She watched Carter and Ryan walk away with Hartwell.

"Does your mother want to see him before we leave, Ryan?" Hartwell asked.

"I think we should take him to the White House first. Mother is hanging on by nerves right now. We'll have the doctor give her something when we get there."

"Very well. The cars are ready for you and your family. We thought we'd do this part with as little ceremony as possible. The Honor Guard will take over at the White House. I'll return for you in a short time."

Ryan saluted the General. "Sir, my father always wore his Annapolis ring. Could you remove it so that I can give it to my mother tonight?" Ryan asked.

Hartwell nodded, gripped Ryan's hand and went back down hall and through the swinging double doors. Ryan watched the man disappear and then returned to his stepmother. David was with her now. Ryan gripped her hand and looked into her frightened eyes.

"We'll be ready to leave in a short time, Mother."

"Ryan—after we get him home, General Hartwell and I are going to Arlington."

"Arlington?" Ryan looked to Carter for an answer.

"To show them where his grave will be," Sharon answered.

Ryan grabbed Carter's arm and pulled him over near the door. David went with them. "What the hell is this bull shit about Arlington? We're taking my father home."

"Your mother has decided that he will be buried in Arlington National Cemetery. There's a spot out there that has some special meaning for them."

"Like hell!" Ryan was furious. "My father goes home. This City killed him. He's going where no one can get to him again."

"Mother says Arlington and Arlington it will be," David said.

"It's none of your business, David."

Carter moved between the two young men. "Listen to me—you're both hurt and angry. You've lost your father—and you need some way to vent your grief, but not on each other and certainly not against your mother. She watched him die this morning. She held his hand while they tried to save his life. She heard the blast and saw him fall. She's going to live with that memory for the rest of her life and now, it's going to be three more days before she can even let down and mourn her loss."

Ryan and David stood with their heads down.

"That man was more than your father, Ryan, or your step-father, David. He was the President—and he was loved by millions of people, all around the world. Do you have any idea how many people will want to come to this city and pay their respects? He belongs to the Nation—and he should lie forever in Arlington."

#

The press was watching all exits from the hospital, so the movement of the hearse and motorcade was not unnoticed. Sharon sat against the left passenger door.

The motorcade moved swiftly accompanied only by policemen on motorcycles.

As they approached the White House, they could see the flowers. No one was prepared for all the flowers that strangers were leaving at the fence. It was a solemn pilgrimage of people trying vainly to ease a pain so deep nothing would ever touch it. It had started right after the news was announced and it was continuing through the night. People moved slowly under the watchful eyes of the Marine Corps Guards. Few spoke a word. They just moved forward, placed a small bouquet in place, paused for a moment to bow their heads in a prayerful farewell and slipped away, moving back to their lives in a world they would never understand again.

The White House was bathed in glaring light and television cameras dotted the lawn. An Honor Guard stood at ramrod attention on the steps as the cortege drove up. Death had once again entered the White House, in the midst of winter, when all men grow weary of their burdens.

The hearse hesitated and the limousines carrying the family members proceeded to the portico and unloaded first. Sharon took her place beside the children and waited as the hearse advanced and the Honor Guard, that would bear his casket inside, moved into position.

It all looks so damn well rehearsed, Sharon thought. *They must always be ready.*

Ryan extended his arm to her and she took it as she began to follow the casket inside. "God, how you must hate this, Cam," she whispered, not realizing she had spoken aloud.

"Did you say something, Mother?"

"It's nothing, Ryan. I was thinking…" her voice trailed off and she turned her attention to the White House staff standing in doorways as the group filed past.

The catafalque looked forlorn in the center of the East Room, waiting for its burden. It was all ceremony—centuries of tradition replacing personal emotions—rigid guards, cadence steps, silent commands, soft movements—homage's to a fallen leader.

Here, President Cameron Marshall would lie, covered by the red, white and blue of his Country, for a day and a night. There was so little time left to be with him.

Flowers were already in place around the room. Ryan steered Sharon to the center, a few feet from where the casket would rest.

Sharon looked small and frail as she stared at the casket being carried into the room.

Still, she shed no tears.

tum tum tum ta tum…
tum tum tum ta tum…

Eternal father grant him rest—the playing of the Naval Hymn brought back memories of the son and that day, not so long ago, when they had taken him home to lie on a hillside, near his father. It had been cold that day, too, only Cameron had been there to comfort her. She had resented his touch that day and found no comfort in his concern. Now…oh, God, now his strong arms could reach out for her no more…there would be no warmth and comfort. She had to be the comforter this day—to the Nation—to the World.

tum tum tum ta tum…

CHAPTER XXIII

Sharon and General Hartwell rode in silence to Arlington. As she had done earlier on the ride to the White House, Sharon stared blindly out the window.

Once they entered the cemetery, Sharon gave the driver directions. The driver followed her instructions and found the place she had described. Sharon asked the driver and Secret Service agents to remain at the car while they walked to the site. Hartwell took Sharon by the arm.

"It had to end this way, didn't it Mitch?" Sharon's statement startled Hartwell.

"What do you mean, Sharon?"

"Don't play games, Mitch. He had to be killed. He was giving them too many problems."

"Don't think that way, Sharon. Let it go. Grieve for your husband and let it go."

"Do you know who they are, Mitch? They're close to him, aren't they—people he trusted."

They stopped walking and Mitch looked at her in the moonlight. "Sharon, don't pursue this. Please, as a friend, I'm asking you to stay out of this."

"What will happen if I don't? Will I be next? If they can kill a President, a First Lady must be a piece of cake. What will it be, another case of fast moving cancer? Make sure everyone takes the secret to the grave—is that how its done, Mitch?"

"Please, Sharon."

"Are you one of them Mitch?"

Mitch took her by her shoulders and turned her toward him. "I was one hundred percent loyal to him, Sharon. I couldn't stop this from happening. I— I really didn't think they would go this far."

They resumed walking in silence for a few moments.

"What happened to the assassin?"

"He was found under a bridge about a mile from the Center in an abandoned car. His neck was broken."

"They're thorough. I've been over and over this—ever since…" she hesitated, "he was shot. I've gone back over all the deaths. This started a long time ago, didn't it?"

"I think it started in Viet Nam."

"My God, Guy?"

"I don't think so, Sharon. Somehow I get the sense he was out of the loop and I don't know why. We agree on the unholy four, I'm sure, but the leader isn't in that group."

"Do you think he knew?"

Hartwell sighed. "I think he had figured it out but he didn't know what to do about it. He started to talk to me one day, and then he changed his mind. I'm not sure I could have convinced him that I was loyal—but I was, Sharon, please believe me."

"I believe you, Mitch and I think he trusted you. I'd give anything to know who the leader is."

"We have to bury all of this with him. No good will come of creating stories about a conspiracy. The tabloids will go crazy and those responsible will dig themselves a safe hole somewhere."

"What about Arnold—the President? Is he involved?"

"Not smart enough—or ambitious enough. Forgive me, Sharon, I shouldn't speak about my Commander-in-Chief like that."

"This conversation is not going to be shared with anyone, Mitch. When we go back to the White House, I'll give the world the ideal grieving widow. And then, I'm going to leave this goddamned city. Promise me one thing, Mitch?"

"What Sharon?"

"If you ever find out who the brains behind this mess is, you'll tell me."

"I promise, Sharon. It's the least I can do for you and Cameron."

Sharon turned into his arms and for the first time since Portland, she sobbed. "God, how I loved him, Mitch."

Tears finally flowed from the wife—who would never forget his face, the gentle touch of his lips, the loving sound of his voice. There would be no more private moments when all she needed was his presence. He had been taken from her in violence so terrible that it would always be remembered in the history of the Nation he loved.

#

Father O'Connor sat stoically in his office watching the reports on the news. Over and over again he saw the chaotic scene at the Convention Center, then the ambulance racing through the streets and the crowd gathering at the hospital.

One station was already recapping the President's life and career.

He got up, turned off the television set and moved to the window. He looked down at the playground and watched innocent children swinging and laughing. They were totally unaware that their world was changing while they played.

"I am so sorry, Cameron. I am so sorry," he whispered as he crossed himself, knelt and said a brief silent prayer. He rose and removed the cross from around his neck. He placed it gently on his desk.

He looked at the President's picture on the cadenza. "It should not have been this way for you," he said, half aloud.

"You had so much to give your Country, but this couldn't be stopped. You understand that, don't you? Some day perhaps those who remain behind will also understand."

As he left his office, he picked up a jump rope from a bookcase shelf. His fingers fumbled with the rope as he climbed the narrow stairs to the attic.

He entered the dusty, cluttered room; looked around, saw an old kitchen chair, picked it up and moved it to a clear space. He climbed onto the chair with difficulty and tied one end of the rope around a rafter.

"Goodbye, Cameron," he said as tears slid down his tired, wrinkled face. "God grant you peace forever."

He put the noose around his neck and kicked over the chair.

#

The first traces of dawn were streaking the Washington sky when Guy took Ann into the East Room for her first look at the casket. The only sound was Ann's sobs.

In a choking voice, she managed to speak. "I can't make myself believe that he's in there. He was so full of life when he left yesterday. You don't watch someone walk onto a plane and then have him home hours later in a casket.

Nothing can happen that fast. This isn't some goddamned movie."

"It only took seconds for that maniac to squeeze the trigger."

"Did he know what happened, Guy?"

"I think he did. There was a look on his face—for an instant. If I had had any idea how this was going to end, we would have stayed in New York. I'm the cause of it all…" Guy choked back a sob in his throat.

"And this Country would have missed a great President." Sharon's calm voice startled Ann and Guy.

"I thought you were asleep," Ann moved close to Sharon and hugged her.

"There is no time to sleep. I have very little time left with him. This is all I have—for a few hours." Sharon took hold of a corner of the flag and pressed the material tight between her fingers. Tears were slipping down her face and she did not wipe them away.

The three of them knelt at the catafalque and wept. The soft candlelight cast their shadows about the room. The guards looked on in stoic silence, witnessing a scene no one else would ever know. Soon the leaders of the world would come to pay their respects and the eyes of everyone would not be averted until the soil of Arlington received his mortal remains.

"I said yes to him, Ann… yesterday. I hope I've done the right thing."

"Oh, Sharon, of course you've done the right thing." Ann embraced her friend. "He loves you very much."

"We haven't known each other very long. Am I confusing a night of passion with love? It seems so right."

"It is right, Sharon. He's a good man and you've got three children to raise. Marry him, Sharon. You'll be proud of him. He's a brilliant man."

As the memory drifted through Sharon's thoughts, she leaned her head against the casket. "It was right, Cam. For the short time I had you, it was right," she whispered.

tum tum tum ta tum…
tum tum tum ta tum…

The muffled drums began the mournful beat for the first time. These sounds would echo around the world as citizens everywhere paused to watch the beginning of the public farewell to President Cameron Marshall.

They had stood, side-by-side, hands just touching, as the people cheered. Only moments ago, his strong, confidence-filled voice had echoed across the land and around the world:

I, Cameron Marshall, do solemnly swear that I will   faithfully execute the Office of the President of the United States and will to the best of my ability, preserve, protect and defend the Constitution of the United States, so help me God.

Sharon remembered it all so clearly now, as she sat in the limousine that was creeping behind the caisson.

That had been an exciting day for all of them. The children were thrilled with the pageantry and the anticipation of spending their first night in the White House.

Today, Ryan and David sat on each side of her, in silence, each lost in their own private pain. They watched the faces of the Honor Guard holding the flags of the fifty-states as the motorcade eased its way down the driveway.

For the first time, Maggie let herself show a human side and her eyes were wet with tears for the man her daughter loved. She held her grandson Nicky close and reached out for her husband's hand.

The caisson, pulled by six grey-white horses with three riders, creaked its way up Pennsylvania Avenue toward the Capitol. A frisky rider-less horse, with sword strapped to the saddle and boots reversed in the stirrups in the ancient tradition of Genghis Kahn, gave his handler a hard time.

Another car carried Gillian, young Guy, Debbie and her husband and Jay's widow. Shala was frightened and her hands trembled. She had not yet come to grips with the grief for her husband and now she had to mourn her father-in-law. She felt Jay's child stir within her. She had made up her mind that she would not stay in America. It was not safe here—she was going home after the funeral.

The motorcade halted at the Capitol and military officers began to open the doors of the limousines. David stepped out first and turned to help his mother. Ryan offered his arm to Maggie and they proceeded to their place at the bottom of the steps. Officers escorted other members of the family into position.

Ann, Guy and Brian stood with the family. Guy clutched Ann's hand and fought back his tears. He was not an emotional man. He had been taught that tears were a sign of weakness and he did not want to appear weak in public. He wanted to be strong for Cameron, but everything was wrong today.

The Marine Band played the National Anthem, and then *Hail to the Chief* as the Honor Guard slid the casket slowly back on the caisson and picked it up.

Sharon's heart had always beaten a little faster when she heard his music. In funeral dirge it was heartbreaking. For a moment she felt the strength go out of her legs and she leaned heavily on David's arm. He slipped his arm around her waist, reached into his coat pocket and got the ammonia vial that the doctor had given him. He passed it under his mother's nose and Sharon regained her composure.

The Honor Guard began the climb...step. . by...step...their progress heavy with sadness, their arms aching, their hearts broken. Cameron had climbed these steps many times, always in a hurry...a young Senator on his way to becoming President. Why were they carrying a man who was never meant to be carried?

Sharon clinched her hand and forced the metal of his ring into her flesh. She felt the pressure and tried to absorb his presence into her own body.

The young Marine carrying his flag seems so like him, Sharon thought— like he must have been before I met him. That young man is suffering, too, because his Commander-in-Chief has fallen.

The family followed up the stairs. Sharon held her head up and kept her eyes on the casket.

The rotunda was filled with Members of Congress, his Cabinet, the Supreme Court, his Secretary, his aides, White House staff, and a few World Leaders who had already arrived in Washington. Many of them remembered the brash young man from New York who was so new to politics, but so quick to grasp the reigns and move on to the White House.

We shouldn't be here today, Guy thought. His mind replayed that fateful summer—the parties—the fishing—days on the beach with the children— young Guy and Gillian falling in love—Cameron meeting Sharon—it was all so carefree.

All of that should have been his life forever. He deserved the simple things that every man is entitled to—but he was destined to be President— I wonder if he knew it would end this way?

The rotunda was silent. No one moved—no one seemed to breathe. The new President inched forward toward the catafalque, following an officer who positioned a wreath for him. President Orbaker looked pale, drawn and frightened. His eyes darted around as he performed his duty, looking for some unseen force to make a move toward him.

Orbaker reached out a cautious hand and let his fingers touch the American flag. "Gladly would I have died in your place, Mr. President." He hesitated, reluctant to move away, then turned, walked to Sharon and gathered her into his arms. They stood in a silent embrace, bound by their shared grief.

President Orbaker gathered his thoughts and moved to the microphones.

"He was educated at Annapolis, tempered by war, inspired by the love of a devoted wife and children and often awed by the responsibilities of his Office. He was a leader who made decisions always believing in the power of truth and right. He was a patriot who was humbled by the legacy of Washington, Jefferson and Lincoln."

"He was not perfect, for he was mortal. We gather here today to remember and weep, because he was mortal."

"We weep today bitter tears that cannot wash away the deed. The world is wet with tears for this wasted life. But, when you weep, weep not for him, for he has gone to serve a higher purpose; weep not for his widow and children, for they will live always with the glowing memory of his love in their hearts; but weep for the World, deprived of his wise leadership, void of his love of justice, desolate in its despair."

"Cameron Marshall will be missed—not today—nor tomorrow—but with each passing day—in all the years that lie before this Nation."

When the President finished speaking, Ryan and David stepped forward and snapped salutes to their father's casket. They turned and returned to their mother, each taking an arm. They escorted her forward where she knelt and whispered a brief prayer. She reached up and let her fingers gently drift across the fabric. It was time to leave. They would return in the morning to get their father for the last time. Now he was to be with the thousands who waited outside to file past and remember.

The line outside exceeded five miles. People waited patiently to reach the rotunda. But no one left the line. With a stubborn determination, they crept forward, knowing that only a casket and a silent, motionless Honor Guard awaited them inside. It did not matter. They would have a few final moments with him, for a personal goodbye.

And the people came, rich and poor, young and old, black, yellow, white, the grieving and the curious. Most had never met him, never even seen him in person, but they came to file through the Capitol and remember that they had been here on this day.

Some came because they loved him and some came because they owed their freedom to him. Some came because he was President. Some came because they hated him and wanted to gloat at the scene.

There was the executive from Chicago who flew to Washington on his personal plane, to say good-bye to a man he had known in a hospital room in Japan. They had never seen each other again, but he always remembered the young Marine.

There were classmates from Annapolis, some still in the service.

There was a young man who accompanied his mother because she had been frantic to get to Washington. She had constantly nagged at him to be the kind of man Cameron Marshall was. He always carried a secret pride because he looked a little like the man. He would wonder all his life why this trip had been so important to his mother.

Some carried flowers to leave with him; others cameras so that when the memory of this day grew dim, they would be able to recall the scene before them.

And through the night, unnoticed by the thousands, members of the family slipped back, one by one, to spend a few moments with him.

> *tum tum tum ta tum…*
> *tum tum tum ta tum…*

A gentle January snow began to transform Washington into a white mirage. The City was stilled—no cars moved—no people rushed along the streets—no horns blared—there was only the mournful beat of the muffled drums—the creaking of the caisson—and the sound of marching feet—this was the final act—there would be no *deus ex machina.*

Once again they followed the casket as it was carried—this time into the National Cathedral. World leaders and other dignitaries were already in place. The two Cardinals met the casket at the door and escorted it to the altar.

Sharon's mind was not on the service. Her thought was far in the past with a young man who had a dream.

I shared that dream blindly. So blind I couldn't see what was happening. She was angry. She rested her head on her fist and stared at the floor. *Oh, Cameron, how could we not have seen what was going on around us?*

The Mass ended.

Once again the ritual of transporting the casket began. Nothing changed in the pageantry that observed its own rhythm, its own pace, its own beat.

As the procession passed the Lincoln Memorial, Sharon looked up at the brooding head of stone and wondered if he too, were sad. The bands were stilled as they passed. Only the muffled drums filled the silence.

tum tum tum ta tum ...
tum tum tum ta tum ...

Now the procession would begin the final phase—the trip across the bridge and into Arlington National Cemetery, with is winding roads and row upon row of white grave markers. Another hero was coming home to be embraced by the earth that held the remains of other heroes, who like him, had given their lives to protect a Nation and its people.

The procession stopped. The muted sounds of car doors closing could be heard as dignitaries disembarked from the limousines...Presidents and Kings, Prime Ministers and Princesses, commoners and royalty moved together to stand beside the final resting place.

The family stood beside the caisson and waited to begin their final steps behind him. Ryan and David held Sharon between them, fearful that the stoicism she showed would finally break and she would collapse. She felt the strength of her sons and through them, felt him. They followed slowly.

As the casket was placed over the open grave, the Marine Band played the National Anthem and then fifty jets roared overhead and one peeled up and away, leaving the missing man formation

They were trailed by Air Force One, which dipped its wings. "Good bye, Mr. President. God speed," the graceful giant whispered.

The prayers at the gravesite were brief. The family sat uncomfortably on cold, hard chairs.

The guns began to thunder...boom...boom...boom...Sharon's body shuttered with each sound. The mournful sound of taps, with the heart-wrenching sob, wafted across the hills.

The white-gloved hands folded the flag with precision into a neat, perfect triangle and handed it to General Hartwell. Salutes were exchanged and Hartwell moved to Sharon.

"With the thanks of a grateful Nation," he whispered, slipping the flag into her trembling hands. He snapped a final salute as she pressed the flag to her heart. He knew that nothing would ever heal his heart, which beat in agony for his friend and the unfulfilled dreams he had for his Country.

Goddamn it to hell, Hartwell thought. *If I ever find out who these bastards are, I'll kill them with my bare hands.*

The funeral ended and Cameron Marshall passed to the ages.

#

Guy paced in his study. He sat at his desk and reached for a yellow, legal tablet and a pencil. In slow deliberate strokes, he began to write.

Today, I buried my best friend.

He took me from the midst of a pleasant country law practice and thrust me into the world of politics. I wrote words for him to speak, counseled him, followed him in triumph and glory, laughed with him, wept with him. I carried his papers, shared his secret briefings, knew the trials and tests of the Presidency, saw the adoration and faith of millions.

In the harsh light of morning, which now seems A lifetime ago, I stood, composed, at the North Portico of the White House and greeted dignitaries who came from around the world to mourn at his casket.

And then, too soon, we left him on an Arlington hillside.

I will take his family home, home to the lake country where he found love and peace. There, beside the chilled waters, I will finally be able to mourn my President, denied his zenith as a statesman.

I shall try to be a father to his children, shall offer comfort to his widow, but never will I be able to replace the memory of a man, husband and father, who was the mecca of fleeting magic, set upon this earth for too brief a time.

I know that he walks with Presidents and Kings, and I know that he feels no animosity for this perpetrated deed, although he must feel the terrible shame that it was carried out by those closest to him. He loved this Country and all of its people. We failed him—I failed him—I let him be used and discarded—and all the tears of the world cannot wash away that failure. But, he would have understood our weakness.

The World has lost a leader, the Nation a President and I—I killed my brother.

He tore the sheet from the tablet and ripped it into little pieces and let the pieces drop from his fingers into the wastepaper basket. He was exhausted. He cupped his head in his hands and stared at the smiling picture of the President.

He reached over to the pencil holder on his desk and picked up a black marking pen. On the top of the page he printed, in big, bold, black letters—CONSPIRACY.

He took up a pencil and wrote Unholy Four near the bottom of the page. He drew a box around the words and an arrow leading upward—there he wrote: Leader? In small print, he wrote, "If not one of the four—who…who orchestrated this deed? What evil mind hatched this plot?"

He was unaware of Ann's presence until he felt her hands massaging his shoulders. She was reading over his shoulder, but made no comment.

"You're tense and exhausted, Guy. Let me fix you a scotch," Ann dug her fingers into his muscles.

"OK, Ann." He winced from the pain of her grip.

Ann slipped a bottle of pills out of her pocket. "Honey, I can't seem to get my sleeping pills open, will you do it for me?"

"Of course." Ann handed him the pill bottle and went to the bar in the family room to get his drink. When she returned, the open pill bottle sat on the desk.

"You only have two pills left, Ann."

"I know. I'll get the prescription refilled tomorrow. Here, drink your scotch." She placed the glass in front of him.

Guy downed half of the contents in one gulp. He looked up at Ann, "It wasn't a dream, was it?"

"No, it wasn't." She crossed the room and sat on the sofa.

Guy finished his drink. "That stuff is hitting me like a ton of bricks. My head is reeling." The glass slipped from his hand and broke on the desk.

Ann got up, went over and tore half dozen sheets from the legal pad. Her voice turned ice cold. "You were the weak link, Guy. If you had been part of the team, we could have controlled the son-of-a-bitch and we wouldn't have had to kill him. Now, he'll be a goddamned hero forever. I should never have married you, except it was a perfect cover."

She took a pencil and knocked over the pill bottle, spilling the two capsules.

"You poor distraught fool. You killed yourself over your best friend's death. Well, let me tell you the final irony. The shooter was your bastard son. And you thought I didn't know. That should fuel a lot of theories."

"Maybe you'll get your thirty seconds of glory after all. I'll find your body in the morning."

"Don't go any where, Guy," she said, with a laugh as she left the room.

Ann went to the phone and dialed a number. When she heard the male voice at the other end, she said, "Proceed."

#

Arnold Orbaker was sitting alone in the oval office when he heard the door open. He looked up and saw Franklin.

"What are you doing here so late?" the new President asked.

Franklin smiled and sat down across from Orbaker. He had a brown envelope in his hand. "Mr. President, we need to talk."

The End